About the Author

THOMAS WOLFE was born in Asheville, North Carolina, in 1900. His other novels include *You Can't Go Home Again, Of Time and the River,* and *Look Homeward, Angel.* He died in 1938.

The Web and the Root

ALSO BY THOMAS WOLFE

Look Homeward, Angel
Of Time and the River
From Death to Morning
The Story of a Novel
The Web and the Rock
You Can't Go Home Again
The Hills Beyond

The Web and the Root

A Selection from

The Web and the Rock

Thomas Wolfe

HARPER**PERENNIAL** MODERN**CLASSICS**

NEW YORK • LONDON • TORONTO • SYDNEY • NEW DELHI • AUCKLAND

HARPER**PERENNIAL** ● MODERN**CLASSICS**

Designed by Joy O'Meara

Library of Congress Cataloging-in-Publication Data is available upon request.

ISBN 978–0–06–157955–4

09 10 11 12 13   OV/RRD   10 9 8 7 6 5 4 3 2 1

Could I make tongue say more than tongue could utter!
Could I make brain grasp more than brain could think!
Could I weave into immortal denseness some small brede of words,
pluck out of sunken depths the roots of living,
some hundred thousand magic words that were as great as all my hunger,
and hurl the sum of all my living out upon three hundred pages—
then death could take my life, for I had lived it ere he took it:
I had slain hunger, beaten death!

Contents

The Web and the Root

The first three chapters of *The Web and the Rock* return to familiar, if slightly disguised, Wolfe territory, Asheville, now called Libya Hill; the Blue Ridge Mountains; and some familiar characters, now sporting new names or relationships to the central figure of the novel. That new figure, grotesque in body but potentially beautiful in spirit, supplants Eugene Gant as a surrogate character. He is called George Webber and must accept, willy-nilly, the nickname "Monk" because of his simian features. The territory may be familiar and the characters readily identifiable with ones Wolfe created for *Look Homeward, Angel* and *Of Time and the River*, but the subject matter, tone, and literary traditions differ significantly from the earlier novels.

Launching a frontal attack on the warped values of the Blue Ridge area, especially among Baptist members of the Joyner side of George's forebears, Wolfe dwells sarcastically on the hypocrisy of Bible-quoting but scripture-disobeying members of that flock, Aunt Mag Joyner being the chief offender. She shares the opinion that drinking whiskey is a greater moral vice than committing murder. Like other members of her Baptist kin, she thinks that divorce is unforgivable. Morally intolerant as she is, she's not above abusing children in her care, and her kin fail to act when mining companies despoil the landscape to dig for mica. In pointing to this rape of mountain property, Wolfe takes a place as an early eco-minded writer.

True to his conceptual plan for moving to a more objective way of writing, Wolfe took measured steps to leave behind the trappings of a Byronic hero, or a Shellyean rebel out to reform the world with idealism so compelling that even the yokels of the world would see the errors of their way. Rather than satisfying himself with a pinprick, he most often struck with heavy hammerblows. This new tone, rigorous in its denunciation and damning in its charges of hypocrisy and accommodation, underscores Wolfe's expressed ambition to be more satiric and probing in this new cycle.

In large measure, Wolfe doffed Joycean and Whitmanesque garb in a revealing letter leading up to his attempt to present an avatar more representative of his maturing vision of American society. Pointedly, he wanted to leave behind the "wounded faun," his portrait of a young American author misunderstood and undervalued by his countrymen, to strip his projected protagonist of what he labeled "Eugene Gant-i-ness." Even though he liked the feel and look of a bardic mantle, he was moving inexorably towards Sinclair Lewis, Theodore Dreiser, Mark Twain, and those penetrating observers of the dark side of American culture: Nathaniel Hawthorne, Herman Melville, and William Faulkner. Lyrical outpourings would diminish as social criticism, satire, and dramatizations of human propensity to evil boiled to the surface of his fiction.

Even as he marched in closer rank with American writers, he looked to foreign writers for models of what he hoped to do in developing a new avatar, variously christened Paul Spangler, Joe Doaks, and George Webber. Spangler would be a kind of modern-day Gulliver, Don Quixote, or Werther, a man who discovered that the real world was quite different from the one he had imagined. Joe Doaks would not have a celebrated literary model but rather would be a man of the people, just one of those stumbling, bumbling humans trying to make his way through the world and getting bumped and bruised but nonetheless hanging tough and exposing—through his common touch, falsity, meanness, and pretense, and expressing, out of a hopefulness that the goodness of the American people would finally prevail—a conviction that the true greatness of the nation lay before it. George

Webber would inherit traits from Spangler and Doaks but would ac-
quire a lineage linking him to a western North Carolina folk hero and
a Pennsylvania brick mason.

The folk hero was Zebulon Vance, like Wolfe a native of Buncombe
County, North Carolina, who served the state as congressman, governor,
and senator. Wolfe reaches back before Vance's time to trace the rise of
the mountain-bred Joyner family, the founding member of which, William "Bear" Joyner, appears in the mold of Daniel Boone, Davy Crockett,
and Mike Finn: a lusty, rough-edged fellow who fathers many children,
one of whom, Zach, takes on the trappings of Vance in his climb to political power and heroic stature. It is from the Joyners that George Webber traces his maternal side, and it is that Joyner side, split in its views
of morals, religion, and regard for the supernatural, that spawns much
of the musing of young George as he stretches out on his Aunt Maw's
lawn at three o'clock one fine afternoon. But readers of Wolfe have to go
to *The Hills Beyond* to find an account of George's Joyner side, since Edward Aswell, his editor at *Harper's,* chose to start George's narrative with
George and not his forebears, thereby repeating a move Maxwell Perkins
made in cutting Wolfe's account of Eugene Gant's ancestors in *Look
Homeward, Angel.* Much as he had worked to put together a connected
narrative and to develop a cast of characters since early 1936, Wolfe
delivered into Aswell's hands portions of the Joyner-Webber material in
various states of completion or mere drafts along with a rough outline
and statement of purpose when he left New York to give a talk at Purdue
University and to travel further west. That trip, crowded by sightseeing
with a team of journalists wanting to prove that many of the great Western parks could be visited in a few days, further exhausted an already
fatigued Wolfe, and precipitated a hospital stay in the Seattle area and his
death in Baltimore on 15 September 1938, a victim of tuberculosis of the
brain. Wolfe had intended, he had assured Aswell, to work hard and long
to make this new work, now being called *You Can't Go Home Again,* the
best piece of writing he had ever done, more objective, more truthfully
autobiographical, without the preening and posturing of Eugene Gant,

with less of a Joycean flavor, and with more of America as Wolfe had seen it, reveled in it, been disappointed and inspired by it. This means he would sometimes be naturalistic, hard-nosed, intent upon dramatizing how Americans came to act and believe as they did. But there would be jollity mixed with somberness, pessimism lightened by optimism, disgust mitigated by a deeply felt conviction that Americans would not let the dream of a democratic nation die. In Wolfe's expansive way of thinking, he was writing one book, one in which he would wreak his vision of America as he positioned himself as a truth-telling protagonist, one more faithful and thoroughly autobiographical than he had drawn in depicting Eugene Gant.

Yet that book existed more as a concept than as a body of writing that could be readily turned into one or more novels. The stacks of material left in Aswell's hands seemed to him a "jigsaw puzzle," an accurate enough description considering that Wolfe had brought together pieces cut from *O Lost/Look Homeward, Angel,* stories previously published in magazines, and sketches and dramatic vignettes he wanted to use in a projected work about America at night, *The Hound of Darkness.* Faced with something he sometimes thought of as a chaotic jumble, Aswell turned to Maxwell Perkins, formerly Wolfe's editor at Scribner's and now his literary executor; Elizabeth Nowell, Wolfe's agent, who was quite familiar with Wolfe's work in progress; and to members of Wolfe's family to seek advice and counsel about how to proceed with the chore of editing and publishing. He particularly wanted Fred Wolfe to identify the real-life counterparts of characters based on persons living in Asheville, and he wanted to assure himself that Wolfe's former mistress, Aline Bernstein, would not file a libel suit if Harper and Brothers published the love story of George Webber and Esther Jack, the fictional embodiments of Wolfe and Bernstein.

Aswell's efforts, though fruitful in many ways, still left him with a disjointed work, a work needing revision, transitional passages, excision of duplicate materials, fuller realization of characters or scenes, and untangling of names. The task was a daunting one, solved, ultimately, by his becoming a coauthor, a role in part acknowledged in a note appearing at the end of *The Hills Beyond,* in which Aswell explained that he had added italicized transitional passages between books. But studies of Wolfe's typescript reveal that Aswell did more than provide bridges. The extent of his creative contribution to the Webber cycle will likely be the work of some doctoral student in American literature, the result of which will be a dissertation or an article in a learned journal. Part of that task has been undertaken and shared by John Halberstadt. Aswell's note on his work to bring Wolfe's stacks of material to print makes the justifiable claim that Wolfe was not thinking of two separate novels, rather one that would be called "You Can't Go Home Again." It was a matter of convenience, wrote Aswell, that Harper and Brothers decided to issue the novel in two parts, naming the first installment after a working title Wolfe was using for part of his stack of manuscript, "The Web and the Rock."

As far as the whole result is concerned, the decision was not a happy one, for Wolfe wished to salvage the love story he had meant to publish as *The October Fair.* To use it in the Webber cycle would demand heavy revision, for the story was truly Eugene Gant's and the style was early Wolfe, not the later Wolfe, who had moved to a leaner style and a more objective way of presenting his characters. The first three chapters of *The Web and the Rock* were later Wolfe, part of the Joyner-Webber cycle, a recasting of Wolfe's boyhood and family relationships, a deeper and more objective evaluation of the forces of southern Appalachia on his thought and personality.

The decision to issue the three initial chapters of *The Web and the Rock* rescues a portion of Wolfe's work that could pass from the American literary scene. As a few of the earliest critical estimates of the whole work asserted, the novel had mismatched, uneven parts, and represented a falling off of Wolfe's powers. Some reviewers, rightfully, complained that the claim made in the author's note, about a more objective manner and a pronounced satiric flavor was not an accurate description of the work. That note, shaped from a letter to Aswell, more properly related to the Webber-Joyner cycle. It certainly did not apply to much of the material in the final four books.

The three books rescued in this edition do indeed merit publication, even if Wolfe was recycling some materials. They are rich, varied, evocative of time and place, and abounding in characters that Wolfe either created from scratch, for example, Nebraska Crane, or had but skimpily developed in the Gant novels, a notable one being Gerald Alsop, who had merely a cameo role in *O Lost* under another name, Jack Harvey, a fictional version of John Skally Terry. No doubt the richest, most varied and evocative book is the first. Its four chapters introduce us to George Webber's world, his Joyner and Webber kin, the Joyners linked to southern Appalachia, John Webber (George's father) to Pennsylvania, the same ancestral heritage of Eugene Gant. But here Wolfe, commenting on mountain-bred civilization, delves far more deeply and concretely into narrowness, clannishness, bigotry, hypocrisy, religion, moral values, superstitions, and beliefs in the occult than he had in the Gant cycle. It is a world that Mark Joyner in Book II will vividly expose and roundly condemn. It is a world that George rejects in favor of the envisioned Golden City of the North. Yet it is a world that Wolfe readers must examine and study if they are to understand the forces that helped shape him. A sense of place emerges graphically and powerfully here in Book I, and to rush through Wolfe's wrestling with his mountain heritage is to miss a vital element in his cultural background. His roots indeed run deep in Blue Ridge soil. His lover's quarrel with his native region adds vinegar, and sometimes gall, to his depiction of mountain folk, including thinly disguised members of his own family.

Although some passages about these mountain folk—these "grills," as W. O. Gant would have called them—read more like sociological notes than facts transformed into fiction, Wolfe enables readers to discern the web George must escape if he is to find his way to the Golden City and become the writer he longs to be. Happily, sociology gives way to character presentation and dramatized events as Wolfe moves to trace the enlarging circles of George's world: his friendship with Nebraska Crane, a part Cherokee boy who later becomes a professional baseball player; his disgust with and loathing of white-trash boys from the Doubleday section of town; his resentment that Aunt Maw would interrupt his reveries to ask him to do a mere chore; his encounter with Jerry Alsop at Pine Rock College (another, less favorable, rendering of the University of North Carolina) over whether Charles Dickens or Feodor Dostoevski was the greater writer; his admiration and adulation of a star athlete, Jim Randolph, who was based on William Folger, a star performer at the Citadel and later the University of North Carolina; his further disagreement with Alsop about the greatest men since Jesus Christ, Alsop's candidates being Woodrow Wilson and the saintly and morally stern president of Pine Rock College; his life among a group of young Southern men trying to find their way in New York City and his conclusion, that Jim Randolph, their ostensible leader, was truly a member of the Lost Generation; and, finally, his decision to go his own way, to use his powers and talents to the utmost to win recognition and fame in the Golden City. As a means of rounding out George's journey from daydreamer to his hope of becoming a successful, celebrated, and loved author, Aswell closed out Book III with a fantasy Wolfe had written much earlier, setting it in Boston and casting it as part of Eugene Gant's means of coping with his lonely feelings in Boston.

Interesting as that journey is, in the literary tradition it is a retelling of a provincial's migration to the big city, where, if all goes well, his talents take him to the pinnacle of fame. Had Wolfe only this well-worn plot to share, readers would likely turn to *The Web and the Rock* as relevant but not powerful foregrounding autobiographical fiction linked to the better-realized George Webber of *You Can't Go Home Again*.

The episodes of the novel that most grab and hold attention, asking readers to contemplate the forces that act and interact in human relations and revealing Wolfe to be a master of his craft, appear in Book II, chapters 7 and 8, the first examining the sadistic brutality of Mrs. Lampley, the butcher's wife, the second the shooting rampage of Dick Prosser and its aftermath. Sensual and earthy herself, vulgar in language and thought but puritanical in her demands on the sexual conduct of her son and daughter, she could pass as a blood relative of the mother in *Maggie: A*

Girl of the Streets. Her economic standing is far better than that of Maggie's mother, whose goodness has been beaten down by a drunken husband and poverty. Mrs. Lampley's brutal treatment of her daughter stems more from sadism than from moral rectitude. Her sadism links her to her townsmen, those who violate the law and lynch Dick Prosser. In turning into fiction an event occurring in Asheville when an African American named Will Harris gunned down several men, Wolfe explored the heart of darkness evident in both Dick and the bloodthirsty posse that riddled his body and hanged it up for view in the town square. Posing a question akin to Melville's in *Billy Budd* when Claggart turns against the handsome young sailor, Wolfe seeks to understand the nature of good and evil. Dick is a deeply religious man, a man who prays, reads the Bible, and gains the trust of his employer and of George and his friend, Randy. What explains his onslaught? How to account for the paradox of his behavior, his gentleness and patience when with George and Randy, but his animal-like ferocity as he rifles down man after man in his murderous march across town? His conduct is a mystery to young George, but the older George, recalling the events after many years have passed, could be helped by contemplating the paired poems of William Blake about the tiger, a creature of "fearful symmetry" and the "meek and mild" lamb. "Did he who made the Lamb make thee?" Nowhere else in Wolfe is there a thornier metaphysical mystery to ponder. In a strategy much like one favored by Nathaniel Hawthorne, Wolfe poses the question and leaves the reader to puzzle through its ambiguity, its ambivalence.

Putting "The Child by Tiger" back in its context as Wolfe's delineation and examination of violence in American life provides ample support for reissuing the first three books of *The Web and the Rock*. This story both underscores and magnifies his deeply felt conviction that to see America at night was to see the nation for what it really was. It must not be lost to American literature nor appreciated alone out of context. Welcome back to the canon of American literature.

John L. Idol, Jr.

BOOK I

The Web and the Root

CHAPTER I

The Child Caliban

Up to the time George Webber's father died, there were some unforgiving souls in the town of Libya Hill who spoke of him as a man who not only had deserted his wife and child, but had consummated his iniquity by going off to live with another woman. In the main, those facts are correct. As to the construction that may be placed upon them, I can only say that I should prefer to leave the final judgment to God Almighty, or to those numerous deputies of His whom He has apparently appointed as His spokesmen on this earth. In Libya Hill there are quite a number of them, and I am willing to let them do the talking. For my own part, I can only say that the naked facts of John Webber's desertion are true enough, and that none of his friends ever attempted to deny them. Aside from that, it is worth noting that Mr. Webber had his friends.

John Webber was "a Northern man," of Pennsylvania Dutch extraction, who had come into Old Catawba back in 1881. He was a brick mason and general builder, and he had been brought to Libya Hill to take charge of the work on the new hotel which the Corcorans were putting up on Belmont Hill, in the center of the town. The Corcorans were rich people who had come into that section and bought up tracts of property and laid out plans for large enterprises, of which the hotel was the central one. The railroad was then being built and would soon be finished. And only a year or two before, George Willetts, the great

Northern millionaire, had purchased thousands of acres of the mountain wilderness and had come down with his architects to project the creation of a great country estate that would have no equal in America. New people were coming to town all the time, new faces were being seen upon the streets. There was quite a general feeling in the air that great events were just around the corner, and that a bright destiny was in store for Libya Hill.

It was the time when they were just hatching from the shell, when the place was changing from a little isolated mountain village, lost to the world, with its few thousand native population, to a briskly-moving modern town, with railway connections to all parts, and with a growing population of wealthy people who had heard about the beauties of the setting and were coming there to live.

That was the time John Webber came to Libya Hill, and he stayed, and in a modest way he prospered. And he left his mark upon it. It was said of him that he found the place a little country village of clapboard houses and left it a thriving town of brick. That was the kind of man he was. He liked what was solid and enduring. When he was consulted for his opinion about some new building that was contemplated and was asked what material would be best to use, he would invariably answer, "Brick."

At first, the idea of using brick was a novel one in Libya Hill, and for a moment, while Mr. Webber waited stolidly, his questioner would be silent; then, rather doubtfully, as if he was not sure he had heard aright, he would say, "Brick?"

"Yes, sir," Mr. Webber would answer inflexibly, "brick. It's not going to cost you so much more than lumber by the time you're done, and," he would say quietly, but with conviction, "it's the only way to build. You can't rot it out, you can't rattle it or shake it, you can't kick holes in it, it will keep you warm in Winter and cool in Summer, and fifty years from now, or a hundred for that matter, it will still be here. I don't like lumber," Mr. Webber would go on doggedly. "I don't like wooden houses. I come from Pennsylvania where they know how to build. Why," he would say, with one of his rare displays of boastfulness, "we've got stone barns up there that are built better and have lasted longer than any house you've got in this whole section of the country. In my opinion there are only two materials for a house—stone or brick. And if I had my way," he would add a trifle grimly, "that's how I'd build all of them."

But he did not always have his way. As time went on, the necessities of competition forced him to add a lumber yard to his brick yard, but that was only a grudging concession to the time and place. His real, his first, his deep, abiding love was brick.

And indeed, the very appearance of John Webber, in spite of physical peculiarities which struck one at first sight as strange, even a little startling, suggested qualities in him as solid and substantial as the houses that he built. Although he was slightly above the average height, he gave the curious impression of being shorter than he was. This came from a variety of causes, chief of which was a somewhat "bowed" formation of his body. There was something almost simian in his short legs, bowed slightly outward, his large, flat-looking feet, the powerful, barrel-like torso, and the tremendous gorillalike length of his arms, whose huge paws dangled almost even with his knees. He had a thick, short neck that seemed to sink right down into the burly shoulders, and close sandy-reddish hair that grew down almost to the edges of the cheek bones and to just an inch or so above the eyes. He was getting bald even then, and there was a wide and hairless swathe right down the center of his skull. He had extremely thick and bushy eyebrows, and the trick of peering out from under them with the head out-thrust in an attitude of intensely still attentiveness. But one's first impression of a slightly simian likeness in the man was quickly forgotten as one came to know him. For when John Webber walked along the street in his suit of good black broadcloth, heavy and well-cut, the coat half cutaway, a stiff white shirt with starched cuffs, a wing collar with a cravat of black silk tied in a thick knot, and a remarkable-looking derby hat, pearl-grey in color and of a squarish cut, he looked the very symbol of solid, middle-class respectability.

And yet, to the surprised incredulity of the whole town, this man deserted his wife. As for the child, another construction can be put on that. The bare anatomy of the story runs as follows:

ABOUT 1885, JOHN Webber met a young woman of Libya Hill named Amelia Joyner. She was the daughter of one Lafayette, or "Fate" Joyner, as he was called, who had come out of the hills of Zebulon County a year or two after the Civil War, bringing his family with him. John Webber married Amelia Joyner in 1885 or 1886. In the next fifteen years they had no children, until, in 1900, their son George was born. And about 1908, after their marriage had lasted more than twenty years, Webber left his wife. He had met, a year or two before, a young woman married to a man named Bartlett: the fact of their relationship had reached the proportions of an open scandal by 1908, when he left his wife, and after that he did not pretend to maintain any secrecy about the affair whatever. He was then a man in his sixties; she was more than twenty years younger, and a woman of great beauty. The two of them lived together until his death in 1916.

It cannot be denied that Webber's marriage was a bad one. It is certainly not my purpose to utter a word of criticism of the woman he married, for, whatever her faults were, they were faults she couldn't help. And her greatest fault, perhaps, was that she was a member of a family that was extremely clannish, provincial, and opinionated—in the most narrow and dogged sense of the word, puritanical—and she not only inherited all these traits and convictions of her early training, they were so rooted into her very life and being that no experience, no process of living and enlargement, could ever temper them.

Her father was a man who could announce solemnly and implacably that he "would rather see a daughter of mine dead and lying in her coffin than married to a man who drank." And John Webber was a man who drank. Moreover, Amelia's father, if anyone had ever dared to put the monstrous suggestion to him, would have been perfectly capable of amplifying the Christian sentiments which have just been quoted by announcing that he would rather see a daughter of his dead and in her grave than married to a man who had been divorced. And John Webber was a man who had been divorced.

That, truly, was calamitous, the cause of untold anguish later—perhaps the chief stumbling block in their whole life together. It also seems to have been the one occasion when he did not deal with her truthfully and honestly in reference to his past life before he came to Libya Hill. He had married a girl in Baltimore in the early Seventies, when he himself had been scarcely more than a stripling old enough to vote. He mentioned it just once to one of his cronies: he said that she was only twenty, "as pretty as a picture," and an incorrigible flirt. The marriage had ended almost as suddenly as it had begun—they lived together less than a year. By that time it was apparent to them both that they had made a ruinous mistake. She went home to her people, and in the course of time divorced him.

In the Eighties, and, for that matter, much later than that, in a community such as Libya Hill, divorce was a disgraceful thing. George Webber later said that, even in his own childhood, this feeling was still so strong that a divorced person was spoken about in lowered voices, and that when one whispered furtively behind his hand that someone was "a grass widow," there was a general feeling that she was not only not all she should be, but that she was perhaps just a cut or two above a common prostitute.

In the Eighties, this feeling was so strong that a divorced person was branded with a social stigma as great as that of one who had been convicted of crime and had served a penal sentence. Murder could have been—and was—far more easily forgiven then divorce. Crimes of violence, in fact, were frequent, and many a man had killed his man and had either escaped scot-free, or, having paid whatever penalty was imposed, had returned to take up a position of respected citizenship in the community.

Such, then, were the family and environment of the woman John Webber married. And after he left her to live with Mrs. Bartlett, he became estranged from all the hard-bitten and puritanical members of the Joyner clan. Not long thereafter, Amelia died. After his wife's death, Webber's liaison with Mrs. Bartlett continued, to the scandal of the public and the thin-lipped outrage of his wife's people.

Mark Joyner, Amelia's older brother, was a man who, after a childhood and youth of bitter poverty, was in the way of accumulating a modest competence in the hardware business. With Mag, his wife, he lived in a bright red brick house with hard, new, cement columns before it—everything about it as hard, new, ugly, bold, and raw as new-got wealth. Mag was a pious Baptist, and her sense of outraged righteousness at the open scandal of John Webber's life went beyond the limits of embittered speech. She worked on Mark, talking to him day and night about his duty to his sister's child, until at last, with a full consciousness of the approval of all good people, they took the boy, George, from his father.

The boy had been devoted to his father, but now the Joyners made him one of them. From this time forth, with the sanction of the courts, they kept him.

GEORGE WEBBER'S CHILDHOOD with his mountain kinsmen was, in spite of his sunny disposition, a dark and melancholy one. His status was really that of a charity boy, the poor relation of the clan. He did not live in the fine new house with his Uncle Mark. Instead, he lived in the little one-story frame house which his grandfather, Lafayette Joyner, had built with his own hands forty years before when he came to town. This little house was on the same plot of ground as Mark Joyner's new brick house, a little to the right and to the rear, obscured and dwarfed by its more splendid neighbor.

Here John Webber's little boy was growing up, under the guardianship of a rusty crone of fate, Aunt Maw, a spinstress, his mother's oldest sister, old Lafayette's first child. Born thirty years before Amelia, Aunt Maw was in her seventies, but like some weird sister who preaches doom forever but who never dies, it seemed that she was ageless and eternal. From this dark old aunt of doom, and from the drawling voices of his Joyner kin, a dark picture of his mother's world, his mother's time, all the universe of the Joyner lives and blood, was built up darkly, was wrought out slowly, darkly, with an undefined but overwhelming horror, in the memory, mind, and spirit of the boy. On Winter evenings, as Aunt Maw talked in her croaking monotone by the light of a greasy little lamp—they never had electric lights in his grandfather's cottage—George heard lost voices in the mountains long ago, the wind-torn rawness, the desolate bleakness of lost days in March along clay-rutted roads in the bleak hills a hundred years ago:

Someone was dead in a hill cabin long ago. It was night. He heard the bowling of the wind about the eaves of March. He was within the cabin. The rude, bare boards creaked to the tread of feet. There was no light except the flickering light of pine, the soft, swift flare of resinous wood, the crumbling ash. Against the wall, upon a bed, lay a sheeted figure of someone who had died. Around the flickering fire flame at the hearth, the drawling voices of the Joyners who could never die and who attended the death of others like certain doom and prophecy. And in the room again there was a soft and sudden flare of pine flame flickering on the faces of the Joyners, a smell of camphor and of turpentine—a slow, dark horror in the blooded memory of the boy he could not utter.

In these and in a thousand other ways, from every intonation of Aunt Maw's life and memory, he heard lost voices in the hills long, long ago, saw cloud shadows passing in the wilderness, listened to the rude and wintry desolation of March winds that howl through the sere grasses of the mountain meadows in the month before the month when Spring is come. It came to him at night, in Winter from a room before a dying fire, in Summer from the porch of his grandfather's little house, where Aunt Maw sat with other rusty, aged crones of her own blood and kin, with their unceasing chronicle of death and doom and terror and lost people in the hills long, long ago. It came to him in all they said and did, in the whole dark image of the world they came from, and something lost and stricken in the hills long, long ago.

And they were always right, invincibly right, triumphant over death and all the miseries they had seen and known, lived and fed upon. And he was of their blood and bone, and desperately he felt somehow like life's criminal, some pariah, an outcast to their invincible rightness, their infallible goodness, their unsullied integrity. They filled him with a nameless horror of the lost and lonely world of the old-time, forgotten hills from which they came, with a loathing, with a speechless dread.

His father was a bad man. He knew it. He had heard the chronicle of his father's infamy recounted a thousand times. The story of his father's crimes, his father's sinfulness, his father's lecherous, godless, and immoral life was written on his heart. And yet the image of his father's world was pleasant and good, and full of secret warmth and joy to him. All of the parts of town, all of the places, lands, and things his father's life had touched seemed full of happiness and joy to him. He knew that it was wicked. He felt miserably that he was tainted with his father's blood. He sensed wretchedly and tragically that he was not worthy to be a death-triumphant, ever-perfect, doom-prophetic Joyner. They filled him with the utter loneliness of desolation. He knew he was not good enough for them, and he thought forever of his father's life, the sinful warmth and radiance of his father's world.

He would lie upon the grass before his uncle's fine new house in the green-gold somnolence of afternoon and think forever of his father, thinking: "Now he's here. At this time of the day he will be here." Again:

"He will be going now along the cool side of the street—uptown—before the cigar store. Now he's there—inside the cigar store. I can smell the good cigars. He leans upon the counter, looking out into the street and talking to Ed Battle, who runs the store. There is a wooden Indian by the door, and there are the people passing back and forth along the cool and narrow glade of afternoon. Here comes Mack Haggerty, my father's friend, into the cigar store. Here are the other men who smoke cigars and chew strong and fragrant plugs of apple tobacco. . . .

"Here is the barber shop next door, the snip of shears, the smell of tonics, of shoe polish and good leather, the incessant drawling voices of the barbers. Now he'll be going in to get shaved. I can hear the strong, clean scraping of the razor across the harsh stubble of his face. Now I hear people speaking to him. I hear the hearty voices of the men, all raised in greeting. They are all men who come out of my father's world—the sinful, radiant, and seductive world, the bad world that I think about so much. All the men who smoke cigars and chew tobacco and go to Forman's barber shop know my father. The good people like the Joyners go along the other side of the street—the shadeless side of afternoon, that has the bright and light. . . .

"Now he has finished at the barber's. Now he goes around the corner quickly to O'Connell's place. The wicker doors flap back together as he passes in. There is a moment's malty reek of beer, a smell of sawdust, lemon, rye, and Angostura bitters. There is the lazy flapping of a wooden fan, a moment's glimpse of the great, polished bar, huge mirrors, bottles, the shine of polished glasses, the brass foot-rail, dented with the heel-marks of a thousand feet, and Tim O'Connell, thick-jowled, aproned, leaning on the bar. . . .

"Now he is out again. See him go along the street. Now he is at the livery stable. I see the great, raw shape of rusty, corrugated tin, the wooden incline, pulped by many hoofs, as it goes down, the great hoofs clumping on the wooden floors, the hoofs kicked swiftly, casually, against the stalls, the wooden floors bestrewn with oaty droppings, the clean, dry whiskings of coarse tails across great polished rumps of glossy brown, the niggers talking gruffly to the horses in the stalls, the low, dark voices, gruff and tender, hoarse voices full of horseplay, the horse smell, and horse knowingness, men and horses both together, close: 'Get over dar! Whar you goin'!' The rubber tires of carriages and buggies, the smooth rumble of the rubber tires upon the battered wooden floors. . . . The little office to the left where my father likes to sit and talk with the livery-stable men, the battered little safe, the old roll-top desk, the creaking chairs, the little, blistered, cast-iron stove, the dirty windows, never washed, the smell of leather, old, worn ledgers, harness. . . ."

So did he think forever of his father's life, his father's places, movements, the whole enchanted picture of his father's world.

HIS WAS, IN fact, a savagely divided childhood. Compelled to grow up in an environment and a household which he hated with every instinctive sense of loathing and repulsion of his being, he found himself longing constantly for another universe shaped in the colors of his own desire. And because he was told incessantly that the one he hated was good and admirable, and the one for which he secretly longed was evil and abominable, he came to have a feeling of personal guilt that was to torment him for many years. His sense of *place,* the feeling for specific locality that later became so strong in him, came, he thought, from all these associations of his youth—from his overwhelming conviction, or prejudice, that there were "good" places and "bad" ones. This feeling was developed so intensely in his childhood that there was hardly a street or a house, a hollow or a slope, a backyard or an alleyway in his own small world that did not bear the color of this prejudice. There were certain streets in town that he could scarcely endure to walk along, and there were certain houses that he could not pass without a feeling of bleak repulsion and dislike.

By the time he was twelve years old, he had constructed a kind of geography of his universe, composed of these powerful and instinctive affections and dislikes. The picture of the "good" side of the universe, the one the Joyners said was bad, was almost always one to which his father was in one way or another attached. It was a picture made up of such specific localities as his father's brick and lumber yard; Ed Battle's cigar and tobacco store—this was a place where he met and passed his father every Sunday morning on his way to Sunday School; John Forman's barber shop on the northwest corner of the Square, and the grizzled, inky heads, the well-known faces, of the negro barbers—John Forman was a negro, and George Webber's father went to his shop almost every day in the week; the corrugated tin front and the little dusty office of Miller and Cashman's livery stable, another rendezvous of his father's; the stalls and booths of the City Market, which was in a kind of great, sloping, concrete basement underneath the City Hall; the fire department, with its arched doors, the wooden stomping of great hoofs, and its circle of shirt-sleeved men—firemen, baseball players, and local idlers—sitting in split-bottom chairs of evenings; the look and feel of cellars everywhere—for this, curiously, was one of his strong obsessions—he always had a love of secret and enclosed places; the interiors of theatres, and the old Opera House on nights when a show was in town; McCormack's drug store, over at the southwest corner of the Square opposite his uncle's hardware store, with its onyx fountain, its slanting wooden fans, its cool and dark interior, and its clean and aromatic smells; Sawyer's grocery store, in one of the old brick buildings over on the north side of the Square, with its groaning plenty, its crowded shelves, its great pickle barrels, flour bins, coffee grinders, slabs of bacon, and its aproned clerks with straw cuffs on their sleeves; any kind of carnival or circus grounds; anything that had to do with railway stations, depots, trains, engines, freight cars, station yards. All of these things, and a thousand others, he had connected in a curious but powerful identity with the figure of his father; and because his buried affections and desires drew him so strongly to these things, he felt somehow that they must be bad because he thought them "good," and that he liked them because he was wicked, and his father's son.

His whole picture of his father's world—the world in which his father moved—as he built it in his brain and all the naïve but passionate intensity of childhood, was not unlike a Currier and Ives drawing, except that here the canvas was more crowded and the scale more large. It was a world that was drawn in very bright and very innocent and very thrilling colors—a world where the grass was very, very green, the trees sumptuous and full-bodied, the streams like sapphire, and the skies a crystal blue.

It was a rich, compact, precisely executed world, in which there were no rough edges and no bleak vacancies, no desolate and empty gaps.

In later years, George Webber actually discovered such a world as this in two places. One was the small countryside community in southern Pennsylvania from which his father had come, with its pattern of great red barns, prim brick houses, white fences, and swelling fields, some green with the perfection of young wheat, others rolling strips of bronze, with red earth, and with the dead-still bloom of apple orchards on the hills—all of it as exactly rich, precise, unwasteful, and exciting as any of his childhood dreams could have imagined it. The other was in certain sections of Germany and the Austrian Tyrol— places like the Black Forest and the Forest of Thuringia, and towns like Weimar, Eisenach, old Frankfort, Kufstein on the Austrian border, and Innsbruck.

CHAPTER 2

Three O'Clock

Twenty-five years ago or thereabouts, one afternoon in May, George Webber was lying stretched out in the grass before his uncle's house in Old Catawba.

Isn't Old Catawba a wonderful name? People up North or out West or in other parts of the world don't know much about it, and they don't speak about it often. But really when you know the place and think about it more and more its name is wonderful.

Old Catawba is much better than South Carolina. It is more North, and "North" is a much more wonderful word than "South," as anyone with any ear for words will know. The reason why "South" *seems* such a wonderful word is because we had the word "North" to begin with: if there had been no "North," then the word "South" and all its connotations would not seem so wonderful. Old Catawba is distinguished by its "Northness," and South Carolina by its "Southness." And the "Northness" of Old Catawba is better than the "Southness" of South Carolina. Old Catawba has the slants of evening and the mountain cool. You feel lonely in Old Catawba, but it is not the loneliness of South Carolina. In Old Catawba, the hill boy helps his father building fences and hears a soft Spring howling in the wind, and sees the wind snake through the bending waves of the coarse grasses of the mountain pastures. And far away he hears the whistle's cry wailed back, far-flung and faint along some mountain valley, as a great train rushes towards the cities of the East. And the heart of the hill boy will know joy because he knows, all world-remote, lonely as he is, that some day he will meet the world and know those cities too.

But in South Carolina the loneliness is not like this. They do not have the mountain cool. They have dusty, sand-clay roads, great mournful cotton fields, with pine wood borders and the nigger shacks, and something haunting, soft, and lonely in the air. These people are really lost. They cannot get away from South Carolina, and if they get away they are no good. They drawl beautifully. There is the most wonderful warmth, affection, heartiness in their approach and greeting, but the people are afraid. Their eyes are desperately afraid, filled with a kind of tortured and envenomed terror of the old, stricken, wounded "Southness" of cruelty and lust. Sometimes their women have the honey skins, they are like gold and longing. They are filled with the most luscious and seductive sweetness, tenderness, and gentle mercy. But the men are stricken. They get fat about the bellies, or they have a starved, stricken leanness in the loins. They are soft-voiced and drawling, but their eyes will go about and go again with fear, with terror and suspicion. They drawl softly in front of the drug store, they palaver softly to the girls when the girls drive up, they go up and down the streets of blistered, sun-wide, clay-dust little towns in their shirtsleeves, and they are full of hearty, red-faced greetings.

They cry: "How are y', Jim? Is it hot enough fer you?"

And Jim will say, with a brisk shake of the head: "Hotter'n what Sherman said war was, ain't it, Ed?"

And the street will roar with hearty, red-faced laughter: "By God! That's a good 'un. Damned if ole Jim didn't have it about right too!"— but the eyes keep going back and forth, and fear, suspicion, hatred, and mistrust, and something stricken in the South long, long ago, is there among them.

And after a day before the drug stores or around the empty fountain in the Courthouse Square, they go out to lynch a nigger. They kill him, and they kill him hard. They get in cars at night and put the nigger in between them, they go down the dusty roads until they find the place that they are going to, and before they get there, they jab little knives into the nigger, not a long way, not the whole way in, but just a little way. And they laugh to see him squirm. When they get out at the place where they are going to, the place the nigger sat in is a pool of blood. Perhaps it makes the boy who is driving the car sick at his stomach, but the older people laugh. Then they take the nigger through the rough field stubble of a piece of land and hang him to a tree. But before they hang him they saw off his thick nose and his fat nigger lips with a rusty knife. And they laugh about it. Then they castrate him. And at the end they hang him.

This is the way things are in South Carolina; it is not the way things are in Old Catawba. Old Catawba is much better. Although such things may happen in Old Catawba, they do not belong to the temper and character of the people there. There is a mountain cool in Old Catawba and the slants of evening. The hill men kill in the mountain meadows—they kill about a fence, a dog, the dispute of a boundary line. They kill in drunkenness or in the red smear of the murder lust. But they do not saw off niggers' noses. There is not the look of fear and cruelty in their eyes that the people in South Carolina have.

Old Catawba is a place inhabited by humble people. There is no Charleston in Old Catawba, and not so many people pretending to be what they are not. Charleston produced nothing, and yet it pretended to so much. Now their pretense is reduced to pretending that they amounted to so much formerly. And they really amounted to very little. This is the curse of South Carolina and its "Southness"—of always pretending you *used to be* so much, even though you are not now. Old Catawba does not have this to contend with. It has no Charleston and it does not have to pretend. They are small, plain people.

So Old Catawba is better because it is more "North." Even as a child, George Webber realized that in a general way it was better to be more North than South. If you get too North, it gets no good. Everything gets frozen and dried up. But if you get too South, it is no good either, and it also gets rotten. If you get too North, it gets rotten, but in a cold, dry way. If you get too South, it gets rotten not in a dry way—which if you're going to get rotten is the best way to get rotten—but in a horrible, stagnant, swampy, stenchlike, humid sort of way that is also filled with obscene whisperings and ropy laughter.

Old Catawba is just right. They are not going to set the world on fire down there, neither do they intend to. They make all the mistakes that people can make. They elect the cheapest sort of scoundrel to the highest offices they are able to confer. They have Rotary Clubs and chain gangs and Babbitts and all the rest of it. But they are not bad.

They are not certain, not sure, in Old Catawba. Nothing is certain or sure down there. The towns don't look like New England towns. They don't have the lovely white houses, the elm green streets, the sure, sweet magic of young May, the certainty and purpose of it all. It is not like that. First there are about two hundred miles of a coastal plain. This is a mournful flat-land, wooded with pine barrens. Then there are two hundred miles or thereabouts of Piedmont. This is rolling, rugged, you can't remember it the way that you remember the lavish, sweet, and wonderful farm lands of the Pennsylvania Dutch with their great barns which dominate the land. You don't remember Old Catawba in this way. No; field and fold and gulch and hill and hollow, rough meadow land, bunched coarsely with wrench grass, and pine land borderings, clay bank and gulch and cut and all the trees there are, the locusts, chestnuts, maples, oaks, the pines, the willows, and the syca-mores, all grown up together, all smashed-down tangles, and across in a sweet wilderness, all choked between with dogwood, laurel, and the rhododendron, dead leaves from last October and the needles of the pine—this is one of the ways that Old Catawba looks in May. And then out of the Piedmont westward you will hit the mountains. You don't hit them squarely, they just come to you. Field and fold and hill and hollow, clay bank and cut and gulch and rough swell and convolu-tion of the earth unutterable, and presently the hills are there.

A certain unknown, unsuspected sharpness thrills you. Is it not there? You do not know, for it cannot be proved. And yet the shifting engines switch along the tracks, you see the weed growth by the track-side, the leak-grey painting of a toolshed hut, the bleak, unforgettable, marvelous yellow of a station of the Southern Railway. The huge black snout of a mountain engine comes shifting down the track to take you up behind, and suddenly you know the hills are there. The heavy coaches ride up past mountain pastures, a rail fence, a clay road, the rock-bright clamors of a mountain water. You feel upon your neck the hot, the thrilling, the immensely intimate, the strange and most famil-iar breath of the terrific locomotive. And suddenly the hills are there. You go twisting up the grades and snake round curves with grinding screech. How near, how homely, how common and how strange, how utterly familiar—the great bulk of the Blue Ridge bears imminent upon you and compels you. You can put your hand out of the slow, toiling train and touch it. And all life is near, as common as your breath, as strange as time.

The towns aren't much to look at. There is no lovely, certain thing the way there is in New England. There are just plain houses, nigger shacks, front porches, most of the current bungalow and country-club atrocities, a Public Square, some old buildings that say "The Weaver Block, 1882," some new ones for Ford agencies, cars parked around the Square.

Down in the East, in Old Catawba, they have some smack of an-cientry. The East got settled first and there are a few old towns down there, the remnants of plantations, a few fine old houses, a lot of nig-gers, tobacco, turpentine, pine woods, and the mournful flat-lands of the coastal plain. The people in the East used to think they were better than the people in the West because they had been there a little longer. But they were not really better. In the West, where the moun-tains sweep around them, the people have utterly common, familiar, plain, Scotch-Irish faces, and names like Weaver, Wilson, Gudger, Joyner, Alexander, and Patton. The West is really better than the East. They went to war in the West, and yet they didn't want to go to war. They didn't have anything to go to war about: they were a plain and common people and they had no slaves. And yet they will always go to war if Leaders tell them to—they are made to serve. They think long and earnestly, debatingly; they are conservative; they vote the right way, and they go to war when big people tell them to. The West is really a region of good small people, a Scotch-Irish place, and that, too, is undefined, save that it doesn't drawl so much, works harder, doesn't loaf so much, and shoots a little straighter when it has to. It is really just one of the common places of the earth, a million or two people with nothing very extraordinary about them. If there had been anything extraordinary about them, it would have come out in their houses, as it came out in the lovely white houses of New England; or it would have come out in their barns, as it came out in the great red barns of the Pennsylvania Dutch. They are just common, plain, and homely—but almost everything of America is in them.

GEORGE WEBBER MUST have known all these things twenty-five years ago as he lay on the grass one afternoon before his uncle's house. He really knew the way things were. People sometimes pretend they don't know the way things are, but they really do. George lay in the grass and pulled some grass blades and looked upon them contentedly and chewed upon them. And he knew the way the grass blades were. He dug bare toes into the grass and thought of it. He knew the way it felt. Among the green grass, he saw patches of old brown, and he knew the way that was too. He put out his hand and felt the maple tree. He saw the way it came out of the earth, the grass grew right around it, he felt the bark and got its rough, coarse feeling. He pressed hard with his fingers, a little rough piece of the bark came off; he knew the way that was too. The wind kept howling faintly the way it does in May. All the young leaves of the maple tree were turned back, straining in the wind. He heard the sound it made, it touched him with some sadness, then the wind went and came again.

He turned and saw his uncle's house, its bright red brick, its hard, new, cement columns, everything about it raw and ugly; and beside it, set farther back, the old house his grandfather had built, the clapboard structure, the porch, the gables, the bay windows, the color of the paint. It was all accidental, like a million other things in America. George Webber saw it, and he knew that this was the way things were. He watched the sunlight come and go, across backyards with all their tangle of familiar things; he saw the hills against the eastern side of town, sweet green, a little mottled, so common, homely, and familiar, and, when remembered later, wonderful, the way things are.

George Webber had good eyes, a sound body, he was twelve years old. He had a wonderful nose, a marvelous sense of smell, nothing fooled him. He lay there in the grass before his uncle's house, thinking: "This is the way things are. Here is the grass, so green and coarse, so sweet and delicate, but with some brown rubble in it. There are the houses all along the street, the concrete blocks of walls, somehow so dreary, ugly, yet familiar, the slate roofs and the shingles, the lawns, the hedges and the gables, the backyards with their accidental structures of so many little and familiar things as hen houses, barns. All common and familiar as my breath, all accidental as the strings of blind chance, yet all somehow fore-ordered as a destiny: the way they are, because they are the way they are!"

There was a certain stitch of afternoon while the boy waited. Bird chirrupings and maple leaves, pervading quietness, boards hammered from afar, and a bumbling hum. The day was drowsed with quietness and defunctive turnip greens at three o'clock, and Carlton Leathergood's tall, pock-marked, yellow-nigger was coming up the street. The big dog trotted with him, breathing like a locomotive, the big dog Storm, that knocked you down with friendliness. Tongue rolling, heavy as a man, the great head swaying side to side, puffing with joy continually, the dog came on, and with him came the pock-marked nigger, Simpson Simms. Tall, lean, grinning cheerfully, full of dignity and reverence, the nigger was coming up the street the way he always did at three o'clock. He smiled and raised his hand to George with a courtly greeting. He called him "Mister" Webber as he always did; the greeting was gracious and respectful, and soon forgotten as it is and should be in the good, kind minds of niggers and of idiots, and yet it filled the boy somehow with warmth and joy.

"Good day dar, Mistah Webbah. How's Mistah Webbah today?"

The big dog swayed and panted like an engine, his great tongue lolling out; he came on with great head down and with the great black brisket and his shoulders working.

Something happened suddenly, filling that quiet street with instant menace, injecting terror in the calm pulse of the boy. Around the corner of the Potterham house across the street came Potterham's bulldog. He saw the mastiff, paused; his forelegs widened stockily, his grimjowled face seemed to sink right down between the shoulder blades, his lips bared back along his long-fanged tusks, and from his baleful redshot eyes fierce lightning shone. A low snarl rattled in the folds of his thick throat, the mastiff swung his ponderous head back and growled, the bull came on, halted, leaning forward on his widened legs, filled with hell-fire, solid with fight.

And Carlton Leathergood's pock-marked yellow negro man winked at the boy and shook his head with cheerful confidence, saying:

"He ain't goin' to mix up wid *my* dawg, Mistah Webbah! . . . No, sah! . . . He knows bettah dan dat! . . . Yes, sah!" cried Leathergood's nigger with unbounded confidence. "He knows too well fo' *dat*!"

The pock-marked nigger was mistaken! Something happened like a flash: there was a sudden snarl, a black thunderbolt shot through the air, the shine of murderous fanged teeth. Before the mastiff knew what had happened to him, the little bull was in and had his fierce teeth buried, sunk, gripped with the lock of death, in the great throat of the larger dog.

What happened after that was hard to follow. For a moment the great dog stood stock still with an eloquence of stunned surprise and bewildered consternation that was more than human; then a savage roar burst out upon the quiet air, filling the street with its gigantic anger. The mastiff swung his great head savagely, the little bull went flying through the air but hung on with imbedded teeth; great drops of bright arterial blood went flying everywhere across the pavement, and still the bull held on. The end came like a lightning stroke. The great head flashed over through the air and down: the bull, no longer dog now—just a wad of black—smacked to the pavement with a sickening crunch.

From Potterham's house a screen door slammed, and fourteen-year-old Augustus Potterham, with his wild red hair aflame, came out upon the run. Up the street, paunch-bellied, stiff-legged, and slouchy-uniformed, bound for town and three o'clock, Mr. Matthews, the policeman, pounded heavily. But Leathergood's nigger was already there, tugging furiously at the leather collar around the mastiff's neck, and uttering imprecations.

But it was all too late. The little dog was dead the moment that he struck the pavement—back broken, most of his bones broken, too; in Mr. Matthews' words, "He never knowed what hit him." And the big dog came away quietly enough, now that the thing was done: beneath the negro's wrenching tug upon his neck, he swung back slowly, panting, throat dripping blood in a slow rain, bedewing the street beneath him with the bright red flakes.

Suddenly, like a miracle, the quiet street was full of people. They came from all directions, from everywhere: they pressed around in an excited circle, all trying to talk at once, each with his own story, everyone debating, explaining, giving his own version. In Potterham's house, the screen door slammed again, and Mr. Potterham came running out at his funny little bandylegged stride, his little red apple-cheeks aglow with anger, indignation, and excitement, his funny, chirping little voice heard plainly over all the softer, deeper, heavier, more Southern tones. No longer the great gentleman now, no longer the noble descendant of the Dukes of Potterham, no longer the blood-cousin of belted lords and earls, the possible claimant of enormous titles and estates in Gloucestershire when the present reigning head should die—but Cockney Potterham now, little Potterham minus all his aitches, little

Potterham the dealer in nigger real estate and the owner of the nigger shacks, indomitable little Potterham forgetting all his grammar in the heat and anger of the moment:

" 'Ere now! Wot did I tell you? I always said 'is bloody dog would make trouble! 'Ere! *Look* at 'im now! The girt bleedin', blinkin' thing! Big as a helefant, 'e is! Wot chance ud a dog like mine *'ave* against a brute like that! 'E ought to be put out of the way—that's wot! You mark my words—you let that brute run loose, an' there won't be a dog left in town—that's wot!"

And Leathergood's big pock-marked nigger, still clutching to the mastiff's collar as he talks, and pleading with the policeman almost tearfully:

"Fo' de Lawd, Mistah Matthews, my dawg didn't do *nuffin*! No, sah! He don't bothah nobody—*my* dawg don't! He wa'nt even noticin' dat othah dawg—you ask *anybody*!—ask Mistah Webbah heah!"— suddenly appealing to the boy with pleading entreaty—"Ain't dat right, Mistah Webbah? You saw de whole thing yo'se'f, didn't you? You tell Mistah Matthews how it was! Me an' my dawg was comin' up de street, a-tendin' to ouah business, I jus' tu'ned my haid to say good-day to Mistah Webbah heah, when heah comes dis othah dawg aroun' de house, jus' a-puffin' an' asnawtin', an' befo' I could say Jack Robinson he jumps all ovah my dawg an' grabs him by de throat—you ask Mistah Webbah if dat ain't de way it happened."

And so it goes, everyone debating, arguing, agreeing, and denying, giving his own version and his own opinion; and Mr. Matthews asking questions and writing things down in a book; and poor Augustus Potterham blubbering like a baby, holding his dead little bulldog in his arms, his homely, freckled face contorted piteously, and dropping scalding tears upon his little dead dog; and the big mastiff panting, dripping blood upon the ground and looking curious, detached from the whole thing, and a little bored; and presently the excitement subsiding, people going away; Mr. Matthews telling the negro to appear in court; Augustus Potterham going away into the house blubbering, with the little bulldog in his arms; Mr. Potterham behind him, still chirping loudly and excitedly; and the dejected, pock-marked nigger and his tremendous dog going away up the street, the big dog dropping big blood flakes on the pavement as he goes. And finally, silence as before, the quiet street again, the rustling of young maple leaves in the light wind, the brooding imminence of three o'clock, a few bright blood-flakes on the pavement, and all else the way that it had always been, and George Webber as before stretched out upon the grass beneath the tree there in his uncle's yard, chin cupped in hands, adrift on time's great dream, and thinking:

"Great God, this is the way things are, I see and know this is the way things are, I understand this is the way things are: and, Great God! Great God! this being just the way things are, how strange, and plain, and savage, sweet and cruel, lovely, terrible, and mysterious, and how unmistakable and familiar all things are!"

Three o'clock!

"CHILD, CHILD!—WHERE ARE you, child?"

So did he always know Aunt Maw was there!

"Son, son!—Where are you, son?"

Too far for finding and too near to seek!

"Boy, boy!—Where *is* that boy?"

Where *you,* at any rate, or any other of the apron-skirted kind, can never come.

"You can't take your eye off him a minute. . . ."

Keep eye *on,* then; it will do no good.

"The moment that your back is turned, he's up and gone. . . ."

And out and off and far away from *you*—no matter if your back is turned or not!

"I can never find him when I need him. . . ."

Need me no needs, sweet dame; when I need you, you shall be so informed!

"But he can *eat,* all right. . . . He's Johnny-on-the-spot when it is time to eat. . . ."

And, pray, what is there so remarkable in *that*? Of course he *eats*—more power to his eating, too. Was Hercules a daffodil; did Adam toy with water cress; did Falstaff wax fat eating lettuces; was Dr. Johnson surfeited on shredded wheat; or Chaucer on a handful of parched corn? No! What is more, were campaigns fought and waged on empty bellies; was Kublai Khan a vegetarian; did Washington have prunes for breakfast, radishes for lunch; was John L. Sullivan the slave of Holland Rusk, or President Taft the easy prey of lady fingers? No! More—who drove the traffic of swift-thronging noon, perched high above the hauling rumps of horses; who sat above the pistoned wheels of furious day; who hurled a ribbon of steel rails into the West; who dug, drove through gulches, bored through tunnels; whose old gloved hands were gripped on the throttles; who bore the hammer, and who dealt the stroke?—did such of these grow faint with longing when they thought of the full gluttony of peanut-butter and ginger snaps? And finally, the men who came back from the town at twelve o'clock, their solid liquid tramp of leather on the streets of noon, the men of labor, sweat, and business coming down the street—his uncle, Mr. Potterham, Mr. Shepperton, Mr. Crane—were fence gates opened, screen doors slammed, and was there droning torpor and the full feeding silence of assuagement and repose—if these men had come to take a cup of coffee and a nap?

"He can *eat*, all right! . . . He's always here when it is time to *eat*!"

It was to listen to such stuff as this that great men lived and suffered, and great horses bled! It was for this that Ajax battled, and Achilles died; it was for this that Homer sang and suffered—and Troy fell! It was for this that Artaxerxes led great armies, it was for this that Caesar took his legions over Gaul; for this that Ulysses had braved strange seas, encompassed perils of remote and magic coasts, survived the Cyclops and Charybdis, and surmounted all the famed enchantments of Circean time—to listen to such damned and dismal stuff as this—the astonishing discovery by a woman that men *eat*!

Peace, woman, to your bicker—hold your prosy tongue! Get back

THE WEB AND THE ROOT

into the world you know, and do the work for which you were intended; you intrude—go back, go back to all your kitchen scourings, your pots and pans, your plates and cups and saucers, your clothes and rags and soaps and sudsy water; go back, go back and leave us; we are fed and we are pleasantly distended, great thoughts possess us; drowsy dreams; we would lie alone and contemplate our navel—it is afternoon!

"Boy, boy!—Where has he got to now! . . . Oh, I could see him lookin' round. . . . I saw him edgin' towards the door! . . . Aha, I thought, he thinks he's very smart . . . but I knew exactly what he planned to do . . . to slip out and to get away before I caught him . . . and just because he was afraid I had a little work for him to do!"

A *little* work! Aye. there's the rub—if only it were not always just a *little* work we had to do! If only in their minds there ever were a moment of *supreme occasion* or *sublime event*! If only it were not always just a *little* thing they have in mind, a *little* work we had to do! If only there were something, just a spark of joy to lift the heart, a spark of magic to fire the spirit, a spark of understanding of the thing we *want* to do, a grain of feeling, or an atom of imagination! But always it is just a *little* work, a *little* thing we have to do!

Is it the little *labor* that she asks that we begrudge? Is it the little *effort* which it would require that we abhor? Is it the little *help* she asks for that we ungenerously withhold, a hate of work, a fear of sweat, a spirit of mean giving? No! It is not this at all. It is that women in the early afternoon are dull, and dully ask dull things of us; it is that women in the afternoon are dull, and ask us always for a *little* thing, and do not understand!

It is that at this hour of day we do not want them near us—we would be alone. They smell of kitchen steam and drabness at this time of day: the depressing moistures of defunctive greens, left-over cabbage, lukewarm boilings, and the dinner scraps. An atmosphere of sudsy water now pervades them; their hands drip rinsings and their lives are grey.

These people do not know it, out of mercy we have never told them; but their lives lack interest at three o'clock—we do not want them, they must let us be.

They have some knowledge for the morning, some for afternoon, more for sunset, much for night; but at three o'clock they bore us, they must leave us be! They do not understand the thousand lights and weathers of the day as we; light is just light to them, and morning morning, and noon noon. They do not know the thing that comes and goes—the way light changes, and the way things shift; they do not know how brightness changes in the sun, and how man's spirit changes like a flick of light. Oh, they do not know, they cannot understand, the life of life, the joy of joy, the grief of grief unutterable, the eternity of living in a moment, the thing that changes as light changes, as swift and passing as a swallow's flight; they do not know the thing that comes and goes and never can be captured, the thorn of Spring, the sharp and tongueless cry!

They do not understand the joy and horror of the day as *we* can feel it; they do not understand the thing we dread at this hour of the afternoon.

To them the light is light, the brief hour passing; their soaps-suds spirits do not contemplate the horror of hot light in afternoon. They do not understand our loathing of hot gardens, the way our spirits dull and sicken at hot light. They do not know how hope forsakes us, how joy flies away, when we look at the mottled torpor of hot light on the hydrangeas, the broad-leaved dullness of hot dock-weeds growing by the barn. They do not know the horror of old rusty cans filled into gaps of rubbish underneath the fence: the loathing of the mottled, hot, and torpid light upon a row of scraggly corn; the hopeless depth of torpid, dull depression which the sight of hot coarse grasses in the sun can rouse to a numb wakefulness of horror in our souls at three o'clock.

It is a kind of torpid stagnancy of life, it is a hopelessness of hope, a dull, numb lifelessness of life! It is like looking at a pool of stagnant water in the dull torpor of the light of three o'clock. It is like being where no green is, where no cool is, where there is no song of unseen birds, where there is no sound of cool and secret waters, no sound of rock-bright, foaming waters; like being where no gold and green and sudden magic is, to be called out to do *little* things at three o'clock.

Ah, Christ, could we make speech say what no speech utters, could we make tongue speak what no tongue says! Could we enlighten their enkitchened lives with a revealing utterance, then they would never send us out to do a *little* thing at three o'clock.

We are a kind that hate clay banks in afternoon, the look of cinders, grimy surfaces, old blistered clapboard houses, the train yards and the coaches broiling on the tracks. We loathe the sight of concrete walls, the fly-speckled windows of the Greek, the strawberry horror of the row of lukewarm soda-pop. At this hour of the day we sicken at the Greek's hot window, at his greasy frying plate that *fries* and oozes with a loathsome sweat in the full torpor of the sun. We hate the row of greasy frankfurters that *sweat* and *ooze* there on the torpid plate, the loathsome pans all oozing with a stew of greasy onions, mashed potatoes, and hamburger steaks. We loathe the Greek's swart features in the light of three o'clock, the yellowed pock-marked pores that sweat in the hot light. We hate the light that shines on motor cars at three o'clock, we hate white plaster surfaces, new stucco houses, and most open places where there are no trees.

We must have coolness, dankness, darkness; we need gladed green and gold and rock-bright running waters at the hour of three o'clock. We must go down into the coolness of a concrete cellar. We like dark shade, and cool, dark smells, and cool, dark, secret places, at the hour of three o'clock. We like cool, strong smells with some cool staleness at that hour. Man smells are good at three o'clock. We like to remember the smells of all things that were in our father's room: the dank, cool pungency of the plug of apple tobacco on the mantelpiece, bit into at one end, and struck with a bright red flag; the smell of the old mantelpiece, the wooden clock, the old calf bindings of a few old books; the smell of the rocking chair, the rug, the walnut bureau, and the cool, dark smell of clothing in the closet.

At this hour of the day we like the smell of old unopened rooms, old packing cases, tar, and the smell of the grape vines on the cool side of the house. If we go out, we want to go out in green shade and gladed coolnesses, to lie down on our bellies underneath the maple trees and work our toes down into the thick green grass. If we have to go to town we want to go to places like our uncle's hardware store, where we can smell the cool, dark cleanliness of nails, hammers, saws, tools, T-squares, implements of all sorts; or to a saddle shop where we can get the smell of leather; or to our father's brick and lumber yard where we can get the smells of putty, glass, and clean white pine, the smell of the mule-teams, and the lumber sheds. It is also good to go into the cool glade of the drug store at this hour, to hear the cool, swift slatting of the wooden fans, and to smell the citrus pungency of lemons, limes, and oranges, the sharp and clean excitements of unknown medicines.

The smell of a street car at this hour of day is also good—a dynamic smell of motors, wood work, rattan seats, worn brass, and steel-bright flanges. It is a smell of drowsy, warm excitement, and a nameless beating of the heart; it speaks of going somewhere. If we go anywhere at this hour of day, it is good to go to the baseball game and smell the grandstand, the old wooden bleachers, the green turf of the playing field, the horsehide of the ball, the gloves, the mitts, the clean resilience of the ash-wood bats, the smells of men in shirt-sleeves, and the sweating players.

"And if there is work to do at three o'clock—if we must rouse ourselves from somnolent repose, and from the green-gold drowsy magic of our meditations—for God's sake give us something *real* to do. Give us great labors, but vouchsafe to us as well the promise of a great accomplishment, the thrill of peril, the hope of high and spirited adventure. For God's sake don't destroy the heart and hope and life and will, the brave and dreaming soul of man, with the common, dull, soul-sickening, mean transactions of these *little* things!

Don't break our heart, our hope, our ecstasy, don't shatter

irrevocably some brave adventure of the spirit, or some brooding dream, by sending us on errands which any stupid girl, or nigger wench, or soulless underling of life could just as well accomplish. Don't break man's heart, man's life, man's song, the soaring vision of his dream with—"Here, boy, trot around the corner for a loaf of bread,"—or "Here, boy; the telephone company has just called up—you'll have to trot around there . . ."—Oh, for God's sake, and *my* sake, *please* don't say '*trot* around'—" . . . and pay the bill before they cut us off!"

Or, fretful-wise, be-flusteredlike, all of a twitter, scattered and de-moralized, fuming and stewing, complaining, whining, railing against the universe because of things undone *you* should have done yourself, because of errors *you* have made yourself, because of debts unpaid *you* should have paid on time, because of things forgotten *you* should have remembered— fretting, complaining, galloping off in all directions, unable to get your thoughts together, unable even to call a child by his proper name—as here:

"Ed, John, Bob—pshaw, boy! *George,* I mean! . . ."

Well, then for God's sake, *mean* it!

"Why, pshaw!—to think that that fool nigger—I could wring her neck when I think of it—well, as I say now. . . ."

Then, in God's name, *say* it!

" . . . why, you *know* . . ."

No! I do *not* know!

" . . . here I was dependin' on her—here she told me she would come—and all the work to be done—and here she's sneaked out on me after dinner—and I'm left here in the lurch."

Yes, of course you are; because you failed to pay the poor wench on Saturday night the three dollars which is her princely emolument for fourteen hours a day of sweaty drudgery seven days a week; because "it slipped your mind," because you couldn't bear to let it go in one gigantic lump—*could* you?—because you thought you'd hang on to the good green smell of money just a *little* longer, didn't you?—let it sweat away in your stocking and smell good just a *little* longer—didn't you?—break the poor brute's heart on Saturday night just when she had her mind all set on fried fish, gin, and f——g, just because you wanted to hold on to three wadded, soiled, and rumpled greenbacks just a *little* longer—dole it out to her a dollar at a time—tonight a dollar, Wednesday night a dollar, Friday night the same . . . and so are left here strapped and stranded and forlorn, where my father would have *paid* and *paid at once,* and kept his nigger and his nigger's loyalty. And all because you are a woman, with a woman's niggard smallness about money, a woman's niggard dealing towards her servants, a woman's selfishness, her small humanity of feeling for the dumb, the suffering, and afflicted soul of man—and so will fret and fume and fidget now, all flustered and undone, to call me forth with:

"Here, boy!—Pshaw, now!—To think that she would play a trick like this!—Why as I say, now—child! child!—I don't know what I shall do—I'm left here all alone—you'll have to trot right down and see if you can find someone at once."

Aye! to call me forth from coolness, and the gladed sweetness of cool grass to sweat my way through Niggertown in the dreary torpor of the afternoon; to sweat my way up and down that grassless, treeless horror of baked clay; to draw my breath in stench and sourness, breathe in the funky nigger stench, sour wash-pots and branch-sewage, nigger privies and the sour shambles of the nigger shacks; to scar my sight and soul with little snot-nosed nigger children fouled with dung, and so bowed out with rickets that their little legs look like twin sausages of fat, soft rubber; so to hunt, and knock at shack-door, so to wheedle, persuade, and cajole, in order to find some other sullen wench to come and sweat her fourteen hours a day for seven days a week—and for three dollars!

Or again, perhaps it will be: "Pshaw, boy!—Why to think that he would play me such a trick!—Why, I forgot to put the sign out—but I thought he knew I needed twenty pounds!—If he'd only asked!—but here he drove right by with not so much as by-your-leave, and here there's not a speck of ice in the refrigerator—and ice cream and iced tea to make for supper.—You'll have to trot right down to the ice-house and get me a good ten-cent chunk."

Yes! A good ten-cent chunk tied with a twist of galling twine, that cuts like a razor down into my sweaty palm; that wets my trouser leg from thigh to buttock; that bangs and rubs and slips and cuts and freezes against my miserable knees until the flesh is worn raw; that trickles freezing drops down my bare and aching legs, that takes all joy from living, that makes me curse my life and all the circumstances of my birth—and all because *you* failed to "put the sign out," all because *you* failed to think of twenty pounds of ice!

Or is it a thimble, or a box of needles, or a spool of thread that *you* need now! Is it for such as *this* that I must "trot around" some place for baking powder, salt or sugar, or a pound of butter, or a package of tea!

For God's sake thimble me no thimbles and spool me no spools! If I must go on errands send me out upon man's work, with man's dispatch, as my father used to do! Send me out with one of his niggers upon a wagon load of fragrant pine, monarch above the rumps of two grey mules! Send me for a wagon load of sand down by the river, where I can smell the sultry yellow of the stream, and shout and holler to the boys in swimming! Send me to town to my father's brick and lumber yard, the Square, the sparkling traffic of bright afternoon. Send me for something in the City Market, the smell of fish and oysters, the green, cool growth of vegetables; the cold refrigeration of hung beeves, the butchers cleaving and sawing in straw hats and gouted aprons. Send me out to life and business and the glades of afternoon; for God's sake, do not torture me with spools of thread, or with the sunbaked clay and shambling rickets of black Niggertown!

"Son, son! . . . Where has that fool boy got to! . . . Why, as I say now, boy, you'll have to trot right down to. . . ."

With baleful, brooding vision he looked towards the house. Say me no says, sweet dame: trot me no trots. The hour is three o'clock, and I would be alone.

So thinking, feeling, saying, he rolled over on his belly, out of sight, on the "good" side of the tree, dug bare, luxurious toes in cool, green grass, and, chin a-cup in his supporting hands, regarded his small universe of three o'clock.

"A LITTLE CHILD, a limber elf"—twelve years of age, and going on for thirteen next October. So, midway in May now, midway to thirteen, with a whole world to think of. Not large or heavy for his age, but strong and heavy in the shoulders, arms absurdly long, big hands, legs thin, bowed out a little, long, flat feet; small face and features quick with life, the eyes deep-set, their look both quick and still; low brow, wide, stick-out ears, a shock of close-cropped hair, a large head that hangs forward and projects almost too heavily for the short, thin neck—not much to look at, someone's ugly duckling, just a boy.

And yet—could climb trees like a monkey, spring like a cat; could jump and catch the maple limb four feet above his head—the bark was already worn smooth and slick by his big hands; could be up the tree like a flash; could go places no one else could go; could climb anything, grab hold of anything, dig his toes in anything; could scale the side of a cliff if he had to, could almost climb a sheet of glass; could pick up things with his toes, and hold them, too; could walk on his hands, bend back and touch the ground, stick his head between his legs, or wrap his legs around his neck; could make a hoop out of his body and roll over like a hoop, do hand-springs and cut flips—jump, climb, and leap as no other boy in town could do. He is a grotesque-looking little creature, yet unformed and unmatured, in his make-up something between a spider and an ape (the boys, of course, call him "Monk")—and yet with an eye that sees and holds, an ear that hears and can remember, a nose that smells out unsuspected pungencies, a spirit swift and mercurial as a flash of light, now soaring like a rocket, wild with ecstasy, outstripping storm and flight itself in the aerial joy of skyey buoyancy; now plunged in nameless, utter, black, unfathomable dejection; now bedded cool in the reposeful grass beneath the maple tree, remote from time and brooding on his world of three o'clock; now catlike on his feet—the soaring rocket of a sudden joy—then catlike spring and catch upon the lowest limb, then like a monkey up the tree, and like a monkey down, now rolling like a furious hoop across the yard—at last, upon his belly in cool grass again, and bedded deep in somnolent repose at three o'clock.

Now, with chin cupped in his hands and broodingly aware, he meditates the little world before him, the world of one small, modest street, the neighbors, and his uncle's house. For the most part, it is the pleasant world of humble people and small, humble houses, most of them worn, shabby, so familiar: the yards, the porches, swings, and railings, and the rocking chairs; the maple trees, the chestnuts and the oaks; the way a gate leans open, half ajar, the way the grass grows, and the way the flowers are planted; the fences, hedges, bushes, and the honeysuckle vines; the alleyways and all the homely and familiar back-yard world of chicken houses, stables, barns, and orchards, and each one with its own familiar hobby, the Potterham's neat back-garden, Nebraska Crane's pigeon houses—the whole, small, well-used world of good, small people.

He sees the near line of eastern hills, with light upon it, the sweet familiarity of massed green. His thought soars westward with a vision of far distances and splendid ranges; his heart turns west with thoughts of unknown men and places and of wandering; but ever his heart turns home to this his own world, to what he knows and likes the best. It is—he feels and senses this obscurely—the place of common man, his father's kind of people. Except for his uncle's raw, new house, the sight of which is a desolation to him, it is the place of the homely, simple houses, and the old, ordinary streets, where the bricklayers, plasterers, and masons, the lumber dealers and the stonecutters, the plumbers, hardware merchants, butchers, grocers, and the old, common, native families of the mountains—his mother's people—make their home.

It is the place of the Springtime orchards, the loamy, dew-wet morning gardens, the peach, cherry, apple blossoms, drifting to the ground at morning in the month of April, the pungent, fragrant, maddening savor of the breakfast smells. It is the place of roses, lilies, and nasturtiums, the vine-covered porches of the houses, the strange, delicious smell of the ripening grapes in August, and the voices—near, strange, haunting, lonely, most familiar—of the people sitting on their porches in the Summer darkness, the voices of the lost people in the darkness as they say good-night. Then boys will hear a screen door slam, the earth grow silent with the vast and brooding ululation of the night, and finally the approach, the grinding screech, the brief halt, the receding loneliness and absence of the last street car going around the corner on the hill, and will wait there in the darkness filled with strangeness, thinking, "I was born here, there's my father, this is I!"

It is the world of the sun-warm, time-far clucking of the sensual hens in the forenoon strangeness of the spell of time, and the coarse, sweet coolness of Crane's cow along the alleyway; and it is the place of the ice-tongs ringing in the streets, the ice saw droning through the dripping blocks, the sweating negroes, and the pungent, musty, and exotic odors of the grocery wagons, the grocery box piled high with new provisions. It is the place of the forenoon housewives with their shapeless gingham dresses, bare legs, slippers, turbaned heads, bare, bony, labor-toughened hands and arms and elbows, and the fresh, clean, humid smell of houses airing in the morning. It is the place of the heavy midday dinners, the smells of roasts of beef, corn on the cob, the deep-hued savor of the big string beans, cooking morning long into the sweet amity and unction of the fat-streaked pork; and above it all is the clean, hungry, humid smell and the streaming freshness of the turnip greens at noon.

It is the world of magic April and October; world of the first green and the smell of blossoms; world of the bedded oak leaves and the smell of smoke in Autumn, and men in shirt-sleeves working in their yards in red waning light of old October as boys pass by them going home from school. It is the world of the Summer nights, world of the dream-strange nights of August, the great moons and the tolling bells; world of the Winter nights, the howling winds, and the fire-full chimney throats—world of the ash of time and silence while the piled coals flare and crumble, world of the waiting, waiting, waiting—for the world of joy, the longed-for face, the hoped-for step, the unbelieved-in magic of the Spring again.

It is the world of warmth, nearness, certitude, the walls of home! It is the world of the plain faces, and the sounding belly laughter; world of the people who are not too good or fine or proud or precious for the world's coarse uses; world of the sons who are as their fathers were before them, and are compacted of man's base, common, stinking clay of fury, blood, and sweat and agony—and must rise or fall out of the world from which they came, sink or swim, survive or perish, live, die, conquer, find alone their way, be baffled, beaten, grow furious, drunken, desperate, mad, lie smashed and battered in the stews, find a door, a dwelling place of warmth and love and strong security, or be driven famished, unassuaged, and furious through the world until they die!

Last of all, it is the world of the true friends, the fine, strong boys who can smack a ball and climb a tree, and are always on the lookout for the thrill and menace of adventure. They are the brave, free, joyful, hope-inspiring fellows who are not too nice and dainty and who have no sneers. Their names are such wonderful, open-sounding names as John, Jim, Robert, Joe, and Tom. Their names are William, Henry, George, Ben, Edward, Lee, Hugh, Richard, Arthur, Jack! Their names are the names of the straight eye and the calm and level glance, names of the thrown ball, the crack of the bat, the driven hit; names of wild, jubilant, and secret darkness, brooding, prowling, wild, exultant night, the wailing whistle and the great wheels pounding at the river's edge.

They are the names of hope, the names of love, friendship, confidence, and courage, the names of life that will prevail and will not be beaten by the names of desolation, the hopeless, sneering, deathloving, and lifehating names of old scorn-maker's pride—the hateful and accursed names that the boys who live in the western part of town possess.

Finally, they are the rich, unusual names, the strange, yet homely, sturdy names—the names of George Josiah Webber and Nebraska Crane.

NEBRASKA CRANE WAS walking down the street upon the other side. He was bare-headed, his shock of Indian coarse black hair standing out, his shirt was opened at his strong, lean neck, his square brown face was tanned and flushed with recent effort. From the big pocket of his pants the thick black fingers of a fielder's mitt protruded, and upon his shoulder he was carrying a well-worn ash-wood bat, of which the handle was wound round tight with tape. He came marching along at his strong and even stride, his bat upon his shoulder, as steady and as unperturbed as a soldier, and, as he passed, he turned his fearless face upon the boy across the street—looked at him with his black-eyed Indian look, and, without raising his voice, said quietly in a tone instinct with quiet friendliness:

"Hi, Monk!"

And the boy who lay there in the grass, his face supported in his hands, responded without moving, in the same toneless, friendly way:

"Hello, Bras."

Nebraska Crane marched on down the street, turned into the alley by his house, marched down it, turned the corner of his house, and so was lost from sight.

And the boy who lay on his belly in the grass continued to look out quietly from the supporting prop of his cupped hands. But a feeling of certitude and comfort, of warmth and confidence and quiet joy, had filled his heart, as it always did when Nebraska Crane passed his house at three o'clock.

The boy lay on his belly in the young tender grass. Jerry Alsop, aged sixteen, fat and priestly, his belly buttoned in blue serge, went down along the other side of the street. He was a grave and quiet little figure, well liked by the other boys, but he was always on the outer fringes of their life, always on the sidelines of their games, always an observer of their universe—a fat and quiet visitant, well-spoken, pleasant-voiced, compactly buttoned in the blue serge that he always wore. . . . There had been one night of awful searching, one hour when all the torment and the anguish in that small, fat life had flared out in desperation. He had run away from home, and they had found him six hours later on the river road, down by the muddy little river, beside the place where all the other boys went to swim, the one hole deep enough to drown. His mother came and took him by the hand; he turned and looked at her, and then the two fell sobbing in each other's arms. . . . For all the rest, he had been a quiet and studious boy, well thought of in the town. Jerry's father was a dry goods merchant, and the family was comfortably off in a modest way. Jerry had a good mind, a prodigious memory for what he read, all things in books came smoothly to him. He would finish high school next year. . . .

Jerry Alsop passed on down the street.

Suddenly, the Webber boy heard voices in the street. He turned his head and looked, but even before he turned his head his ear had told him, a cold, dry tightening of his heart, an acrid dryness on his lips, a cold, dry loathing in his blood, had told him who they were.

Four boys were coming down the street in raffish guise; advancing scattered and disorderly, now scampering sideways, chasing, tussling in lewd horseplay with each other, smacking each other with wet towels across the buttocks (they had just come from swimming in Jim Rheinhardt's cow pond in the Cove), filling the quiet street with the intrusions of their raucous voices, taking the sun and joy and singing from the day.

They slammed yard gates and vaulted fences; they dodged round trees, ducked warily behind telephone poles, chased each other back and forth, gripped briefly, struggling strenuously, showed off to each other, making raucous noises, uttering mirthless gibes. One chased another around a tree, was deftly tripped, fell sprawling to the roar of their derision, rose red and angry in the face, trying mirthlessly to smile, hurled his wet, wadded towel at the one who tripped him—missed and was derided, picked his towel up, and to save his ugly face and turn derision from him cried out—"Pee-e-nuts!"—loudly passing Pennock's house.

The boy surveyed them with cold loathing—this was wit!

They filled that pleasant street with raucous gibes, and they took hope and peace and brightness from the day. They were unwholesome roisterers, they did not move ahead in comradeship, but scampered lewdly, raggedly around, as raucous, hoarse, and mirthless as a gob of phlegm: there was no warmth, no joy or hope or pleasantness in them; they filled the pleasant street with brutal insolence. They came from the west side of town, he knew them instinctively for what they were—the creatures of a joyless insolence, the bearers of the hated names.

Thus Sidney Purtle, a tall, lean fellow, aged fifteen, and everything about him pale—pale eyes, pale features, pale lank hair, pale eyebrows and a long, pale nose, pale lips and mouth carved always in a pale and ugly sneer, pale hands, pale hair upon his face, pale freckles, and a pale, sneering, and envenomed soul:

"Georgeous the Porgeous!" A pale sneer, a palely sneering laugh; and as he spoke the words he smacked outward with his wet and loathsome rag of towel. The boy ducked it and arose.

Carl Hooton stood surveying him—a brutal, stocky figure, brutal legs outspread, red-skinned, red-handed, and red-eyed, red-eyebrowed, and an inch of brutal brow beneath the flaming thatch of coarse red hair:

"Well, as I live and breathe," he sneered (the others smirked appreciation of this flaming wit), "it's little Jocko the Webber, ain't it?"

"Jockus the Cockus," said Sid Purtle softly, horribly—and smacked the wet towel briefly at the boy's bare leg.

"Jockus the Cockus—hell!" said Carl Hooton with a sneer, and for a moment more looked at the boy with brutal and derisory contempt. "Son, you ain't *nothin'*," he went on with heavy emphasis, now turning to address his fellows—"Why that little monk-faced squirrel's—they ain't even dropped yet."

Loud appreciative laughter followed on this sally; the boy stood there flushed, resentful, staring at them, saying nothing. Sid Purtle moved closer to him, his pale eyes narrowed ominously to slits.

"Is that right, Monkus?" he asked, with a hateful and confiding quietness. A burble of unwholesome laughter played briefly in his throat, but he summoned sober features, and said quietly, with menacing demand: "Is that right, or not? Have they fallen yet?"

"Sid, Sid," whispered Harry Nast, plucking at his companion's sleeve; a snicker of furtive mirth crossed his rat-sharp features. "Let's find out how well he's hung."

They laughed, and Sidney Purtle said:

"Are you hung well, Monkus?" Turning to his comrades, he said gravely, "Shall we find out how much he's got, boys?"

And suddenly alive with eagerness and mirthful cruelty, they all pressed closer around the boy, with secret, unclean laughter, saying:

"Yes, yes—come on, let's do it! Let's find out how much he's got!"

"Young Monkus," said Sid Purtle gravely, putting a restraining hand upon his victim's arm, "much as it pains us all, we're goin' to examine you."

"Let go of me!" The boy wrenched free, turned, whirled, backed up against the tree; the pack pressed closer, leering faces thrusting forward, pale, hateful eyes smeared with the slime of all their foul and secret jubilation. His breath was coming hoarsely, and he said: "I told you to let go of me!"

"Young Monkus," said Sid Purtle gravely, in a tone of quiet reproof, wherein the dogs of an obscene and jeering mirth were faintly howling—"Young Monkus, we're surprised at you! We had expected you to behave like a little gentleman—to take your medicine like a little man. . . . Boys!"

He turned, addressing copemates in a tone of solemn admonition, grave surprise: "It seems the little Monkus is trying to get hard with us. Do you think we should take steps?"

"Yes, yes," the others eagerly replied, and pressed still closer round the tree.

And for a moment there was an evil, jubilantly attentive silence as they looked at him, naught but the dry, hard pounding of his heart, his quick, hard breathing, as they looked at him. Then Victor Munson moved forward slowly, his thick, short hand extended, the heavy volutes of his proud, swart nostrils swelling with scorn. And his voice, low-toned and sneering, cajoling with a hateful mockery, came closer to him coaxingly, and said:

"Come, Monkus! Come little Monkus! Lie down and take your medicine, little Monk! . . . Here Jocko! Come Jocko! Here Jocko! Come Jocko!—Come and get your peanuts—Jock, Jock, Jock!"

Then while they joined in hateful laughter, Victor Munson moved forward again, the swart, stub fingers, warted on the back, closed down upon the boy's left arm; and suddenly he drew in his breath in blind, blank horror and in bitter agony, he knew that he must die and never draw his shameful breath in quietude and peace, or have a moment's hope of heartful ease again; something blurred and darkened in blind eyes—he wrenched free from the swart, stub fingers, and he struck.

The blind blow landed in the thick, swart neck and sent it gurgling backwards. Sharp hatred crossed his vision now, and so enlightened it; he licked his lips and tasted bitterness, and, sobbing in his throat, he started towards the hated face. He arms were pinioned from behind. Sid Purtle had him, the hateful voice was saying with a menacing and now really baleful quietude:

"Now, wait a minute! Wait a minute, boys! . . . We were just playin' with him, weren't we, and he started to get hard with us! . . . Ain't that right?"

"That's right, Sid. That's the way it was, all right!"

"We thought he was a man, but he turns out to be just a little sorehead, don't he? We were just kiddin' him along, and he has to go and get sore about it. You couldn't take it like a man, could you?" said

Sidney Purtle, quietly and ominously into the ear of his prisoner; at the same time he shook the boy a little— "You're just a little cry-baby, ain't you? You're just a coward, who has to hit a fellow when he ain't lookin'?"

"You turn loose of me," the captive panted, "I'll show you who's the cry-baby! I'll show you if I have to hit him when he isn't looking!"

"Is that so, son?" said Victor Munson, breathing hard.

"Yes, that's so, son!" the other answered bitterly.

"Who says it's so, son?"

"I say it's so, son!"

"Well, you don't need to go gettin' on your head about it!"

"I'm not the one who's gettin' on his head about it; *you* are!"

"Is *that* so?"

"Yes, *that's* so!"

There was a pause of labored breathing and contorted lips; the acrid taste of loathing and the poisonous constrictions of brute fear, a sense of dizziness about the head, a kind of hollow numbness in the stomach pit, knee sockets gone a trifle watery; all of the gold of just a while ago gone now, all of the singing and the green; no color now, a poisonous whiteness in the very quality of light, a kind of poisonous intensity of focus everywhere; the two antagonists' faces suddenly keen, eyes sharp with eager cruelty, pack-appetites awakened, murder-sharp now, lusts aware.

"You'd better not be gettin' big about it," said Victor Munson slowly, breathing heavily, "or somebody'll smack you down!"

"You know anyone who's going to do it?"

"Maybe I do and maybe I don't, I'm not sayin'. It's none of your business."

"It's none of your business either!"

"Maybe," said Victor Munson, breathing swarthily, and edging forward an inch or so—"Maybe I'll make it some of my business!"

"You're not the only one who can make it your business!"

"You know of anyone who wants to make it anything?"

"Maybe I do and maybe I don't."

"Do you *say* that you do?"

"Maybe I do and maybe I don't. I don't back down from saying it."

"Boys, boys," said Sidney Purtle, quietly, mockingly. "You're gettin' hard with each other. You're usin' harsh language to each other. The first thing you know you'll be gettin' into trouble with each other—about Christmas time," he jeered quietly.

"If he wants to make anything out of it," said Victor Munson bitterly, "he knows what he can do."

"You know what you can do, too!"

"Boys, boys," jeered Sidney Purtle softly.

"Fight! Fight!" said Harry Nast, and snickered furtively. "When is the big fight gonna begin?"

"Hell!" said Carl Hooton coarsely, "they don't want to fight. They're both so scared already they're ready to—in their pants. Do you want to fight, Munson?" he said softly, brutally, coming close and menacing behind the other boy.

"If he wants to make something of it—" the Munson boy began again.

"Well, then, make it!" cried Carl Hooton, with a brutal laugh, and at the same moment gave the Munson boy a violent shove that sent him hurtling forward against the pinioned form of his antagonist. Sid Purtle sent his captive hurtling forward at the Munson boy; in a second more, they were crouching toe to toe, and circling round each other. Sid Purtle's voice could be heard saying quietly:

"If they want to fight it out, leave 'em alone! Stand back and give 'em room!"

"Wait a minute!"

The words were spoken almost tonelessly, but they carried in them such a weight of quiet and inflexible command that instantly all the boys stopped and turned with startled surprise, to see where they came from.

Nebraska Crane, his bat upon his shoulder, was advancing towards them from across the street. He came on steadily, neither quickening nor changing his stride, his face expressionless, his black Indian gaze fixed steadily upon them.

"Wait a minute!" he repeated as he came up.

"What's the matter?" Sidney Purtle answered, with a semblance of surprise.

"You leave Monk alone," Nebraska Crane replied.

"What've we done?" Sid Purtle said, with a fine show of innocence.

"I saw you," said Nebraska with toneless stubbornness, "all four of you ganged up on him; now leave him be."

"Leave him *be*?" Sid Purtle now protested.

"You heard me!"

Carl Hooton, more brutal and courageous and less cautious than Sid Purtle, now broke in truculently:

"What's it to you? What business is it of yours what we do?"

"I make it my business," Nebraska answered calmly. "Monk," he went on, "you come over here with me."

Carl Hooton stepped before the Webber boy and said:

"What right have you to tell us what to do?"

"Get out of the way," Nebraska said.

"Who's gonna make me?" said Carl Hooton, edging forward belligerently.

"Carl, Carl—come on," said Sid Purtle in a low, warning tone. "Don't pay any attention to him. If he wants to get on his head about it, leave him be."

There were low, warning murmurs from the other boys.

"The rest of you can back down if you like," Carl Hooton answered, "but I'm not takin' any backwash from him. Just because his old man is a policeman, he thinks he's hard. Well, I can get hard, too, if he gets hard with me."

"You heard what I told you!" Nebraska said. "Get out of the way!"

"You go to hell!" Carl Hooton answered. "I'll do as I damn please!"

Nebraska Crane swung solidly from the shoulders with his baseball bat and knocked the red-haired fellow sprawling. It was a crushing blow, so toneless, steady, and impassive in its deliberation that the boys turned white with horror, confronted now with a murderous savagery of purpose they had not bargained for. It was obvious to all of them that the blow might have killed Carl Hooton had it landed on his head; it was equally and horribly evident that it would not have mattered to Nebraska Crane if he *had* killed Carl Hooton. His black eyes shone like agate in his head, the Cherokee in him had been awakened, he was set to kill. As it was, the blow had landed with the sickening thud of ash-wood on man's living flesh, upon Carl Hooton's arm; the arm was numb from wrist to shoulder, and three frightened boys were now picking up the fourth, stunned, befuddled, badly frightened, not knowing whether a single bone had been left unbroken in his body, whether he was permanently maimed, or whether he would live to walk again.

"Carl—Carl—are you hurt bad? How's your arm?" said Sidney Purtle.

"I think it's broken," groaned that worthy, clutching the injured member with his other hand.

"You—you—you hit him with your bat," Sid Purtle whispered. "You—you had no right to do that."

"His arm may be broken," Harry Nast said, in an awed tone.

"I meant to break it," Nebraska said calmly. "He's lucky that I didn't break his God-damn head."

They looked at him with horrified astonishment, with a kind of fascinated awe.

"You—you could be arrested for doing that!" Sid Purtle blurted out. "You might have killed him!"

"Wouldn't have cared if I had!" Nebraska said firmly. "He ought to be killed! Meant to kill him!"

Their eyes were fixed on him in a stare wide with horror. He returned their look in Indian-wise, and moved forward a step, still holding his bat firm and ready at his shoulder.

"And I'll tell you this—and you can tell the rest of 'em when you get back to *your* side of town. Tell 'em I'm ready to brain the first West Side —— who comes here looking for trouble. And if any of you ever bother Monk again, I'll come right over there and climb your frame," Nebraska Crane asserted. "I'll come right over there and beat you to death. . . . Now you clear out! We don't want you on our street no longer! You get out of here!"

He advanced upon them slowly, his hard black eyes fixed firmly on them, his hands gripped ready on his bat. The frightened boys fell back, supporting their injured comrade, and, muttering furtively among themselves, limped hastily away down the street. At the corner they turned, and Sid Purtle put his hands up to his mouth and, with a sudden access of defiance, yelled back loudly:

"We'll get even with you yet! Wait till we get you over on our side of town!"

Nebraska Crane did not reply. He continued to stare steadily towards them with his Indian eyes, and in a moment more they turned and limped away around the corner and were lost from sight.

When they had gone, Nebraska took his bat off his shoulder, leaned gracefully on it, and, turning towards the white-faced boy, surveyed him for a moment with a calm and friendly look. His square brown face, splotched large with freckles, opened in a wide and homely smile; he grinned amiably and said:

"What's the trouble, Monkus? Were they about to get you down?"

"You—you—why, Nebraska!" the other boy now whispered—"you might have killed him with that bat."

"Why," Nebraska answered amiably, "what if I had?"

"Wuh—wuh—wouldn't you care?" young Webber whispered, awe-struck, his eyes still with wonder, horror, fascinated disbelief.

"Why, not a bit of it!" Nebraska heartily declared. "Good riddance to bad rubbish if I *had* killed him! Never liked that redhead of his'n, anyway, and don't like none of that crowd he runs with—that whole

West Side gang! I've got no use for none of 'em, Monkus—never did have!"

"B-but, Bras," the other stammered, "wouldn't you be *afraid*?"

"Afraid? Afraid of what?"

"Why, why—that you might have killed him."

"Why, that's nothin' to be afraid of!" said Nebraska. "Anyone's likely to get killed, Monk. You're likely to have to kill someone almost *any* time! Why, look at my old man. He's been killin' people all his life—ever since he's been on the police force, anyway! I reckon he's killed more people than he could remember—he counted up to seventeen one time, an' then he told me that there was one or two others he'd clean lost track of! Yes!" Nebraska continued triumphantly, "and there was one or two *before* he joined the force that no one ever knowed of—I reckon that was way back there when he was just a boy, so long ago he's plumb lost track of it! Why my old man had to kill a nigger here along—oh, just a week or so ago—and he never turned a hair! Came home to supper, an' took off his coat, hung up his gun and cottridge belt, washed his hands and set down at the table, and had got halfway through his supper before he even thought of it. Says to my maw, all of a sudden, says—'Oh, yes! I clean forgot to tell you! I had to shoot a nigger today!' 'That so?' my maw says. 'Is there any other news?' So they went on talkin' about first one thing and then another, and in five minutes' time I'll bet you both of them had forgotten clean about it! . . . Pshaw, Monk!" Nebraska Crane concluded heartily, "you oughtn't even to *bother* about things like that. Anyone's liable to have to kill someone. *That* happens every day!"

"Y-y-y-yes, Bras," Young Webber faltered—"b-b-but what if anything should happen to *you*?"

"Happen?" cried Nebraska, and looked at his young friend with frank surprise. "Why what's goin' to happen to you, Monk?"

"W-w-why—I was thinking that sometimes *you* might be the one who gets killed *yourself*."

"*Oh!*" Nebraska said, with a nod of understanding, after a

moment's puzzled cogitation. "That's what you mean! Why, yes, Monk, that *does* sometimes happen! But," he earnestly continued, "it's got no *right* to happen! You ought not to *let* it happen! If it happens it's your own fault!"

"*L-l-let! Fault!* How do you mean, Bras?"

"Why," Nebraska said patiently, but with just a shade of resignation, "I mean it won't happen to you if you're *careful.*"

"*C-c-careful?* How do you mean careful, Bras?"

"Why, Monk," Nebraska now spoke with a gruff, though kind, impatience, "I mean if you're careful not to *let* yourself be killed! Look at my old man, now!" he proceeded with triumphant logic—"Here he's been killin' people in one way or 'nother goin' on to thirty years now—leastways way before both you an' *me* was born! An he's never been killed his-self *one* time!" he triumphantly concluded. "And *why?* Why, Monk, because my old man always took good care to kill the other feller before the other feller could kill him. As long as you do *that,* you'll be all right."

"Y-y-yes, Bras. But if you g-g-get yourself in trouble?"

"Trouble?" said Nebraska, staring blankly. "Why what trouble is there to get into? If *you* kill the other feller before he kills you, *he's* the one who gets in trouble. *You're* all right; I thought *anyone* could see that much!"

"Y-y-yes, Bras. I do see that. But I was thinking about getting arrested . . . and being locked up . . . and having to go to jail—that kind of trouble."

"Oh, *that* kind of trouble!" Nebraska said a little blankly, and considered the question for a moment. "Well, Monk, if you get arrested, you get *arrested*—and that's all there is to that! Why, pshaw, boy—*anyone* can get arrested; that's likely to happen to anybody. My old man's been arrestin' people all his life. I reckon he wouldn't have any notion how many people he's arrested and locked up! . . . Why yes, and he's even been arrested and locked up a few times himself, but he never let that bother him a *bit.*"

"F-f-for *what,* Bras? What did he get arrested for?"

"Oh—for killin' people, an' doin' things like that! You know how it is, Monk. Sometimes the relatives or neighbors, or the wives and children of people that he killed would raise a rumpus—say he didn't have no right to kill 'em—some such stuff as that! But it always come out all right—it always *does!*" cried Nebraska earnestly. "And why? Why because, like the old man says, this is America, an' we're a *free* country—an' if someone gets in your way an' bothers you, you have to kill him—an' that's all there is to it! . . . If you have to go to court an' stand trial, you go to court an' stand trial. Of course, it's a lot of trouble an' takes up your time—but then the jury lets you off, an' that's all there is to it! . . . I know my old man always says that this is the only country in the world where the poor man has a chance! In Europe he wouldn't have the chance a snowball has in hell! And why? Why because, as my old man says, in Europe the laws are all made for the rich, a poor man never can get justice *there*—what justice there *is* is all for the kings an' dukes an' lords an' ladies, an' such people as that. But a poor man—why, Monk," Nebraska said impressively, "if a poor man in *Europe* went an' killed a man, almost anything might happen to him— that's just how rotten an' corrupt the whole thing is over there. You ask my old man about it sometime! He'll tell you! . . . But, pshaw, boy!" he now continued, with a resumption of his former friendly and good-humored casualness, "you got nothing in the world to worry about! If any of that West Side gang comes back an' tries to bother you, you let *me* know, and I'll take care of 'em! If we've got to kill someone, we'll have to kill someone—but you oughtn't even to let it worry you! . . . And now, so long, Monk! You let *me* know if anything turns up and I'll take care of it!"

"Th-thanks, Bras! I sure appreciate . . ."

"Pshaw, boy! Forget about it! We got to stick together on *our* side of town. We're neighbors! You'd do the same for me, I knew *that!*"

"Yes, I would, Bras. Well, good-bye."

"Good-bye, Monk. I'll be seein' you 'fore long."

And quiet, steady, unperturbed, moving along at even steps, his calm, brave face and Indian eyes fixed forward, his baseball bat held firmly on his shoulder, the Cherokee boy moved off, turned right into his alley, and was lost from sight.

NEBRASKA CRANE WAS the best boy in the town, but Sid Purtle was poor white trash and a mountain grill. If Sid Purtle had been any good, his people never would have named him Sid. George Webber's uncle had said that they were nothing but mountain grills no matter if they did live out upon Montgomery Avenue on the West Side of town; that's all that they had been to start with, that's what he called them, and that's what they were, all right. Sid! That was a fine name, now! A rotten, dirty, sneering, treacherous, snot-nosed, blear-eyed, bitch of a name! Other rotten sneering names were Guy, Clarence, Roy, Harry, Victor, Carl and Floyd.

Boys who had these names were never any good—a thin-lipped, sneer-mouthed, freckled, blear-eyed set of hair-faced louts, who had unpleasant knuckly hands, and a dry, evil, juiceless kind of skin. There was always something jeering, ugly, unwholesome, smug, complacent, and triumphant about these people. Without knowing why, he always wanted to smash them in the face, and not only hated everything about them, but he hated the "very ground they walked on," the houses they lived in, the streets on which they lived, the part of town they came from, together with their fathers, mothers, sisters, brothers, cousins, aunts, and close companions.

He felt that they were not only foully different from the people that he liked in all the qualities that made for warmth, joy, happiness, affection, friendship, and the green-gold magic of enchanted weather—he felt there was also in them a physical difference, so foul and hateful that they might be creatures of another species. In blood, bone, brains, white-haired, juiceless-looking flesh, in sinew, joint, and tissue, in the very spittle of their mouths—which would be a vilely ropy, glutinously murky stuff of the very quality of their blear eyes and their sneering

lips—as well as in all the delicate combining nerves, veins, jellies, ce-
ments, and fibrous webs that go to knit that marvelous tenement, that
whole integument of life that is a human body, these people whose very
names he hated would be found to be made of a vile, base, incalculably
evil stuff. It was a substance that was as different from the glorious stuff
of which the people that he liked were made as a foul excrement of fecal
matter from the health and relish of sound, wholesome, life-begetting
food. It was a substance not only of the mind and spirit but of the very
texture of the body, so that it seemed they had been begot from acid and
envenomed loins, and nurtured all their lives on nameless and abominable rations. He could not have eaten of the food their mothers cooked
for them without choking and retching at each mouthful, feeling that
he was swallowing some filth or foulness with every bite he took.

And yet, they seemed to score an evil and unfathomable triumph
everywhere he met them. It was a triumph of death over life; of sneering mockery and ridicule over gaiety, warmth, and friendly ease; of
wretchedness, pain, and misery over all the powerful music of joy; of
the bad, sterile, and envenomed life over the good life of hope, happiness, and the glorious belief and certitude of love.

They were the dwellers in accursed streets, the very bricks of which
you hated so you had to fight your way along each grim step of the
hated pavement. They were the walkers underneath accursed skies,
who evilly rejoiced in the broad, wet, wintry lights of waning March,
and in all the cruel, houseless, hopeless, viscous, soul-engulfing lights
and weathers of misery, weariness, and desolation.

They were the people that you never met in all the green-gold magic
of enchanted weather. They were the accursed race who never came
to you in places where strong joy was—in sorceries of gladed green by
broken, rock-cold waters starred by the poignant and intolerable enchantments of the dandelions. No! They were the bathers in the humid,
shadeless waters where the soul sank down. They came to no encircled
pools of greenery; the brave shout was not in them, and they sang no
songs.

In a thousand barren and desolate places, a thousand lights and weathers of the soul's grey horror, in the brutal, weary heat of August in raw concrete places, or across rude paths of gluey clay beneath the desolate wintry reds of waning Sunday afternoons in March, they moved forever with the triumphant immunity of their evil lives. They breathed without weariness, agony, or despair of soul an accursed air from which your own life recoiled with a shuddering revulsion; they sneered at you forever while you drowned.

They were the vultures of the world, who swoop forever over stricken fields, and, with an evil and unfailing prescience of woe, they always come upon you at your life's worst hour. If your bowels were wretched, queasy, sick, and diarrheic; if your limbs were feverish, feeble, watery, and sick; your skin, dry, loose, and itchy; your stomach retching with disgusting nausea, your eyes running, your nose leaking snottily, and your guts stuffed full of the thick, grey, viscous misery of a cold—then, certain as death and daylight they would be there, gloating on your wretchedness with the evil and triumphant superiority of their sneering faces.

Similarly, if the grey and humid skies of desolation pressed down upon your spirit; if the broad, wet lights of shame were eating nakedly into your unhoused, unwalled, unprotected flesh; if the nameless and intolerable fear—huge, soft, grey, and shapeless—was pressing at you from the immense and planetary vacancy of timeless skies; if grey horror drowned you, and every sinew, power, exultant strength and soaring music of your life, together with the powerful, delicate, and uncountable fabric of the nerves lay snarled, palsied, and unedged, leaving you stricken, wrecked, impotent, and shuddering in the hideous shipwreck of your energies: then they, *they*—Sid, Carl, Guy, Harry, Floyd, Clarence, Victor, Roy, that damned, vile, sneering horde of evil-loving, pain-devouring, life-destroying names—would be there certain as a curse, to dip their dripping beaks into your heart, to feed triumphant on your sorrow while you strangled like a mad dog in your wretchedness, and died!

And oh! to die so, drown so, choke and strangle, bleed so wretchedly to death—and die! die! die! in horror and in misery, untended and unfriended by these ghouls of death! Oh, death could be triumphant—death in battle, death in love, death in friendship and in peril, could be glorious if it were proud death, gaunt death, lean, lonely, tender, loving, and heroic death, who bent to touch his chosen son with mercy, love, and pity, and put the seal of honor on him when he died!

Yes, death could be triumphant! Death could come sublimely if it came when the great people of the living names were with you. Heroic fellowship of friendship, joy, and love, their names were John, George, William, Oliver, and Jack; their names were Henry, Richard, Thomas, James, and Hugh; their names were Edward, Joseph, Andrew, Emerson, and Mark! Their names were George Josiah Webber and Nebraska Crane!

The proud, plain music of their names itself was anthem for their glorious lives, and spoke triumphantly to him of the warmth, the joy, the certitude and faith of that heroic brotherhood. It spoke to him of great deeds done and mighty works accomplished, of glorious death in battle, and a triumph over death himself if only they were there to see him greet him when he came. Then might he say to them, with an exultant cry: "Oh brothers, friends, and comrades, dear rivals with me in the fellowship of glorious deeds, how dearly I have loved my life with you! How I have been your friendly rival and your equal in all things! How proudly and sublimely have I lived!—Now see how proudly and sublimely I can die!"

To die so, in this fellowship of life, would be glory, joy, and triumphant death for any man! But to die wretchedly and miserably, unfed, famished, unassuaged; to die with queasy guts and running bowels, a dry skin, feeble limbs, a nauseous and constricted heart; to die with rheumy eyes, and reddened, running nostrils; to die defeated, hopeless, unfulfilled, your talents wasted, your powers misused, unstruck, palsied, come to naught—the thought of it was not to be endured, and he swore that death itself would die before he came to it.

To die there like a dull, defeated slave in that ghoulish death-triumphant audience of Sid, Roy, Harry, Victor, Carl, and Guy!—to die defeated with those sneering visages of scorn-maker's pride upon you, yielding to that obscene company of death-in-life its foul, final victory—oh, it was intolerable, intolerable! Horror and hatred gripped him when he thought of it, and he swore that he would make his life prevail, beat them with the weapons of certitude, nail their grisly hides upon the wall with the shining and incontrovertible nails of joy and magic, make their sneering mouths eat crow, and put the victorious foot of life upon the proud, bowed neck of scorn and misery forever.

NEBRASKA CRANE WAS a fellow that he liked. That was a queer name, sure enough, but there was also something good about it. It was a square, thick, muscular, brawny, browned and freckled, wholesome kind of name, plain as an old shoe and afraid of nothing, and yet it had some strangeness in it, too. And that was the kind of boy Nebraska Crane was.

Nebraska's father had been a policeman, was now a captain on the force; he came from back in Zebulon County; he had some Cherokee in him. Mr. Crane knew everything; there was nothing that he could not do. If the sun came out the fourteenth day of March, he could tell you what it meant, and whether the sun would shine in April. If it rained or snowed or hailed or stormed three weeks before Easter, he could prophesy the weather Easter Sunday. He could look at the sky and tell you what was coming; if an early frost was on its way to kill the peach trees, he could tell you it was on its way and when it would arrive; there was no storm, no sudden shift in weather that he could not "feel in his bones" before it came. He had a thousand signs and symptoms of foretelling things like these—the look of the moon or the look of a cloud, the feel of the air or the direction of the wind, the appearance of the earliest bird, the half-appearance of the first blade of grass. He could feel storm coming, and could smell the thunder. It all amounted to a kind of great sixth sense out of nature, an almost supernatural intuition. In addition to—or as a consequence of—all these things, Mr. Crane raised the finest vegetables of anyone in town—the largest, perfectest tomatoes, the biggest potatoes, the finest peas and greens and onions, the most luscious strawberries, the most beautiful flowers.

He was, as may be seen, a figure of some importance in the community, not only as a captain of police, but as a sort of local prophet. The newspaper was constantly interviewing him about all kinds of things—changes in weather, prospects for a cold Winter, a hot Summer, or a killing frost, a state of drought, or an excess of rain. He always had an answer ready, and he rarely failed.

Finally—and this, of course, made his person memorably heroic to the boys—he had at one time in his life been a professional wrestler (a good one too; at one time, it was said, "the champion of the South"), and although he was now approaching fifty, he occasionally consented to appear in local contests, and give an exhibition of his prowess. There had been one thrilling Winter, just a year or two before, when Mr. Crane, during the course of a season, had met a whole series of sinister antagonists—Masked Marvels, Hidden Menaces, Terrible Turks, Mighty Swedes, Demon Dummies, and all the rest of them.

George Webber remembered all of them; Nebraska had always taken him on passes which his father gave him. The thought of the very approach of these evenings was enough to put the younger boy into a fever of anticipation, a frenzy of apprehension, an agonized unrest. He could not understand how Mr. Crane or Nebraska could face one of these occasions, with all of its terrible moments of conflict, victory or defeat, injury or mutilation, broken bones or fractured ligaments, with no more perturbation than they would show when sitting down to eat their evening meal.

And yet it was true! These people—son and father both—seemed to have come straight from the heart of immutable and unperturbed nature. Warmth they had, staunch friendliness, and the capacity for savage passion, ruthless murder. But they had no more terror than a mountain. Nerve they had, steel nerve; but as for the cold anguish of the aching and constricted pulse, the dry, hard ache and tightness of the throat, the hollow numbness of the stomach pit, the dizzy lightness of the head, the feeling of an unreal buoyancy before the moment of attack—they seemed to know no more about these things than if they had been made of oak!

Time after time on days when Mr. Crane was due to wrestle at the City Auditorium, the boy had watched him pass the house. Time after time he had searched the policeman's square-cut face for signs of anguish or tension to see if the strange, hard features showed any sign of strain, if the square, hard jaw was grimly clenched, the hard eyes worried, if there were any signs of fear, disorder, apprehension in his step, his look, his tone, his movement, or his greeting. There was none. The policeman never varied by a jot. A powerful, somewhat shambling figure of a man, a little under six feet tall, with a thick neck, coarsely seamed and weathered with deep scorings, long arms, big hands, gorillalike shoulders, and a kind of shambling walk, a little baggy at the knees—a figure of an immense but rather worn power—he passed by in his somewhat slouchy uniform, seamed down the trouser-legs with stripes of gold, turned in at his house and mounted the front porch steps, with no more excitement than he would show on any other day of the week. And yet the male population of the whole town would be buzzing with excited speculation on the outcome of the match, and the hearts of boys would thud with apprehensive expectation at the very thought of it.

Later on, when dark had come, a half hour or so before the time scheduled for the match, Mr. Crane would leave his house, bearing underneath his arm a bundle wrapped up in a newspaper, which contained his old wrestling trunks and shoes; and with the same deliberate, even, bag-kneed stride, turn his steps in the direction of the town and the City Auditorium—and, Great God! his approaching and now terribly imminent encounter with the Bone-Crushing Swede, the Masked Marvel, or the Strangler Turk!

A few minutes later Nebraska would come by Monk's house and whistle piercingly; the Webber boy would rush out of the house and down the steps still gulping scalding coffee down his aching throat—and then the two of them would be off on their way to town!

What nights they were—the nights of smoke-smell, stillness, and the far-off barking of a dog, a fire of oak leaves at the corner, and the leaping fire-dance of the boys around it—great nights of the approaching contest of the wrestlers, the nights of frost and menace, joy and terror—and October!

Oh, how each step of the way to town was pounded out beneath the rhythm of the pounding heart! How tight the throat, how dry the mouth and lips! How could Nebraska walk on so steadily, and look so cool! Arrived before the Auditorium, and the press of people, the calcium glare of hard white lights, the excited babble of the voices. Then the inside, seats down front in the big, draughty, thrilling-looking place, the great curtain with "Asbestos" written on it, horseplay and loudmouthed banter in the crowd, the shouts of raucous boys, catcalls at length, foot-stamping, imperative hand-clapping, the bare and thrilling anatomy of the roped-in square. At last the handlers, timekeepers, and referees; and last of all—the principals!

Oh, the thrill of it! The anguish and the joy of it—the terror and the threat of it—the dry-skinned, hot-eyed, fever-pounding pulse of it, the nerve-tight, bursting agony of it! In God's name, how could flesh endure it! And yet—there they were, the *fatal, fated,* soon-to-be-at-bitter-arm's-length *two* of them—and Mr. Crane as loose as ashes, as cold as a potato, patient as a dray-horse, and as excited as a bale of hay!

But in the other corner—hah, now! hisses, jeers, and catcalls for the likes of you!—the Masked Marvel sits and waits, in all the menaceful address and threat of villainous disguisement. Over his bullet head and squat gorilla-neck a kind of sinister sack of coarse black cloth has been pulled and laced and tied! It is a horrible black mask with baleful eye-slits through which the beady little eyes seem to glitter as hard and wicked as a rattlesnake's; the imprint of his flat and brutal features shows behind it, and yet all so weirdly, ominously concealed that he looks more like a hangman than anything else. He looks like some black-masked and evil-hooded thing that does the grim and secret bidding of the Inquisition or the Medici; he looks like him who came in darkness to the Tower for the two young princes; he looks like the Klu Klux Klan; he looks like Jack Ketch with a hood on; he looks like the guillotine where Sidney Carton was the twenty-third; he looks like the Red Death, Robespierre, and The Terror!

As he sits there, bent forward brutishly, his thick, short fingers haired upon the back, an old bathrobe thrown round his brutal shoulders, the crowd hoots him, and the small boys jeer! And yet there is alarmed apprehension in their very hoots and jeers, uneasy whisperings and speculations:

"Good God!" one man is saying in an awed and lowered tone, "look at that neck on him—it's like a bull!"

"For God's sake, take a look at those shoulders!" says another, "look at his arms! His wrists are thick as most men's legs! Look at those arms, Dick; they could choke a bear!"

Or, an awed whisper: "Damn! It looks as if John Crane is in for it!"

All eyes now turn uneasily to Mr. Crane. He sits there in his corner quietly, and a kind of old, worn, patient look is on him. He blinks and squints unconcernedly into the hard glare of the light above the ring, he rubs his big hand reflectively over the bald top of his head, scratches the side of his coarse, seamed neck. Someone shouts a greeting to him from the audience: he looks around with an air of slight surprise, surveys the crowd with eyes as calm and hard as agate, locates the person who has called to him, waves in brief greeting, then leans forward patiently on his knees again.

The referee crawls through the ropes upon the mat, converses learnedly across the ropes but too intimately for hearing with Dr. Ned Revere, compares notes with him, looks very wise and serious, at length calls the two gladiators, attended by their handlers, bucket carriers, towel swingers, seconds, and sponge throwers, to the center of the mat, admonishes them most earnestly, sends them to their corners—and the bout begins.

The two men go back to their corners, throw their battered bathrobes off their shoulders, limber up a time or two against the ropes, a bell clangs, they turn and face each other and come out.

They come out slowly, arms bear-wise, half extended, the paws outward, circling, crouching, crafty as two cats. Mr. Crane in wrestler's garb is even looser and more shambling than in uniform; everything about him sags a little, seems to slope downward with a kind of worn, immensely patient, slightly weary power. The big shoulders slope, the great chest muscles sag and slope, the legs sag at the knees, the old full-length wrestler's trunks are wrinkled and also sag a little; there are big, worn knee-pads for the work down on the mat, and they also have a worn and baggy, kangaroolike look.

Mr. Crane shuffles cautiously about, but the Masked Marvel shifts and circles rapidly; he prances back and forth upon his bulging legs that seem to be made of rubber; he crouches and looks deadly, he feints and leaps in for a hold, which Mr. Crane evades with a shuffling ease. The crowd cheers wildly! The Masked Marvel dives and misses, falls sprawling. Mr. Crane falls on him, gets a hammerlock; the Masked Marvel bridges with his stocky body, squirms out of it, locks Mr. Crane's thick neck with vicelike power; the big policeman flings his body backward, gets out of it, is thrown to the corner of the ring. The two men come to grips again—the house is mad!

Oh, the thrill of it! The fear and menace of it, the fierce, pulse-pounding joy and terror of it! The two-hour-long grunting, panting, sweating, wheezing, groaning length of it! The exultant jubilation of it when Mr. Crane came out on top; the dull, dead, hopeless misery when Mr. Crane was on the bottom! And above all the inhuman mystery, secrecy, and the sinister disguisement of it all!

What did it matter that the Terrible Turk was really just a muscular Assyrian from New Bedford, Massachusetts? What did it matter if the Demon Dummy was really a young helper in the roundhouse of the Southern Railway Company? What did it matter if all this sinister array of Bone-Crushing Swedes, Horrible Huns, Desperate Dagoes, and Gorilla Gobs were for the most part derived from the ranks of able-bodied plasterers from Knoxville, Tennessee, robust bakers from Hoboken, ex-house-painters from Hamtramck, Michigan, and retired cow-hands from Wyoming? Finally, what did it matter that this baleful-eyed executioner of a Masked Marvel was really only the young Greek who worked behind the counter at the Bijou Café for Ladies and Gents down by the railway depot? What did it matter that this fact was proved one night when the terrible black hood was torn off? It was a shock, of course, to realize that the Bone-Crushing Menace, the very sight of whom struck stark terror to the heart, was just a rather harmless and good-natured Greek who cooked hamburger sandwiches for railway hands. But when all was said and done, the thrill, the threat, the danger were the same!

To a boy of twelve they *were* mysteries, they were Marvels, they were Menaces and Terrors—and the man who dared to meet them was a hero. The man who met them without a flicker of the eye was a man of steel. The man who shambled out and came to grips with them— and heaved and tugged, escaped their toils, or grunted in their clutches for two hours—that man was a man of oak, afraid of nothing, and as enduring as a mountain. That man did not know what fear was—and his son was like him in all ways, and the best and bravest boy in town!

Nebraska Crane and his family were recent-comers to this part of town. Formerly, he had lived out in "the Doubleday Section"; perhaps this was one reason why he had no fear.

Doubleday was a part of the town where fellows named Reese and Dock and Ira lived. These were ugly names; the fellows carried knives in their pockets, had deadly, skull-smashing fights with rocks, and grew up to be hoboes, poolroom loafers, pimps and bullies living off a whore. They were big, loutish, hulking bruisers with bleared features, a loose, blurred smile, and yellowed fingers in which they constantly held the moist fag-end of a cigarette, putting it to their lips from time to time to draw in on it deeply with a hard, twisted mouth and lidded eyes, a general air of hardened and unclean debauchery as they flipped the cigarette away into the gutter. Then they would let the smoke trickle slowly, moistly from their nostrils—as if the great spongy bellows of the lungs was now stained humidly with its yellow taint—and then speak out of the sides of their mouths in hard, low, knowing tones of bored sophistication to their impressed companions.

These were the fellows who grew up and wore cheap-looking, flashy clothes, bright yellow, box-toed shoes, and loud-striped shirts, suggesting somehow an unwholesome blending of gaudy finery and bodily filth. At night and on Sunday afternoons, they hung around the corners of disreputable back streets, prowled furtively about in the dead hours of the night past all the cheap clothing stores, pawn shops, greasy little white-and-negro lunchrooms (with a partition down the middle), the pool rooms, the dingy little whore-hotels—the adepts of South Main Street, the denizens of the whole, grimy, furtive underworld of a small town's nighttime life.

They were the bruisers, brawlers, cutters, slashers, stabbers, shooters of a small town's life; they were the pool-room thugs, the runners of blind tigers, the brothel guardians, the kept and pampered bullies of the whores. They were the tough town drivers with the thick red necks and leather leggings, and on Sunday, after a week of brawls, dives, stews, the stale, foul air of nighttime evil in the furtive places, they could be seen racing along the river road, out for a bawdy picnic with their whore. On Sunday afternoon they would drive along as brazen as you please beside the sensual, warm, and entrail-stirring smell, the fresh, half-rotten taint and slowness of the little river, that got in your bowels, heavy, numb, and secret, with a rending lust each time you smelled it. They they would stop at length beside the road, get out, and take their woman up the hill into the bushes for an afternoon of dalliance underneath the laurel leaves, embedded in the thick green secrecies of a Southern growth that was itself as spermy,

humid, hairy with desire, as the white flesh and heavy carnal nakedness of the whore.

These were the boys from Doubleday—the boys named Reese and
Dock and Ira—the worst boys in the school. They were always older
than the other boys, stayed in the same class several years, never passed
their work, grinned with a loutish, jeering grin whenever the teachers upbraided them for indolence, stayed out for days at a time and
were finally brought in by the truant officer, got into fist fights with
the principal when he tried to whip them, and sometimes hit him in
the eye, and at length were given up in despair, kicked out in disgrace
when they were big brutes of sixteen or seventeen years, having never
got beyond the fourth grade.

These were the boys who taught the foul words to the little boys,
told about going to the whore houses, jeered at those who had not gone
and said you could not call yourself a man until you had gone and "got
yourself a little." Further, Reese McMurdie, who was sixteen, as big and
strong as a man, and the worst boy in the school, said you couldn't call
yourself a man until you'd caught a dose. He said he'd had his first one
when he was fourteen years old, boasted that he'd had it several times
since then, and said it was no worse than a bad cold. Reese McMurdie
had a scar that turned your flesh sick when you looked at it; it ran the
whole way from the right-hand corner of his mouth to the corner of his
ear. He had got it in a knife-fight with another boy.

Ira Dingley was almost as bad as Reese. He was fifteen, not so big
and heavy as the other boy, but built as solid as a bullock. He had a red,
small, brutal kind of face, packed with energy and evil, and one little red
eye that went glowering malignantly and truculently around at the whole
world. He was blind in his other eye and wore a black shade over it.

One time, when there had been the great, jubilant shout of "Fight!
Fight!" from the playing field at recess, and the boys had come running
from all directions, Monk Webber had seen Ira Dingley and Reese Mc-
Murdie facing each other in the circle, edging closer truculently with
fists clenched, until someone behind Reese had given him a hard shove

that sent him hurtling into Ira. Ira was sent flying back into the crowd, but when he came out again, he came out slowly, crouched, his little red eye fixed and mad with hate, and this time he had the knife-blade open, naked, ready in his hand.

Reese, who had been smiling after he was pushed, with a foul, loose smile of jeering innocence, now smiled no more. He edged cautiously away and back as Ira came on, his hard eyes fixed upon his enemy, his thick hand fumbling in his trousers for the knife. And while he fumbled for his knife, he edged back slowly, talking with a sudden, quiet, murderous intensity that froze the heart:

"All right, you son-of-a-bitch!" he said, "Wait till I git my knife out!" Suddenly, the knife was out and open; it was an evil six-inch blade that opened on a spring. "If that's what you want, I'll cut your God-damned head off!"

And now all of the boys in the crowd were stunned, frightened, hypnotized by the murderous fascination of those two shining blades from which they could not take their eyes, and by the sight of the two boys, their faces white, contorted, mad with fear, despair, and hate, as they circled continuously around. The strong terror of their heavy breathing filled the air with menace, and communicated to the hearts of all the boys such a sense of horror, fascination, and frozen disbelief that they were unwilling to continue, afraid to intervene, and yet unable to move or wrench themselves away from the sudden, fatal, and murderous reality of the fight.

Then as the two boys came close together, Nebraska Crane suddenly stepped in, thrust them apart with a powerful movement, and at the same time said with a good-natured laugh, and in a rough, friendly, utterly natural tone of voice that instantly conquered everyone, restored all the boys to their senses and brought breath and strength back to the light of day again:

"You boys cut it out," he said. "If you want to fight, fight fair with your fists."

"What's it to you?" said Reese menacingly, edging in again with his knife held ready in his hand. "What right you got to come buttin' in? Who told you it was any business of yours?" All the time he kept edging closer with his knife held ready.

"No one told me," said Nebraska, in a voice that had lost all of its good nature and that was now as hard and unyielding in its quality as his tar-black eyes, which he held fixed, steady as a rifle, as his foe came on. "Do you want to make anything out of it?" he said.

Reese looked back at him for a moment, then his eyes shifted, and he sidled off and half withdrew, still waiting, unwilling to depart, muttering threats. In a moment the boys broke up in groups, dispersed, and enemies sidled uneasily away, each with his partisans, and the threatened fight was over. Nebraska Crane was the bravest boy in school. He was afraid of nothing.

Ira, Dock, and Reese! These were the savage, foul, and bloody names, and yet there was a menaceful wild promise in them, too. World of the "mountain grills," the poor whites, the nameless, buried, hopeless atoms of the wilderness, their lives yet had a lawless, sinful freedom of their own. Their names evoked the wretched, scabrous world of slum-town rickets whence they came; a painful, haunting, anguished memory of the half-familiar, never-to-be-forgotten, white-trash universe of Stumptown, Pigtail Alley, Doubleday, Depot Street, and that foul shamble of a settlement called, for God knows what ironic reason, Strawberry Hill—that sprawled its labyrinthine confusion of unpaved, unnamed, miry streets and alleys and rickety shacks and houses along the scarred, clay-barren flanks of the hills that sloped down towards the railway district in the western part of town.

It was a place that Monk had seen only a few times in his whole life, but that always, then and forever, as long as he lived, would haunt him with the horrible strangeness and familiarity of a nightmare. For although that world of rickets was a part of his home town, it was a part so unfamiliar to all the life he knew the best that when he saw it first, he came upon it with a sense of grotesque discovery, and after he had gone from it he could hardly believe that it was there, and would think of it years later with a sense of pain and anguish, saying:

"Here is the town, and here the streets, and here the people—and all, save *that,* familiar as my father's face; all, save *that,* so near that we could touch it with our hand. All of it was ours in its remotest patterns—all save *that,* save *that*! How could we have lived there with it and beside it, and have known it so little? Was it really there?"

Yes, it was there—strangely, horribly there, never-to-be-forgotten, never wholly to be remembered or believed, haunting the soul forever with the foul naturalness of a loathsome dream. It was there, immutably, unbelievably there, and what was most strange and terrible about it was that he recognized it instantly—that world of Ira, Dock, and Reese—the first time that he saw it as a child; and even as his heart and bowels sickened with their nauseous disbelief of recognition, he knew it, lived it, breathed it utterly to the last remotest degradation of its horror.

And for that reason he hated it. For that reason, nausea, fear, disgust, and horror overwhelmed the natural sense of pity which that wretched life evoked. It haunted him the moment that he saw it with a sense of buried memory, loathsome rediscovery, and it seemed to him that, so far from being different from these people, he was of them, body and brain and blood to the last atom of his life, and had escaped from them only by some unwarranted miracle of chance, some hideous insecurity of fortune that might return him into the brutish filth and misery and ignorance and hopelessness of that lost world with the same crude fickleness by which he had escaped.

No birds sang in that barren world. Beneath its skies of weary desolation the cry of all-exultant joy, the powerful, swelling anthem of youth, certitude, and victory burst from no man's heart, rose with a wild and uncontrollable shout from no man's throat. In Summer the heat beat down upon that baked and barren hill, upon the wretched streets, and on all the dusty, shadeless roads and alleys of the slum, and there was no pity in the merciless revelations of the sun. It shone with a huge and brutal impassivity upon the hard red dirt and dust, on shack and hut and rotting tenement.

It shone with the same impartial cruelty on mangy, scabby, nameless dogs, and on a thousand mangy, scabby nameless little children—hideous little scarecrows with tow hair, their skinny little bodies unrecognizably scurfed with filth and scarred with running sores, staring at one forever with gaunt, empty eyes as they grubbed in the baked, dusty, beaten, grassless dirt before some dreary shack, or scrabbled wretchedly about, eaten by swarming flies, in the sun-stench of a little lean-to porch, the very planks of which were as dry, hard, baked, and wretched-looking as the beaten earth in which they merged.

And the sun shone also on the slattern women of the district, revealing them to all their foul unloveliness, their loathsome and inexplicable fecundities—the Lonies, Lizzies, Lotties, Lenas of the district, the Sals, the Molls, the Millies and Bernices—as well as on all their wretched little progeny of Iras, Docks, and Reeses, their Asas, Jeters, Greeleys, Zebs, and Roys. They stood there at the edge of a ramshackle porch, tall and gaunt and slatternly, while their grimy little tow-haired brats scrabbled wretchedly around the edges of their filthy, lop-edged skirts. They stood there, those foul, unlovely women, with their gaunt, staring faces, sunken eyes, toothless jaws, and corrupt, discolored mouths, rilled at the edges with a thin brown line of snuff.

They stood there like some hopeless, loveless, wretched drudge of nature, bearing about them constantly the unbroken progressions of their loathsome fertility. In their arms they held their latest, youngest, wretched little child, swaddled in filthy rags, and staring forth at one with its blue, drowned eyes, its peaked and grimy little face, its nostrils and its upper lip gummed thickly with two ropes of snot. And in their pregnant bellies, which they proposed from their gaunt, unlovely figures like some dropsical ripeness foully fructifying in the sun, they carried the last and most revolting evidence of the germinal sequence of maternity, which thus was odiously revealed in every stage of its disgusting continuity—from sagging breast to swollen womb and thence to the grimy litter of their filth-bespattered brats that crawled and scrambled round their foul skirts on the porch. The idiot proliferations of blind nature which these wretched rakes and hags and harridans of women so nakedly and brutally revealed as they stood there stupidly proposing their foul, swollen bellies in the merciless and shameful light of the hot sun filled Monk with such a feeling of choking and wordless fury, loathing, and disgust that every natural emotion of pity and sorrow was drowned out below the powerful flood tide of revulsion, and his antagonism to the women and their wretched children was scarcely to be distinguished from blind hatred.

For pity, more than any other feeling, is a "learned" emotion; a child will have it least of all. Pity comes from the infinite accumulations of man's memory, from the anguish, pain, and suffering of life, from the full deposit of experience, from the forgotten faces, the lost men, and from the million strange and haunting visages of time. Pity comes upon the nick of time and stabs us like a knife. Its face is thin and dark and burning, and it has come before we know it, gone before we can grasp or capture it; it leaves a shrewd, deep wound, but a bitter, subtle one, and it always comes most keenly from a little thing.

It comes without a herald or a cause we can determine at some moment of our lives when we are far and lost from all the scenes that pity comes from; and how, why, where it comes we cannot say. But suddenly in the city—in the great and million-footed city—pity comes to us at evening when the dust and fury of another city day is over, and we lean upon the sills of evening in an ancient life. Then pity comes to us; we will remember children's voices of long ago, the free, full shout of sudden, gleeful laughter from a child that we once knew, full of exulting innocence, the songs that we sang on Summer porches long ago, a note of pride in our mother's voice and her grave, worn eyes of innocence as she boasted of a little thing, the simple words that a woman we once loved had said in some forgotten moment when she left us for another day.

Then pity is there, is there at once with its dark face and sudden knife, to stab us with an anguish that we cannot utter, to rend us with its agony of intolerable and wordless regret, to haunt us with the briefness of our days, and to tear our hearts with anguish and wild sorrow. And for what? For what? For all we want that never may be captured, for all we thirst for that never may be found. For love that must grow old and be forever dying, for all the bone, brain, passion, marrow, sinew of our lives, our hearts, our youth, that must grow old and bowed and barren, wearied out!

And oh! for beauty, that wild, strange song of magic, aching beauty, the intolerable, unutterable, ungraspable glory, power, and beauty of this world, this earth, this life, that is, and is everywhere around us, that we have seen and known at ten thousand moments of our lives, that has broken our hearts, maddened our brains, and torn the sinews of our lives asunder as we have lashed and driven savagely down the kaleidoscopic fury of the years in quest of it, unresting in our frenzied hope that some day we shall find it. hold it, fix it, make it ours forever—and that now haunts us strangely, sorrowfully, with its wild song and aching ecstasy as we lean upon the sills of evening in the city. We feel the sorrow and the hush of evening in the city, the voices, quiet, casual, lonely, of the people, far cries and broken sounds, and smell the sea, the harbor, and the huge, slow breathing of deserted docks, and know that there are ships there! And beauty swells like a wild song in our heart, beauty bursting like a great grape in our throat, beauty aching, rending, wordless, and unutterable, beauty in us, all around us, never to be captured—and we know that we are dying as the river flows! Oh, then will pity come, strange, sudden pity with its shrewd knife and the asp of time to stab us with a thousand wordless, lost, forgotten, little things!

And how, where, why it came we cannot say, but we feel pity now for all men who have ever lived upon the earth, and it is night, now, night, and the great stars are flashing in the lilac dark, the great stars are flashing on a hundred million men across America, and it is night, now, night, and we are living, hoping, fearing, loving, dying in the darkness, while the great stars shine upon us as they have shone on all men dead and living on this earth, on all men yet unborn, and yet to live who will come after us!

Yet, when Monk looked at these foul, pregnant hags in slum-town's gulch and hill and hollow, he could feel no pity, but only loathing, sickness of the flesh, disgust and nameless fear and dread and horror, so overwhelming in their tidal flood that he looked upon the filth and misery of these people with a shuddering revulsion and hated them because of it. For joy, faith, hope, every swelling certitude of glory, love, and triumph youth can know went dead and sick and rotten in that foul place. In the casual, filthy, and incessant littering of these ever-pregnant hags was evident not a love for life, but a contempt and carelessness for it so vile and criminal that it spawned its brood of rickety, scabby, mangy, foredoomed brats as indifferently as a bitch might drop its litter, and with a murderous nonchalance and bestial passivity that made man less than dung and instantly destroyed every proud illusion of the priceless value, dignity, and sanctity of his individual life.

How had man been begotten? Why, they had got him between brutish snores at some random waking of their lust in the midwatches of the night! They had got him in a dirty corner back behind a door in the hideous unprivacy of these rickety wooden houses, begotten, him standing in a fearful secrecy between apprehensive whisperings to make haste, lest some of the children hear! They had got him in some bestial sudden wakening of lust and hunger while turnip greens boiled with their humid fragrance on the stove! He had been begotten in some casual and forgotten moment which they had snatched out of their lives of filth, poverty, weariness, and labor, even as a beast will tear at chunks of meat; begotten in the crude, sudden, straddling gripe of half-rape on the impulsion of a casual opportunity of lust; begotten instantly as they were flung back rudely on the edge of an untidy bed in the red waning light of some forgotten Saturday when work was done, the week's wages given, the week's brief breathing space of rest, repose, and brutal dalliance come! He had been begotten without love, without beauty, tenderness, magic, or any nobleness of spirit, by the idiot, blind hunger of lust so vile that it knew no loathing for filth, stench, foulness, haggish ugliness, and asked for nothing better than a bag of guts in which to empty out the accumulations of its brutish energies.

The thought of it was not to be endured, and suddenly the boy cranes his neck, he grips his throat hard with his fingers, he squirms like something caught in a steel trap, a bestial grimace contracts his features—it is like drowning, drowning, not to be endured. The congress of their foul and bloody names—the loathsome company of these Iras, Docks and Reeses, the Jeters, Zebs and Greeleys of these poor-white slums—return to torment memory now with the white sear of horrible and instant recognition. Why? Because these people are the mountain people. These people are the poor-white litter of the hills. These people—Oh! it is intolerable, but true—these people came out of his mother's world, her life! He hears lost voices in the mountains long ago! They return to him from depths of sourceless memory, from places he has never viewed, from scenes that he has never visited—the whole deposit of inheritance, the lives and voices of lost people in the hills a hundred years ago.

They were a sharp-distinguished and strong-fibered people of his mother's stock, a race eccentric, powerful, thoughtful, honest, energetic—much better than this brutish and degraded kind. They were a race that lived upon the mountain slopes and river bottoms of old wild and rugged Zebulon; a kind that mined for mica in the hills, and hewed for tan-bark on the mountains; a kind that lived along a brawling mountain stream, and tilled the good land of the bottoms. It was a kind apart from these, hard-bitten in its pride, and hard-assured in its complacence, scornful in its own superiority, conceited, individual, strongly marked—but kinsman of this kind, as well.

He hears lost voices of his kinsmen in the mountains one hundred years before—and all as sad, faint, and remote as far-faint voices in a valley, all passing sad as a cloud shadow passing in the wilderness, all lonely, lost, and sad as strange, lost time. All hill-remote and lonely they come to him—the complacent, drawling voices of the death-triumphant Joyners long ago!

The vision changes, and again he sees the scar and squalor of the white-trash slum, the hill-man's rickets come to town—and it is night; there is a shrew's cry from the inner depth and darkness of some name-less house, lit only by the greasy, murky, and uneven light of a single lamp. It comes from scream and shout and curse, from drunken cry and stamping boot, from rancid flesh, fat pork, and rotting cabbage, and from his memory of a foul, sallow slut, gap-toothed, gaunt and shapeless as a pole—who stands there at the border of the rotting porch, her wisp of lank, unwashed hair screwed to a knot upon her head, proposing her pregnant belly for the fourteenth time.

Drowning! Drowning! Not to be endured! The abominable memory shrivels, shrinks, and withers up his heart in the cold constriction of its fear and loathing. The boy clutches at his throat, cranes with a livid face at the edges of his collar, draws one hand sharply up, and lifts his foot as if he has received a sudden, agonizing blow upon the kidneys. Less than his mother's stock he knows, far less in sense, mind, will, energy, and character—they yet have come from the same wil-derness, the same darkness, the same nature from which his mother's people came—and their mark is on him, never to be changed—their taint is in him, never to be drawn out. Bone of their bone, blood of their blood, flesh of their flesh, by however various and remote a web, he is of them, they are in him, he is theirs—has seen, known, felt, and has distilled into his blood every wild passion, criminal desire, and rending lust they have known. And the blood of the murdered men, the rivers of blood of the murdered men which has soaked down quietly in the wilderness, which has soaked quietly away with all its million mute and secret tongues into the stern, the beautiful, the un-yielding substance of the everlasting earth, is his, has stained his life, his flesh, his spirit, and is on his head as well as theirs!

And suddenly, like a man who is drowning and feels a rock beneath his feet; like a man lost, dying, freezing, famished, almost spent in the dark and howling desolation of the strange wilderness, who sees a light, comes suddenly upon a place of shelter, warmth, salvation, the boy's spirit turns and seizes on the image of his father. The image of his father's life, that image of decent order, gaunt cleanliness and dispatch, the image of warmth, abundance, passionate energy and joy. returns to the boy now with all that is beautiful and right in it, to save him, to heal him instantly, to restore him from the horror and abomination of that memory in which his spirit for a moment drowned.

And at the moment that he sees the huge salvation of his father's figure, he also sees his father's house, his life, the whole world that he has made and shaped with his own single power, his unique color, his one soul. And instantly he sees as well his father's country, the land from which his father came, the beautiful, rich country which the boy has never seen with his own eyes, but which he has visited ten thousand times with his heart, his mind, until that country is as much a part of him as if he had been born there. It is the unknown land which all of us have known and have longed to find in youth. It is the undiscovered complement of all that we have seen and known, the lost half of our dark heart, the secret hunger, need, and magic working in our blood; and though we have not seen it, we recognize it instantly as the land we know the minute that we come to it.

And now, like an image of certitude, peace, joy, security, and abundance to restore his life out of the filth and shambles of that other vision, he sees his father's land. He sees the great red barns, the tidy houses, the thrift, the comfort, and the loveliness, the velvet pastures, meadows, fields, and orchards, the red-bronze soil, the nobly-swelling earth of southern Pennsylvania. And at the moment that he sees it, his spirit comes out of the brutal wilderness, his heart is whole and sound and full of hope again. There are new lands.

And at the same moment he sees the image of the brave companionship of Nebraska Crane. What is there to fear? What is there to fear on earth if Nebraska Crane is there? Nebraska stands there in his life like the image of that heroic integrity in life which cannot be touched or conquered, which is outside a man, and to which his own life must be united if he will be saved. So what is there to fear as long as Nebraska Crane—the free, the frank, the friendly, the fierce, the secret, and the unafraid—is there to show him with his life where he can go? What boys who live out on the West Side, for all their manners, customs, looks, and ways, for all their names and cunning stratagems, can he fear, as long as Nebraska Crane is there with him?

No—though they stood there massed against him in the whole concert of their hateful qualities, all the Sidneys, Roys, Carls, Victors, Guys, and Harrys of the earth—though he had to meet them on their own earth of red waning March and Sunday afternoons, what nameless and accursed horror can quench utterly the fearless light, the dark integrity of that fierce and lonely flame? He could breathe in their poisonous and lifeless air, stand houseless, naked, unprepared beneath their desolate skies—he could yet endure, meet them, beat them, carry the victorious power of his own world in his own life, and make exultant joy, all-conquering certitude, triumphant sense, and lusty love prevail forever above the wretchedness and scornful doubt of their own life-denying lives—if only Nebraska Crane were there to see him do it!

So the old wild joy of three o'clock has risen in his heart again—wordless, tongueless as a savage cry, with all its passion, pain, and ecstasy—and he sees the world, the East, the West, the lands and cities of the earth in triumph, for Nebraska Crane is there!

GEORGE WEBBER AND Nebraska Crane! The splendid names flash in the sun, soar to the westward, wing together over the roof of the whole world, together back again, are there!

George Webber! George Josiah and Josiah George! Josiah George Nebraska Webber and Crane George!

"My name is George Josiah Webber!" cried the boy, and sprang erect.

"GEORGE JOSIAH WEBBER!"

The great name flashed then through the shining air; flashed, too, the great name to the flashing of the leaves; all of the maple leaves a-spangle with the proud flash of the great, proud name!

"GEORGE JOSIAH WEBBER!" cried the boy again; and all the gold-proud afternoon was ringing with the sound; flashed, too, the aspen leaves, and flashed the honeysuckle hedge a-tremble; flashed, too, and bent each blade of velvet grass.

"My name is George Josiah Webber!"

Flashed the proud name to the brazen pounding of the courthouse bell; flashed, too, and rose and struck upon the ponderous, solemn strokes of three!

"ONE! . . . TWO! . . . THREE!"

And then upon the stroke the black boys came:

"Hi, Paul! . . . Hey, Paul! . . . How are you, Paul?" the black boys cried and flashed before him.

"My name is George Josiah Webber!" cried the boy.

Solemnly, in perfect line, the black boys wheeled, swept round platoon-wise, faultless in formation, and with spin-humming wheels rode slowly back in lines of eight, squads-righted perfectly, and, halting on their wheels in perfect order, with grave inquiry greeted him:

"How's ole Paul today?"

"My name," the boy said firmly, "is not Paul! My name is George!"

"Oh, no, it's not, Paul!" cried the black boys, grinning amiably. "Yo' name is *Paul*!"

It was a harmless mockery, some unknown and unknowledgeable jest, some secret, playful banter of their nigger soul. God knows what they meant by it. They could not have said themselves what made them call him by this name, but Paul he was to them, and every day at three o'clock, before the markets opened up again, the black boys came and flashed before him—called him "*Paul*."

And he contended stubbornly, would not give in, always insisted that his name was George, and somehow—God knows how!—the unyielding argument filled his heart with warmth, and delighted the black boys, too.

Each day at three o'clock he knew that they would come and call him "Paul." each day at three o'clock he waited for them, with warmth, with joy, with longing and affection, with a strange sense of ecstasy and magic, with fear they might not come. But each day at three o'clock, hard on the market's opening and the booming of the courthouse bell, the black boys came and flashed before him.

He knew that they would come. He knew they could not fail him. He knew that he delighted them, that they adored the look of him— the long-armed, big-handed, and flat-footed look of him. He knew that all his words and movements—his leaps and springs, his argument and stern insistence on his proper name—gave them an innocent and enormous pleasure. He knew, in short, that there was nothing but warm liking in their banter when they called him "Paul."

Each day, therefore, he waited on their coming—and they always came! They could not have failed him, they would have come if all hell had divided them. A little before three o'clock, each day of the week except Sundays, the black boys roused themselves from their siesta in the warm sun round the walls of the City Market, saying:

"It's time to go and see ole Paul!"

They roused themselves out of the pleasant reek of cod-heads rotting in the sun, decaying cabbage leaves and rotten oranges; they roused themselves from drowsy places in the sun, delicious apathy, from the depth and dark of all their African somnolence—and said:

"We got to go now! Ole Paul is waitin' for us! Stay with us, footses; we is on ouah way!"

And what a way it was! Oh, what a splendid, soaring, flashing, winglike way! They came like streaks of ebon lightning; they came like ravens with a swallow-swoop; they came like shot out of a gun, and like a thunderbolt; they came like demons—but they came!

He heard them coming from afar, he heard them racing down the street, he heard the furious thrum of all their flashing wheels, and then they flashed before him, they were there! They shot past, eight abreast, bent over, pedaling like black demons; they shot past on their flashing wheels, the fibrous market baskets rattling lightly; and as they flashed before him, they cried "Paul!"

Then, wheeling solemnly in squadrons, they rode slowly, gravely back, and wheeled and faced him, steady and moveless on their wheels, and said, "Hi, Paul! . . . How's ole Paul today!"

Then the parade began. They did amazing things, performed astounding evolutions on their wheels; they flashed by in fours, and then by twos; they did squads-right, retreated or advanced in echelon, swooped past in single file like soaring birds, rode like demons soaring in the wind.

Then madness seized them, and desire for individual excellence, a lust for championship, wild inventiveness, whimsical caprice. They shouted with rich nigger laughter, howled derisory comments at their fellows, strove to outdo one another—to win applause and approbation—all for Paul! They swooped down the street with lightlike swiftness and a bullet speed; they swooped down in terrific spirals, snaking from one side to the other, missing curbs by hair-line fractions of an inch; they shot past, stooping like a cowboy from the saddle, and snatching up their ragged caps as they shot past. They shouted out to one another things like these:

"Outa my way, ole Liver Lips! I got somethin' dat I got to show to Paul!"

"Hey, Paul—look at ole Slewfoot ride dat wheel!"

"Move ovah deh, M'lasses! Let ole Paul look at someone who *can* ride!"

"Get outa my way, Big Niggah, 'fo' I rides all ovah you! I'm goin' to show Paul somethin' dat he nevah saw befo'!—How's dis one, Paul?"

And so they soared and swooped and flashed, their rich black voices calling back to him, their warm good voices bubbling with black laughter, crying, "Paul!"

And then they were off like furies riding for town and the reopening of the markets, and their rich, warm voices howled back to him with affectionate farewell:

"Good-bye, Paul!"

"So long, Paul."

"We'll be seein' you, Paul!"

"My name," he shouted after them, "is George Josiah Webber!"

Flashed and rose the splendid name as proud and shining as the day.

And answered faintly, warm with pleasant mockery, upon the wind:

"Yo' name is Paul! Paul! Paul!"

And coming faintly, sadly, haunting as a dream:

"—is Paul! Paul! Paul!"

CHAPTER 3

Two Worlds Discrete

When Aunt Maw spoke, at times the air would be filled with unseen voices, and the boy knew that he was listening to the voices of hundreds of people he had never seen, and knew instantly what those people were like and what their lives had been. Only a word, a phrase, an intonation of that fathomless Joyner voice falling quietly at night with an immense and tranquil loneliness before a dying fire, and the unknown dead were moving all around him, and it seemed to him that now he was about to track the stranger in him down to his last dark dwelling in his blood, explore him to his final secrecy, and make all the thousand strange, unknown lives in him awake and come to life again.

And yet Aunt Maw's life, her time, her world, the fathomless intonations of that Joyner voice, spoken quietly, interminably at night, in the room where the coal-fire flared and crumbled, and where slow time was feeding like a vulture at the boy's heart, could overwhelm his spirit in tides of drowning horror. Just as his father's life spoke to him of all things wild and new, of exultant prophecies of escape and victory, of triumph, flight, new lands, the golden cities—of all that was magic, strange, and glorious on earth—so did the life of his mother's people return him instantly to some dark, unfathomed place in nature, to all that was tainted by the slow-smouldering fires of madness in his blood, some ineradicable poison of the blood and soul, brown, thick, and brooding, never to be cured or driven out of him, in which at length he must drown darkly, horribly, unassuaged, unsavable, and mad.

Aunt Maw's world came from some lonely sea-depth, some huge abyss and maw of drowning time, which consumed all things it fed upon except itself—consumed them with horror, death, the sense of drowning in a sea of blind, dateless Joyner time. Aunt Maw fed on sorrow with a kind of tranquil joy. In that huge chronicle of the past which her terrific memory wove forever, there were all the lights and weathers of the soul—sunlight, Summer, singing—but there was always sorrow, death and sorrow, the lost, lonely lives of men there in the wilderness. And yet she was not sorrowful herself. She fed on all the loneliness and death of the huge, dark past with a kind of ruminant and invincible relish, which said that all men must die save only these triumphant censors of man's destiny, these never-dying, all-consuming Joyner witnesses of sorrow, who lived, and lived forever.

This fatal quality of that weblike memory drowned the boy's soul in desolation. And in that web was everything on earth—except wild joy.

HER LIFE WENT back into the wilderness of Zebulon County before the Civil War.

"Remember!" Aunt Maw would say in a half-amused and half-impatient voice, as she raised the needle to the light and threaded it. "Why, you fool boy, you!" she would exclaim in scornful tones, "What are you thinkin' of! Of course I can remember! Wasn't I right there, out in Zebulon with all the rest of them, the day they came back from the war? . . . Yes, sir, I saw it all." She paused, reflecting. "So here they came," she continued tranquilly, "along about ten o'clock in the morning—you could hear them, you know, long before they got there—around that bend in the road—you could hear the people cheerin' all along the road—and, of course, I began to shout and holler along with all the rest of them," she said, "I wasn't goin' to be left out, you know," she went on with tranquil humor, "—and there we were, you know, all lined up at the fence there—father and mother and your great-uncle Sam. Of course, you never got to know him, boy, but he was there, for he'd come home sick on leave at Christmas time. He was still limpin' around from that wound he got—and of course it was all over or everyone knew it *would* be before he got well enough to go on back again. Hm," she laughed shortly, knowingly, as she squinted at her needle, "At least that's what he said——"

"What, Aunt Maw?"

"Why, that he was waitin' for his wound to heal, but, pshaw!"— she spoke quietly, shaking her head—"Sam was *lazy*—oh, the laziest feller I ever saw in all my life!" she cried. "Now if the truth were told, *that* was all that was wrong with him—and let me tell you something; it didn't take long for him to get well when he saw the war was comin' to an end and he wouldn't have to go on back and join the rest of them. He was limpin' around there one day leanin' on a cane as if every step would be his last, and the next day he was walkin' around as if he didn't have an ache or a pain in the world. . . .

" 'That's the quickest recovery *I* ever heard of, Sam,' father said to him. 'Now if you've got some more medicine out of that same bottle, I just wish you'd let me have a little of it.'—Well, then, so Sam was there." She went on in a moment, "And of course Bill Joyner was there—old Bill Joyner, your great-grandfather, boy—as hale and hearty an old man as you'll ever see!" she cried.

"Bill Joyner . . . why he must have been all of eighty-five right then, but you'd never have known it to look at him! Do anything! Go anywhere! Ready for anything!" she declared. "And he was that way, sir, right up to the hour of his death—lived over here in Libya Hill then, mind you, fifty miles away, but if he took a notion that he'd like to talk to one of his children, why he'd stand right out and come, without waitin' to get his hat or anything. Why yes! didn't he turn up one day just as we were all settin' down to dinner, without a hat or coat or anything!" she cried. " 'Why, what on earth!' said mother. 'Where did you come from, Uncle Bill?'—she called him Uncle Bill, you know. 'Oh,

I came from Libya Hill,' says he. 'Yes, but how did you get here?' she says—asks him, you know. 'Oh, I walked it,' he says. 'Why, you know you didn't!' mother says, 'And where's your hat and coat?' she says. 'Oh, I reckon I came without 'em,' he said, 'I was out workin' in my garden and I just took a notion that I'd come to see you all, so I didn't stop to get my hat or coat,' he said, 'I just came on!' And that's just exactly what he'd done, sir," she said with a deliberate emphasis. "He just took the notion that he'd like to see us all, and he lit right out, without stoppin' to say hello or howdy-do to anybody!"

She paused for a moment, reflecting. Then, nodding her head slightly, in confirmation, she concluded:

"But that was Bill Joyner for you! That's just the kind of feller that he was."

"So he was there that day?" said George.

"Yes, sir. He was right there standin' next to father. Father was a Major, you know," she said, with a strong note of pride in her voice, "but he was home on leave at the time the war ended. Why yes! he came home every now and then all through the war. Bein' a Major, I guess he could get off more than the common soldiers," she said proudly. "So he was there, with old Bill Joyner standin' right beside him. Bill, of course—he'd come because he wanted to see Rance, and he knew he'd be comin' back with all the rest of them. Of course, child," she said, shaking her head slightly, "none of us had seen your great-uncle Rance since the beginning of the war. He had enlisted at the very start, you know, when war was declared, and he'd been away the whole four years. And oh! they told it, you know, they told it!" she half-muttered, shaking her head slightly with a boding kind of deprecation, "what he'd been through—the things he'd had to do—whew-w!" she said suddenly with an expostulation of disgust— "Why, the time they took him prisoner, you know, and he escaped, and had to do his travelin' by night, sleepin' in barns or hidin' away somewheres in the woods all day, I reckon—and that was the

THE WEB AND THE ROOT 83

time—whew-w!— 'Go away,' I said, 'it makes me shudder when I think of it!'—why that he found that old dead mule they'd left there in the road—and cut him off a steak and eaten it—'And the best meat,' says, 'I ever tasted!'—Now that will give you some idea of how hungry he must have been!

"Well, of course, we'd heard these stories, and none of us had seen him since he went away, so we were all curious to know. Well, here they came, you know, marchin' along on that old river road, and you could hear all the people cheerin', and the men a-shoutin' and the women folks a-cryin', and here comes Bob Patten. Well then, of course we all began to ask him about Rance, said, 'Where is he? Is he here?'

" 'Oh, yes, he's here, all right,' said Bob, 'He'll be along in a minute now. You'll see him—and if you don't see him'"—suddenly she began to laugh—" 'if you don't see him,' says Bob, *'why, by God, you'll smell him!'* That's just the way he put it, you know, came right out with it, and of course, they had to laugh. . . . But, child, child!" with strong distaste she shook her head slightly—"That awful—oh! that *awful, awful,* odor! Poor feller! I don't reckon he could help it! But he always had it. . . . Now he was clean enough!" she cried out with a strong emphasis, "Rance always kept himself as clean as anyone you ever saw. And a good, clean-livin' man, as well," she said.

"Never touched a drop of licker in *all* his life," she said decisively, "No, sir—neither him nor father.—Oh father! father!" she cried proudly, "Why father wouldn't let anyone come near him with the smell of licker on his breath! And let me tell you something!" she said solemnly, "If he had known that papa drank, he'd never have let your mother marry him!—Oh! he wouldn't have let him enter his house, you know—he would have considered it a disgrace for any member of his family to associate with anyone who drank!" she proudly said. "And Rance was the same—he couldn't endure the sight or taste of it—but *oh!*" she gasped, "that awful, awful odor—that old, rank body-smell that nothing could take out!—awful, awful," she whispered. Then for a moment she stitched silently. "And of course," she said, "that's what they say about him—that's what they called him———"

"What, Aunt Maw?"

"Why," she said—and here she paused again, shaking her head in a movement of strong deprecation, "to think of it!—to think, they'd have no more decency or reverence than to give a man a name like that! But, then, you know what soldiers are—I reckon they're a pretty rough, coarse-talkin' lot, and of course they told it on him—that was the name they gave him, the one they called him by."

"What?"

She looked at him quietly for a moment with a serious face, then laughed.

"Stinkin' Jesus," she said shyly. "Whew-w!" she gently shrieked. "'Oh, you know they wouldn't say a thing like that!' I cried—but that was it, all right. To think of it! . . . And of course, poor fellow, he knew it, he recognized it, says, 'I'd do anything in the world if I could only get rid of it,' says, 'I reckon it's a cross the Lord has given me to bear.' . . . But there it was—that—old—rank—thing!—Oh, awful, *awful*!" she whispered, peering downward at the needle. "And say! yes! Didn't he tell us all that day when he came back that the Day of Judgment was already here upon us?—Oh! said Appomattox Courthouse marked the comin' of the Lord and Armageddon—and for us all to get ready for great changes! And, yes! don't I remember that old linen chart—or map, I reckon you might call it—that he kept strung around his neck, all rolled up in a ball, and hangin' from a string? It proved, you know, by all the facts and figures in the Bible that the world was due to end in 1865. . . . And there he was, you know, marchin' along the road with all the rest of them, with that old thing a-hangin' round his neck, the day they all came back from the war."

She stitched quietly with deft, strong fingers for a moment, and then, shaking her head, said sadly:

"Poor Rance! But I tell you what! He was *certainly* a good man," she said.

RANCE JOYNER HAD been the youngest of all old Bill Joyner's children. Rance was a good twelve years the junior of Lafayette, George Webber's grandfather. Between them had been born two other brothers—John, killed at the battle of Shiloh, and Sam. The record of Rance Joyner's boyhood, as it had survived by tongue, by hearsay, which was the only record these men had, was bare enough in its anatomy, but probably fully accurate.

"Well, now I tell you how it was," Aunt Maw said. 'The rest of them used to tease him and make fun of him. Of course, he was a simple-minded sort of feller, and I reckon he'd believe anything they told him. Why, yes! Didn't father tell me how they told him Martha Alexander was in love with him, and got him to believin' it, and all!—And here Martha, you know, was the belle of the neighborhood, and could pick and choose from anyone she liked! But didn't they write him all sorts of fool love letters then, pretendin' to come from Martha, and tellin' him to meet her at all sorts of places—up on the Indian Mound, and down in the holler, or at some old stump, or tree, or crossroads—oh! anywheres!" she cried, "just to see if he'd be fool enough to go! And then, when she didn't turn up, wouldn't they write him another letter, sayin' her father was suspicious and watchin' her like a hawk! And didn't they tell him then that Martha had said she'd like him better if he grew a beard! And then they told him, you know, they had a special preparation all fixed up that would make his beard grow faster if he washed his face in it, and then didn't they persuade him to wash his face in old blue indigo water that was used to dye wool in, and didn't he go around there for weeks as blue in the face as a monkey! . . .

"And didn't he come creepin' up behind her after church one day, and whisper in her ear: 'I'll be there. Just swing the light three times and slip out easy when you're ready, and I'll be there waitin' for you!'—Why, he almost frightened the poor girl out of her wits. 'Oh!' she screamed, you know, and hollered for them to come and get him, 'Oh! Take him! Take him away!'—thinkin' he'd gone crazy—and of course that let the cat out of the bag. They had to tell it then, the joke they'd played on him." She smiled quietly, shaking her head slightly, with the sad and faintly troubled mirth of things far and lost.

"But, I want to tell you," she said gravely in a moment, "they can say all they like about your great-uncle Rance, but he was always an upright and honest man. He had a good heart," she said quietly, and in these words there was an accolade. "He was always willin' to do anything he could to help people when they needed it. And he wouldn't wait to be asked, neither! Why, didn't they tell it how he practically carried Dave Ingram on his back as they retreated from Antietam, rather than let him lay there and be taken!—Of course, he was strong—why, strong as a mule!" she cried. "He could stand anything.—They told it how he could march all day long, and then stay up all night nursin' the sick and tendin' to the wounded."

She paused and shook her head. "I guess he'd seen some awful things," she said. "I reckon he'd been with many a poor feller when he breathed his last—they had to admit it, sir, when they came back! Now, they can laugh at him all they please, but they had to give him his due! Jim Alexander said, you know, he admitted it, 'Well, Rance has preached the comin' of the Lord and a better day upon the earth, and I reckon we've all laughed at him at times for doin' it—but let me tell you, now,' he says, 'he always practiced what he preached. If everybody had as good a heart as he's got, we'd have that better day he talks about right now!' "

She sewed quietly for a moment, thrusting the needle through with her thimbled finger, drawing the thread through with a strong, pulling movement of her arm.

"Now, child, I'm goin' to tell you something," she said quietly. "There are a whole lot of people in this world who think they're pretty smart—but they never find out anything. Now I suppose that there are lots of smarter people in the world than Rance—I guess they looked on him as sort of simple-minded—but let me tell you something! It's not always the smartest people who know the most—and there are things I could tell you—things I know about!" she whispered with an omened tone, then fell to shaking her head slightly again, her face contracted in a portentous movement—"Child! Child! . . . I don't know what you'd call it . . . what explanation you could give for it—but it's mighty strange when you come to think about it, isn't it?"

"But what? What is it, Aunt Maw?" he demanded feverishly.

She turned and looked him full in the face for a moment. Then she whispered:

"He's been—*Seen*! . . . I *Saw* him once myself! . . . He's been *Seen* all through his life," she whispered again. "I know a dozen people who have *Seen* him," she added quietly. She stitched in silence for a time.

"Well, I tell you," she presently said, "the first time that they *Saw* him he was a boy—oh! I reckon along about eight or nine years old at the time. I've heard father tell the story many's the time," she said, "and mother was there and knew about it, too. That was the very year that they were married, sir, that's exactly when it was," she declared triumphantly. "Well, mother and father were still livin' there in Zebulon, and old Bill Joyner was there, too. He hadn't yet moved into town, you know. Oh, it was several years after this before Bill came to Libya Hill to live, and father didn't follow him till after the war was over. . . . Well, anyway," she said, "Bill was still out in Zebulon, as I was sayin', and the story goes that it was Sunday morning. So after breakfast the whole crowd of them start out for church—all of them except old Bill, you know, and I reckon he had something else to do, or felt that it was all right for *him* to stay at home so long as all the others went. . . . Well, anyhow," she smiled, "Bill didn't go to church, but he saw them go, you know! He *saw* them go!" she cried. "He stood there in the door and watched them as they went down the road—father and Sam and mother, and your great-uncle Rance. Well, anyway, when they had gone—I reckon it was some time later—Bill went out into the kitchen. And when he got there he saw the lid of the wool-box was open. Of course father was a hatter and he kept the wool from which he made the felt out in the kitchen in this big box.—Why, it was big enough for a grown man to stretch out full length in, with some to spare, and of course it was as good a bed as anyone could want. I know that when father wanted to take a nap on Sunday afternoons, or get off somewheres by himself to study something over, he'd go back and stretch out on the wool.

" 'Well,' thinks Bill, 'now who could ever have gone and done such a trick as that? Fate told them'—that's what he called my father, Lafayette, you know—'Fate told them to keep that box closed,' and he walks over, you know, to put the lid down—and there he *was*, sir!" she cried strongly—"There he *was*, if you please, stretched out in the wool and fast asleep—why, Rance, you know! Rance! There he *was*! . . . 'Aha!' thinks Bill, 'I caught you that time, didn't I? Now he's just sneaked off from all the others when he thought my back was turned, and he's crawled back here to have a snooze when he's supposed to be in church.' That's what Bill thought, you know. 'Now if he thinks he's goin' to play any such trick as that on me, he's very much mistaken. But we'll see,' thinks Bill, 'We'll just wait and see. Now, I'm not goin' to wake him up,' says Bill, 'I'll go away and let him sleep—but when the others all get back from church I'm goin' to ask him where he's been. And if he tells the truth—if he confesses that he crawled into the wool-box for a nap, I won't punish him. But if he tries to lie out of it,' says Bill, 'I'll give him such a thrashin' as he's never had in all his life before!'

"So he goes away then and leaves Rance there to sleep. Well, he waited then, and pretty soon they all came back from church, and, sure enough, here comes Rance, trailin' along with all the rest of them. 'Rance,' says Bill, 'How'd you like the sermon?' 'Oh,' says Rance, smilin' an' grinnin' all over, you know, 'it was fine, father, fine,' he says. 'Fine, was it?' Bill says, 'You enjoyed it, did you?' 'Oh, why, yes!' he says, 'I enjoyed it fine!' 'Well, now, that's good,' says Bill, 'I'm glad to hear that,' says he. 'What did the preacher talk about?' he says.

"Well, then, you know, Rance started in to tell him—he went through the preacher's sermon from beginnin' to end, he told him everything that was in it, even to describin' how the preacher talked and all.

"And Bill listened. He didn't say a word. He waited till Rance got through talkin'. Then he looked at him, and shook his head. 'Rance,' he says, 'I want you to look me in the eye.' And Rance looked at him, you know, real startled-like; says, 'Why, yes, father, what is it? What's wrong?' he says. Then Bill looked at him, and shook his head. Says, 'Rance, Rance, I'd have let you go if you had told the truth about it, but,' says, 'Rance—you have *lied* to me,' 'Why, no, father,' says Rance, 'No, I haven't. What do you mean?' he says. And Bill looked at him; says, 'Rance—you have not been to church,' says, 'I found you in the wool-box fast asleep, and that is where you've been all morning. Now,' says Bill, 'you come with me,' and took him by the shoulder. 'Oh, father, I haven't done anything'—begins to cry, you know, says, 'Don't whip me, don't whip me—I haven't lied to you—I'll swear to you I haven't.' 'You come with me,' says Bill—begins to pull and drag him along, you know, 'and when I'm through with you you'll never lie to me again.'

"And that," she said, "that was where *father*—my father, your grandfather—stepped into the picture. He stepped between them and stopped Bill Joyner from going any further. Of course, father was a grown man at the time. 'No,' says father, 'you mustn't do that,' he says, 'You're makin' a mistake. You can't punish him for not attendin' church today.' 'Why, what's the reason I can't?' Bill Joyner said. 'Because,' said father, 'he was *there*. He's been with us every minute of the time since we left home this morning. And he heard the sermon,' father said, 'He's tellin' you the truth—I'll swear to that—because he was sittin' next to me all the time.'

"And then, of course, the others all chimed in, mother and Sam, said, 'Yes, he's tellin' you the truth, all right. He was right there with us all the time, and we'd have known if he left us.' Then Bill was bitter against them all, of course, thinkin' they had all joined against him in an effort to shield Rance in a lie. 'To think,' he said, 'that children of mine would turn against me in this way! To think that you'd all join together in a lie in order to shield him. Why, you're worse than he is,' he said, 'for you're abettin' him and leadin' him on, and you'—he said to father—'*you* are certainly old enough to know better,' says, 'Fate, I didn't think it of you, I didn't think you'd help him to lie like this.' And father said, 'No.' He looked him in the eye, said, 'No, father, no one is helpin' him to lie. He's not tellin' you a lie. We're all tellin' the truth—and I can prove it.'—Why yes, didn't it turn out then that the preacher and all the folks at church had seen him and were willin' to testify that he was there?—'Now I don't know what it is you saw,' said father, 'but whatever it was, it wasn't Rance. At least, it wasn't the Rance you see here, for he's been with us every moment.' And then Bill looked at him and saw that he was tellin' him the truth, and they say Bill Joyner's face was a study.

" 'Well,' he said, 'this is a strange thing! God only knows what will come out of it! Rance has been *Seen*!" '

She paused; then turned to look straight and silent at George. In a moment she shook her head slightly, with boding premonition.

"And let me tell you something," she whispered. "That wasn't the only time, either!"

THERE WERE, IN fact, from this time on, an increasing number of such apparitions. The news of the first one had spread like wildfire through the whole community: the uncanny story of the boy's discovery in the wool-box when his corporeal body was two miles distant at the church became instantly common property, and inflamed the wonder and imagination of all who heard it.

And, as seems to be almost the invariable practice in these cases, the public did not question at all the evidence which was dubious; they questioned only that which was indubitable, and, finding it to be confirmed beyond the shadow of a doubt, swallowed the whole, hook, line, and sinker! They took it instantly for granted that Bill Joyner had seen the boy, or "at least, seen something, now—that's one thing sure." But was Rance really present at the church that day? Had he been with the other members of his family from first to last? Had there been any opportunity for him to "slip away" and leave them without their knowing it? To all this there was only one answer—testified to by a hundred people. He *had* been present at the church from first to last; he had been seen, greeted, and remembered by minister, sexton, deacons, choir, and congregation, not only before, but also after services. Therefore, the fact was now established in their minds with an unshakable conviction. There was no longer any possible doubt about it—Rance had been *Seen*.

Then, about eight months after this, when the story of this ghostly apparition was still fresh in people's minds, and made matter for awed conversation when they gathered, another extraordinary incident occurred!

One evening, towards the end of a harsh and ragged day in March, a neighbor of the Joyners' was driving hard into the backwoods village of Blankenship, which stood about two miles distant from his home. Night was coming on fast; it was just the few minutes of brief, fading grey that end a Winter's day, and the man, whose name was Roberts, was driving along the hard, clay-rutted road as fast as the rickety rig in which he sat, and the old grey horse he drove, could carry him. His wife had been seized suddenly by a cramp or colic, or so they called it, and now lay at home in bed in mortal pain until Roberts should reach town and fetch help back to her.

Just outside of town as the troubled man was urging on his nag to greater speed, he encountered Rance Joyner. The boy was trudging steadily along the road in the grey light, coming from town and going towards home, and, according to the story Roberts told, Rance was carrying a heavy sack of meal which he had plumped over his right shoulder and supported with his hand. As the man in the buggy passed him, the boy half turned, paused, looked up at him, and spoke. In this circumstance there was nothing unusual. Roberts had passed the boy a hundred times coming or going to the town on some errand.

On this occasion, Roberts said he returned the boy's greeting somewhat absently and curtly, weighted down as his spirit was with haste and apprehension, and drove on without stopping. But before he had gone a dozen yards the man recalled himself and pulled up quickly, intending to shout back to the boy the reason for his haste, and to ask him to stop at his house on the way home, do what he could to aid the stricken woman, and wait there till the man returned with help. Accordingly, Roberts pulled up, turned in his seat, and began to shout his message down the road. To his stupefaction, the road was absolutely bare. Within a dozen yards the boy had vanished from his sight, "as if," said Roberts, "the earth had opened up and swallered him." But even as the man sat staring, gape-mouthed with astonishment, the explanation occurred to him:

"Thar were some trees thar down the road a little piece, a-settin' at the side of the road, and I jest figgered," he said delicately, "that Rance had stepped in behind one of 'em fer a moment, so I didn't stop no more. Hit was gettin' dark an' I was in a hurry, so I jest drove on as hard as I could."

Roberts drove in to town, got the woman's sister whom he had come to fetch, and then returned with her as hard as he could go. But even as he reached home and drove up the rutted lane, a premonition of calamity touched him. The house was absolutely dark and silent: there was neither smoke nor sound nor any light whatever, and, filled with a boding apprehension, he entered. He called his wife's name in the dark house, but no one answered him. Then, he raised the smoky lantern which he carried, walked to the bed where his wife lay, and looked at her, seeing instantly that she was dead.

That night the people from the neighborhood swarmed into the house. The women washed the dead woman's body, dressed her, "laid her out," and the men sat round the fire, whittled with knives, and told a thousand drawling stories of the strangeness of death and destiny. As Roberts was recounting for the hundredth time all of the circumstances of the death, he turned to Lafayette Joyner, who had come straightway when he heard the news, with his wife and several of his brothers:

" . . . and I was jest goin' to tell Rance to stop and wait here till I got back, but I reckon it was just as well I didn't—she would have been dead a-fore he got here, and I reckon it might have frightened him to find her."

Fate Joyner looked at him slowly with a puzzled face.

"Rance?" he said.

"Why, yes," said Roberts, "I passed him comin' home just as I got to town—and I reckon if I hadn't been in such a hurry I'd a-told him to stop off and wait till I got back."

The Joyners had suddenly stopped their whittling. They looked upward from their places round the fire with their faces fixed on Roberts' face in a single, silent, feeding, fascinated stare, and he paused suddenly, and all the other neighbors paused, feeling the dark, premonitory boding of some new phantasmal marvel in their look.

"You say you passed Rance as you were goin' in to town?" Fate Joyner asked.

"Why, yes," said Roberts, and described again all of the circumstances of the meeting.

And, still looking at him, Fate Joyner slowly shook his head.

"No," said he, "you never saw Rance. It wasn't Rance that you saw."

The man's flesh turned cold.

"What do you mean?" he said.

"Rance wasn't there," said Fate Joyner. "He went to visit Rufus Alexander's people a week ago, and he's fifty miles away from here right now. That's where he is tonight," said Fate quietly.

Roberts' face had turned grey in the firelight. For several moments he said nothing. Then he muttered:

"Yes. Yes, I see it now. By God, that's it, all right."

Then he told them how the boy had seemed to vanish right before his eyes a moment after he had passed him—"as if—as if," he said, "the earth had opened up to swaller him."

"And that was it?" he whispered.

"Yes," Fate Joyner answered quietly, "that was it."

He paused, and for a moment all the feeding, horror-hungry eyes turned with slow fascination to the figure of the dead woman on the bed, who lay, hands folded, in composed and rigid posture, the fire-flames casting the long flicker of their light upon her cold, dead face.

"Yes, that was it," Fate Joyner said. "She was dead then, at that moment—but you—you didn't know it," he added, and quietly there was feeding a deep triumph in his voice.

THUS, THIS GOOD-HEARTED and simple-minded boy became, without his having willed or comprehended it, a supernatural portent of man's fate and destiny. Rance Joyner, or rather, his spiritual substance, was seen by dusk and darkness on deserted roads, was observed crossing fields and coming out of woods, was seen to toil up a hill along a narrow path at evening—and then to vanish suddenly. Often, these apparitions had no discernible relation to any human happening; more often, they were precedent, coincident, or subsequent to some fatal circumstance. And this ghostly power was not limited to the period of his boyhood. It continued, with increasing force and frequency, into the years of his manhood and maturity.

Thus, one evening early in the month of April, 1862, the wife of Lafayette Joyner, coming to the door of her house—which was built on the summit of a hill, or ledge, above a little river—suddenly espied Rance toiling up the steep path that led up to the house. In his soiled and ragged uniform, he looked footsore, unkempt, dusty, and unutterably weary—"as if," she said, "he had come a long, long ways"—as indeed, he must have done, since at that moment he was a private soldier in one of Jackson's regiments in Virginia.

But Lafayette Joyner's wife could see him plainly as he paused for a moment to push open a long gate that gave upon the road below her, halfway down the hill. She turned, she said, in her excitement for a moment, to shout the news of his approach to others in the house, and in that instant he had vanished from her sight. When she looked again, no one was there; the scene was fading into night and stillness, and the woman wrung her hands in her despair, saying:

"Oh, Lord! Oh, Lord! What's to become of us? What's happened now?"

Such was her story. And, as always, it confirmed a fatal event. On that day in April, more than two hundred miles to the westward, the bloody battle of Shiloh had been fought in Tennessee, and at that moment, although the news did not get back to them for several weeks, one of the brothers, John, was lying on the field, his shattered face turned upward, dead.

SUCH, THEN, WERE some of the stories Aunt Maw told to George. And always, when she spoke so in the night, as the coal-fire flared and crumbled in the grate, and the huge demented winds of darkness howled around them and the terror of strong silence fed forever at his heart—he could hear the thousand death-devouring voices of the Joyners speaking triumphantly from the darkness of a hundred years, the lost and lonely sorrow of the hills, and somehow smell incredibly— always and forever!—the soft, fragrant ash of the pine blaze, the pungent sharpness of the whittled wood, the winy warmth and fullness of mellow apples. And horribly, somehow, to these odors were always added the death-evoking smells of turpentine and camphor—which were a lost memory of infancy, when his mother had taken him, a child of two, to such a room—warmth, apples, Joyner room, and all—to see his grandfather the night before he died.

Upon a thousand lost and lonely roads in the ever-lost and ever-lonely hills he heard the unctuous, drawling voices of the Joyners. He saw them toiling up a wooded hill in sad, hushed, evening light to vanish like a wraith into thin air; and the terrible prophecies of old wars and battles, and of all the men who had that day been buried in the earth, were in that instant apparition and farewell! He saw them in a thousand little houses of the wilderness, in years more far and lonely than the years of Vercingetorix, coming in at darkness always to watch the night away beside the dead, to sit in semi-darkness in some neighbor's ill-starred house, to sit around the piny fire-flame's dance of death, and with triumphant lust to drawl and whittle night away while the pine logs flamed and crumbled to soft ash and their voices spoke forever their fated and invincible auguries of sorrow.

What was it Aunt Maw thus evoked by the terrific weavings of her memory? In the boy's vision of that world, the Joyners were a race as lawless as the earth, as criminal as nature. They hurled their prodigal seed into the raw earth of a mountain woman's body, bringing to life a swarming progeny which lived or died, was extinguished in its infancy or fought its way triumphantly to maturity against the savage enemies of poverty, ignorance, and squalor which menaced it at every step. They bloomed or perished as things live or die in nature—but the triumphant Joyners, superior to all loss or waste, lived forever as a river lives. Other tribes of men came up out of the earth, flourished for a space, and then, engulfed and falling, went back into the earth from which they came. Only the Joyners—these horror-hungry, time-devouring Joyners—lived, and would not die.

And *he* belonged to that fatal, mad, devouring world from whose prison there was no escape. He belonged to it, even as three hundred of his blood and bone had belonged to it, and must unweave it from his brain, distill it from his blood, unspin it from his entrails, and escape with demonic and exultant joy into his father's world, new lands and mornings and the shining city—or drown like a mad dog, die!

FROM THE FIRST years of coherent memory, George had the sense of the overpowering immanence of the golden life. It seemed to him that he was always on the verge of finding it. In his childhood it was all around him, impending numbly, softly, filling him with an intolerable exultancy of wordless joy. It wrenched his heart with its wild pain of ecstasy and tore the sinews of his life asunder, but yet it filled his soul with the triumphant sense of instant release, impending discovery—as if a great wall in the air would suddenly be revealed and sundered, as if an enormous door would open slowly, awfully, with the tremendous majesty of an utter and invisible silence. He never found a word for it, but he had a thousand spells and prayers and images that would give it coherence, shape, and meanings that no words could do.

He thought that he could twist his hand a certain way, or turn his wrist, or make a certain simple movement of rotation into space (as boys will learn the movement to unsolve a puzzle of linked chains, or as an expert in the mysteries of locks can feel the bearings faintly, softly, rolling through his finger tips, and know the instant that he finds the combination to unlock the safe)—and that by making this rotation with his hand, he would find the lost dimension of that secret world, and instantly step through the door that he had opened.

And he had other chants and incantations that would make that world reveal itself to him. Thus, for a period of ten years or more, he had a spell for almost everything he did. He would hold his breath along a certain block, or take four breaths in pounding down the hill from school, or touch each cement block upon a wall as he went past, and touch each of the end-blocks where the steps went up two times, and if he failed to touch them twice, go back and touch the whole wall over from the start.

And on Sunday he would always do the second thing: he would never do the first on Sunday. All through the day, from midnight Saturday until midnight Monday morning, he would always do the second thing he thought about and not the first. If he woke up on Sunday morning and swung over to the left side to get out of bed, he would swing back and get out on the right. If he started with the right sock, he would take it off and pull the left one on instead. And if he wanted first to use one tie, he would discard it and put on another.

And so it went the whole day through on Sunday. In every act and moment of his life that day he would always do the second thing he thought about instead of the first. But then when midnight came again, he would, with the same fanatic superstition, do the first thing that he thought about; and if he failed in any detail of this ritual, he would be as gloomy, restless, and full of uneasy boding doubts as if all the devils of mischance were already out in force against him, and posting on their way to do him harm.

These spells, chants, incantations, and compulsions grew, interwove, and constantly increased in the complexity and denseness of their web until at times they governed everything he did—not only the way he touched a wall, or held his breath while pounding down a hill from school, or measured out a block in punctual distances of breathing, or spanned the cement blocks of sidewalks in strides of four, but even in the way he went along a street, the side he took, the place he had to stop and look, the place he strode by sternly even when he wanted bitterly to stay and look, the trees out in his uncle's orchard that he climbed until he had to climb a certain tree four times a day and use four movements to get up the trunk.

And this tyrannic mystery of four would also get into the way he threw a ball, or chanted over Latin when preparing it, or muttered παιδενσω four times in the Subjunctive of the First Aorist, or ἐθηκα in the Indicative Active of the First. And it was also in the way he washed his neck and ears, or sat down at a table, split up kindling (using four strokes of the axe to make a stick), or brought up coal (using four scoops of the shovel to fill the scuttle).

Then there were also days of stern compulsion when he could look at only a single feature of people's faces. On Monday he would look upon men's noses, on Tuesday he would stare into their teeth, on Wednesday he would peer into their eyes, save Thursday for their hands, and Friday for their feet, and sternly meditate the conformation of their brows on Saturday, saving Sunday always for the second feature that occurred to him—eyes when feet were thought of, teeth for eyes, and foreheads when his fine first rapture had been noses. And he would go about this duty of observing with such a stern, fanatical devotion, peering savagely at people's teeth or hands or brows, that sometimes they looked at him uneasily, resentfully, wondering what he saw amiss in their appearance, or shaking their heads and muttering angrily as they passed each other by.

At night, he said his prayers in rhymes of four—for four, eight, sixteen, thirty-two were somehow the key numbers in his arithmetic of sorcery. He would say his one set prayer in chants of four times four, until all the words and meanings of the prayer (which he had composed himself with four times four in mind) were lost, and all that he would follow would be the rhythm and the number of the chant, muttered so rapidly that the prayer was just a rapid blur—but muttered always sixteen times. And if he failed to do this, or doubted he had got the proper count, then he could not sleep or rest after he got into bed, and would get up instantly and go down upon his knees again, no matter how cold or raw the weather was, no matter how he felt, and would not pause until he did the full count to his satisfaction, with another sixteen thrown in as penalty. It was not piety he felt, it was not thought of God or reverence or religion: it was just superstitious mystery, a belief in the wizard-charm of certain numbers, and the conviction that he had to do it in this way in order to have luck.

Thus, each night he paid his punctual duty to "their" dark authorities, in order to keep himself in "their" good graces, to assure himself that "they" would not forsake him, that "they" would still be for him, not against him, that "they"—immortal, secret, "they" that will not give us rest!—would keep him, guard him, make his life prevail, frustrate his evil enemies, and guide him on to all the glory, love, and triumph, and to that great door, the huge, hinged, secret wall of life—that immanent and unutterable world of joy which was so near, so strangely, magically, and intolerably near, which he would find at any moment, and for which his life was panting.

ONE DAY A circus came to town, and as the boy stood looking at it there came to him two images which were to haunt all the rest of his childhood, but which were now for the first time seen together with an instant and a magic congruence. And these were the images of the circus and his father's earth.

He thought he had joined a circus and started on the great tour of the nation with it. It was Spring: the circus had started in New England, and worked westward and then southward as the Summer and Autumn came on. His nominal duties—for in his vision every incident, each face and voice and circumstance, was blazing real as life itself—were those of ticket seller. But in this tiny show everyone did several things, so he also posted bills, and bartered with the tradesmen and farmers in new places for fresh food. He became very clever at this work—some old, sharp, buried talent for shrewd trading that had come to him from his mountain blood now aided him. He could get the finest, freshest meats and vegetables at the lowest prices. The circus people were tough and hard, they always had a fierce and ravenous hunger, they would not accept bad food and cooking, they fed stupendously, and they always had the best of everything.

Usually the circus would arrive at a new town very early in the morning, before daybreak. He would go into town immediately: he would go to the markets, or with farmers who had come in for the circus. He felt and saw the purity of first light, he heard the sweet and sudden lutings of first birds, and suddenly he was filled with the earth and morning in new towns, among new men. He walked among the farmers' wagons, and he dealt with them on the spot for the prodigal plenty of their wares—the country melons bedded in sweet hay, the cool, sweet pounds of butter wrapped in clean, wet cloths, with dew and starlight still upon them, the enormous battered cans foaming with fresh milk, the new-laid eggs which he bought by the gross and hundred dozen, the tender, limey pullets by the score, the delicate bunches of green scallions, the heavy red ripeness of huge tomatoes, the sweet-leaved lettuces, crisp as celery, the fresh-podded peas and the succulent young beans, as well as the potatoes spotted with the loamy earth, the winy apples, the peaches, and the cherries, the juicy corn stacked up in shocks of luring green, and the heavy, blackened rinds of the home-cured hams and bacons.

As the markets opened, he would begin to trade and dicker with the butchers for their finest cuts of meat. They would hold great roasts up in their gouted fingers, they would roll up tubs of fresh-ground sausage, they would smack with their long palms the flanks of beeves and porks. He would drive back to the circus with a wagon full of meat and vegetables.

At the circus ground the people were already in full activity. He could hear the wonderful timed tattoo of sledges on the driven stakes, the shouts of men riding animals down to water, the slow clank and pull of mighty horses, the heavy rumble of the wagons as they rolled down off the circus flat cars. By now the eating tent would be erected, and, as he arrived, he could see the cooks already busy at their ranges, the long tables set up underneath the canvas with their rows of benches, their tin plates and cups. There would be the amber pungency of strong coffee, and the smell of buckwheat batter.

Then the circus people would come in for breakfast. The food they ate was as masculine and fragrant as the world they dwelt in. It belonged to the warmed, stained world of canvas, the clean and healthful odor of the animals, and the wild, sweet, lyric nature of the land on which they lived as wanderers. And it was there for the asking with a fabulous and stupefying plenty, golden and embrowned. They ate stacks of buckwheat cakes, smoking hot, soaked in hunks of yellow butter, which they carved at will with a wide, free gesture from the piled prints on the table, and which they garnished with ropes of heavy black molasses, or with maple syrup. They ate big steaks for breakfast, hot from the pan and thick with onions; they ate whole melons, crammed with the ripeness of the deep-pink meat, rashers of bacon, and great platters of fried eggs, or eggs scrambled with calves' brains. They helped themselves from pyramids of fruit piled up at intervals on the table—plums, peaches, apples, cherries, grapes, oranges, and bananas. They had great pitchers of thick cream to pour on everything, and they washed their hunger down with pint mugs of strong, deep-savored coffee.

For their midday meal they would eat fiercely, hungrily, with wolfish gusto, mightily with knit brows and convulsive movements of their corded throats. They would eat great roasts of beef with crackled hides, browned in their juices, rare and tender; hot chunks of delicate pork with hems of fragrant fat; delicate young broiled chickens; twelve-pound pot roasts, cooked for hours in an iron pot with new carrots, onions, sprouts, and young potatoes; together with every vegetable that the season yielded—huge roasting ears of corn, smoking hot, piled like cordwood on two-foot platters, tomatoes cut in slabs with wedges of okra and succotash, and raw onions, mashed potatoes whipped to a creamy batter, turnips, fresh peas cooked in butter, and fat, strong beans seasoned with the flavor of big chunks of pork. In addition they had every fruit that the place and time afforded: hot crusty apple, peach, and cherry pies, encrusted with cinnamon; puddings and cakes of every sort; and blobbering cobblers inches deep.

Thus the circus moved across America, from town to town, from state to state, eating its way from Maine into the great plains of the West, eating its way along the Hudson and the Mississippi Rivers, eating its way across the prairies and from the North into the South.

Abroad in this ocean of earth and vision, the boy thought of his father's land, of its great red barns, its clear familiarity and its haunting strangeness, and its lovely and tragic beauty. He thought of its smell of harbors and its rumors of the sea, the city, and the ships, its wine-ripe apples and its brown-red soil, its snug, weathered houses, its lyric, unutterable ecstasy.

A wonderful thing happened. One morning he awoke suddenly to find himself staring straight up at the pulsing splendor of the stars. At first he did not know where he was. The circus train had stopped in the heart of the country, for what reason he did not know. He could hear the languid and intermittent breathing of the engine, the strangeness of men's voices in the dark, the casual stamp of the horses in their cars, and all around him the attentive and vital silence of the earth.

Suddenly he raised himself from the pile of canvas on which he slept. It was the moment just before dawn: against the east the sky had already begun to whiten with the first faint luminosity of day, the invading tides of light crept up the sky, drowning the stars out as they went. The train had halted by a little river, which ran swift and deep close to the tracks, and now he knew that what at first he thought had been the sound of silence was the swift and ceaseless music of the river.

There had been rain the night before, and now the river was filled with the sweet, clean smell of earthy deposits. He could see the delicate white glimmer of young birch trees leaning from the banks, and on the other side he saw the winding whiteness of a road. Beyond the road, and bordering it, there was an orchard with a wall of lichened stone. As the wan light grew, the earth and all its contours emerged sharply. He saw the worn and ancient design of lichened rocks, the fertile soil of the ploughed fields; he saw the kept order, the frugal cleanliness, with its mild tang of opulent greenery. Here was an earth with fences as big as a man's heart, but not so great as his desire, and this earth was like a room he once lived in. He returned to it as a sailor to a small, closed harbor, as a man, spent with the hunger of his wandering, comes home.

Instantly he recognized the scene. He knew he had come at last into his father's land. Here was his home, brought back to him while he slept, like a forgotten dream. Here was his heart's desire, his father's country, the earth his spirit dwelt in. He knew every inch of the land-scape, and he knew past reason, doubt, or argument that home was not three miles away.

He got up at once and leaped down to the earth: he knew where he would go. Along the track there was the slow swing and dance of the brakemen's lamps. Already the train was in motion, its bell tolled, and the heavy trucks rumbled away from him. He began to walk back along the tracks, for less than a mile away, he knew, where the stream boiled over the lip of a dam, there was a bridge. When he reached the bridge a deeper light had come: the old red brick of the mill emerged sharply and fell sheer into bright, shining waters.

He crossed the bridge and turned left along the road. Here it moved away from the river, among fields and through dark woods— dark woods bordered with stark poignancy of fir and pine, with the noble spread of maples, shot with the naked whiteness of birch. Sharp thrummings, woodland flitters, broke the silence. The tongue-trilling chirrs arose now, and little brainless cries, liquefied lutings. Smooth drops and nuggets of bright gold they were.

He went along that road where, he knew, the house of his father's blood and kin lay hidden. At length, he came around a bending of the road, he left the wooded land, he passed by hedges, and saw the old white house, set in the shoulder of the hill, clean and cool below the dark shelter of its trees. A twist of morning smoke coiled through its chimney.

Then he turned into the road that led up to the house, and at this moment the enormous figure of a powerful old man appeared around the corner, prophetically bearing a smoked ham in one huge hand. And when the boy saw the old man, a cry of greeting burst from his throat, and the old man answered with a roar of welcome that shook the earth. The old man dropped his ham, and waddled forward to meet the boy: they met half down the road, and the old man crushed him in his hug. They tried to speak but could not, they embraced again and in an instant all the pain of loneliness and the fierce hungers of desire were scoured away like a scum of frost from a bright glass.

At this moment also, two young men burst from the house and came running down the road to greet him. They were powerful and heavy youths, and, like their father, they recognized the boy instantly, and in a moment he was engulfed in their mighty energies, borne up among them to the house. As they ate breakfast, he told them of his circus wanderings and they told him what had befallen them. And they understood all that he wanted to say but could not speak, and they surrounded him with love and lavish heapings of his plate.

Such were the twin images of the circus and his father's land which now, as he stood there looking at the circus, fused instantly to a living whole and came to him in a blaze of light. And in this way, before he had ever seen or set his foot upon it, he came for the first time to his father's earth.

Thus, day by day, in the taut and tangled web of this boy's life, the two hemispheres that touched but never joined, contended, separated, recombined, and wove again. First came the old dark memory of time-haunted man and the lost voices in the hills a hundred years ago, the world-lost and hill-haunted sorrow of the time-triumphant Joyners. Then his spirit flamed beyond the hills, beyond lost time and sorrow, to his father and his father's earth; and when he thought of him his heart grew warm, the hot blood thudded in his veins, he leapt all barriers of the here and now, and northward, gleaming brightly there beyond the hills, he saw a vision of the golden future in new lands.

CHAPTER 4

The Golden City

Always and forever when the boy thought of his father, and of the proud, the cold, the secret North, he thought, too, of the city. His father had not come from there, yet strangely, through some subtle chemistry of his imagination, some magic of his boy's mind and heart, he connected his father's life and figure with the bright and shining city of the North.

In his child's picture of the world, there were no waste or barren places: there was only the rich tapestry of an immense and limitlessly fertile domain forever lyrical as April, and forever ready for the harvest, touched with the sorcery of a magic green, bathed forever in a full-hued golden light. And at the end, forever at the end of all the fabled earth, there hung the golden vision of the city, itself more fertile, richer, more full of joy and bounty than the earth it rested on. Far-off and shining, it rose upward in his vision from an opalescent mist, upborne and sustained as lightly as a cloud, yet firm and soaring with full golden light. It was a vision simple, unperplexed, carved from deep substances of light and shade, and exultant with its prophecy of glory, love, and triumph.

He heard, far off, the deep and beelike murmur of its million-footed life, and all the mystery of the earth and time was in that sound. He saw its thousand streets peopled with a flashing, beautiful, infinitely varied life. The city flashed before him like a glorious jewel, blazing with countless rich and brilliant facets of a life so good, so bountiful, so strangely and constantly beautiful and interesting, that it seemed intolerable that he should miss a moment of it. He saw the streets swarming with the figures of great men and glorious women, and he walked among them like a conqueror, winning fiercely and exultantly by his talent, courage, and merit the greatest tributes that the city had to offer, the highest prize of power, wealth, and fame, and the great emolument of love. There would be villainy and knavery as black and sinister as hell, but he would smash it with a blow, and drive it cringing to its hole. There would be heroic men and lovely women, and he would win and take a place among the highest and most fortunate people on the earth.

Thus, in a vision hued with all the strange and magic colors of his adolescence, the boy walked the streets of his great legendary city. Sometimes he sat among the masters of the earth in rooms of manlike opulence: dark wood, heavy leathers of solid, lavish brown, were all around him. Again he walked in great chambers of the night, rich with the warmth of marble and the majesty of great stairs, sustained on swelling columns of a rich-toned onyx, soft and deep with crimson carpets in which the foot sank down with noiseless tread. And through this room, filled with a warm and undulant music, the deep and mellow thrum of violins, there walked a hundred beautiful women, and all were his, if he would have them. And the loveliest of them all was his. Long of limb and slender, yet lavish and deep of figure, they walked with proud, straight looks on their fragile and empty faces, holding their gleaming shoulders superbly, and their clear, depthless eyes alive with love and tenderness. A firm and golden light fell over them, and over all his love.

He also walked in steep and canyoned streets, blue and cool with a frontal steepness of money and great business, brown and rich somehow with the sultry and exultant smell of coffee, the good green smell of money, and the fresh, half-rotten odor of the harbor with its tide of ships.

Such was his vision of the city—adolescent, fleshly, and erotic, but drunk with innocence and joy, and made strange and wonderful by the magic lights of gold and green and lavish brown in which he saw it. For, more than anything, it was the light. The light was golden with the flesh of women, lavish as their limbs, true, depthless, tender as their glorious eyes, fine-spun and maddening as their hair, as unutterable with desire as their fragrant nests of spicery, their deep melon-heavy breasts. The light was golden like a morning light that shines through ancient glass into a room of old dark brown. The light was rich brown shot with gold, lavish brown like old stone houses gulched in morning on a city street. The light was also blue, like morning underneath the frontal cliff of buildings, vertical, cool blue, hazed with thin morning mist, cold-flowing harbor blue of clean, cool waters, rimed brightly with a dancing morning gold.

The light was amber-brown in vast, dark chambers shuttered from young light, where, in great walnut beds, the glorious women stirred in sensual warmth their lavish limbs. The light was brown-gold like ground coffee, merchants, and the walnut houses where they lived; brown-gold like old brick buildings grimed with money and the smell of trade; brown-gold like morning in great gleaming bars of swart mahogany, the fresh wet beer-wash, lemon rind, and the smell of Angostura bitters. Then it was full-golden in the evening in the theatres, shining with full-golden warmth and body on full-golden figures of the women, on fat red plush, and on the rich, faded, slightly stale smell, and on the gilt sheaves and cupids and the cornucopias, on the fleshly, potent, softly-golden smell of all the people. And in great restaurants the light was brighter gold, but full and round like warm onyx columns, smooth, warmly-tinted marble, old wine in dark, rounded, age-encrusted bottles, and the great blonde figures of naked women on rose-clouded ceilings. Then the light was full and rich, brown-golden like great fields in Autumn; it was full-swelling golden light like mown fields, bronze-red picked out with fat, rusty-golden sheaves of corn, and governed by huge barns of red and the mellow, winy fragrance of the apples.

That vision of the city was gathered from a thousand isolated sources, from the pages of books, the words of a traveler, a picture of Brooklyn Bridge with its great, winglike sweep, the song and music of its cables, even the little figures of the men with derby hats as they advanced across it. These and a thousand other things all built the picture of the city in his mind, until now it possessed him and had got somehow, powerfully, exultantly, ineradicably, into everything he did or thought or felt.

That vision of the city blazed outward not only from those images and objects which would evoke it literally, as the picture of the Bridge had done: it was now mixed obscurely and powerfully into his whole vision of the earth, into the chemistry and rhythm of his blood, into a million things with which it had no visible relation. It came in a woman's laughter in the street at night, in sounds of music and the faint thrumming of a waltz, in the guttural rise and fall of the bass violin; and it was in the odor of new grass in April, in cries half-heard and broken by the wind, and in the hot daze and torpid drone of Sunday afternoon.

It came in all the sounds and noises of a carnival, in the smell of confetti, gasoline, the high, excited clamors of the people, the wheeling music of the carousel, the sharp cries and strident voices of the barkers. And it was in the circus smells and sounds as well—in the ramp and reek of lions, tigers, elephants, and in the tawny camel smell. It came somehow in frosty Autumn nights, in clear, sharp, frosty sounds of Hallowe'en. And it came to him intolerably at night in the receding whistle-wail of a distant and departing train, the faint and mournful tolling of its bell, and the pounding of great wheels upon the rail. It came also in the sight of great strings of rusty freight cars on the tracks, and in the sight of a rail, shining with the music of space and flight as it swept away into the distance and was lost from sight.

In things like these, and countless others, the vision of the city would come alive and stab him like a knife.

BOOK II

The Hound of Darkness

Until his sixteenth year, George Webber, whom the boys called "Monk"—a name that was to stick to him throughout his life and come to seem more natural than the one his parents gave him—grew up among his Joyner kin. And he was one of them, knit closely in the web and fabric of their narrow, mountain-rimmed, and self-sufficient world. And yet he was a Webber, too, a fact of family shame and secret pride to him, and something from beyond the mountains was at work within his spirit.

Thus the strong, conflicting pulls of Joyner and of Webber blood which met but never fused in his own veins produced a ceaseless ebb and flow within his mind and heart, and from these motions of his spirit came a strangely sentient vision of the world, a richly varied tapestry of life, woven in contrasting tones of light and dark, of sunshine and deep shadow.

CHAPTER 5

Aunt Mag and Uncle Mark

For Mark Joyner's wife, Aunt Mag, the boy George had little love.

She was of a family of mountain peasants, and she had done everything she could to advance her position in life by a liberal use of Mark's purse.

"She needn't give herself airs," said Aunt Maw. "When Mark first saw her, she was hoein' corn in a field."

Childless at forty-five, Mag was a tall, rather gaunt, white-faced woman, with cold eyes, a thin nose, and a bitter, sneering mouth. She had been handsome, but for twenty years she had been under the spell of a neurosis which had held her in the unshakable conviction that she was suffering from consumption, cancer, heart disease, and pernicious anæmia. She was under constant medical attention. She spent half her waking hours extended in white terror on her bed, in a room chemical with shelves and tables full of bottles, and sealed against a draft of air.

She was, as a matter of fact, a strong, healthy, and well-nourished woman.

George sometimes went along with Aunt Maw when she crossed the intervening strip of lawn to visit Mag in her new and ugly house of bright red brick. They would find her in her sealed room in a sickening enervation of red-hot stove heat.

"Come here!" Aunt Mag would say in her harsh, sneering voice, drawing the boy's unwilling figure beside her bed. "Lord a' mercy!" she would add, staring up into his face with her bitter laugh. "He smells like a Webber! Do your feet stink, boy?"

These pleasantries, delivered to the accompaniment of sneering laughter, and a bending down of her thin, pious mouth as she pretended to sniff the air with disgust, did not increase George's love for his aunt.

"You don't know how lucky you are, boy!" she would scream at him. "You ought to get down on your knees every night and thank the Lord for having a good Christian home like this! Where would you be if it wasn't for me? I made your Uncle Mark take you in! If it wasn't for me, you'd have been sent to an orphan asylum—that's where you'd be!"

Under this goading, the boy would mumble his gratitude, but in his heart he often wished he *had* been sent to an orphanage.

MAG WAS A Baptist, and very active in her church. She donated liberally; she fattened the preacher at her Sunday table; above all, she contributed large sums for the maintenance of the Baptist orphanage, and kept in her service at all times two or three children whom she had taken under her generous wing. This charity got the thick coatings of flattery which assure a Baptist of success on earth and favor in heaven. The minister, speaking to his Sunday hundreds, would say:

" . . . And now I know we will all be glad to hear that the heart of another orphan child has been made happy through the generosity of Sister Joyner, who, in the great goodness of her heart, is giving a comfortable home to Betsy Belcher, a little girl who lost both her parents before she was eight years old. This makes the sixth orphan that the good woman has taken into her loving care. I know, when we see her giving to the Lord so freely, that there are others here who will be led to give a little in the furtherance of the great work which the good Brothers and Sisters at the orphanage are doing."

And as Mag, bridling and ludicrously humble, advanced to the pulpit after the preacher's harangue, he would bend with greased unction over her hand, saying:

"And how is the good woman today?"

Mag took in these wretched children and made them drudges of all trades about the house. One of them was a boy of fourteen whose name was Willie, a thick-headed, smiling, perpetually bewildered idiot. Willie never played with the boys in the neighborhood because he was always kept busy doing chores, and George rarely saw him except on his visits of duty to Aunt Mag, when the orphan boy would be summoned into her room on a fire-building errand.

"Did you ever see such an idiot?" Mag would say, with her sneering laugh. "Lord a' mercy!"

And the boy would smile back at her, doubtfully, idiotically, fearfully, not knowing why.

One time Willie was left with Aunt Maw when Mark and Mag went to Florida. He worked like a dog. Aunt Maw stuffed him with food and gave him a little room in which to sleep. She did not abuse him. She and George laughed constantly at him, and he was absurdly pleased and grateful to know that he amused them, smiling his wide, idiot grin.

His hair was a tangled, uncut jungle which fell in matted lengths almost to his shoulder. Nebraska Crane told him solemnly, one day, that he was an experienced barber, and Willie submitted joyfully to the operation. Nebraska capped his large head with an inverted chamber pot, and laughed quietly from time to time as he sheared off all the hair that fell below the edges of the pot. And Willie, under the pot, continued to smile at them in friendly, puzzled idiocy while Nebraska and George caved slowly inward with laughter.

MAG HAD TWO nephews who lived in the big house with her and Mark. They were the sons of her brother who had died, and when the mother of the boys died not long after their father, Mag had taken them in. Since they were her own blood, she had brought them up with as much misguided indulgence as though they had been her sons, and had lavished upon them all the affection of which her narrow and thwarted nature was capable. Mark's money was poured out for their benefit with a liberal hand, Mag having made it a cardinal point, in her system of educating them for their high position in life as her nearest kin, to deny them nothing.

The older, Earl, was a heavy, florid, coarsely handsome young man with a loud, vacant, infectious laugh. He was well liked in the town. He had devoted all his time to the study of golf as a fine art, and was one of the best players in Libya Hill. It pleased Mag to know that he was a member of the Country Club. Her conception of gentility was a life of complete idleness spent in the company of "the best people."

The other nephew, the little golden apple of Mag's delight, was named Tad. He was now a young man of seventeen or eighteen, with a shiny red, porky face and an annoying, satisfied laugh. Tad had avoided expertly all of the inconvenient toil of life. He had all his aunt's skill in calling on physical collapse to aid him, and Mag was convinced that a weak heart ran in her family and that the boy had inherited it.

Tad, too delicate for the rough uses of a school, received his instruction at home, peripatetically, in the Greek manner, between three and four o'clock in the afternoon, from a withered hack who ran a small school for boys, and who, for a substantial sum, winked considerately and assured Mag that her nephew had already received the equivalent of a university education.

A good part of his time Tad spent in his "laboratory," a little gabled room in the attic to which he brought the subjects of his experiments—small, panting birds, vibrating cats, stray curs—noting with minute curiosity their sensory responses when he drove pins into their eyes, cut off portions of their tails, or seared them with a heated poker.

"That boy's a born naturalist," said Mag.

Mark Joyner was frugal for himself, but open-handed with Mag. He had toast and two boiled eggs for breakfast, which he cooked on top of a little wood stove in his room, estimating among his friends the cost of kindling, eggs, and bread at twelve cents. Later he used the hot water for shaving.

"By God!" said the townsmen, "that's the reason he's got it!"

He sought for his clothing among the Jews; he smoked rank, weedy "threefers"; he cobbled his own shoes; he exulted equally in his parsimony to himself and his liberality to his household. From the first years of his marriage he had given Mag a generous allowance, which had increased as his business prospered, and she had turned over a considerable part of it to her two nephews. They were her own blood, and whatever she had was theirs.

Most of the time Mag held her husband in iron subjection, but there was a hidden volcano of anger in him that increased from year to year of his living with her, and when it was roused, all her weapons of harsh laughter, incessant nagging, and chronic invalidism were impotent. He would grow silent, doing his utmost to control himself, and in the effort contorting his lips in a terrible grimace; but finally his emotion would become too much for him, and he would storm out of the house, away from Mag and the sound of her voice, and, turning his gaunt face towards the western hills, he would tramp through the woods for hours until his spirit grew calm again.

CHAPTER 6

The Street of the Day

When George Webber was a child, Locust Street, the street on which he lived with his Joyner relatives, seemed fixed for him into the substance of immemorial antiquity. It had a beginning and a history, he had no doubt, but a history that began so long ago that countless men had come and lived and died and been forgotten since the street began, and no man living could remember when that was. Moreover, it seemed to him that every house and tree and garden had been framed to the pattern of an immutable design: they were there because they had to be there, they were built that way because that was the only way in which they could be built.

This street held for him a universe of joy and magic which seemed abundant for a thousand lives. Its dimensions were noble in their space and limitless surprise. Its world of houses, yards, and orchards and its hundred people seemed to him to have the incomparable grandeur of the first place on earth, the impregnable authority of the center of the universe.

In later years, George plainly saw that the world in which he lived had been a little place. All of the dimensions of the street had dwindled horribly. The houses that had seemed so imposing in their opulence and grandeur, the lawns that were so spacious, the backyards and the vistaed orchards that went on in limitless progressions of delight and new discovery that never had an end—all this had shrunken pitifully, incredibly, and now looked close, and mean, and cramped. Yet even then, years later, the street and all its million memories of a buried life awoke for him with the blazing and intolerable vividness of a dream. It was a world which he had known and lived with every atom of his blood and brain and spirit, and every one of its thousand images was rooted into the structure of his life forever, as much a part of him as his inmost thoughts.

AT FIRST IT was just the feel of the grass and the earth and the ground under your naked feet in May when you were going barefoot for the first time and walking gingerly. It was the cool feel of the sand up through your toes, and the feel of the soft tar in the streets and walking on a wall of concrete blocks, and the feel of cool, damp earth in shaded places. It was the feel of standing on the low edge of a roof or in a barn loft opening or on the second story of a house that was being built and daring another boy to jump; and looking over, waiting, knowing you must jump; and looking down, and waiting, daring, taunting, with a thudding heart, until you jumped.

And then it was the good feel of throwing a small, round, heavy stone through the window of a vacant house when the red and ancient light of evening was blazing on its windows; and it was like feeling a baseball in your hands for the first time in the Spring, and its round and solid weight at the end of your arm and the way it shot away like a bullet the first time when you threw it with a feeling of terrific power and speed and it smacked into the odorous, well-oiled pocket of the catcher's mitt. And then it was like prowling round in dark, cool cellars, thinking you would come upon a buried treasure any moment, and finding rows of cobwebbed bottles and the rusty frame of an old bicycle.

Sometimes it was like waking up on Saturday with the grand feeling of Saturday morning leaping in your heart, and seeing the apple blossoms drifting to the earth, and smelling sausage and ham and coffee, and knowing there would be no school today, no dreadful, morning, schoolhouse bell today, no thudding heart, and pounding legs,

and shuddering nerves and bolted and uneasy food, and sour, distressful coffee in your guts, because there would be no school today and it
was golden, shining, and triumphant Saturday.

And then it was like Saturday night, and joy and menace in the
air, and everyone waiting to get out on the streets and go "uptown,"
and taking a hot bath, and putting on clean clothes and eating supper,
and going uptown on the nighttime streets of Saturday where joy and
menace filled the air about you, and where glory breathed upon you,
and yet never came, and getting far down towards the front and seeing Broncho Billy shoot the bad men dead three times until the last
show of the night was over, and a cracked slide was shone on the screen
which said "Good Night."

Then it was like Sunday morning, waking, hearing the bus outside, smelling the coffee, brains and eggs, and buckwheat cakes, feeling peaceful, sweetly happy, not exultant as on Saturday, a slumberous,
drowsy, and more mournful joy, the smell of the Sunday newspapers,
and the Sunday morning light outside, bright, golden, yet religious
light, and church bells, people putting on good clothes to go to church,
and the closed and decent streets of Sunday morning, and going by the
cool side where the tobacco store was, and the Sunday morning sports
inside who didn't have to go to church, and the strong, clean, pungent
smell of good tobacco, and the good smell and feel of the church,
which was not so much like God as like a good and decent substance
in the world—the children singing, "Shall we gather at the River the
Bew-tee-ful the Bew-tee-ful R-hiv-er!"—and the drone of voices from
the class rooms later on, and the dark walnut, stained-glass light in the
church, and decent, never-gaudy people with good dinners waiting for
them when they got home, and the remote yet passionate austerity of
the preacher's voice, the lean, horselike nobility of his face as he craned
above his collar saying "heinous"—and all remote, austere, subdued,
and decent as if God were there in walnut light and a choker collar:
and then the twenty-minute prayer, the organ pealing a rich benison,
and people talking, laughing, streaming out from the dutiful, weekly,

walnut disinfection of their souls into bright morning-gold of Sunday light again, and standing then in friendly and yet laughing groups upon the lawn outside, and steaming off towards home again, a steady liquid Sunday shuffle of good leather on the quiet streets—and all of it was good and godly, yet not like God, but like an ordered destiny, like Sunday morning peace and decency and good dinners, money in the bank, and strong security.

And then it was the huge winds in great trees at night—the remote, demented winds—the sharp, clean raining of the acorns to the earth, and a demon's whisper of evil and unbodied jubilation in your heart, speaking of triumph, flight, and darkness, new lands, morning, and a shining city.

And then it was like waking up and knowing somehow snow was there before you looked, feeling the numb, white, brooding prescience of soft-silent, all-engulfing snow around you and then hearing it, soft, almost noiseless, fluff and fall to earth, and the scraping of a shovel on the sidewalk before the house.

And then it was like stern and iron Winter, and days and nights that ate intolerably the slow grey ash of time away, and April that would never come, and waiting, waiting, waiting dreamily at night for something magical that never happened, and bare boughs that creaked and swayed in darkness, and the frozen shapes of limbs that swung stiff shadows on the street below a light, and your aunt's voice filled with the fathomless sea-depths of Joyner time and horror, and of a race that lived forever while you drowned.

And then it was like the few days that you liked school, when you began and ended in September and in June. It was like going back to school again in September and getting some joy and hope out of the book-lists that the teacher gave you the first day, and then the feel and look and smell of the new geography, the reader and the composition books, the history, and the smells of pencils, wooden rules, and paper in the bookstore, and the solid, wealthy feel of the books and bookstrap, and taking the books home and devouring them—the new, richly illustrated geography and history and reading books—devouring them with an insatiate joy and hunger until there was nothing new left in them, and getting up in the morning and hearing the morning schoolhouse bell, and hoping it would not be so bad this year after all.

And it was like waiting in May for school to end, and liking it, and feeling a little sad because it would soon be over, and like the last day when you felt quite sorrowful and yet full of an exultant joy, and watched the high school graduate, and saw the plaster casts of Minerva and Diana, the busts of Socrates, Demosthenes, and Caesar, and smelled the chalk, the ink, the schoolroom smells, with ecstasy, and were sorry you were leaving them.

And you felt tears come to your own eyes as the class sang its graduation song with words to the tune of "Old Heidelberg," and saw the girls weeping hysterically, kissing each other and falling on the neck of Mr. Hamby, the Principal, swearing they would never forget him, no, never, as long as they lived, and these had been the happiest days of their lives, and they just couldn't bear it—boo-hoo-hoo!—and then listened to the oration of the Honorable Zebulon N. Meekins, the local Congressman, telling them the world had never seen a time when it needed leaders as it does at present and go—go—go my young friends and be a Leader in the Great World that is waiting for you and God Bless You All—and your eyes were wet, your throat was choked with joy and pain intolerable as Zebulon N. Meekins spoke these glorious words, for as he spoke them the soft, bloom-laden wind of June howled gusty for a moment at the eaves, you saw the young green of the trees outside and smelled a smell of tar and green and fields thick with the white and yellow of daisies bending in the wind, and heard far-faint thunder on the rails, and saw the Great World then, the far-shining, golden, and enchanted city, and heard the distant, murmurous drone of all its million-footed life, and saw its fabulous towers soaring upward from an opalescent mist, and knew that some day you would walk its streets a conqueror and be a Leader among the most beautiful and fortunate people in the world: and you thought the golden tongue of Zebulon Nathaniel Meekins had done it all for you, and gave no credit to the troubling light that came and went outside, from gold to grey and back to gold again, and none to the young green of June and the thick-starred magic of the daisy fields, or to the thrilling schoolhouse smells of chalk and ink and varnished desks, or to the thrilling mystery, joy, and sadness, the numb, delicious feel of glory in your guts—no you gave no credit to these things at all, but thought Zeb Meekins' golden tongue had done it all to you.

And you wondered what the schoolrooms were like in Summer when no one was there, and wished that you could be there alone with your pretty, red-haired, and voluptuous-looking teacher, or with a girl in your class who sat across the aisle from you, and whose name was Edith Pickleseimer, and who had fat curls, blue eyes of sweet tranquillity, and a tender, innocent smile, and who wore short little skirts, clean blue drawers, and you could sometimes see the white and tender plumpness of her leg where the straps and garter buckles that held up her stockings pressed into it, and you thought of being here with her alone, and yet all in a pure way too.

And sometimes it was like coming home from school in October, and smelling burning leaves upon the air, and wading in the oak leaves in the gutter, and seeing men in shirt-sleeves with arm bands of a ruffled blue upon the sleeves raking the leaves together in their yards, and feeling, smelling, hearing ripeness, harvest, in the air, and sometimes frost at night, silence, frost-white moonlight through the windows, the distant barking of a dog, and a great train pounding at the rails, a great train going in the night, the tolling bell, the lonely and departing whistle-wail.

THESE LIGHTS AND shapes and tones of things swarmed in the boy's mind like a magic web of shifting, iridescent colors. For the place where he lived was not just a street to him—not just a strip of pavement and a design of weathered, shabby houses: it was the living integument of his life, the frame and stage for the whole world of childhood and enchantment.

Here on the corner of Locust Street, at the foot of the hill below his uncle's house, was the wall of concrete blocks on which Monk sat at night a thousand times with the other boys in the neighborhood, conspiring together in lowered voices, weaving about their lives a huge conspiracy of night and mystery and adventure, prowling away into the dark to find it, whispering and snickering together in the dark, now prowling softly in the shadows, halting sharply, whispering, "Wait a minute!"—now in full, sudden, startled flight and terror with a rush of feet, going away from—nothing. Now talking, conspiring mysteriously again upon the wall of concrete blocks, and prowling off desperately into the dark of streets, yards, and alleys, filled exultantly with the huge and evil presence of the dark, and hoping, with a kind of desperate terror and resolve, for something wicked, wild, and evil in the night, as jubilant and dark as the demonic joy that rose wildly and intolerable in their hearts.

This also was the corner where he saw two boys killed one day. It was a day in Spring, in afternoon, and heavy, grey, and wet to feel, all of the air was cool, and damp, full of the smell of earth and heavy green. He was on his way uptown, and Aunt Maw was cleaning up in the dining room and looking after him as he went down Locust Street, past the Shepperton house and past the house across the street where Nebraska Crane lived. He had a good feeling because he was going to buy chocolate and maple syrup for candy making, and because the air was heavy, grey, and green, and he felt some intolerable joy was in the air.

Then he turned the corner into Baird Street, and Albert and Johnny Andrews were coming towards him, coasting in their wagon, Albert steering; and Johnny raised his hand and yelled at him as he went by, and Albert yelled but did not raise his hand. And then Monk turned to watch them as they whizzed around the corner and saw the high-wheeled Oldsmobile that young Hank Bass drove run over them. And he remembered that the car belonged to Mr. Pendergraft, the fine-looking lumber man, who was rich and lived out on Montgomery

Avenue in the swell part of town, and had two sons named Hip and Hop who went to Sunday School with Monk and grinned at people and were tongue-tied and had harelips. He saw the car hit the boys, smash their wagon into splinters, and drag Albert on his face for fifty yards. And Albert's wagon had been painted bright yellow, and on the sides had been printed the word "Leader."

Albert's face was smashed to currant jelly on the street, and Monk could see it scrape for fifty yards along the pavement like a bloody rag before the car was stopped; and when he got there they were getting Albert out from beneath the car. He could smell the sultry odors of the car, the smell of worn rubber, oil and gasoline, and heavy leathers, and the smell of blood; and everywhere people were rushing from their houses shouting, and men were going down beneath the car to get Albert out, and Bass was standing there with a face the color of green blubber, and cold sweat standing on his forehead, and his pants staining where he'd messed himself, and Albert was nothing but a bloody rag.

Mr. Ernest Pennock, who lived next door to Uncle Mark, got Albert out and lifted him in his arms. Ernest Pennock was a big, red-faced man with a hearty voice, the uncle of Monk's friend, Sam Pennock. Ernest Pennock was in shirt-sleeves and wore arm bands of ruffled blue, and Albert's blood got all over Ernest Pennock's shirt as he held Albert in his arms. Albert's back was broken and his legs were broken and the raw splinters of the bones were sticking through his torn stockings, and all the time he kept screaming:

"O mama save me O mama, mama save me O mama save me!"

And Monk was sick to his guts because Albert had shouted at him and been happy just a minute ago, and something immense and merciless that no one understood had fallen from the sky upon him and broken his back and no one could save him now.

The car had run over Johnny but had not dragged him, and he had no blood upon him, only two blue sunken marks upon his forehead. And Mr. Joe Black, who lived two doors below the Joyners at the corner, and was the foreman of the street-car men and stood up in the Public Square all day and gave orders to the motormen every fifteen minutes when the cars came in, and married one of the daughters of Mr. McPherson, the Scotchman who lived across the street above the Joyners, had picked Johnny up and was holding him and talking gently to him, and saying in a cheerful voice, half to Johnny, half to himself and the other people:

"This boy's not hurt, yes, sir, he just got bruised a bit, he's going to be a brave man and be all right again before you know it."

Johnny moaned a little, but not loudly, and there was no blood on him, and no one noticed Johnny, but Johnny died then while Joe Black talked to him.

And then Mrs. Andrews came tearing around the corner, wearing an apron and screaming like a demented hag, and she clawed her way through the crowd of people about Albert, and snatched him out of Ernest Pennock's arms, and kissed him till her face was covered with his blood, and kept screaming:

"Is he dead? Is he dead? Why don't you tell me if he's dead?"

Then suddenly she stopped screaming when they told her that it was not Albert but Johnny who was dead—grew calm, silent, almost tranquil, because Albert was her own child, and Johnny was an adopted child; and although she had always been good to Johnny, all the people in the neighborhood said later:

"You see, don't you? It only goes to show you! You saw how quick she shut up when she heard it wasn't her own flesh and blood."

But Albert died anyway two hours later at the hospital.

Finally—and somehow this was the worst of all—Mr. Andrews came tottering towards the people as they gathered around Albert. He was an insurance salesman, a little scrap of a man who was wasting away with some horrible joint disease. He was so feeble that he could not walk save by tottering along on a cane, and his great staring eyes and sunken face and large head, that seemed too heavy for the scrawny neck and body that supported it, went waggling, goggling, jerking about from side to side with every step he took, and his legs made sudden and convulsive movements as if they were going to fly away beneath him as he walked. Yet this ruin of a man had gotten nine children, and was getting new ones all the time. Monk had talked about this with the other boys in lowered voices, and with a feeling of horror and curiosity, for he wondered if his physical collapse had not come somehow from all the children he had got, if some criminal excess in nature had not sapped and gutted him and made his limbs fly out below him with these movements of convulsive disintegration; and he felt a terrible fascination and revulsion of the spirit because of the seminal mystery of nature that could draw forth life in swarming hordes from the withered loins of a walking dead man such as this.

But finally he had come around the corner, goggling, waggling, jerking onward with his huge, vacant, staring eyes, towards the bloody place where two of his children had been killed; and this, together with the strong congruent smells of rubber, leather, oil and gasoline, mixed with the heavy, glutinous sweetness of warm blood, and hanging there like a cloud in the cool, wet, earthy air of that grey-green day that just a moment before had impended with such a wordless and intolerable prescience of joy, and now was filled with horror, nausea, and desperate sickness of the soul—this finally was the memory that was to fix that corner, the hour, the day, the time, the words and faces of the people, with a feeling of the huge and nameless death that waits around the corner for all men, to break their backs and shatter instantly the blind and pitiful illusions of their hope,

HERE WAS THE place, just up the hill a little way from this treacherous corner, right there in front of Shepperton's house, where another accident occurred, as absurd and comic as the first was tragic and horrible.

One morning about seven o'clock, in the Spring of the year when all the fruit trees were in blossom, George was awakened instantly as he lay in his room, with a vision of cherry blossoms floating slowly to the earth, and at the same time with the memory of a terrific collision—a savage grinding and splintering of glass, steel, and wood—still ringing in his ears. Already he could hear people shouting to one another in the street, and the sound of footsteps running. The screen door slammed in his uncle's house next door, and the boy heard his Uncle Mark howl to someone in an excited tone:

"It's down here on Locust Street! Merciful God, they'll all be killed!"

And he was off, striding down the street.

But already George was out of bed, had his trousers on, and, without stopping for stockings, shoes, or shirt, he went running onto the porch, down the steps, and out into the street as hard as he could go. People were running along in the same direction, and he could see his uncle's figure in the rapidly growing crowd gathered in front of Shepperton's about a big telephone post which had been snapped off like a match stick near the base and hung half-suspended from the wires.

As he pounded up, the fragments of the car were strewn over the pavement for a distance of fifty yards—a wheel here, a rod there, a lamp, a leather seat at other places, and shattered glass everywhere. The battered and twisted wreckage of the car's body rested solidly and squatly upon the street before the telephone post which it had snapped with its terrific impact, and in the middle of all this wreckage Lon Pilcher was solemnly sitting, with a stupid look upon his face and the rim of the steering wheel wrapped around his neck. A few feet away, across the sidewalk, and upon the high-banked lawn of the Shepperton house, Mr. Matthews, the fat, red-faced policeman, was sitting squarely on his solid bottom, legs thrust out before him, and with the same look of stupid and solemn surprise on his face that Lon Pilcher had.

Uncle Mark and some other men pulled Lon Pilcher from the wreckage of his car, took the steering wheel from around his neck, and assured themselves that by some miracle of chance he was not hurt. Lon, recovering quickly from the collision which had stunned him, now began to peer owlishly about at the strewn remnants of his car, and finally, turning to Uncle Mark with a drunken leer, he said:

"D'ye think it's damaged much, Mr. Joyner? D'ye think we can fix her up again, so she will run?" Here he belched heavily, covered his mouth with his hand, and said, "Excuse me," and began to prowl drunkenly among the strewn fragments.

Meanwhile Mr. Matthews, recovering from his shock, now clambered down clumsily from the bank and pounded heavily towards Lon, shouting:

"I'll arrest ye! I'll arrest ye! I'll take ye to the lockup and arrest ye, that's what I'll do!"—a threat which now seemed somewhat superfluous since he had arrested Lon some time before.

It now developed that Lon had been cruising about the town all night with some drunken chorus girls in his celebrated Cadillac, model 1910; that the policeman had arrested him at the head of the Locust Street hill, and had commanded Lon to drive him to the police station; and then, during that terrific dash downhill which had ended in the smash-up near the corner, had screamed frantically at his driver:

"Stop! Stop! Let me out! You're under arrest! Damn you, I'll arrest ye fer this, as sure as you're born!"

And, according to witnesses, at the moment of collision the fat policeman had sailed gracefully through the shining morning air, described two somersaults, and landed solidly and squarely upon his bottom, with such force that he was stunned for several minutes, but still kept muttering all the time:

"Stop! Stop! Or I'll arrest ye!"

HERE WAS THE house, across the street from Shepperton's and just above Nebraska Crane's house, where Captain Suggs lived. He was a cripple, with both legs amputated far above the knee. The rest of him was a gigantic hulk, with enormous shoulders, powerful, thick hands, and a look of brutal power and determination about his great, thick neck and his broad, clean-shaven, cruel-lipped mouth. He got about on crutches when he had his wooden stumps on him; at other times he crawled about on the stump ends of his amputated legs, which were protected by worn leather pads. He had had one leg shot off at Cold Harbor, and the other was mangled and had to be amputated. In spite of his mutilation and his huge bulk, he could move with amazing speed when he wanted to. When he was angered, he could use his crutch as a club and could floor anyone within a radius of six feet. His wife, a little, frail woman, was thoroughly submissive.

His son, "Fielder" Suggs, was a little past thirty and on his way to fortune. At one time in his career he had been a professional baseball player. Later, with money enough for one month's rent, Fielder leased a vacant store and installed there the first moving picture projection camera the town had known. Now he owned the Princess and the Gaiety on the Square, and his career was a miracle of sudden wealth.

HERE WAS THE place upon the street before McPherson's house where the horse slipped and fell on the icy pavement one cold night in January, and broke its leg. There were dark faces of men around the house, and presently George heard two shots, and his Uncle Mark came back with a sad look on his face, shaking his head regretfully and muttering, "What a pity! What a pity!"—and then began to denounce the city government bitterly for making the pavements so slippery and the hill so steep. And light and warmth went from the boy's life, and the terror of the dark was all about him.

HERE WAS THE alleyway that ran past his uncle's house on the lower side and was bordered by a lane of lonely pines, and there was the huge, clay-caked stump of a tree where the boys would go Christmas morning and on the Fourth of July to explode their firecrackers on the stump. Rufus Higginson, who was Harry's older brother, came there one Fourth of July with a toy cannon and a large yellow paper bag filled with loose powder, and he threw a match away into the powder bag, and even as he bent to get more powder it exploded in his face.

He rushed screaming like a madman down the alley, his face black as a negro's and his eyes blinded, and he rushed through his house from room to room, and no one could quiet him or get him to stop running because the pain was so intense. The doctor came and picked the powder out, and for weeks he bathed his face in oil; and his face turned into one solid scab, which then peeled off and left no scar at all, when everyone said he "would be scarred for life."

ON UP THE hill past his uncle's new, brick house, and beside it, and to the rear, the little frame house which his grandfather had built more than forty years before and where George now lived with his Aunt Maw; on up the hill past Pennock's house and Higginson's old house; on up past Mr. McPherson's house across the street, which always looked new and clean and tidy, and bright with new paint; on up to the top of the hill where Locust Street came into Charles, and on the left hand, was the huge, old, gabled house of brown, with its great porches, parlors, halls of quartered oak, and carriage entrances, and the enormous, lordly oaks in front of it. Some wealthy people from South Carolina lived there. They had a negro driver and a carriage that came up the driveway for them every day, and they never spoke to the other people on the street because they were too fine for them and moved in higher circles.

Across Charles Street, on the corner, was a brick house in which a woman lived with her aged mother. The woman was a good soul, with fluffy, sandy-reddish hair, a hooked nose, a red face, and teeth that stuck out. Everyone called her "Pretty Polly" because she looked like a parrot and had a parrot's throaty voice. She played the piano for the moving picture shows at the Gaiety Theatre, and every night when she stopped playing the people in the audience would cry out:

"Music, Polly, music! Please, Polly, music, Polly! Pretty Polly, please!"

She never seemed to mind at all, and would play again.

"Pretty Polly" had a beau named James Mears, better known as

"Duke" Mears, because he was always smartly dressed in correct riding costume, or at least what he believed to be the correct riding costume of the English aristocracy. He wore a derby hat, a stock, a fawn-colored weskit with the last and lowest button nonchalantly left unbuttoned, a close-fitting checked riding coat, riding trousers and magnificent, shining riding boots and spurs, and he carried a riding crop. He always wore this costume. He wore it when he got up in the morning, he wore it when he walked across the Square, he wore it when he went down the main street of the town, he wore it when he got into a street car, he wore it when he went to Miller and Cashman's livery stable.

Duke Mears had never been on a horse in his life, but he knew more about horses than anyone else. He talked to them and loved them better than he loved people. George saw him one Winter night at the fire which burned down the livery stable, and he yelled like a madman when he heard the horses screaming in the fire; they had to hold him and throw him to the ground and sit on him to keep him from going in to get the horses. Next day the boy went by and the stable was a mass of smoking timbers, and he could smell the wet, blackened embers, caked with ice, and the acrid smell of the put-out fire, and the sickening smell of roasted horse flesh. Teams were dragging the dead horses out with chains, and one dead horse had burst in two across the belly and its blue roasted entrails had come bulging out with a hideous stench he could not blow out of his nostrils.

ON THE OTHER corner of Locust Street and Charles, facing the house where "Pretty Polly" lived, was the Leathergood house; and farther along Charles Street, up the hill in the direction of the Country Club, was Mrs. Charles Montgomery Hopper's boarding house.

Everyone knew Mrs. Charles Montgomery Hopper. No one had ever seen or heard of Mr. Charles Montgomery Hopper. No one knew where he came from, no one knew where she got him, no one knew where they had lived together, no one knew who he was, or where he lived and died and was buried. It may very well be that he did not exist, that he never existed at all. Nevertheless, by the vociferous use of this imposing and resounding name, year after year, in a loud, aggressive, and somewhat raucous voice, Mrs. Charles Montgomery Hopper had convinced everyone, bludgeoned, touted everyone into the unquestioning acceptance of the fact that the name of Charles Montgomery Hopper was a very distinguished one, and that Mrs. Charles Montgomery Hopper was a very distinguished person.

In spite of the fact that she ran a boarding house, it was never referred to as a boarding house. If one telephoned and asked if this was Mrs. Hopper's boarding house, one of two things was likely to happen if Mrs. Hopper was the one who answered. The luckless questioner would either have the receiver slammed up violently in his face, after having his ears blistered by the scathing invective of which Mrs. Hopper was the complete mistress; or he would be informed, in tones that dripped with acid, that it was *not* Mrs. Hopper's boarding house, that Mrs. Hopper did not *have* a boarding house, that it was Mrs. Hopper's *residence*—then, also, he would have the receiver slammed up in his face.

None of the boarders ever dared to refer to the fact that the lady had a boarding house, and that they paid her money for their board. Should anyone be so indelicate as to mention this, he must be prepared to pay the penalty for his indiscretion. He would be informed that his room was needed, that the people who had engaged it were coming the next day, and at what time could he have his baggage ready. Mrs. Hopper had even her boarders cowed. They were made to feel that a great and distinguished privilege had been extended to them when they were allowed to remain even for a short time as guests in Mrs. Hopper's residence. They were made to feel also that this fact had somehow miraculously removed from them the taint of being ordinary boarders. It gave them a kind of aristocratic distinction, gave them a social position of which few people could boast, enrolled them under Mrs. Hopper's approving seal in the Bluebook of the 400. So here was a boarding house that was no boarding house at all. Call it, rather, a kind of elegant house party which went on perpetually, and to which the favored few who were invited were also graciously permitted to contribute with their funds.

Did it work? Whoever has lived here in America must know how well it worked, how cheerfully, how meekly, how humbly, with what servility, the guests at Mrs. Hopper's house party endured that lean and scrawny fare, endured discomfort, cold, bad plumbing, and untidy housekeeping, even endured Mrs. Hopper and her voice, her domination and her dirge of abuse, if only they could remain there in the circle of the elect, not boarders really, but distinguished people.

That small company of the faithful returned from year to year to Mrs. Hopper's palace. Season after season, Summer after Summer, the rooms were booked up solid. Occasionally a stranger tried to make an entrance—some parvenu, no doubt, trying to buy his way into the protected circles of the aristocracy, some low bounder with money in his pocket, some social climber. Well, they looked him over with a very cold and fishy eye at Mrs. Charles Montgomery Hopper's, remarked that they did not seem to remember his face, and had he ever been to Mrs. Charles Montgomery Hopper's house before. The guilty wretch would stammer out a confused and panicky admission that this, indeed, was his first visit. A cold silence then would fall upon the company. And, presently, someone would say that he had been coming there every Summer for the past fourteen years. Another would remark that his first visit was the year before the year the War with Spain broke out. Another one would modestly confess that this was just his eleventh year and that at last he really felt that he belonged; it took ten years, he added, to feel at home. And this was true.

So they came back year after year, this little circle of the elect. There were old man Holt and his wife, from New Orleans. There was Mr. McKethan, who stayed there all the time. He was a jeweler's assistant, but his folks came from down near Charleston. He belonged. There was Miss Bangs, an antique spinstress, who taught in the public schools of New York City and soon would have her pension, and thereafter, it was thought, would retire forever, four seasons of the year, to the elegant seclusion of Mrs. Hopper's house. And there was Miss Millie Teasdale, the cashier at McCormack's pharmacy. She came from New York also, but now she was a "permanent" at Mrs. Hopper's house.

In the kitchen at Mrs. Charles Montgomery Hopper's was Jenny Grubb, a negro woman of forty who had been there fifteen years or more. She was plump, solid, jolly, and so black that, as the saying went, charcoal would make a white mark on her. Her rich and hearty laughter, that had in it the whole black depth and warmth of Africa, could be heard all over the house. She sang forever, and her rich, strong, darkly-fibered voice could also be heard all day long. During the week she worked from dawn till after dark, from six in the morning till nine at night. On Sunday afternoon she had her day of rest. It was the day she had been preparing for, the day she had been living for all week. But Sunday afternoon was really not a day of rest for Jenny Grubb: it was a day of consecration, a day of wrath, a day of reckoning. It was potentially always the last day of the world, the day of sinners come to judgment.

Every Sunday afternoon at three o'clock, when Mrs. Hopper's clients had been fed. Jenny Grubb was free for three hours and made the most of it. She went out the kitchen door and round the house and up the alley to the street. She had already begun to mutter darkly and forebodingly, to herself. By the time she had crossed Locust Street and got two blocks down the hill towards town, her broad figure had begun to sway rhythmically. By the time she reached the bottom of the Central Avenue hill and turned the corner, began to mount again at Spring Street towards the Square, she had begun to breathe stertor-ously, to moan in a low tone, to burst into a sudden shout of praise or malediction. By the time she got to the Square, she was primed and ready. As she turned into the Square, that torpid and deserted Sunday Square of three o'clock, a warning cry burst from her.

"O sinners, I'se a-comin'!" Jenny yelled, although there were no sinners there.

The Square was bare and empty, but it made no difference. Swaying with a rhythmical movement of her powerful and solid frame, she propelled herself rapidly across the Square to the appointed corner, warning sinners as she came. And the Square was empty. The Square was always empty. She took up her position there in the hot sun, on the corner where McCormack's drug store and Joyner's hardware store faced each other. For the next three hours she harangued the heated, vacant Square.

From time to time, each quarter of the hour, the street cars of the town came in and crossed, halted and stopped. The motormen got down with their control rods in their hands, moved to the other end; the conductors swung the trolleys around. The solitary loafer leaned against the rail and picked his teeth, half-listening idly to black Jenny Grubb's harangue. And then the cars moved out, the loafer went away, and Jenny still harangued the vacant Square.

CHAPTER 7

The Butcher

Every afternoon, up the hill before Mark Joyner's house, wheezed and panted the ancient, dilapidated truck in which Mr. Lampley, the butcher, delivered his tender, succulent steaks and chops and roasts, and his deliciously fragrant home-made sausage, headcheese, liverwurst, and fat red frankfurters. To the boy, George Webber, this glamorous and rickety machine seemed to gain glory and enchantment as the years went on and the deposits of grease and oil, together with the warm odors of sage and other spices with which he seasoned his fresh pork sausage and a dozen more of his home-made delicacies, worked their way in and through the rich, stained texture of its weathered, winelike wood. Even years later, in the transforming light of time, it seemed to him strange, important, and immense to remember Mr. Lampley, to remember his wife, his daughter, and his son, the wholesome, fragrant, and delicate quality of their work—and something as savage and wild as nature in the lives of all of them.

Mr. Lampley had come to town as a stranger twenty years before, and a stranger he had always been since coming there. Nothing was known of his past life or origins. He was a small and hideously battered figure of a man, as compact and solid as a bullock, and with a deadly stillness and toneless quietness about all his words and movements that suggested a controlled but savagely illimitable vitality. His small, red face, which had the choleric and flaring color of the Irishman, had been so horribly drawn and twisted on one side by a hideous cut, inflicted, it was said, by another butcher with a meat cleaver in a fight long before he came to town, that it was one livid and puckered seam from throat to forehead, and even the corners of his hard lips were drawn and puckered by the scar. Moreover, the man never seemed to bat his eyelids, and his small black eyes—as hard, as black, as steady as any which ever looked out upon the light of day—glared at the world so unflinchingly, with such a formidable and deadly gaze that no man could stand their stare for long, that one's words trembled, stammered, and faltered foolishly away as one tried to utter them, and all attempts at friendliness or intimacy were blasted and withered in a second before those two unwinking eyes. Therefore no one knew him, no one sought his friendship twice: in all the years he had lived in the town he had made, beyond his family, not one intimate or friendly connection.

But if Mr. Lampley was formidable in his own toneless and un-winking way, his wife was no less formidable in quite another. He had married a woman native to that section, and she was one of those creatures of an epic animality and good nature whose proportions transcend the descriptive powers of language, and who can be measured by no scale of law or judgment. Of her, it could only be said that she was as innocent as nature, as merciful as a river in flood, as moral as the earth. Full of good nature and a huge, choking scream of laughter that swelled boundlessly from her mighty breast, she could in an instant have battered the brains out of anyone who crossed her or roused the witless passion of her nature; and she would never have felt a moment's pity or regret for doing so, even if she had paid the penalty with her life.

She was one of a large family of country people, all built on the same tremendous physical proportions, the daughter of an epic brute who had also been a butcher.

Physically, Mrs. Lampley was the biggest woman George had ever seen. She was well over six feet tall, and must have weighed more than two hundred pounds, and yet she was not fat. Her hands were ham-like in their size and shape, her arms and legs great swelling haunches of limitless power and strength, her breast immense and almost depthless in its fullness. She had a great mass of thick, dark red hair; eyes as clear, grey, and depthless as a cat's; a wide, thin, rather loose, and cruel mouth; and a skin which, while clear and healthy-looking, had somehow a murky, glutinous quality—the quality of her smile and her huge, choking laugh—as if all the ropy and spermatic fluids of the earth were packed into her.

There was nothing to measure her by, no law by which to judge her: the woman burst out beyond the limit of all human valuations, and for this reason she smote terror to George's heart. She could tell stories so savage in their quality that the heart was sickened at them, and at the same time throw back her great throat and scream with laughter as she told them—and her laughter was terrible, not because it was cruel, but because the substance of which cruelty is made was utterly lacking in her nature.

Thus she would describe incidents out of the life of her father, the butcher, in a strangely soft, countrified tone of voice, which always held in it, however, a suggestion of limitless power, and the burble of huge, choking laughter that would presently burst from her:

"There used to be a cat down there at the market," she drawled, "who was always prowlin' and snoopin' around to get at his meat, you know," she went on confidentially in a quiet, ropy tone, and with a faint smile about her mouth. "Well," she said, with a little heaving chuckle of her mighty breasts, "the old man was gittin' madder an' madder all the time, an' one day when he found the cat had been at his meat again, he says to me—you know, I used to keep his books fer him—the old man turns to me, an' says, 'If I ketch that son-of-a-bitch in here again I'm goin' to cut his head off—' " Here she paused to chuckle, her great throat swelling with its burble of laughter and her mighty bosom swelling. "I could see he was gittin' mad, you know," she said in that almost unctuous drawl, "and I knew that cat was goin' to git in trouble if he didn't mind! . . . Well, sir," she said, beginning to gasp a little, "it wasn't ten minutes afore the old man looked up an' saw the cat over yonder on the chopping block fixin' to git at a great big side of beef the old man had put there! . . . Well, when the old man sees that cat he lets out a yell you could hear from here across the Square! 'You son-of-a-bitch!' he says, 'I told you I'd kill you if I caught you here again!'—and he picks up a cleaver," she gasped, "and throws it at that cat as hard as he could let fly, and—har!—har!—har!—har!"—she screamed suddenly, her great throat swelling like a bull's, and a wave of limitless laughter bursting from her and ending in a scream—"he ketches that damn cat as perty as anything you ever saw, an' cuts him plumb in two—har!—har!—har!—har—!"—And this, time her huge laughter seemed too immense even for her mighty frame to hold, and the tears ran down her cheeks as she sank back gasping in her chair. "Lord! Lord!" she gasped. "That was the pertiest thing I ever see! I liked to laffed myself to death," she panted, and then, still trembling, began to wipe at her streaming eyes with the back of one huge hand.

Again, one day, she told this merry story of her honored sire:

"A nigger came in there one day," she said, "an' told the old man to cut him off a piece of meat an' wrap it up for him. When the old man gave it to him, the nigger begins to argue with him," she said, "an' to give him some back-talk, claimin' the old man was cheatin' him on the weight an' tryin' to charge him too much fer it! Well, sir," she said, beginning to gasp a little, "the old man picks up a carving knife an' he makes one swipe across the counter at that nigger with it—and—har!—har!—har!"—her huge laugh burst out of her mighty breast again and welled upward to a choking, ropy scream, "—that nigger! —that nigger!—his guts came rollin' out into his hands like sausage meat!" she gasped. "I wish't you could have seen the look upon his face!" she panted. "He just stood there lookin' at them like he don't know what to do with them—and har!—har!—har!"—she cast her swelling throat back and roared with laughter, subsiding finally to huge, gasping mirth—"that was the funniest thing I ever see! If you could a-seen the look upon that nigger's face!" she panted, wiping at her streaming eyes with the back of her huge paw.

WHENEVER A TALL, strong, powerfully-built man came for the first time into the butcher's little shop, Mrs. Lampley would immediately comment on his size and strength in a flattering and good-natured tone, but with something speculative and hard in her eye as she surveyed him, as if she was coldly calculating his chances with her in a knockdown fight. Many men had observed this look of appraisal, and George had heard men say that there was something so savagely calculating in it that it had made their blood run cold. She would look them over with a good-natured smile, but with a swift narrowing of her cat-grey eyes as she sized them up, meanwhile saying in a bantering and hearty tone of voice:

"Say! You're a right big feller, ain't you? I was lookin' at you when you came in—you could hardly git through the door," she chuckled. "I said to myself, 'I'd hate to git mixed up in any trouble with him,' I says, 'I'll bet a feller like that could hit you an awful lick if you git him mad. . . .' How much do you weigh?" she would then say, still smiling, but with those cold, narrowed, grey eyes measuring the unhappy stranger up and down.

And when the wretched man had stammered out his weight, she would say softly, in a contemplative fashion: "Uh-huh!" And after going over him a moment longer with those merciless and slitlike eyes, she would say, with an air of hearty finality: "Well, you're a big 'un, sure enough! I'll bet you'll be a big help to your paw an' maw when you get your growth—har! —har!—har!—har!" And the choking scream of laughter would then burst from her Atlantean breasts and bull-like throat.

When she spoke of her husband she always referred to him as "Lampley," and this was the way she always addressed him. Her tone when she spoke of him certainly had in it nothing that could be described as affection, for such a feeling would have had no more place in her nature than a swan upon the breast of the flood-tide Mississippi, but her tone had in it a note of brutal and sensual satisfaction that somehow told plainly and terribly of a perfect marriage of savage and limitless sexual energies, and of a mate in the battered figure of that little bullock man who could match and fit this mountain of a woman perfectly in an epic, night-long bout of lust and passion.

Mrs. Lampley spoke constantly, openly, vulgarly, and often with a crude, tremendous humor, of the sexual act, and although she never revealed the secrets of her own marriage bed—if a union so savage, complete, and obvious as the one between herself and her husband could be called a secret—she did not for a moment hesitate to publish her opinions on the subject to the world, to give young married couples, or young men and their girls, advice that would make them flush to the roots of their hair, and to scream with merriment when she saw their confusion.

Her son, Baxter, at this time a youth of eighteen, had just a year or two before taken a young girl by force, a well-developed and seductive red-haired girl of fourteen. This event, so far from causing his mother any distress, had seemed to her so funny that she had published it to the whole town, describing with roars of laughter her interview with the girl's outraged mother:

"Why, hell yes!" she said. "She came down here to see me, all broke out in a sweat about it, sayin' Baxter had ruined her daughter an' what was I goin' to do about it!—'Now, you look a-here!' I said. 'You jist git down off your high horse! He's ruined no one,' I says, 'for there was no one to ruin to begin with'—har!—har!—har!—har!"—the full, choking scream burst from her throat—"'Now,' I says, 'if she turns out to be a whore, she'll come by it natural'—har!—har!—har!—har!— 'an' Baxter didn't make her one,' I says. 'What do you mean? What do you mean?' she says—oh! gittin' red as a ripe termater an' beginnin' to shake her finger in my face—'I'll have you put in jail fer slander,' she says, 'that's what I'll do!' 'Slander!' I says, 'Slander! Well, if it's slander,' I says, 'the law has changed since my day and time. It's the first time

I ever knew you could slander a whore,' I says, 'by callin' her by her right name.' 'Don't you call my daughter no name like that,' she says, oh, madder'n a wet hen, you know—'Don't you dare to! I'll have you arrested,' she says. 'Why, God-damn you!' I says—that's just the way I talked to her, you know, 'everyone knows what your daughter is!' I says, 'so you git on out of here,' I says, 'before I git mad an' tell you something you may not like to hear!'—and I'm tellin' you, she went!" And the huge creature leaned back gasping for a moment.

"Hell!" she went on quietly in a moment, "I asked Baxter about it and he told me. 'Baxter,' I says, 'that woman has been here now an' I want to know: did you jump on that girl an' take it from her?' 'Why, mama,' he says, 'take it from her? Why, she took it from me!' says Baxter—har!—har!—har!—har!"—the tremendous laughter filled her throat and choked her. " 'Hell!' says Baxter, 'she throwed me down an' almost broke my back! If I hadn't done like I did I don't believe she'd ever a-let me out of there!'—har!—har!—har!—har!—I reckon ole Baxter figgered it might as well be him as the next one," she panted, wiping at her streaming eyes. "I reckon he figgered he might as well git a little of it while the gittin' was good. But Lord!" sighed, "I laffed about that thing until my sides was sore—har!—har!—har!—har!— har!"—and the enormous creature came forward in her creaking chair again, as the huge laughter filled her, and made the walls tremble with its limitless well of power.

Towards her own daughter, however, whose name was Grace, and who was fifteen at this time, Mrs. Lampley was virtuously, if brutally, attentive. In both the children the inhuman vitality of their parents was already apparent, and in the girl, especially, the measureless animal power of her mother had already developed. At fifteen, she was a tremendous creature, almost as tall as her mother, and so fully matured that the flimsy little cotton dresses she wore, and which would have been proper for most children of her age, were almost obscenely in-adequate. In the heavy calves, swelling thighs, and full breasts of this great, white-fleshed creature of fifteen years there was already evident a tremendous seductiveness; men looked at her with a terrible fascination and felt the wakening of unreasoning desire, and turned their eyes away from her with a feeling of strong shame.

Over this girl's life already there hung the shadow of fatality. Without knowing why, one felt certain that this great creature must come to grief and ruin—as one reads that giants die early, and things which are too great in nature for the measure of the world destroy themselves. In the girl's large, vacant, and regularly beautiful face, and in the tender, empty, and sensual smile which dwelt forever there, this legend of unavoidable catastrophe was plainly written.

The girl rarely spoke, and seemed to have no variety of passion save that indicated by her constant, limitlessly sensual, and vacant smile. And as she stood obedient and docile beside her mother, and that huge creature spoke of her with a naked frankness, and as the girl smiled always that tender, vacant smile as if her mother's words had no meaning for her, the feeling of something inhuman and catastrophic in the natures of these people was overwhelming:

"Yes," Mrs. Lampley would drawl, as the girl stood smiling vacantly at her side. "She's growed up here on me before I knowed it, an' I got to watch her all the time now to keep some son-of-a-bitch from knockin' her up an' ruinin' her. Here only a month or two ago two of these fellers down here at the livery stable—you know who I mean," she said carelessly, and in a soft, contemptuous voice—"that dirty, good-fer-nothin' Pegram feller an' that other low-down bastard he runs around with—what's his name, Grace?" she said impatiently, turning to the girl.

"That's Jack Cashman, mama," the girl answered in a soft and gentle tone, without changing for a second the tender, vacant smile upon her face.

"Yeah, that's him!" said Mrs. Lampley. "That low-down Cashman—if I ever ketch him foolin' around here again I'll break his neck, an' I reckon he knows it, too," she said grimly. "Why, I let her out, you know, one night along this Spring, to mail some letters," she went on in an explanatory tone, "an' told her not to be gone more'n half an hour—an' these two fellers picked her up in a buggy they was drivin' an' took her fer a ride way up the mountain side. Well, I waited an' waited till ten o'clock had struck, an' still she didn't come. An' I walked the floor, an' walked the floor, an' waited—an' by that time I was almost out of my head! I'll swear, I thought I would go crazy," she said slowly and virtuously. "I didn't know what to do. An' finally, when I couldn't stand it no longer, I went upstairs an' waked Lampley up. Of course, you know Lampley," she chuckled. "*He* goes to bed early. He's in bed every night by nine o'clock, and *he* ain't goin' to lose sleep over nobody. Well, I waked him up," she said slowly. " 'Lampley,' I says, 'Grace's been gone from here two hours, an I'm goin' to find her if I have to spend the rest of the night lookin' for her.'—'Well how you goin' to find her,' he says, 'if you don't know where she's gone?'—'I don't know,' I says, 'but I'll find her if I've got to walk every street an' break into every house in town—an' if I find some son-of-a-bitch has taken advantage of her, I'll kill him with my bare hands,' " said Mrs. Lampley. " 'I'll kill the two of them together—for I'd rather see her layin' dead than know she's turned out to be a whore'—that's what I said to him," said Mrs. Lampley.

During all this time, the girl stood obediently beside the chair in which her mother sat, smiling her tender, vacant smile, and with no other sign of emotion whatever.

"Well," said Mrs. Lampley slowly, "then I heard her. I heard her while I was talkin' to Lampley, openin' the door easylike an' creepin' up the stairs. Well, I didn't say nothin'—I just waited until I heard her tiptoe in along the hall past Lampley's door—an' then I opened it an' called to her. 'Grace,' I said, 'where've you been?'—Well," said Mrs. Lampley with an air of admission, "she told me. She never tried to lie to me. I'll say that fer her, she's never lied to me yet. If she did," she added grimly, "I reckon she knows I'd break her neck."

And the girl stood there passively, smiling all the time.

"Well, then." said Mrs. Lampley, "she told me who she'd been with and where they'd been. Well—I thought I'd go crazy!" the woman said slowly and deliberately. "I took her by the arms an' looked at her. 'Grace,' I said, 'you look me in the eye an' tell me the truth—did those two fellers do anything to you?'—'No,' she says.—'Well, you come with me,' I says, 'I'll find out if you're telling me the truth, if I've got to kill you to git it out of you.' "

And for a moment the huge creature was silent, staring grimly ahead, while her daughter stood beside her and smiled her gentle and imperturbably sensual smile.

"Well," said Mrs. Lampley slowly, as she stared ahead, "I took her down into the cellar—and," she said with virtuous accents of slight regret, "I don't suppose I should have done it to her, but I was so worried—so worried," she cried strangely, "to think that after all the bringin' up she'd had, an' all the trouble me an' Lampley had taken tryin' to keep her straight—that I reckon I went almost crazy. . . . I reached down an' tore loose a board in an old packin' case we had down there," she said slowly, "an' I beat her! I *beat* her," she cried powerfully, "until the blood soaked through her dress an' run down on the floor. . . . I beat her till she couldn't stand," cried Mrs. Lampley, with an accent of strange maternal virtue in her voice, "I beat her till she got down on her knees an' begged for mercy—now *that* was how hard I beat her," she said proudly. "An' you know it takes a lot to make Grace cry—she won't cry fer nothin'—so you may know I beat her mighty hard," said Mrs. Lampley, in a tone of strong satisfaction.

And during all this time the girl just stood passively with her sweet and vacant smile, and presently Mrs. Lampley heaved a powerful sigh of maternal tribulation, and, shaking her head slowly, said:

"But, Lord! Lord! They're a worry an' a care to you from the moment that they're born! You sweat an' slave to bring 'em up right—an' even then you can't tell what will happen. You watch 'em day an' night—an' then the first low-down bastard that comes along may git 'em out an' ruin 'em the first time your back is turned!"

And again she sighed heavily, shaking her head. And in this grotesque and horribly comic manifestation of motherly love and solicitude, and in the vacant, tender smile upon the girl's large, empty face there really was something moving, terribly pitiful, and unutterable.

WHENEVER GEORGE THOUGHT of this savage and tremendous family, his vision always returned again to Mr. Lampley himself, whose last, whose greatest secrecy, was silence. He talked to no one more than the barest necessity of business speech demanded, and when he spoke, either in question or reply, his speech was as curt and monosyllabic as speech could be, and his hard, blazing eyes, which he kept pointed as steady as a pistol at the face of anyone to whom he spoke or listened, repelled effectively any desire for a more spacious conversation. Yet, when he did speak, his voice was never surly, menacing, or snarling. It was a low, hard, toneless voice, as steady and unwavering as his hard black eyes, yet not unpleasant in its tone or timbre; it was, like everything about him save the naked, blazing eyes—hard, secret, and contained. He simply fastened his furious and malignant little eyes on one and spoke as brief and short as possible.

"Talk!" a man said. "Why, hell, he don't need to talk! He just stands there and lets those eyes of his do all the talkin' for him!" And this was true.

Beyond this bare anatomy of speech, George had heard him speak on only one occasion. This had been one day when he had come to make collections for the meat he had delivered. At this time it was known in the town that Mr. Lampley's son, Baxter, had been accused of stealing money from the man he worked for, and that—so ran the whispered and discreditable rumor—Baxter had been compelled to leave town. On this day when Mr. Lampley came to make collections, Aunt Maw, spurred by her native curiosity, and the desire that people have to hear the confirmation of their worst suspicions from the lips of those who are most painfully concerned, spoke to the butcher with the obvious and clumsy casualness of tone that people use on these occasions:

"Oh, Mr. Lampley," she said, as if by an afterthought when she had paid him, "say—by the way—I was meanin' to ask you. What's become of Baxter? I was thinkin' just the other day, I don't believe I've seen him for the last month or two."

During all the time she spoke, the man's blazing eyes never faltered in their stare upon her face, and they neither winked nor wavered as he answered.

"No," he said, in his low, hard, toneless voice. "I don't suppose you have. He's not livin' here any more. He's in the navy."

"What say?" Aunt Maw cried eagerly, opening the screen door a trifle wider and moving forward. "The navy?" she said sharply.

"Yes, ma'am," said Mr. Lampley tonelessly, "the navy. It was a question of join the navy or go to jail. I gave him his choice. He joined the navy," Mr. Lampley said grimly.

"What say? Jail?" she said eagerly.

"Yes, ma'am," Mr. Lampley replied. "He stole money from the man he was workin' for, as I reckon maybe you have heard by now. He done something he had no right to do. He took money that did not belong to him," he said with a brutal stubbornness. "When they caught him at it they came to me and told me they'd let him go if I'd make good the money that he'd stolen. So I said to him: 'All right. I'll give 'em the money if you join the navy. Now, you can take your choice—it's join the navy or go to jail. What do you want to do?' He joined the navy," Mr. Lampley again concluded grimly.

As for Aunt Maw, she stood for a moment reflectively, and now, her sharp curiosity having been appeased by this blunt and final statement, a warmer, more engaging sentiment of friendliness and sympathy was awakened in her:

"Well, now, I tell you what," she said hopefully, "I believe you did just the thing you should have done. I believe that's the very thing Baxter needs. Why, yes!" she now cried cheerfully. "He'll go off there and see the world and meet up with all kinds of people, and learn to keep the proper sort of hours and lead a good, normal, healthy sort of life—for there's one thing sure," she said oracularly, "you can't violate the laws of nature. If you do, you'll have to pay for it some day as sure as you're born," she said solemnly, as she shook her head, "as sure as you're born."

"Yes, ma'am," said Mr. Lampley in his low, toneless voice, keeping his little blazing eyes fixed straight upon her.

"Why, yes," Aunt Maw cried again, and this time with the vigorous accents of a mounting cheerful certitude, "they'll teach that boy a trade and regular habits and the proper way to live, and you mark my words, everything's goin' to turn out good for him," she said with heartening conviction. "He'll forget all about this trouble. Why, yes!—the whole thing will blow right over, people will forget all about it. Why, say! everyone is liable to make a mistake sometime, aren't they?" she said persuasively. "That happens to everyone—and I'll bet you. I'll bet you anything you like that when that boy comes back—"

"He ain't comin' back," said Mr. Lampley.

"What say?" Aunt Maw cried in a sharp, startled tone.

"I said he ain't comin' back," said Mr. Lampley.

"Why what's the reason he's not?" she said.

"Because if he does," said Mr. Lampley, "I'll kill him. And he knows it."

She stood looking at him for a moment with a slight frown.

"Oh, Mr. Lampley," she said quietly, shaking her head with a genial regret, "I'm sorry to hear you say that. I don't like to hear you talk that way."

He stared at her grimly for a moment with his furious, blazing eyes.

"Yes, ma'am," he said, as if he had not heard her. "I'll kill him. If he ever comes back here, I'll kill him. I'll beat him to death," he said.

Aunt Maw looked at him, shaking her head a little, saying with a closed mouth: "Huh, huh, huh, huh."

He was silent.

"I never could stand a thief," he said at length. "If it'd been anything else, I could've forgotten it. But a thief!" for the first time his voice rose hoarsely on a surge of passion. "Ah-h-h!" he muttered, stroking his head, and now there was a queer note of trouble and bewilderment in his hard tone. "You don't know! You don't know," he said, "the trouble I have had with that boy! His mother an' me done all we could for him. We worked hard an' we tried to raise him right—but we couldn't do nothing with him," he muttered. "He was a bad egg." He looked at her quietly a moment with his little, blazing eyes. Then he said, slowly and deliberately, and with a note of strong rising virtue in his voice, "I beat him, I beat him till he couldn't stand up—I beat him till the blood ran down his back—but it didn't do no more good than if I was beatin' at a post," he said. "No, ma'am. I might as well have beaten at a post."

And now his voice had a queer, hard note of grief, regret, and resignation in it, as if a man might say: "All that a father could do for a son I did for mine. But if a man shall beat his son until the blood runs down his back, and still that son learns neither grace nor penitence, what more can a father do?"

He paused a moment longer, with his eyes fixed hard upon her.

"No, ma'am," he concluded, in his low, toneless voice, "I never expect to see his face again. He'll never come back here. He knows I'll kill him if he does." Then he turned and walked off towards his ancient vehicle while Aunt Maw stood watching him with a troubled and regretful face.

AND HE HAD told the truth. Baxter never did come back. He was as lost to all of them as if he had been dead. They never saw him again.

But George, who heard all this, remembered Baxter suddenly. He remembered his part-brutal, part-corrupted face. He was a creature criminal from nature and entirely innocent. His laugh was throaty with a murky, hoarse, and hateful substance in it; there was something too glutinously liquid, rank, and coarse in his smile; and his eyes looked wet. He had too strange and sudden and too murderously obscure a rage for the clear, hard passions most boys knew. He had a knife with a long, curved blade, and when he saw negroes in the street he put his hand upon his knife. He made half-sobbings in his throat when his rage took hold of him. Yet he was large, quite handsome, well-proportioned. He was full of rough, sudden play, and was always challenging a boy to wrestle with him. He could wrestle strongly, rudely, laughing hoarsely if he flung somebody to the ground, enjoying a bruising struggle, and liking to pant and scuffle harshly with skinned knees upon the earth; and yet he would stop suddenly if he had made his effort but found his opponent stronger than he was, and succumb inertly, with a limp, sudden weakness, smiling, with no pride or hurt, as his opponent pinned him to the earth.

There was something wrong in this; and there was something ropy, milky, undefined in all the porches of his blood, so that, George felt, had Baxter's flesh been cut or broken, had he bled, there would have been a ropy, milkweed mucus before blood came. He carried pictures in his pockets, photographs from Cuba, so he said, of shining naked whores in their rank white flesh and hairiness, in perverse and Latin revels with men with black mustaches, and he spoke often of experiences he had had with girls in town, and with negro women.

All this George remembered with a rush of naked vividness.

But he remembered also a kindness, a warmth and friendliness, equally strange and sudden, which Baxter had; something swift and eager, wholly liberal, which made him wish to share all he had— the sausages and sandwiches which he brought with him to school, together with all his enormous and delicious lunch—offering and thrusting the rich bounty of his lunch box, which would smell with an unutterable fragrance and delight, at the other boys with a kind of eager, asking, and insatiable generosity. And at times his voice was gentle, and his manner had this same strange, eager, warm, and almost timid gentleness and friendliness.

George remembered passing the butcher shop once, and from the basement, warm with its waft of fragrant spices, he suddenly heard Baxter screaming:

"Oh, I'll be good! I'll be good!"—and that sound from this rough, brutal boy had suddenly pierced him with an unutterable sense of shame and pity.

This, then, was Baxter as George had known him, and as he remembered him when the butcher spoke of him that day. And as the butcher spoke his hard and toneless words of judgment, George felt a wave of intolerable pity and regret pass over him as he remembered Baxter (although he had not known him well or seen him often), and knew he never would come back again.

CHAPTER 8

The Child by Tiger

One day after school, Monk and several of the boys were
playing with a football in the yard at Randy Shepperton's. Randy was calling signals and handling the ball.
Nebraska Crane was kicking it. Augustus Potterham was too clumsy
to run or kick or pass, so they put him at center where all he'd have to
do would be to pass the ball back to Randy when he got the signal. To
the other boys, Gus Potterham was their freak child, their lame duck,
the butt of their jokes and ridicule, but they also had a sincere affection
for him; he was something to be taken in hand, to be protected and
cared for.

There were several other boys who were ordinarily members of
their group. They had Harry Higginson and Sam Pennock, and two
boys named Howard Jarvis and Jim Redmond. It wasn't enough to
make a team, of course. They didn't have room enough to play a game
even if they had had team enough. What they played was really a kind
of skeletonized practice game, with Randy and Nebraska back, Gus at
center, two other fellows at the ends, and Monk and two or three more
on the other side, whose duty was to get in and "break it up" if they
could.

It was about four o'clock in the afternoon, late in October, and
there was a smell of smoke, of leaves, of burning in the air. Bras had
just kicked to Monk. It was a good kick too—a high, soaring punt that
spiraled out above Monk's head, behind him. He ran back and tried to

get it, but it was far and away "over the goal line"—that is to say, out in the street. It hit the street and bounded back and forth with that peculiarly erratic bounce a football has.

The ball rolled away from Monk down towards the corner. He was running out to get it when Dick Prosser, Sheppertons' new negro man, came along, gathered it up neatly in his great black paw, and tossed it to him. Dick turned in then, and came on around the house, greeting the boys as he came. He called all of them "Mister" except Randy, and Randy was always "Cap'n"—"Cap'n Shepperton." This formal address—"Mr." Crane, "Mr." Potterham, "Mr." Webber, "Cap'n" Shepperton—pleased them immensely, gave them a feeling of mature importance and authority.

"Cap'n Shepperton" was splendid! It was something more to all of them than a mere title of respect. It had a delightful military association, particularly when Dick Prosser said it. Dick had served a long enlistment in the U. S. army. He had been a member of a regiment of crack negro troops upon the Texas border, and the stamp of the military man was evident in everything he did. It was a joy just to watch him split up kindling. He did it with a power, a clean precision, a kind of military order, that was astounding. Every stick he cut seemed to be exactly the same length and shape as every other. He had all of them neatly stacked against the walls of the Shepperton basement with such regimented faultlessness that it almost seemed a pity to disturb their symmetry for the use for which they were intended.

It was the same with everything else he did. His little whitewashed basement room was as spotless as a barracks room. The bare board floor was always cleanly swept, a plain, bare table and a plain, straight chair were stationed exactly in the center of the room. On the table there was always just one object—an old Bible with a limp cover, almost worn out by constant use, for Dick was a deeply religious man. There was a little cast-iron stove and a little wooden box with a few lumps of coal and a neat stack of kindling in it. And against the wall, to the left, there was an iron cot, always precisely made and covered cleanly with a coarse grey blanket.

The Sheppertons were delighted with him. He had come there looking for work just a month or two before, "gone around to the back door" and modestly presented his qualifications. He had, he said, only recently received his discharge from the army, and was eager to get employment, at no matter what wage. He could cook, he could tend the furnace, he could do odd jobs, he was handy at carpentry, he knew how to drive a car—in fact, it seemed to the boys that there was very little that Dick Prosser could not do.

He could certainly shoot. He gave a modest demonstration of his prowess one afternoon, with Randy's "twenty-two," that left them gasping. He just lifted that little rifle in his powerful black hands as if it were a toy, without seeming to take aim, pointed it towards a strip of tin on which they had crudely marked out some bull's-eye circles, and he simply peppered the center of the bull's eye, putting twelve holes through a space one inch square, so fast they could not even count the shots.

He knew how to box, too. Randy said he had been a regimental champion. At any rate, he was as cunning and crafty as a cat. He never boxed with the boys, of course, but Randy had two sets of gloves, and Dick used to coach them while they sparred. There was something amazingly tender and watchful about him. He taught them many things, how to lead, to hook, to counter, and to block, but he was careful to see that they did not hurt each other. Nebraska, who was the most powerful of the lot, could hit like a mule. He would have killed Gus Potterham in his simple, honest way if he had ever been given a free hand. But Dick, with his quick watchfulness, his gentle and persuasive tact, was careful to see this did not happen.

He knew about football, too, and that day, as Dick passed the boys, he paused, a powerful, respectable-looking negro of thirty years or more, and watched them for a moment as they played.

Randy took the ball and went up to him.

"How do you hold it, Dick?" he said. "Is this right?"

Dick watched him attentively as he gripped the ball and held it back above his shoulder. The negro nodded approvingly and said:

"That's right, Cap'n Shepperton. You've got it. Only," he said gently, and now took the ball in his own powerful hand, "when you gits a little oldah, yo' handses gits biggah and you gits a bettah grip."

His own great hand, in fact, seemed to hold the ball as easily as if it were an apple. And, holding it so a moment, he brought it back, aimed over his outstretched left hand as if he were pointing a gun, and rifled it in a beautiful, whizzing spiral thirty yards or more to Gus. He then showed them how to kick, how to get the ball off of the toe in such a way that it would rise and spiral cleanly.

He showed them how to make a fire, how to pile the kindling, where to place the coal, so that the flames shot up cone-wise, cleanly, without smoke or waste. He showed them how to strike a match with the thumbnail of one hand and keep and hold the flame in the strongest wind. He showed them how to lift a weight, how to "tote" a burden on their shoulders in the easiest way. There was nothing that he did not know. They were all so proud of him. Mr. Shepperton himself declared that Dick was the best man he'd ever had, the smartest darky that he'd ever known.

And yet? He went too softly, at too swift a pace. He was there upon them sometimes like a cat. Looking before them sometimes, seeing nothing but the world before them, suddenly they felt a shadow at their back, and, looking up, would find that Dick was there. And there was something moving in the night. They never saw him come or go. Sometimes they would waken, startled, and feel that they had heard a board creak, the soft clicking of a latch, a shadow passing swiftly. All was still.

"Young white fokes—O young white gentlemen"—his soft voice ending in a moan, a kind of rhythm in his lips—"O young white fokes, I'se tellin' *you*—" that soft, low moan again—"you gotta love each othah like a brothah." He was deeply religious and went to church three times a week. He read his Bible every night.

Sometimes Dick would come out of his little basement room and his eyes would be red, as if he had been weeping. They would know, then, that he had been reading his Bible. There would be times when he would almost moan when he talked to them, a kind of hymnal chant, a religious ecstasy, that came from some deep intoxication of the spirit, and that transported him. For the boys, it was a troubling and bewildering experience. They tried to laugh it off and make jokes about it But there was something in it so dark and strange and full of a feeling they could not fathom that their jokes were hollow, and the trouble in their minds and in their hearts remained.

Sometimes on these occasions his speech would be made up of some weird jargon of Biblical phrases and quotations and allusions, of which he seemed to have hundreds, and which he wove together in the strange pattern of his emotion in a sequence that was meaningless to them but to which he himself had the coherent clue.

"O young white fokes," he would begin, moaning gently, "de dry bones in de valley. I tell you, white fokes, de day is comin' when He's comin' on dis earth again to sit in judgment. He'll put de sheep upon de right hand and de goats upon de left—O white fokes, white fokes—de Armageddon days' a-comin', white fokes—an' de dry bones in de valley."

Or again, they could hear him singing as he went about his work, in his deep, rich voice, so full of warmth and strength, so full of Africa, singing hymns that were not only of his own race, but that were familiar to them all. They didn't know where he learned them. Perhaps they were remembered from his army days. Perhaps he had learned them in the service of former masters. He drove the Sheppertons to church on Sunday morning, and would wait for them throughout the service. He would come up to the side door of the church while the service was going on, neatly dressed in his good, dark suit, holding his chauffeur's hat respectfully in his hand, and stand there humbly and listen during the course of the entire sermon.

And then when the hymns were sung, and the great rich sound

would swell and roll out into the quiet air of Sunday, Dick would stand and listen, and sometimes he would join quietly in the song. A number of these favorite hymns the boys heard him singing many times in a low, rich voice as he went about his work around the house. He would sing "Who Follows in His Train?"—or "Alexander's Glory Song," or "Rock of Ages," or "Onward, Christian Soldiers."

And yet? Well, nothing happened—there was just "a flying hint from here and there"—and the sense of something passing in the night.

Turning into the Square one day, as Dick was driving Mr. Shepperton to town, Lon Pilcher skidded murderously around the corner, side-swiped Dick, and took the fender off. The negro was out of the car like a cat and got his master out. Mr. Shepperton was unhurt. Lon Pilcher climbed out and reeled across the street, drunk as a sot in mid-afternoon. He swung viciously, clumsily, at the negro, smashed him in the face. Blood trickled from the flat black nostrils and from the thick, liver-colored lips. Dick did not move. But suddenly the whites of his eyes were shot with red, his bleeding lips bared for a moment over the white ivory of his teeth. Lon smashed at him again. The negro took it full in the face again; his hands twitched slightly but he did not move. They collared the drunken sot and hauled him off and locked him up. Dick stood there for a moment, then he wiped his face and turned to see what damage had been done to the car. No more now, but there were those who saw it, who remembered later how the eyes went red.

Another thing. The Sheppertons had a cook named Pansy Harris. She was a comely negro wench, young, plump, black as the ace of spades, a good-hearted girl with a deep dimple in her cheeks and faultless teeth, bared in a most engaging smile. No one ever saw Dick speak to her. No one ever saw her glance at him, or him at her—and yet that dimpled, plump, and smilingly good-natured wench became as mournful-silent and as silent-sullen as midnight pitch. She sang no more. No more was seen the gleaming ivory of her smile. No more was heard the hearty and infectious exuberance of her warm, full-throated laugh. She went about her work as mournfully as if she were going to a funeral. The gloom deepened all about her. She answered sullenly now when spoken to.

One night towards Christmas she announced that she was leaving. In response to all entreaties, all efforts to find the reason for her sudden and unreasonable decision, she had no answer except a sullen repetition of the assertion that she had to leave, Repeated questionings did finally wring from her a statement that her husband wanted her to quit, that he needed her at home. More than this she would not say, and even this excuse was highly suspected, because her husband was a Pullman porter, home only two days a week, and well accustomed to do himself such housekeeping tasks as she might do for him.

The Sheppertons were fond of her. The girl had been with them for several years. They tried again to find the reason for her leaving. Was she dissatisfied? "No'm"—an implacable monosyllable, mournful, unrevealing as the night. Had she been offered a better job elsewhere? "No'm"—as untelling as before. If they offered her more wages, would she stay with them? "No'm"—again and again, sullen and unyielding; until finally the exasperated mistress threw her hands up in a gesture of defeat and said: "All right then, Pansy. Have it your own way, if that's the way you feel. Only for heaven's sake, don't leave us in the lurch. Don't leave us until we get another cook."

This, at length, with obvious reluctance, the girl agreed to. Then, putting on her hat and coat, and taking the paper bag of "leavings" she was allowed to take home with her at night, she went out the kitchen door and made her sullen and morose departure.

This was on Saturday night, a little after eight o'clock.

THAT SAME AFTERNOON Randy and Monk had been fooling around the Shepperton basement, and, seeing that Dick's door was slightly ajar, they stopped at the opening and looked in to see if he was there. The little room was empty, and swept and spotless as it had always been.

But they did not notice that! They saw *it*! At the same moment their breaths caught sharply in a gasp of startled wonderment. Randy was the first to speak.

"Look!" he whispered. "Do you see it?"

See it? Monk's eyes were glued upon it. Had he found himself staring suddenly at the flat head of a rattlesnake his hypnotized surprise could have been no greater. Squarely across the bare boards of the table, blue-dull, deadly in its murderous efficiency, lay an automatic army rifle. They both knew the type. They had seen them all when Randy went to buy his little "twenty-two" at Uncle Morris Teitlebaum's. Beside it was a box containing one hundred rounds of ammunition, and behind it, squarely in the center, face downward, open on the table, was the familiar cover of Dick's old, worn Bible.

Then he was on them like a cat. He was there like a great, dark shadow before they know it. They turned, terrified. He was there above them, his thick lips bared above his gums, his eyes gone small and red as rodents'.

"Dick!" Randy gasped, and moistened his dry lips. "Dick!" he fairly cried now.

It was all over like a flash. Dick's mouth closed. They could see the whites of his eyes again. He smiled and said softly, affably, "Yes suh, Cap'n Shepperton. Yes suh! You gent-mun lookin' at my rifle?"—and he stepped across the sill into the room.

Monk gulped and nodded his head and couldn't say a word, and Randy whispered, "Yes." And both of them still stared at him with an expression of appalled and fascinated interest.

Dick shook his head and chuckled. "Can't do without my rifle, white fokes. No suh!" He shook his head good-naturedly again, "Ole Dick, he's—he's—he's an ole *ahmy* man, you know. He's gotta have his rifle. If they take his rifle away from him, why that's jest lak takin' candy away from a little baby. Yes suh!" he chuckled again, and picked the weapon up affectionately. "Ole Dick felt Christmas comin' on—he—he—I reckon he must have felt it in his bones," he chuckled, "so I been savin' up my money—I jest thought I'd hide this heah and keep it as a big surprise fo' the young white fokes," he said. "I was jest gonna put it away heah and keep it untwill Christmas morning. Then I was gonna take the young white fokes out and show 'em how to shoot."

They had begun to breathe more easily now, and, almost as if they were under the spell of the Pied Piper of Hamelin, they had followed him step by step into the room.

"Yes suh," Dick chuckled, "I was jest fixin' to hide this gun away and keep it hid twill Christmas day, but Cap'n Shepperton—hee!" he chuckled heartily and slapped his thigh—"you can't fool ole Cap'n Shepperton! He was too quick fo' me. He jest must've smelled this ole gun right out. He comes right in and sees it befo' I has a chance to tu'n around. . . . Now, white fokes," Dick's voice fell to a tone of low and winning confidence, "Ah's hopin' that I'd git to keep this gun as a little surprise fo' you. Now that you's found out, I'll tell you what I'll do. If you'll jest keep it a surprise from the other white fokes twill Christmas day, I'll take all you gent'mun out and let you shoot it. Now cose," he went on quietly, with a shade of resignation, "if you want to tell on me you can—but"—here his voice fell again, with just the faintest yet most eloquent shade of sorrowful regret—"Ole Dick was lookin' fahwad to this. He was hopin' to give all the white fokes a supprise Christmas day."

They promised earnestly that they would keep his secret as if it were their own. They fairly whispered their solemn vow. They tiptoed away out of the little basement room, as if they were afraid their very footsteps might betray the partner of their confidence.

This was four o'clock on Saturday afternoon. Already, there was a somber moaning of the wind, grey storm clouds sweeping over. The threat of snow was in the air.

SNOW FELL THAT night. It began at six o'clock. It came howling down across the hills. It swept in on them from the Smokies. By seven o'clock the air was blind with sweeping snow, the earth was carpeted, the streets were numb. The storm howled on, around houses warm with crackling fires and shaded light. All life seemed to have withdrawn into thrilling isolation. A horse went by upon the street with muffled hoofs.

George Webber went to sleep upon this mystery, lying in the darkness, listening to that exultancy of storm, to that dumb wonder, that enormous and attentive quietness of snow, with something dark and jubilant in his soul he could not utter.

Snow in the South is wonderful. It has a kind of magic and a mystery that it has nowhere else. And the reason for this is that it comes to people in the South not as the grim, unyielding tenant of the Winter's keep, but as a strange and wild visitor from the secret North. It comes to them from darkness, to their own special and most secret soul there in the South. It brings to them the thrilling isolation of its own white mystery. It brings them something that they lack, and that they have to have; something that they have lost, but now have found: something that they have known utterly, but had forgotten until now.

In every man there are two hemispheres of light and dark, two worlds discrete, two countries of his soul's adventure. And one of these is the dark land, the other half of his heart's home, the unvisited domain of his father's earth.

And this is the land he knows the best. It is the earth unvisited— and it is his, as nothing he has seen can ever be. It is the world intangible that he has never touched—yet more his own than something he has owned forever. It is the great world of his mind, his heart, his spirit, built there in his imagination, shaped by wonder and unclouded by the obscuring flaws of accident and actuality, the proud, unknown earth of the lost, the found, the never-here, the ever-real America, unsullied, true, essential, built there in the brain, and shaped to glory by the proud and flaming vision of a child.

Thus, at the head of those two poles of life will lie the real, the truthful image of its immortal opposite. Thus, buried in the dark heart of the cold and secret North, abides forever the essential image of the

South; thus, at the dark heart of the moveless South, there burns forever the immortal splendor of the North.

So had it always been with George. The other half of his heart's
home, the world unknown that he knew the best, was the dark North.
And snow swept in that night across the hills, demonic visitant, to
restore that land to him, to sheet it in essential wonder. Upon this mystery he fell asleep.

A LITTLE AFTER two o'clock next morning he was awakened by the
ringing of a bell. It was the fire bell of the City Hall, and it was beating
an alarm—a hard, fast stroke that he had never heard before. Bronze
with peril, clangorous through the snow-numbed silence of the air, it
had a quality of instancy and menace he had never known before. He
leaped up and ran to the window to look for the telltale glow against
the sky. But it was no fire. Almost before he looked, those deadly
strokes beat in upon his brain the message that this was no alarm for
fire. It was a savage, brazen tongue calling the town to action, warning
mankind against the menace of some peril—secret, dark, unknown,
greater than fire or flood could ever be.

He got instantly, in the most overwhelming and electric way, the
sense that the whole town had come to life. All up and down the
street the houses were beginning to light up. Next door, the Shepperton house was ablaze with light, from top to bottom. Even as he
looked Mr. Shepperton, wearing an overcoat over his pajamas, ran
down the steps and padded out across the snow-covered walk towards
the street.

People were beginning to run out of doors. He heard excited cries
and shouts and questions everywhere. He saw Nebraska Crane come
pounding up the middle of the street. He knew that he was coming for
him and Randy. As Bras ran by Shepperton's, he put his fingers to his
mouth and whistled piercingly. It was a signal they all knew.

Monk was already almost dressed by the time he came running in
across the front yard. He hammered at the door; Monk was already

there. They both spoke at once. He had answered Monk's startled question before he got it out.

"Come on!" he said, panting with excitement, his Cherokee black eyes burning with an intensity Monk had never seen before. "Come on!" he cried. They were halfway out across the yard by now. "It's that nigger! He's gone crazy and is running wild!"

"Wh-wh-what nigger?" Monk gasped, pounding at his heels.

Even before he spoke Monk had the answer. Mr. Crane had already come out of his house and crossed the street, buttoning his heavy policeman's overcoat and buckling his girdle as he came. He had paused to speak for a moment to Mr. Shepperton, and Monk heard Mr. Shepperton say quickly, in a low voice:

"Which way did he go?"

Then he heard somebody cry, "It's that nigger of Shepperton's!"

Mr. Shepperton turned and went quickly back across his yard towards the house. His wife and two girls stood huddled in the open doorway. The snow had drifted in across the porch. The three women stood there, white, trembling, holding themselves together, their arms thrust in the side sleeves of their kimonos.

The telephone in Shepperton's house was ringing like mad but no one was paying any attention to it. Monk heard Mrs. Shepperton say quickly as her husband ran up the steps, "Is it Dick?" He nodded and passed her brusquely, going towards the phone.

At this moment, Nebraska whistled piercingly again upon his fingers, and Randy Shepperton ran past his mother and sped down the steps. She called sharply to him. He paid no attention to her. When he came up, Monk saw that his fine, thin face was white as a sheet. He looked at Monk and whispered:

"It's—it's Dick!" And in a moment, "They say he's killed four people!"

"With—?" Monk couldn't finish.

Randy nodded dumbly, and they both stared there for a minute, two white-faced boys, aware now of the full and murderous significance of the secret they had kept, the confidence they had not violated, with a sudden sense of guilt and fear as if somehow the crime lay on their shoulders.

Across the street a window banged up in the parlor of Suggs' house and Old Man Suggs appeared in the window clad only in his nightgown, his brutal old face inflamed with excitement, his shock of silvery white hair awry, his powerful shoulders and his thick hands gripping his crutches.

"He's coming this way!" he bawled to the world in general. "They say he lit out across the Square! He's heading out in this direction!"

Mr. Crane paused to yell back impatiently over his shoulder, "No, he went down South Main Street. He's heading for Wilton and the river. I've already heard from headquarters."

Automobiles were beginning to roar and sputter all along the street. Even at that time, over half the people on the street had them. Across the street Monk could hear Mr. Potterham sweating with his Ford. He would whirl the crank a dozen times or more, the engine would catch for a moment, cough and splutter, and then die again. Gus ran out of doors with a kettle of boiling water and began to pour it feverishly down the radiator spout.

Mr. Shepperton was already dressed. They saw him run down the back steps towards the carriage house. Randy, Bras, and Monk streaked down the driveway to help him. They got the old wooden doors open. He went in and cranked the car. It was a new Buick. It responded to their prayers and started up at once. Mr. Shepperton backed out into the snowy drive. They all clambered up onto the running board. He spoke absently, saying:

"You boys stay here. Randy, your mother's calling you."

But they all tumbled in and he didn't say a word.

He came backing down the driveway at top speed. They turned into the street and picked up Mr. Crane. As they took the corner into Charles Street, Fred Sanford and his father roared past them in their Oldsmobile. They lit out for town, going at top speed. Every house along Charles Street was lighted up. Even the hospital was ablaze with light. Cars were coming out of alleys everywhere. They could hear people shouting questions and replies at one another. Monk heard one man shout, "He's killed six men!"

Monk didn't know how fast they went, but it was breakneck speed with streets in such condition. It didn't take them over five minutes to reach the Square, but when they got there it seemed as if the whole town was there ahead of them. Mr. Shepperton pulled the car up and parked in front of the City Hall. Mr. Crane leaped out and went pounding away across the Square without another word to them.

Everyone was running in the same direction. From every corner, every street that led into the Square, people were streaking in. One could see the dark figures of running men across the white carpet of the Square. They were all rushing in to one focal point.

The southwest corner of the Square where South Main Street came into it was like a dog fight. Those running figures streaking towards that dense crowd gathered there made Monk think of nothing else so much as a fight between two boys upon the playgrounds of the school at recess time. The way the crowd was swarming in was just the same.

But then he *heard* a difference. From that crowd came a low and growing mutter, an ugly and insistent growl, of a tone and quality he had never heard before, but, hearing it now, he knew instantly what it meant. There was no mistaking the blood note in that foggy growl. And the three of them, the three boys, looked at one another with the same question in the eyes of all.

Nebraska's coal black eyes were shining now with a savage sparkle even they had never had before. The awakened blood of the Cherokee was smoking in him. "Come on," he said in a low tone, exultantly. "They mean business this time, sure. Let's go!" And he darted away towards the dense and sinister darkness of the crowd.

Even as they followed him they heard behind them, at the edge of Niggertown, coming towards them now, growing, swelling at every instant, one of the most savagely mournful and terrifying sounds that night can know. It was the baying of the hounds as they came up upon the leash from Niggertown. Full-throated, howling deep, the savagery of blood was in it, and the savagery of man's guilty doom was in it, too.

They came up swiftly, fairly baying at the boys' heels as they sped across the snow-white darkness of the Square. As they got up to the crowd they saw that it had gathered at the corner where Mark Joyner's hardware store stood. Monk's uncle had not yet arrived but they had phoned for him; he was already on the way. But Monk heard Mr. Shepperton swear beneath his breath in vexation:

"Damn, if I'd only thought—we could have taken him!"

Facing the crowd which pressed in on them so close and menacing that they were almost flattened out against the glass, three or four men were standing with arms stretched out in a kind of chain, as if trying to protect with the last resistance of their strength and eloquence the sanctity of private property.

George Gallatin was Mayor at that time, and he was standing there shoulder to shoulder and arm to arm with Hugh McPherson. Monk could see Hugh, taller by half a foot than anyone around him, his long, gaunt figure, the gaunt passion of his face, even the attitude of his outstretched bony arms, strangely, movingly Lincolnesque, his one good eye (for he was blind in the other) blazing in the cold glare of the corner lamp with a kind of cold, inspired, Scotch passion.

"Wait a minute! Stop! You men wait a minute!" he cried. His words cut out above the shouts and clamor of the mob like an electric spark. "You'll gain nothing, you'll help nothing if you do this thing."

They tried to drown him out with an angry and derisive roar. He shot his big fist up into the air and shouted at them, blazed at them with that cold single eye, until they had to hear. "Listen to me!" he cried. "This is no time for mob law. This is no case for lynch law. This is a time for law and order. Wait till the sheriff swears you in. Wait until Mark Joyner comes. Wait——"

He got no further. "Wait, hell!" cried someone. "We've waited long enough! We're going to get that nigger!"

The mob took up the cry. The whole crowd was writhing angrily now, like a tormented snake. Suddenly there was a flurry in the crowd, a scattering. Somebody yelled a warning at Hugh McPherson. He ducked quickly, just in time. A brick whizzed past him, smashing the plate-glass window into fragments.

And instantly a bloody roar went up. The crowd surged forward, kicked the fragments of jagged glass away. In a moment the whole mob was storming into the dark store. Mark Joyner got there just too late. He said later that he heard the smash of broken glass just as he turned the corner to the Square from College Street. He arrived in time to take out his keys and open the front doors, but as he grimly remarked, with a convulsive movement of his lips, it was like closing the barn doors after the horse had been stolen.

The mob was in and they looted him. They helped themselves to every rifle they could find. They smashed open cartridge boxes and filled their pockets with the loose cartridges. Within ten minutes they had looted the store of every rifle, every cartridge in the stock. The whole place looked as if a hurricane had hit it. The mob was streaming out into the street, was already gathering around the dogs a hundred feet or so away, who were picking up the scent at that point, the place where Dick had halted last before he had turned and headed south, downhill along South Main Street, towards the river.

The hounds were scampering about, tugging at the leash, moaning softly with their noses pointed to the snow, their long ears flattened down. But in that light and in that snow it almost seemed no hounds were needed to follow Dick. Straight down the center of the sheeted car tracks, the negro's footsteps led away. By the light of the corner lamps one could follow them until they vanished downhill in the darkness.

But now, although the snow had stopped, the wind was swirling through the street and making drifts and eddies in the snow. The footprints were fading rapidly. Soon they would be gone.

The dogs were given their head. They went straining on, softly, sniffing at the snow; behind them the dark masses of the mob closed in and followed. The three boys stood there watching while they went. They saw them go on down the street and vanish. But from below, over the snow-numbed stillness of the air, the vast, low mutter of the mob came back to them.

Men were clustered now in groups. Mark Joyner stood before his shattered window, ruefully surveying the ruin. Other men were gathered around the big telephone pole at the corner, measuring, estimating its width and thickness, pointing out two bullet holes that had been drilled cleanly through.

And swiftly, like a flash, running from group to group, like a powder train of fire, the full detail of that bloody chronicle of night was pieced together.

THIS WAS WHAT had happened.

Somewhere between nine and ten o'clock that night, Dick Prosser had gone to Pansy Harris' shack in Niggertown. Some said he had been drinking when he went there. At any rate, the police had later found the remnants of a gallon jug of raw corn whiskey in the room.

What had happened in the shack from that time on was never clearly known. The woman evidently had protested, had tried to keep him out, but eventually, as she had done before, succumbed. He went in. They were alone. What happened then, what passed between them, was never known. And, besides, no one was greatly interested. It was a crazy nigger with a nigger wench. She was "another nigger's woman"; probably she had "gone with" Dick. This was the general assumption, but no one cared. Adultery among negroes was assumed.

At any rate, some time after ten o'clock that night—it must have been closer to eleven, because the train of the negro porter, Harris, was late and did not pull into the yards until 10:20—the woman's husband appeared upon the scene. The fight did not start then. According to the woman, the real trouble did not come until an hour or more after his return.

The men drank together. Each was in an ugly temper. Dick was steadily becoming more savagely inflamed. Shortly before midnight they got into a fight. Harris slashed at Dick with a razor. In a second they were locked together, rolling about and fighting like two madmen on the floor. Pansy Harris went screaming out of doors and across the street into a dingy little grocery store.

A riot call was telephoned at once to police headquarters at the City Hall. The news came in that a crazy nigger had broken loose on Valley Street in Niggertown, and to send help at once. Pansy Harris ran back across the street towards her little shack.

As she got there, her husband, with blood streaming from his face, staggered out across the little lean-to porch into the street, with his hands held up protectively behind his head in a gesture of instinctive terror. At the same moment, Dick Prosser appeared in the doorway of the shack, deliberately took aim with his rifle, and shot the fleeing negro squarely through the back of the head. Harris dropped forward on his face into the snow. He was dead before he hit the ground. A huge dark stain of blood-soaked snow widened out around him. Dick Prosser took one step, seized the terrified negress by the arm, hurled her into the shack, bolted the door, pulled down the shades, blew out the lamp, and waited.

A few minutes later, two policemen arrived from town. They were a young constable named Willis, who had but recently got on the force, and John Grady, a lieutenant. The policemen took one look at the bloody figure in the snow, questioned the frightened keeper of the grocery store, and then, after consulting briefly, produced their weapons and walked out into the street.

Young Willis stepped softly down onto the snow-covered porch of the shack, flattened himself against the wall between the window and the door, and waited. Grady went around to the side, produced his flashlight, flashed it against the house and through the window, which on this side was shadeless. At the same moment Grady said in a loud voice:

"Come out of there!"

Dick's answer was to shoot him cleanly through the wrist. At the same moment Willis kicked the door in with a powerful thrust of his foot, and, without waiting, started in with pointed revolver. Dick shot him just above the eyes. The policeman fell forward on his face.

Grady came running out around the house, crossed the street, rushed into the grocery store, pulled the receiver of the old-fashioned telephone off the hook, rang frantically for headquarters, and yelled out across the wire that a crazy nigger had killed Sam Willis and a negro man, and to send help.

At this moment Dick, coatless and without a hat, holding his rifle crosswise in his hands, stepped out across the porch into the street, aimed swiftly through the dirty window of the dingy little store and shot John Grady as he stood there at the phone. Grady fell dead with a bullet that entered just below his left temple and went out on the other side.

Dick, now moving in a long, unhurried stride that covered the ground with catlike speed, turned up the snow-covered slope of Valley Street and began his march towards town. He moved right up the center of the street, shooting cleanly from left to right as he went. Halfway up the hill, the second-story window of a negro tenement flew open. An old negro man, the janitor of an office building in the Square, stuck out his ancient head of cotton wool. Dick swiveled and shot casually from his hip. The shot tore the top of the old negro's head off.

By the time Dick reached the head of Valley Street, they knew he was coming. He moved steadily along, leaving his big tread cleanly in the middle of the sheeted street, shifting a little as he walked, swinging his gun crosswise before him. This was the negro Broadway of the town, the center of the night life of the negro settlement. But where those pool rooms, barber shops, drug stores, and fried-fish places had been loud with dusky life ten minutes before, they were now silent as the ruins of Egypt. The word was flaming through the town that a crazy nigger was on the way. No one showed his head.

Dick moved on steadily, always in the middle of the street, reached the end of Valley Street and turned into South Main—turned right, uphill, in the middle of the car tracks, and started towards the Square. As he passed the lunchroom on the left he took a swift shot through the window at the counter man. The fellow ducked behind the counter. The bullet crashed into the wall above his head.

Meanwhile, the news that Dick was coming was crackling through the town. At the City Club on Sondley Street, three blocks away, a group of the town's leading gamblers and sporting men was intent in a haze of smoke above a green baize table and some stacks of poker chips. The phone rang. The call was for Wilson Redmond, the police court magistrate.

Wilson listened for a moment, then hung the phone up casually. "Come on, Jim," he said in casual tones to a crony, Jim McIntyre, "there's a crazy nigger loose. He's shooting up the town. Let's go get him." And with the same nonchalance he thrust his arms into the overcoat which the white-jacketed negro held for him, put on his tall silk hat, took up his cane, pulled out his gloves, and started to depart. Wilson, like his comrade, had been drinking.

As if they were going to a wedding party, the two men went out into the deserted, snow-white streets, turned at the corner by the post office, and started up the street towards the Square. As they reached the Square and turned into it they heard Dick's shot into the lunchroom and the crash of glass.

"There he is, Jim!" said Wilson Redmond happily. "Now I'll have some fun. Let's go get him." The two gentlemen moved rapidly across the Square and into South Main Street.

Dick kept coming on, steadily, at his tireless, easy stride, straight up the middle of the street. Wilson Redmond started down the street to get him. He lifted hisgold-headed cane and waved it at Dick Prosser.

"You're under arrest!" Wilson Redmond said.

Dick shot again, and also from the hip, but something faltered this time by the fraction of an inch. They always thought it was Wilson Redmond's tall silk hat that fooled him. The bullet drilled a hole right through the top of Judge Redmond's tall silk hat, and it went flying away. Wilson Redmond faded into the doorway of a building and fervently wished that his too, too solid flesh would melt.

Jim McIntyre was not so lucky. He started for the doorway but Wilson got there first. Dick shot cleanly from the hip again and blew Jim's side in with a fast shot. Poor Jim fell sprawling to the ground, to rise and walk again, it's true, but ever thereafter with a cane. Meanwhile, on the other side of the Square, at police headquarters, the sergeant had sent John Chapman out to head Dick off. Mr. Chapman was perhaps the best-liked man on the force. He was a pleasant, florid-faced man of forty-five, with curling brown mustaches, congenial and good-humored, devoted to his family, courageous, but perhaps too kindly and too gentle for a good policeman.

John Chapman heard the shots and ran forward. He came up to the corner by Joyner's hardware store just as Dick's shot sent poor Jim McIntyre sprawling to the ground. Mr. Chapman took up his position there at the corner behind the telephone pole. From this vantage point he took out his revolver and shot directly at Dick Prosser as he came up the street.

By this time Dick was not over thirty yards away. He dropped quietly upon one knee and aimed. Mr. Chapman shot again and missed. Dick fired. The high-velocity bullet bored through the post a little to one side. It grazed the shoulder of John Chapman's uniform and knocked a chip out of the monument sixty yards or more behind him in the center of the Square.

Mr. Chapman fired again and missed. And Dick, still coolly poised upon his knee, as calm and steady as if he were engaging in a rifle practice, fired again, drilled squarely through the center of the pole, and shot John Chapman through the heart. Mr. Chapman dropped dead.

Then Dick rose, pivoted like a soldier in his tracks, and started back down the street, right down the center of the car tracks, straight as a string, right out of town.

THIS WAS THE story as they got it, pieced together like a train of fire among the excited groups of men that clustered there in trampled snow before the shattered glass of Joyner's store.

And the rifle? Where did he get it? From whom had he purchased it? The answer to this, too, was not long in coming.

Mark Joyner denied instantly that the weapon had come from his store. At this moment there was a flurry in the crowd and Uncle Morris Teitlebaum, the pawnbroker, appeared, gesticulating volubly, clinging to a policeman. Bald-headed, squat, with the face of an old monkey, he protested shrilly, using his hands eloquently, and displaying craggy nuggins of gold teeth as he spoke.

"Vell," he said, "vhat could I do? His moaney vas good!" he said plaintively, lifting his hands and looking around with an expression of finality. "He comes with his moaney, he pays it down like every-bodies—I should say no?" he cried, with such an accent of aggrieved innocence that, in spite of the occasion, a few people smiled.

Uncle Morris Teitlebaum's pawn shop, which was on the right-hand side of South Main Street, and which Dick had passed less than an hour before in his murderous march towards town, was, unlike Joyner's hardware store, securely protected at night by strong bars over the doors and show windows.

But now, save for these groups of talking men, the town again was silent. Far off, in the direction of the river and the Wilton Bottoms, they could hear the low and mournful baying of the hounds. There was nothing more to see or do. Mark Joyner stooped, picked up some fragments of the shattered glass, and threw them in the window. A policeman was left on guard, and presently all five of them—Mr. Shepperton, Mark Joyner, and the three boys—walked back across the Square and got into the car and drove home again.

• • •

BUT THERE WAS no more sleep for anyone that night. Black Dick had murdered sleep. Towards daybreak snow began to fall again. It continued through the morning. It was piled deep in gusting drifts by noon. All footprints were obliterated. The town waited, eager, tense, wondering if the man could get away.

They did not capture him that day, but they were on his trail From time to time throughout the day news would drift back to them. Dick had turned east along the river to the Wilton Bottoms and, following the river banks as closely as be could, he had gone out for some miles along the Fairchilds road. There, a mile or two from Fairchilds, he crossed the river at the Rocky Shallows.

Shortly after daybreak a farmer from the Fairchilds section had seen him cross a field. They picked the trail up there again and followed it across the field and through a wood. He had come out on the other side and got down into the Cane Creek section, and there, for several hours, they lost him. Dick had gone right down into the icy water of the creek and walked upstream a mile or so. They brought the dogs down to the creek, to where he broke the trail, took them over to the other side and scented up and down.

Towards five o'clock that afternoon they picked the trail up on the other side, a mile or more upstream. From that point on they began to close in on him. He had been seen just before nightfall by several people in the Lester township. The dogs followed him across the fields, across the Lester road, into a wood. One arm of the posse swept around the wood to head him off. They knew they had him. Dick, freezing, hungry, and unsheltered, was hiding in that wood. They knew he couldn't get away. The posse ringed the wood and waited until morning.

At seven-thirty the next morning he made a break for it. He almost got away. He got through the line without being seen, crossed the Lester road, and headed back across the fields in the direction of Cane

Creek. And there they caught him. They saw him plunging through the snowdrift of a field. A cry went up. The posse started after him.

Part of the posse were on horseback. The men rode in across the field. Dick halted at the edge of the wood, dropped deliberately upon one knee, and for some minutes held them off with rapid fire. At two hundred yards he dropped Doc Lavender, a deputy, with a bullet through the throat.

The posse came in slowly, in an encircling, flank-wise movement. Dick got two more of them as they closed in, and then, as slowly and deliberately as a trained soldier retreating in good order, still firing as he went, he fell back through the wood. At the other side he turned and ran down through a sloping field that bordered on Cane Creek. At the creek edge he turned again, knelt once more in the snow, and aimed.

It was Dick's last shot. He didn't miss. The bullet struck Wayne Foraker, another deputy, dead center in the forehead and killed him in his saddle. Then the posse saw the negro aim again, and nothing happened. Dick snapped the cartridge breech open savagely, then hurled the gun away. A cheer went up. The posse came charging forward. Dick turned, stumblingly, and ran the few remaining yards that separated him from the cold and rock-bright waters of the creek.

And here he did a curious thing—a thing that in later days was a subject of frequent and repeated speculation, a thing that no one ever wholly understood. It was thought that he would make one final break for freedom, that he would wade the creek and try to get away before they got to him. Instead, arrived at the creek, he sat down calmy on the bank, and, as quietly and methodically as if he were seated on his cot in an army barracks, he unlaced his shoes, took them off, placed them together neatly at his side, and then stood up like a soldier, erect, in his bare feet, and faced the mob.

The men on horseback reached him first. They rode up around him and discharged their guns into him. He fell forward in the snow, riddled with bullets. The men dismounted, turned him over

on his back, and all the other men came in and riddled him. They
took his lifeless body, put a rope around his neck, and hung him to
a tree. Then the mob exhausted all their ammunition on the riddled
carcass.

BY NINE O'CLOCK that morning the news had reached the town.
Around eleven o'clock the mob came back, along the river road. A
good crowd had gone out to meet it at the Wilton Bottoms. The sheriff
rode ahead. Dick's body had been thrown like a sack and tied across
the saddle of the horse of one of the deputies he had killed.

It was in this way, bullet-riddled, shot to pieces, open to the venge-
ful and the morbid gaze of all, that Dick came back to town. The mob
came back right to its starting point in South Main Street. They halted
there before an undertaking parlor, not twenty yards away from where
Dick had halted last and knelt to kill John Chapman. They took that
ghastly mutilated thing and hung it in the window of the undertaker's
place, for every woman, man, and child in town to see.

And it was so they saw him last. Yes, they all had their look. In the
end, they had their look. They said they wouldn't look, Randy and
Monk. But in the end they went. And it has always been the same with
people. It has never changed. It never will. They protest. They shudder.
And they say they will not go. But in the end they always have their
look.

Nebraska was the only one of the boys who didn't lie about it. With
that forthright honesty that was part of him, so strangely wrought of
innocence and of brutality, of heroism, cruelty, and tenderness, he announced at once that he was going, and then waited impatiently, spit-
ting briefly and contemptuously from time to time, while the others
argued out their own hypocrisy.

At length they went. They saw it—that horrible piece of torn
bait—tried wretchedly to make themselves believe that once this
thing had spoken to them gently, had been partner to their confidence, object of their affection and respect. And they were sick with

nausea and fear, for something had come into their lives they could not understand.

The snow had stopped. The snow was going. The streets had been pounded into dirty mush, and before the shabby undertaking place the crowd milled and jostled, had their fill of horror, could not get enough.

Within, there was a battered roll-top desk, a swivel chair, a cast-iron stove, a wilted fern, a cheap diploma cheaply framed, and, in the window, that ghastly relic of man's savagery, that horrible hunk of torn bait. The boys looked and whitened to the lips, and craned their necks and looked away, and brought unwilling, fascinated eyes back to the horror once again, and craned and turned again, and shuffled in the slush uneasily, but could not go. And they looked up at the leaden reek of day, the dreary vapor of the sky, and, bleakly, at these forms and faces all around them—the people come to gape and stare, the pool-room loafers, the town toughs, the mongrel conquerors of earth—and yet, familiar to their lives and to the body of their whole experience, all known to their landscape, all living men.

And something had come into life—into their lives—that they had never known about before. It was a kind of shadow, a poisonous black-ness filled with bewildered loathing. The snow would go, they knew; the reeking vapors of the sky would clear away. The leaf, the blade, the bud, the bird, then April, would come back again—and all of this would be as if it had never been. The homely light of day would shine again familiarly. And all of this would vanish as an evil dream. And yet not wholly so. For they would still remember the old dark doubt and loathing of their kind, of something hateful and unspeakable in the souls of men. They knew that they would not forget.

Beside them a man was telling the story of his own heroic ac-complishments to a little group of fascinated listeners. Monk turned and looked at him. He was a little ferret-faced man with a furtive and uneasy eye, a mongrel mouth, and wiry jaw muscles.

"I was the first one to git in a shot," he said. "You see that hole there?" He pointed with a dirty finger, "That big hole right above the eye?"

They turned and goggled with a drugged and feeding stare.

"That's mine," the hero said, and turned briefly to the side and spat tobacco juice into the slush. "That's where I got him. Hell, after that he didn't know what hit him. The son-of-a-bitch was dead before he hit the ground. We all shot him full of holes then. The whole crowd came and let him have it. But that first shot of mine was the one that got him. But, boy!" he paused a moment, shook his head, and spat again. "We sure did fill him full of lead. Why, hell yes," he declared positively, with a decisive movement of his head, "we counted up to 287. We must have put 300 holes in him."

And Nebraska, fearless, blunt, outspoken, as he always was, turned abruptly, put two fingers to his lips and spat between them, widely and contemptuously.

"Yeah—*we*!" he grunted. "*We* killed a big one! *We*—we killed a b'ar, we did! . . . Come on, boys," he said gruffly, "let's be on our way!"

And, fearless and unshaken, untouched by any terror or any doubt, he moved away. And two white-faced, nauseated boys went with him.

A DAY OR two went by before anyone could go into Dick's room again. Monk went in with Randy and his father. The little room was spotless, bare, and tidy as it had always been. Nothing had been changed or touched. But even the very bare austerity of that little room now seemed terribly alive with the presence of its recent black tenant. It was Dick's room. They all knew that. And somehow they all knew that no one else could ever live there again.

Mr. Shepperton went over to the table, picked up Dick's old Bible that still lay there, open and face downward, held it up to the light and looked at it, at the place that Dick had marked when he last read in it. And in a moment, without speaking to them, he began to read in a quiet voice:

"The Lord is my shepherd; I shall not want. He maketh me to

lie down in green pastures: He leadeth me beside the still waters. He restoreth my soul: He leadeth me in the paths of righteousness for His name's sake. Yea, though I walk through the valley of the shadow of death, I will fear no evil: for Thou art with me. . . ."

Then Mr. Shepperton closed the book and put it down upon the table, the place where Dick had left it. And they went out the door, he locked it, and they went back into that room no more, forever.

THE YEARS PASSED, and all of them were given unto time. They went their ways. But often they would turn and come again, these faces and these voices of the past, and burn there in George Webber's memory again, upon the muted and immortal geography of time.

And all would come again—the shout of the young voices, the hard thud of the kicked ball, and Dick moving, moving steadily, Dick moving, moving silently, a storm-white world and silence, and something moving, moving in the night. Then he would hear the furious bell, the crowd a-clamor and the baying of the dogs, and feel the shadow coming that would never disappear. Then he would see again the little room, the table and the book. And the pastoral holiness of that old psalm came back to him, and his heart would wonder with perplexity and doubt.

For he had heard another song since then, and one that Dick, he knew, had never heard and would not have understood, but one whose phrases and whose imagery, it seemed to him, would suit Dick better:

> Tiger! Tiger! burning bright
> In the forests of the night,
> What immortal hand or eye
> Could shape thy fearful symmetry?

* * *

What the hammer? what the chain?
In what furnace was thy brain?
What the anvil? what dread grasp
Dare its deadly terrors clasp?

When the stars threw down their spears,
And water'd heaven with their tears,
Did he smile his work to see?
Did he who made the Lamb make thee?

What THE HAMMER? *What* the chain? No one ever knew. It was a mystery and a wonder. It was unexplained. There were a dozen stories, a hundred clues and rumors; all came to nothing in the end. Some said that Dick had come from Texas, others that his home had been in Georgia. Some said it was true that he had been enlisted in the army, but that he had killed a man while there and served a term at Leavenworth. Some said he had served in the army and had received an honorable discharge; but had later killed a man and had served a term in the state prison in Louisiana. Others said that he had been an army man but that he had "gone crazy," that he had served a period in an asylum when it was found that he was insane, that he had escaped from this asylum, that he had escaped from prison, that he was a fugitive from justice at the time he came to them.

But all these stories came to nothing. Nothing was ever proved. Nothing was ever found out. Men debated and discussed these things a thousand times—who and what he had been, what he had done, where he had come from—and all of it came to nothing. No one knew the answer.

He came from darkness. He came out of the heart of darkness, from the dark heart of the secret and undiscovered South. He came by night, just as he passed by night. He was night's child and partner, a token of the wonder and the mystery, the other side of man's dark soul, his nighttime partner, and his nighttime foal, a symbol of those things that pass by darkness and that still remain, of something still and waiting in the night that comes and passes and that will abide, a symbol of man's evil innocence, and the token of his mystery, a projection of his own unfathomed quality, a friend, a brother, and a mortal enemy, an unknown demon—our loving friend, our mortal enemy, two worlds together—a tiger and a child.

CHAPTER 9

Home from the Mountain

The winter when he was fifteen years of age, on Sundays and in the afternoons after school, George would go for long walks with his uncle on the mountains above the town and in the coves and valleys on the other side. There had always been a quality of madness in his uncle, and his years of living bound to Mag had sharpened it, intensified it, built it up and held it to the point of passion and demonic fury where at times he shook and trembled with the frenzy of it and had to get away, out of that house, to calm his tortured soul. And when this happened to Mark Joyner, he hated all his life and everything about it, and sought the desolation of the mountains. There, in bleak and wintry winds, he found as nowhere else on earth some strange and powerful catharsis.

THESE EXPEDITIONS WROUGHT upon the spirit of the boy the emotions of loneliness, desolation, and wild joy with a strong and focal congruence of desire, a blazing intensity of sensual image, he had never known before. Then as never before, he saw the great world beyond the wintry hills of home, and felt the huge, bitter conflict of those twin antagonists, those powers discrete that wage perpetual warfare in the lives of all men living—wandering forever and the earth again.

Wild, wordless, and unutterable, but absolutely congruent in his sense of their irreconcilable and inexplicable coherence, his spirit was torn as it had never been before by the strange and bitter unity of that savage conflict, that tormenting oneness of those dual and contending powers of home and hunger, absence and return. The great plantation of the earth called him forth forever with an intolerable longing of desire to explore its infinite mystery and promise of glory, power, and triumph, and the love of women, its magic wealth and joy of new lands, rivers, plains, and mountains, its crowning glory of the shining city. And he felt the strong, calm joy of evening for doors and fences, a light, a window, and a certain faith, the body and the embrace of a single and unwearied love.

The mountains in the Wintertime had a stern and demonic quality of savage joy that was, in its own way, as strangely, wildy haunting as all of the magic and the gold of April. In Spring, or in the time-enchanted spell and drowse of full, deep Summer, there was always something far and lonely, haunting with ecstasy and sorrow, desolation and the intolerable, numb exultancy of some huge, impending happiness. It was a cow bell, drowsy, far and broken in a gust of wind, as it came to him faintly from the far depth and distance of a mountain valley; the receding whistle-wail of a departing train, as it rushed eastward, seaward, towards the city, through some green mountain valley of the South; or a cloud shadow passing on the massed green of the wilderness, and the animate stillness, the thousand sudden, thrumming, drumming, stitching, unseen little voices in the lyric mystery of tangled undergrowth about him.

His uncle and he would go toiling up the mountain side, sometimes striding over rutted, clay-baked, and frost-hardened roads, sometimes beating their way downhill, with as bold and wild a joy as wilderness explorers ever knew, smashing their way through the dry and brittle undergrowth of barren Winter, hearing the dry report of bough and twig beneath their feet, the masty spring and crackle of brown ancient leaves, and brown pine needles, the elastic, bedded compost of a hundred buried and forgotten Winters.

Meanwhile, all about them, the great trees of the mountain side, at once ruggedly familiar and strangely, hauntingly austere, rose grim and barren, as stern and wild and lonely as the savage winds that warred forever, with a remote, demented howling, in their stormy, tossed, and leafless branches.

And above them the stormy wintry skies—sometimes a savage sky of wild, torn grey that came so low its scudding fringes whipped like rags of smoke around the mountain tops; sometimes an implacable, fierce sky of wintry grey; sometimes a sky of rags and tatters of wild, wintry light, westering into slashed stripes of rugged red and incredible wild gold at the gateways of the sun—bent over them forever with that same savage and unutterable pain and sorrow, that ecstasy of wild desire, that grief of desolation, that spirit of exultant joy, that was as gleeful, mad, fierce, lonely, and enchanted with its stormy and unbodied promises of flight, its mad swoopings through the dark over the whole vast sleeping wintriness of earth, as that stormy and maniacal wind, which seemed, in fact, to be the very spirit of the joy, the sorrow, and the wild desire he felt.

That wind would rush upon them suddenly as they toiled up rocky trails, or smashed through wintry growth, or strode along the hardened, rutted roads, or came out on the lonely, treeless bareness of a mountain top. And that wind would rush upon him with its own wild life and fill him with its spirit. As he gulped it down into his aching lungs, his whole life seemed to soar, to swoop, to yell with the demonic power, flight, and invincible caprice of the wind's huge well until he no longer was nothing but a boy of fifteen, the nephew of a hardware merchant in a little town, one of the nameless little atoms of this huge, swarming earth whose most modest dream would have seemed ridiculous to older people had he dared to speak of it.

No. Under the immense intoxication of that great, demented wind, he would become instantly triumphant to all this damning and overwhelming evidence of fact, age, prospect, and position. He was a child of fifteen no longer. He was the overlord of this great earth, and he looked down from the mountain top upon his native town, a conqueror. Not from the limits of a little, wintry town, lost in remote and lonely hills from the great heart, the time-enchanted drone and distant murmur of the shining city of this earth, but from the very peak and center of this world he looked on his domains with the joy of certitude and victory, and he knew that everything on earth that he desired was his.

Saddled in power upon the wild back of that maniacal force, not less wild, willful, and all-conquering than the steed that carried him, he would hold the kingdoms of the earth in fee, inhabit the world at his caprice, swoop in the darkness over mountains, rivers, plains, and cities, look under roofs, past walls and doors, into a million rooms, and know all things at once, and lie in darkness in some lonely and forgotten place with a woman, lavish, wild, and secret as the earth. The whole earth, its fairest fame of praise, its dearest treasure of a great success, its joy of travel, all its magic of strange lands, the relish of unknown, tempting foods, its highest happiness of adventure and love—would all be his: flight, storm, wandering, the great sea and all its traffic of proud ships, and the great plantation of the earth, together with the certitude and comfort of return—fence, door, wall, and roof, the single face and dwelling-place of love.

But suddenly these wild, demonic dreams would fade, for he would hear his uncle's voice again, and see the gaunt fury of his bony figure, his blazing eye, the passionate and husky anathema of his trembling voice, as, standing there upon that mountain top and gazing down upon the little city of his youth, Mark Joyner spoke of all the things that tortured him. Sometimes it was his life with Mag, his young man's hopes of comfort, love, and quiet peace that now had come to nought but bitterness and hate. Again his mind went groping back to older, deeper-buried sorrows. And on this day as they stood there, his mind went back, and, turning now to George and to the wind that howled there in his face, he suddenly brought forth and hurled down from that mountain top the acid of an ancient rancor, denouncing now the memory of old Fate, his father. He told his hatred and his loathing of his father's life, the deathless misery of his own youth, which lived for him again in all its anguish even after fifty years had passed.

"As each one of my unhappy brothers and sisters was born," he declared in a voice so husky and tremulous with his passionate resentment that it struck terror to the boy's heart, "I cursed him—cursed the day that God had given him life! And still they came!" he whispered, eyes ablaze and furious, in a voice that almost faltered to a sob. "Year after year they came with the blind proliferation of his criminal desire—into a house where there was scarcely roof enough to shelter us—in a vile, ramshackle shamble of a place." he snarled, "where the oldest of us slept three in a bed, and where the youngest, weakest, and most helpless of us all was lucky if he had a pallet of rotten straw that he could call his own! When we awoke at morning our famished guts were aching!—*aching*!" he howled, "with the damnable gnawing itch of hunger!—My dear child, my dear, dear child!" he exclaimed, in a transition of sudden and terrifying gentleness—"May *that*, of all life's miseries, be a pang you never have to suffer!—And we lay down at night always unsatisfied—oh always! *always*! *always*!" he cried with an impatient gesture of his hand—"to struggle for repose like restless animals—crammed with distressful bread—swollen with fatback and boiled herbs out of the fields, while your honored grandfather—the *Major*! . . . The *Major*!" he now sneered, and suddenly he contorted his gaunt face in a grotesque grimace and laughed with a sneering, deliberated, forced mirth.

"Now, my boy," he went on presently in a more tranquil tone of patronizing tolerance, "you have no doubt often heard your good Aunt Maw speak with the irrational and incondite exuberance of her sex," he continued, smacking his lips together audibly with an air of relish as he pronounced these formidable words—"of that paragon of all the moral virtues—her noble sire, the *Major*!" Here he paused to laugh sneeringly again. "And perhaps, boylike, you have conceived in your imagination a picture of that distinguished gentleman that is

somewhat more romantic than the facts will stand! . . . Well, my boy,"
he went on deliberately, with the birdlike turn of his head as he looked
at the boy, "lest your fancy be seduced somewhat by illusions of aristocratic grandeur, I will tell you a few facts about that noble man. . . . He
was the self-appointed Major of a regiment of backwoods volunteers, of
whom no more be said than that they were, if possible, less literate than
he! . . . You are descended, it is true," he went on with his calm precise
deliberation, "from a warlike stock—but none of them my dear child,
were Brigadiers—no, not even Majors," he sneered, "for the highest
genuine rank I ever heard of them attaining was the rank of corporal—
and that proud dignity was the office of the Major's pious brother—I
refer, of course, my boy, to your great-uncle, Rance Joyner! . . .

"Rance! Rance!"—here he contorted his face again—"Gods! What
a name! No wonder he smote fear and trembling to the Yankee heart!
. . . The *sight* of him was certainly enough to make them stand stock-
still at the height of an attack! And the *smell* of him would surely be
enough to strike awe and wonder in the hearts of mortal men—I refer,
of course," he said sardonically, "to the average run of base humanity,
since, as you well know, neither your grandfather nor his brother, Holy
Rance, nor any other Joyner that I know," he jeered, "could be com-
pared to mortal men. We admit that much ourselves. For all of us, my
boy, were not so much conceived like other men as willed here by an
act of God, created by a visitation of the Holy Ghost, trailing clouds of
glory as we came," he sneered, "and surely you must have discovered by
this time that it is our unique privilege to act as prophets, messengers,
and agents, of the deity here on earth—to demonstrate God's ways
to man—to reveal the inmost workings of His providence and all the
mysterious secrets of the universe to other men who have not been so
sanctified by destiny as we. . . .

"But be that as it may," he went on, with one of his sudden and
astonishing changes from howling fury to tolerant and tranquil admis-
siveness. "I believe there was no question of your holy great-uncle's
valor. Yes, sir!" he continued, "I have heard them say that he could kill

at fifty or five hundred yards, and always wing his bullet with a gospel text to make it holy! . . . Why, my dear child," the boy's uncle cried, "there was as virtuous a ruffian as ever split a skull! He blew their brains out with a smile of saintly charity, and sang hosannas over them as they expired! He sanctified the act of murder, and assured them as they weltered in their blood that he had come to them as an angel of mercy bearing to them the gifts of immortal life and everlasting happiness in exchange for the vile brevity of their earthly lives, which he had taken from them with such sweet philanthropy. He shot them through the heart and promised them all the blessings of the Day of Armageddon with so soft a tongue that they fairly wept for joy and kissed the hand of their redeemer as they died! . . .

"Yes," he went on tranquilly, "there is no question of your greatuncle's valor—or his piety—but still, my boy, his station was a lowly one—he never reached a higher rank than corporal! And there were others, too, who fought well and bravely in that war—but they, too, were obscure men! Your great-uncle John, a boy of twenty-two, was killed in battle on the bloody field of Shiloh. . . . And there are many others of your kinsmen, who fought, died, bled, were wounded, perished, or survived in that great war—but none of them, my dear child, was a Major! . . . There was only one *Major*!" he bitterly remarked. "Only your noble grandsire was a *Major*!"

Thus, for a moment, in the fading light of that Winter's day, he paused there on the mountain top above the town, his gaunt face naked, lonely, turned far and lost, into the fierce wintry light of a flaming setting sun, into the lost and lonely vistas of the western ranges, among those hills which had begotten him. When he spoke again his voice was sad and quiet and calmly bitter, and somehow impregnated with that wonderful remote and haunting quality that seemed to come like sorcery from some far distance—a distance that was itself as far and lonely in its haunting spatial qualities as those fading western ranges where his face was turned.

"The Major," he quietly remarked, "my honored father—Major

Lafayette Joyner!—Major of Hominy Run and Whooping Holler, the martial overlord of Sandy Mush, the Bonaparte of Zebulon County and the Pink Beds, the crafty strategist of Frying Pan Gap, the Little Corporal of the Home Guards who conducted that great operation on the river road just four miles east of town," he sneered, "where two volleys were fired after flying hooves of two of General Sherman's horse thieves—with no result except to hasten their escape! . . . The Major!" his voice rose strangely on its note of husky passion. "That genius with the master talent who could do all things—except keep food in the cupboard for a week!" Here he closed his eyes tightly and laughed deliberately again.

"Why, my dear boy!" his uncle said, "he could discourse for hours on end most learnedly—oh! *most* learnedly!" he howled derisively, "on the beauty and perfection of the Roman Aqueducts while the very roof above us spouted water like a sieve! . . . Was it the secret of the Sphinx, the sources of the Nile, what songs the sirens sang, the exact year, month, week, day, hour, and moment of the Field of Armageddon with the Coming of the Lord upon the earth, together with all judgments, punishments, rewards, and titles he would mete to us—and particularly to his favored son, the *Major!*" sneered the boy's uncle. "Oh, I can assure you, my dear child, he knew about it all! Earth had no mysteries, the immortal and imperturbable skies of time no secrets, the buried and sunken life of the great ocean no strange terrors, nor the last remotest limits of the sidereal universe no marvels which that mighty brain did not at once discover, and would reveal to anyone who had the fortitude to listen! . . .

"Meanwhile," his uncle snarled, "we lived like dogs, rooting into the earth for esculent herbs that we might stay our hunger on, gorging ourselves on wild berries plucked from roadside hedges, finding a solitary ear of corn and hugging it to our breasts as we hurried home with it as if we had looted the golden granaries of Midas, while the *Major*—the *Major*—surrounded by the rabble-rout of all his progeny, the youngest of whom crawled and scrambled in their dirty rags about his feet while the great man sat enthroned on the celestial lights of his poetic inspiration, his great soul untainted by all this earthly misery about him, composing verses," sneered his uncle, "to the lady of his dreams. 'My lady's hair!'" he howled derisively. " 'My lady's *hair!*" And for a moment, blind with his gaunt, tortured grimace, he kicked and stamped one leg convulsively at the earth—"Oh, sublime! *Sublime!*" he howled huskily at length. "To see him there lost in poetic revery— munching the cud of inspiration and the frayed end of a pencil—his eyes turned dreamily upon the distant hills—slowly stroking his luxu- riant whiskers with the fingers of those plump white hands of which he was so justly proud!" his uncle sneered—"dressed in his fine black broadcloth suit and white boiled shirt that *she*—poor, patient, and devoted woman that she was—who never owned a store dress in her whole life—had laundered, starched, and done up for her lord and master with such loving care. . . .

"My dear child," he went on in a moment, in a voice that had become so husky, faint, and tremulous that it scarcely rose above a whisper. "My dear, dear child!" he said, "may your life never know the anguish, frenzy, and despair, the hideous mutilations of the soul, that passion of inchoate hatred, loathing, and revulsion, that I felt towards my father—my own *father!*—with which my own life was poisoned in my youth!—Oh! To see him sitting there so smug, so well-kept and complacent, so invincibly assured in his self-righteousness, with his unctuous, drawling voice of limitless self-satisfaction, his pleased laughter at his own accursed puns and jests and smart retorts, his insa- tiable delight in all that he—he *alone*—had ever seen, done, thought, felt, tasted, or believed—perched there on the mountainous summit of his own conceit—while the rest of us were starving—writing poems to his lady's hair—his lady's *hair*—while *she*, poor woman—that poor, dead, lost, and unsung martyr of a woman that I have the honor to acknowledge as my mother," he said huskily, "did the drudgery of a nigger as he sat there in his fine clothes writing verses—kept life in us somehow, those of us who managed to survive," he said bitterly, "when she had so little of her own to spare—scrubbed, sewed, mended, cooked—when there was anything at all to cook—and passively yielded to that sanctimonious lecher's insatiable and accursed lust— drudging, toiling, drudging to the very moment of our birth—until we dropped full-born out of our mother's womb even as she bent above her labors at the tub. . . . Is it any wonder that I came to hate the very sight of him—venerable whiskers, thick lips, white hands, broadcloth, unctuous voice, pleased laughter, smug satisfaction, invincible conceit, and all the tyranny of his narrow, vain, inflexible, small soul?—why, damn him," the boy's uncle whispered huskily. "I have seen the time I could have taken that fat throat and strangled it between my hands, blood, bone, body, father of my life though he might be—oh!" he howled, "damn'bly, indubitably, *was!*"

And for a moment his gaunt face burned into the western ranges, far, lost, and lonely in the red light, westering to wintry dark.

"The Major!" he muttered quietly at length. "You have heard your good Aunt Maw speak, no doubt, about the Major—of his erudition and intelligence, the sanctified infallibility of all his judgments, of his fine white hands and broadcloth clothes, the purity of his moral charac- ter, of how he never uttered a profane word, nor allowed a drop of liquor in his house—nor would have let your mother marry your father had he known that your father was a drinking man. That paragon of morals, virtues, purities, and manners—that final, faultless, and inspired judge and critic of all things!—Oh, my dear boy!" he howled faintly, with his husky and contemptuous laugh—"she is a woman—therefore governed by her sentiment; a woman—therefore blind to logic, the evidence of life, the laws of ordered reason; a woman—therefore at the bottom of her heart a Tory, the slave of custom and conformity; a woman— therefore cautious and idolatrous; a woman—therefore fearful for her nest; a woman—therefore the bitter enemy of revolt and newness, hat- ing change, the naked light of truth, the destruction of time-honored superstitions, however cruel, false, and shameful they may be. Oh! she is a woman and she does not know! . . .

THE HOUND OF DARKNESS 193

"She does not *know*!" the boy's uncle howled with his contemptuous laugh. "My dear child, I have no doubt that she has told you of
her father's wisdom, erudition, and his faultless elegance of speech.
. . . Pah-h!" he sneered. "He was a picker-up of unconsidered trifles—
a reader of miscellaneous trash—the instant dupe for every remedy,
nostrum, cure-all that any traveling quack might offer to him, and
the gullible believer of every superstitious prophesy, astrological omen,
ghost-story, augury, or portent that he heard. . . . Why, my boy," his
uncle whispered, bending towards him with an air of horrified revelation, "he was a man who used big words when he had no sense of their
real meaning—a fellow who would try to impress some backwoods
yokel with fine phrases which he didn't understand himself. Yes! I have
heard him talk so even in the presence of people of some education and
intelligence—I have seen them nudge and wink at one another over
the spectacle he was making of himself—and I confess to you I had to
turn my head away and blush for shame," his uncle whispered fiercely,
his eyes blazing, "for *shame* to think my own father could expose himself in that degrading fashion."

And for a moment he stared gauntly into the fading ranges of the
west, and was silent. When he spoke again, his voice had grown old
and weary, bitter with quiet fatality:

"Moral virtues—purity of character—piety—fine words—no
profanity—yes! I suppose my father had them all," said Uncle Mark
wearily. "No liquor in the house—yes, that was true enough—and
also it is true there was no food, no human decency, no privacy. Why,
my dear boy," he whispered suddenly, turning to the boy again with
that birdlike tilt of the head and that abrupt and startling transition
to a shamefaced intimacy of whispered revelation—"do you know that
even after I had reached the age of twenty years and we had moved to
Libya Hill, we all slept together—eight of us—in the same room where
my mother and my father slept?—And for three days!" he cried suddenly and savagely—"Oh! for three damnable, never-to-be-forgotten
days of shame and horror that left their scar upon the lives of all of

us, the body of my grandfather. Bill Joyner, lay there in the house and rotted—*rotted*!" his voice broke in a sob, and he struck his gaunt fist blindly, savagely into the air, "rotted in Summer heat until the stench of him had got into our breath, our blood, our lives, into bedding and food and clothes, into the very walls that sheltered us—and the memory of him became for us a stench of shame and horror that nothing could wash away, that filled our hearts with hatred and loathing for our blood and kind—while my father, Lafayette Joyner, and that damned, thick-lipped, drawling, sanctimonious, lecher of a nigger-Baptist prophet—your great-uncle, Holy Rance!" he snarled savagely, "sat there smugly with that stench of rotting death and man's corrupt mortality thick in their nostrils—calmly discussing, if you please, the lost art of embalming as it was practiced by the ancient Egyptians—which *they*, they alone, of course, of all men living," he snarled bitterly, "had rediscovered—and were prepared to practice on that rotting and putrescent corpse!"

Then he was silent for a moment more. His face, gaunt and passionate, which in repose, after its grotesque contortions of scorn, rage, humor and disgust, was so strangely, nobly tranquil in its lonely dignity, burned with a stern and craggy impassivity in the red, wintry glow of the late sun.

"And yet there was some strangeness in us all," he went on in a remote, quiet, husky tone that had in it the curious and haunting quality of the distance and passion which his voice could carry as no other the boy had ever heard, "something blind and wild as nature—a sense of our inevitable destiny. Oh! call it not conceit!" his uncle cried. "Conceit is such a small thing, after all! Conceit is only mountain-high, world-wide, or ocean-deep!—This thing we had in us could match its will against the universe, the rightness of its every act against the huge single voice and bitter judgment of the world, its moral judgments against God himself.—Was it murder? Why, then, the murder was not in ourselves, but in the very flesh and blood of those we murdered. Their murder rushed out of their sinful lives to beg for bloody execution at our hands. The transgressor assaulted the very blade of our knives with his offending throat. The wicked man did willfully attack the sharp point of our bayonet with his crime-calloused heart, the offender in the sight of God rushed on us, thrust his neck into our guiltless hands and fairly broke it, in spite of all that we could do! . . .

"My dear child, surely you must know by now," his uncle cried, as he turned on him with the fixed, blazing glare of his eyes, his set grimace of scorn and fury—"surely you have learned by now that a Joyner is incapable of doing wrong. Cruelty, blind indifference to everything except oneself, brutal neglect, children criminally begotten in casual gratification of one's own lust, children born unwanted and untended into a world of misery, poverty, and neglect where they must live or die or sicken or be strong according to their own means, in a struggle to survive as barbarously savage as the children of an Indian tribe endure—why, these are faults that might be counted crimes in other men, but in a Joyner are considered acts of virtue!— No, he can see the starved eyes of his children staring at him from the shadows as they go comfortless and famished to their beds, and then go out upon his porch to listen to the million little sounds of night, and meditate the glory of the moon as it comes up across the hill behind the river! He can breathe the sweet, wild fragrance of a Summer's night and dreamily compose a lyric to the moon, the lilac, and his lady's hair, while his daughter coughs her life out from the darkness of the wretched house—and find no fault or error in his life whatever! . . .

"Oh, did I not live and know it all?" his uncle cried, "that agony of life and death, blind chance, survival or extinction—till the mind went mad, man's heart and faith were broken, to see how little was the love we had, how cruel, vile, and useless was the waste!—My brother Edward died when he was four years old: there in the room with all of us he lay for a week upon his trundle bed—oh! we let him die beneath our very eyes!" his uncle cried, striking his fist into the air with a kind of agony of loss and pain—"he died beneath the very beds we slept in, for his trundle bed was pushed each night beneath the big bed where my mother and my father slept. We stood there staring at him with the eyes of dumb, bewildered, foolish oxen, while his body stiffened, his heels drew backward towards his head in the convulsions of his agony—and that damned sanctimonious, well-pleased voice drawled on and on with the conceit of its interminable assurance, 'giving it as my theory,' " snarled the boy's uncle—"though all things else were lacking in that house, there never was a dearth of theory—that unplumbed well of wisdom could give theories till you died. And Edward died, thank God, before the week was out," his uncle quietly went on. "He died suddenly one night at two o'clock while the Great Theorist snored peacefully above him—while all the rest of us were sleeping! He screamed once—such a scream as had the whole blind agony of death in it—and by the time we got a candle lighted and had pulled his little bed out on the floor, that wretched and forsaken child was dead! His body was as stiff as a poker and bent back like a bow even as the Noble Theorist lifted him—he was dead before our eyes before we knew it—dead even as that poor woman who had borne him rushed screaming out of doors like a demented creature—running, stumbling, God knows where, downhill, into the dark—the wilderness—towards the river—to seek help somehow at a neighbor's when the need for help was past. And his father was holding that dead child in his arms when she returned with that unneeded help. . . .

"Oh, my child," his uncle whispered, "if you could have seen the look on that woman's face as she came back into that room of death again—if you could have seen her look first at the child there in his arms, and then at him, and seen him shake his head at her and say, 'I knew that he was gone before you went out of the door, but I didn't have the heart to call you back and let you know'—oh! if you could have heard the sanctimonious, grief-loving unction of that voice, that feeding gluttony and triumphant vanity of sorrow that battened on his own child's life and said to me, as it had said a thousand times, more plain than any words could do: 'I! I! I! Others will die, but I remain! Death, sorrow, human agony, and loss, all the grief, error, misery, and mischance that men can suffer occurs here for the enlargement of this death-devouring, all-consuming, time-triumphant universe of *I, I, I!*'—Why, damn him," said his uncle huskily, "I had no words to nail him with a curse, no handle to take hold of my complaint—he had escaped as always like oil running through my fingers, speaking those unctuous words of piety and sorrow that none could challenge—but I hated him like hell and murder in my heart—I could have killed him where he stood!"

BUT NOW, AS the boy and his uncle stood there on the mountain top looking into the lonely vistas of the westering sun, watching its savage stripes of gold and red as it went down in the smoky loneliness and receding vistas of the great ranges of the west, the wind would fill the boy's heart with unwalled homelessness, a desire for houses, streets, and the familiar words again, a mighty longing for return.

For now black night, wild night, oncoming, secret, and mysterious night, with all its lonely wilderness of storm, demented cries, and unhoused wandering was striding towards them like an enemy. And around them on the lonely mountain top they heard the whistling of the wind in coarse, sere grasses, and from the darkening mountain side below them they could hear the remote howlings of the wind as it waged its stern, incessant warfare in the stormy branches of the bare and lonely trees.

And instantly he would see the town below now, coiling in a thousand fumes of homely smoke, now winking into a thousand points of friendly light its glorious small design, its aching, passionate assurances of walls, warmth, comfort, food, and love. It spoke to him of something deathless and invincible in the souls of men, like a small light in a most enormous dark that would not die. Then hope, hunger, longing, joy, a powerful desire to go down to the town again would fill his heart. For in the wild and stormy darkness of oncoming night there was no door, and the thought of staying there in darkness on the mountain top was not to be endured.

Then his uncle and he would go down the mountain side, taking the shortest, steepest way they knew, rushing back down to the known limits of the town, the streets, the houses, and the lights, with a sense of furious haste, hairbreadth escape, as if the great beast of the dark was prowling on their very heels. When they got back into the town, the whole place would be alive with that foggy, smoky, immanent, and strangely exciting atmosphere of early Winter evening and the smells of supper from a hundred houses. The odors of the food were brawny, strong, and flavorsome, and proper to the Winter season, the bite and hunger of the sharp, strong air. There were the smells of frying steak, and fish, and the good fat fragrance of the frying pork chops. And there were the smells of brawny liver, frying chicken, and, most pungent and well-savored smell of all, the smell of strong, coarse hamburger and the frying onions.

The grand and homely quality of this hamburger-onion smell had in it not only the deep glow and comfort of full-fed, hungry bellies, but somehow it made the boy think also of a tender, buxom, clean, desirable young wife, and of the glorious pleasures of the night, the bouts of lusty, loving dalliance when the lights were out, the whole house darkened, and the stormy and demented winds swooped down out of the hills to beat about the house with burly rushes. That image filled his heart with swelling joy, for it evoked again the glorious hope of the plain, priceless, and familiar happiness of a wedded love that might belong to any man alive—to butcher, baker, farmer, engineer, and clerk, as well as to poet, scholar, and philosopher.

It was an image of a wedded love forever hungry, healthy, faithful, clean, and sweet, never false, foul, jaded, wearied out, but forever loving, lusty in the dark midwatches of the night when storm winds beat about the house. It was at once the priceless treasure and unique possession of one man, and it was, like hamburger steak and frying onions, the plain glory and impossible delight of all humanity, which every man alive, he thought, might hope to win.

Thus the strong and homely fragrance of substantial food smells proper to the Winter evoked a thousand images of warmth, closed-in security, roaring fires, and misted windows, mellow with their cheerful light. The doors were shut, the windows were all closed, the houses were all living with that secret, golden, shut-in life of Winter, which somehow pierced the spirit of a passer-by with a wild and lonely joy, a powerful affection for man's life, which was so small a thing against the drowning horror of the night, the storm, and everlasting darkness, and yet which had the deathless fortitude to make a wall, to build a fire, to close a door.

The sight of these closed golden houses with their warmth of life awoke in him a bitter, poignant, strangely mixed emotion of exile and return, of loneliness and security, of being forever shut out from the palpable and passionate integument of life and fellowship, and of being so close to it that he could touch it with his hand, enter it by a door, possess it with a word—a word that, somehow, he could never speak, a door that, somehow, he would never open.

BOOK III

The Web and the World

When George Webber's father died, in 1916, the boy was left disconsolate. True, he had been separated from his father for eight years, but, as he said, he had always had the sense that he was there. Now, more strongly than before, he felt himself caught fast in all that web of lives and times long past but ever present in which his Joyner blood and kin enmeshed him, and some escape from it became the first necessity of his life.

Fortunately, John Webber left his son a small inheritance—enough to put the boy through college, and, with careful management, to help him get his bearings afterwards. So that Autumn, with sadness and with exultation, he bade good-bye to all his Joyner relatives and set forth on his great adventure.

And, after college, he dreamed a dream of glory in new lands, a golden future in the bright and shining city.

CHAPTER 10

Olympus in Catawba

One September day in 1916, a skinny, adolescent boy, tugging at a cheap valise, and wearing a bob-tail coat and a pair of skin-tight trousers that made up in brevity and in anatomical frankness what they lacked in length, was coming up along one of the pleasant paths that bisect the lovely campus of an old college in the middle South, pausing from time to time to look about him in a rather uncertain and bewildered manner, and doubtfully to consult a piece of paper in his hand on which some instruction had evidently been written. He had just put down his valise again, and was looking at the piece of paper for the sixth or seventh time, when someone came out of the old dormitory at the head of the campus, ran down the steps, and came striding down the path where the boy was standing. The boy looked up and gulped a little as the creature of pantheresque beauty, moving with the grace, the speed, the delicacy of a great cat, bore down swiftly on him.

At that moment the overwhelmed boy was physically incapable of speech. If his life had depended on it, he could not have produced sounds capable of human hearing or understanding; and if he had been able to, he would certainly not have had the effrontery to address them to a creature of such magnificence that he seemed to have been created on a different scale and shape for another, more Olympian, universe than any the skinny, adolescent boy had ever dreamed of. But fortunately the magnificent stranger himself now took the matter in hand. As he came up at his beautiful pacing stride, pawing the air a little, delicately, in a movement of faultless and instinctive grace, he glanced swiftly and keenly at the youth with a pair of piercing, smokily luminous grey eyes, smiled with the most heartening and engaging friendliness—a smile touched with tenderness and humor—and then, in a voice that was very soft and Southern, a little husky, but for all its agreeable and gentle warmth, vibrant with a tremendous latent vitality, said:

"Are you looking for something? Maybe I can help you."

"Y-y-yes, sir," the boy stammered in a moment, gulped again, and then, finding himself incapable of further speech, he thrust the crumpled paper towards his questioner with trembling hand.

The magnificent stranger took the paper, glanced at it swiftly with that peculiar, keen intensity of his smoky eyes, smiled instantly, and said:

"Oh. McIver. You're looking for McIver. Freshman, are you?"

"Y-yes, sir," the boy whispered.

For a moment more the magnificent young man looked keenly at the boy, his head cocked appraisingly a little to one side, a look of deepening humor and amusement in his grey eyes and in the quality of his pleasant smile. At length he laughed, frankly and openly, but with such a winning and friendly humor that even the awed youth could not be wounded by it.

"Damned if you ain't a bird!" the magnificent young man said, and stood there a moment longer, shrewdly, humorously appraising his companion, with his powerful hands arched lightly on his hips in a gesture which was unconsciously as graceful as everything he did. "Here," he said quietly, "I'll show you what to do, freshman." He placed his powerful hands on the boy's skinny shoulders, faced him around, and then, speaking gently, he said, "You see this path here?"

"Y-yes. sir."

"You see that building down there at the end of it—that building with the white columns out in front?"

"Yes, sir."

"Well," the young Olympian said quietly and slowly, "that's McIver. That's the building that you're looking for. Now," he continued very softly, "all you got to do is to pick up your valise, walk right along this path, go up those steps there, and go into the first door on your right. After that, they'll do the rest. That's where you registah." He paused a moment to let this information sink in, then, giving the boy a little shake of the shoulders, he said gently: "Now do you think you've got that straight? You think you can do what I told you to do?"

"Y-yes, sir."

"All right!" and, with the amazing speed and grace with which he did everything, the Olympian released him, cast up his fine head quickly, and laughed a deep, soft, immensely winning laugh. "All right, freshman," he said. "On your way. And don't let those sophomores sell you any radiators or dormitories until you get yourself fixed up."

And the boy, stammering awed but grateful thanks, picked up his valise hastily and started off to do the bidding of the tall Olympian. As he went down the path he heard again the low, deep, winning laugh, and, without turning his head, he knew that Olympian was standing there, following him with his piercing, smoky eyes, with his hands arched on his hips in that gesture of instinctive and unconscious grace.

Monk Webber would never be able to forget that incident. The memory of it burned in his brain as vividly as ever after more than twenty years. For he was that skinny, adolescent boy, and the Olympian, although he did not know it then, was the magnificent creature known to his earthly comrades as Jim Randolph.

YEARS LATER, MONK would still affirm that James Heyward Randolph was the handsomest man he ever saw. Jim was a creature of such power and grace that the memory of him later on was like a legend. He was, alas, a legend even then.

He was a man who had done brilliant and heroic things, and he looked the part. It seemed that he had been especially cast by nature to fulfill the most exacting requirements of the writers of romantic fiction. He was a Richard Harding Davis hero, he was the hero of a book by Robert W. Chambers, he was a Jeffery Farnol paragon, he was all the Arrow collar young men one had ever seen in pictures, all the football heroes from the covers of the *Saturday Evening Post,* he was all of these rolled into one, and he was something more than all of these. His beauty was conformed by a real manliness, his physical perfection by a natural and incomparable grace, the handsome perfection and regularity of his features by qualities of strength, intelligence, tenderness, and humor that all the heroes of romantic fiction can counterfeit but do not attain.

Jim was a classic type of the tall, young American. He was perhaps a fraction under six feet and three inches tall, and he weighed 192 pounds. He moved with a grace and power that were incomparable. Whenever one saw him walking along the street, one got an overwhelming impression that he was weaving and "picking his holes" behind the interference, and that he was just about to shake loose around the ends in a touchdown gallop. He moved by a kind of superb pacing rhythm that suggested nothing on earth so much as a race horse coming from the paddocks down to the starting line. He paced upon the balls of his feet, as lightly and delicately as a cat, and there was always the suggestion that his powerful arms and hands were delicately pawing the air, a gesture not pronounced but unmistakable, and, like his walk, his carriage, everything about him, suggested a tremendous catlike power and speed—pent, trembling, geared for action, ready to be unleashed, like the leap of a panther.

Everything about him had this fine-drawn, poised, and nervous grace of a thoroughbred animal. The predominant characteristics were leanness, grace, and speed. His head was well-shaped, rather small. He had black hair, which was closely cropped. His ears also were well-shaped and set close to the head. His eyes were grey and very deep-set, under heavy eyebrows. In moments of anger or deep feeling of any kind his eyes could darken smokily, almost into black. Ordinarily they had the luminous grey potency, the sense of tremendous latent vitality, of a cat. This well-shaped head was carried proudly upon a strong, lean neck and a pair of wide, powerful shoulders. The arms were long, lean, powerfully muscled; the hands also were large and powerful. The whole body was shaped like a wedge: the great shoulders sloped down to a narrow waist, then the figure widened out somewhat to the lean hips, then was completed with the ranging power and grace of the long legs. Jim's speech and voice also maintained and developed the impression of catlike power. His voice was rather soft and low, very Southern, a little husky, full of latent passion, tenderness, or humor, and indicative, as only a voice can be, of the tremendous pantheresque vitality of the man.

He was a member of a good South Carolina family, but his own branch of it had been impoverished. From his high school days the burden of self-support had rested on his own shoulders, and, as a result of this necessity, he had accumulated a variety of experience that few men knew in the course of a whole lifetime. It seemed that he had done everything and been everywhere. When Monk first knew him at college, he was already twenty-two or twenty-three years old, several years older than most of the students, and in experience twenty years older. The range and variety of his brief life had been remarkable. He had taught for a year or two in a country school. He had shipped for a year's cruise on a freighter out of Norfolk, had been in Rio and in Buenos Aires, had gone up and down the whole Ivory Coast of Africa, had made the round of the Mediterranean ports, had known and "had" women (he was given to this kind of boasting) "on four continents and in forty-seven states of the Union." He had peddled books in Summer through the sweltering grain states of the Middle West. He had even been a traveling salesman for a period, and in this capacity had "been in every state but one." This was Oregon, which was, of course, the state where he had failed to "have" a woman, a deficiency which seemed to trouble him no little, and which he swore that he would remedy if the good Lord spared him just a little more.

In addition to all this, he had played professional—or "semiprofessional"—baseball for a season or two in one of the mill towns of the South. His description of this episode was riotous. He had played under an assumed name in order to protect as best he could his amateur standing and his future as a college athlete. His employer had been the owner of a cotton mill. His salary had been $150 a month and traveling expenses. And for this stipend it had been his duty to go to the mill offices once a week and empty out the waste paper baskets. In addition to this, every two weeks the manager of the team would take him to a pool room, carefully place a ball exactly in front of the pocket and two inches away from it, and then bet his young first baseman $75 that he could not knock it in.

EVEN AT THE time when Monk knew him first at college, Jim had become, for the youth of two states at any rate, an almost legendary figure. The event which sealed him in their hearts, which really gave him a kind of immortality among all the people who will ever go to Pine Rock College was this:

Twenty years ago, one of the greatest sporting occasions in the South was the football game which took place annually between Pine Rock and the old college of Monroe and Madison in Virginia. They were two small colleges, but two of the oldest institutions in the South, and the game on Thanksgiving day was sanctified by almost every element of tradition and of age that could give it color. It was a good deal more than a football game, a great deal more than a contest between two powerful championship teams, for even at that time there were in the South better football teams, and games which, from the point of view of athletic prowess, were more important. But the game between Monroe and Madison and Pine Rock was like the Oxford-Cambridge race along the Thames, or like the Army-Navy game, or like the annual contest between Yale and Harvard—a kind of ceremony, a historic event whose tradition had grown through a series that had lasted even then for almost twenty years and through the associations of two old colleges whose histories were inextricably woven into the histories of their states. For this reason, not only for hundreds of students and thousands of alumni, but for hundreds of thousands of people in both states, the game upon Thanksgiving day had an interest and an importance that no other game could have.

The greatest team Pine Rock ever knew was that team they had that year, with Raby Bennett, back, Jim Randolph hinged over with his big hands resting on his knees, and Randy Shepperton crouched behind the line calling signals for the run around end. Jim could run only to the right; no one ever knew the reason why, but it was true. They always knew where he was going, but they couldn't stop him.

That was the year that Pine Rock beat Monroe and Madison for the first time in nine years. That was the year of years, the year they had been waiting for through all those years of famine, the year they had hoped for so long that they had almost ceased to hope that it would ever come, the year of wonders. And they knew when it came. They felt it in the air all Autumn. They breathed it in the smell of smoke, they felt it in the tang of frost, they heard it coming in the winds that year, they heard it coming as acorns rattled to the ground. They knew it, breathed it, talked it, hoped and feared and prayed for it. They had waited for that year through nine long seasons. And now they knew that it had come.

That was the year they really marched on Richmond. It is hard to tell about it now. It is hard to convey to anyone the passion, the exultant hope, of that invasion. They do not have it now. They fill great towns at night before the game. They go to night clubs and to bars. They dance, they get drunk, they carouse. They take their girls to games, they wear fur coats, they wear expensive clothing, they are drunk by game time. They do not really see the game, and they do not care. They hope that their machine runs better than the other machine, scores more points, wins a victory. They hope their own hired men come out ahead, but they really do not care. They don't know what it is to care. They have become too smart, too wise, too knowing, too assured, to care. They are not youthful and backwoodsy and naïve enough to care. They are too slick to care. It's hard to feel a passion just from looking at machinery. It's hard to get excited at the efforts of the hired men.

It was not that way that year. They cared a lot—so much, in fact, they could feel it in their throats, taste it in their mouths, hear it thudding in the pulses of their blood. They cared so much that they could starve and save for it, hoard their allowances, shave their expenses to the bone, do without the suit of clothes to replace the threadbare one they owned. They were poor boys, most of them. The average expenditure among them was not more than $500 a year, and two-thirds of them worked to earn the greater part of that. Most of them had come from the country, from the little country towns up in the mountains, in the Piedmont, down in the pine lands of the coast. A lot of them were hayseeds, off the farm. And the rest of them had come from little towns. There weren't any big towns. They didn't have a city in the state.

They were, in point of fact, the student body of an old, impoverished, backwoods college. And they had the finest life. It was the finest place with all its old provincialism, the bare austerity of its whitewashed dormitory rooms, its unfurnished spareness, its old brick and its campus well, its world remotion in the Piedmont uplands of an ancient state. It beat any other place "all hollow." It beat Harvard, it beat Princeton, it beat Yale. It was a better life than Cambridge or than Oxford had to offer. It was a spare life, a hard life, an impoverished kind of life, in many ways a narrow and provincial kind of life, but it was a wonderfully true and good life, too.

It was a life that always kept them true and constant to the living sources of reality, a life that did not shelter them or cloister them, that did not make snobs of them, that did not veil the stern and homely visage of the world with some romantic softening of luxury and retreat. They all knew where they had come from. They all knew where their money came from, too, because their money came so hard. They knew all about, not only their own lives, but about the lives of whole state. It is true they did not know much about any other life, but they knew that through and through. They knew what was going on around them. They knew the life of the whole village. They knew every woman, man, and child. They knew the histories and characters of each. They knew their traits, their faults, their meannesses and virtues; they were full of knowledge, humor, and observation. It was a good life. It was a spare one, and perhaps it was a narrow one, but they had what they had, they knew what they knew.

And they knew that they were going to win that year. They saved up for it. They would have made that trip to Richmond if they had had to march there. It was not hard for Monk. He got to go by the exercise of a very simple economic choice. He had the choice of getting a new overcoat or of going to Richmond, and like any sensible boy he took Richmond.

I said that he had the choice of Richmond or of a *new* overcoat. It would be more accurate to say he had the choice of Richmond or *an* overcoat. He didn't have an overcoat. The only one that he had ever had had grown green with age, had parted at the seams a year before he came to college. But he had money for a new one now, and he was going to spend that money for the trip to Richmond.

Somehow Jim Randolph heard about it—or perhaps he just guessed it or inferred it. The team was going up two nights before the game. The rest of them were coming up next day. They had a bonfire and a rousing rally just before the team went off, and after it was over Jim took Monk in his room and handed him his own sweater.

"Put this on," he said.

Monk put it on.

Jim stood there in the old, bare dormitory room, his strong hands arched and poised upon his hips, and watched him while he did it.

"Now put on your coat," he said.

Monk put his coat on over it.

Jim looked at him a moment, then burst out in a laugh.

"God almighty!" he cried. "You're a bird!"

And a bird he was! The big sweater engulfed him, swallowed him like an enormous blanket: the sleeves came out a good four inches longer than the sleeves of his own coat, the sweater hit him midway between his buttocks and his knees and projected shockingly below the coat. It was not a good fit but it was a warm one, and Jim, after looking at him again and slowly shaking his head with the remark, "Damned if you aren't a bird!" seized his valise and put on his hat. (He wore a black or grey felt hat with a wide brim, not quite the slouch hat of a Southern politician, for Jim was always neat and digni-fied in dress, but a hat that, like all his other garments, contributed to his appearance a manlike strength and maturity.) Then, turning to the boy, he said sternly:

"All right, freshman. You wear that sweater when you go to Rich-mond. If I catch you up there running around in the cold with that little shavetail coat of yours, I'll beat yo' —— till you can't sit down." And suddenly he laughed, a quiet, husky, tender, and immensely win-ning laugh. "Good-bye, son," he said. He put his big hand on Monk's shoulder. "Go ahead and wear the sweater. Don't mind how it looks. You keep warm. I'll see you after the game." Then he was gone.

Wear it! From that time on Monk lived in it. He clung to it, he cherished it, he would have fought and bled and died for it as a vet-eran in Lee's army would have fought for his commander's battle flag. It was not only Jim's sweater. It was Jim's sweater initialed with the great white "P R" that had been won and consecrated upon the field of many a glorious victory. It was not only Jim's sweater. It was Jim's *great* sweater, the most famous sweater in the whole school—it seemed to Monk, the most famous sweater on earth. If the royal ermine of His Majesty the King-Emperor of Great Britain and India had been suddenly thrown around his shoulders, he could not have been more powerfully impressed by the honor of his investiture.

And everyone else felt the same way. All the freshmen did, at any rate. There was not a boy among them who would not have cheerfully

and instantly torn off his overcoat and thrust it at Monk if he thought
Monk would have swapped the sweater with him.

And that was the way he went to Richmond.

BUT HOW TO tell the wonder and glory of that trip? George Webber
has been wide and far since then. He has pounded North and South
and East and West across the continent on the crack trains of the nation. He has lain on his elbow in the darkness in his berth, time and
again, and watched the haunted and the ghost-wan visage of Virginia
stroke by in the passages of night. So, too, he has crossed the desert,
climbed through the Sierras in the radiance of blazing moons, has
crossed the stormy seas a dozen times and more and known the racing
slant and power of great liners, has pounded down to Paris from the
Belgian frontiers at blind velocities of speed in the rocketing trains, has
seen the great sweep and curve of lights along the borders of the Mediterranean on the coasts of Italy, has known the old, time-haunted, elfin
magic of the forests of Germany, in darkness also. He has gone these
ways, has seen these things and known these dark wonders, but no voyage he ever made, whether by nighttime or by day, had the thrill, the
wonder, and the ecstasy of that trip when they went up to Richmond
twenty years ago.

The bonfire and the leaping flames, the students cheering, weaving, dancing, the red glow upon the old red brick, the ivy sere and
withered by November, the wild, young faces of eight hundred boys,
the old bell tolling in the tower. And then the train. It was a desolate
little train. It seemed to be a relic of the lost Confederacy. The little,
wheezing engine had a fan-shaped funnel. The old wooden coaches
were encrusted with the cinders and the grime of forty years. Half of
the old red seats of smelly plush were broken down. They jammed into
it till the coaches bulged. They hung onto the platforms, they jammed
the aisles, they crawled up on the tender, they covered the whole grimy
caravan like a swarm of locusts. And finally the old bell tolled mournfully, the whistle shrieked, and, to the accompaniment of their lusty

cheers, the old engine jerked, the rusty couplings clanked and jolted—they were on their way.

Flashing away to the main line junction, fourteen miles away, the engine was derailed, but that did not faze them. They clambered out and swarmed around it, and by main strength and enthusiasm they helped the ancient engineer to crowbar, jack, and coax and lift her back onto the rusty track. They got there finally to the junction and found the train that had been chartered for them waiting. Ten dusty, grimy coaches of the Seaboard Air Line waited for them. They clambered in, found places if they could. Ten minutes later they were on the way to Richmond. All through the night they pounded up out of the South, across Virginia, and they came to Richmond with the first grey light of dawn.

George Webber has been to that old town a good many times since then, but never as he came there first, out of the South by darkness, out of the South with the unuttered hope, the unspoken wildness, the fever of the impossible unknown joy, burning, burning, burning through the night. They got to Richmond just at break of day. They swarmed out cheering. They swarmed out into the long-deserted stretch of Gay Street. And then they started out, the whole noisy, swarming horde of them, up that deserted street, past all the darkened stores and shops, mounting the hill, up to the capitol. The dome of the old capitol was being tinged with the first rays of morning light as they came up. The air was sharp and frosty. The trees in the park around the capitol and the hill had the thrilling, clean austerity of morning, of first light, of frost, and of November.

It was a thrilling experience, for many of them a completely new experience, the experience of seeing a great city—for to most of them old Richmond seemed to be a great city—waking into life, to the beginning of another day. They saw the early street cars rattle past and clatter over switch points with a wonder and a joy that no one who looked at street cars ever felt before. If they had been the first street cars in the world, if they had been thrilling and enchanted vehicles newly brought from Mars, or from the highways of the moon, they could not have seemed more wonderful to them. Their paint was brighter than all other paint, the brilliance of their light was far more brilliant, the people in them reading morning papers, stranger, more exciting, than any people they had ever seen.

They felt in touch with wonder and with life, they felt in touch with magic and with history. They saw the state house and they heard the guns. They knew that Grant was pounding at the gates of Richmond. They knew that Lee was digging in some twenty miles away at Petersburg. They knew that Lincoln had come down from Washington and was waiting for the news at City Point. They knew that Jubal Early was swinging in his saddle at the suburbs of Washington. They felt, they knew, they had their living hands and hearts upon the living presence of these things, and upon a thousand other things as well. They knew that they were at the very gateways of the fabulous and unknown North, that great trains were here to do their bidding, that they could rocket in an hour or two into the citadels of gigantic cities. They felt the pulse of sleep, the heartbeats of the sleeping men, the drowsy somnolence and the silken stir of luxury and wealth of lovely women. They felt the power, the presence, and the immanence of all holy and enchanted things, of all joy, all loveliness, and all the beauty and the wonder that the world could offer. They knew, somehow, they had their hands upon it. The triumph of some impending and glorious fulfillment, some impossible possession, some incredible achievement was thrillingly imminent. They knew that it was going to happen—soon. And yet they could not say how or why they knew it.

They swarmed into the lunchrooms and the restaurants along Broad Street; the richer of them sought the luxury of great hotels. They devoured enormous breakfasts, smoking stacks of wheat cakes, rations of ham and eggs, cup after cup of pungent, scalding coffee. They gorged themselves, they smoked, they read the papers. The humblest lunchroom seemed to them a paradise of gourmets.

Full morning came, and clean, cold light fell slant-wise on the street with golden sharpness. Everything in the world seemed impossibly good and happy, and all of it, they felt, was theirs. It seemed that everyone in Richmond had a smile for them. It seemed that all the people had been waiting for them through the night, had been preparing for them, were eager to give them the warmest welcome of affectionate hospitality. It seemed not only that they expected Pine Rock's victory, but that they desired it. All of the girls, it seemed to them, were lovely, and all of them, they felt, looked fondly at them. All of the people of the town, they thought, had opened wide their hearts and homes to them. They saw a banner with their colors, and it seemed to them that the whole town was festooned in welcome to them. The hotels swarmed with them. The negro bellboys grinned and hopped to do their bidding. The clerks who waited smiled on them. They could have everything they wanted. The whole town was theirs. Or so they thought.

The morning passed. At one-thirty they went out to the playing field. And they won the game. As Monk remembered it, it was a dull game. It was not very interesting except for the essential fact that they won it. They had expected too much. As so often happens when so much passion, fervor, hot imagination has gone into the building of a dream, the consummation was a disappointment. They had expected to win by a big score. They were really much the better team, but all their years of failure had placed before them a tremendous psychical impediment. They won the game by a single touchdown. The score was 6 to 0. They even failed to kick goal after touchdown. It was the first time during the course of the entire season that Randy's toe had failed him.

But it was better that the game ended as it did. It was Jim's game. There was no doubt of that. It was completely and perfectly his own. Midway in the third quarter he did exactly what he was expected to do. Pacing out to the right, behind the interference, weaving and pawing delicately at the air, he found his opening and shook loose, around the end, for a run of 57 yards to a touchdown. They scored six points, and all of them were Jim's.

Later, the whole thing attained the clean, spare symmetry of a legend. They forgot all other details of the game entirely. The essential fact, the fact that would remain, the picture that would be most vivid, was that it was Jim's game. No game that was ever played achieved a more classical and perfect unity for the projection of its great protagonist. It was even better that he scored just that one touchdown, made just that one run. If he had done more, it would have spoiled the unity and intensity of their later image. As it was, it was perfect. Their hero did precisely what they expected him to do. He did it in his own way, by the exercise of his own faultless and incomparable style, and later on that was all they could remember. The game became nothing. All they saw was Jim, pacing and weaving out around right end, his right hand pawing delicately at the air, the ball hollowed in the crook of his long left arm, and then cutting loose on his race-horse gallop.

That was the apex of Jim Randolph's life, the summit of his fame. Nothing that he could do after that could dim the perfect glory of that shining moment. Nothing could ever equal it. It was a triumph and a tragedy, but at that moment Jim, poor Jim, could only know the triumph of it.

NEXT YEAR THE nation went to war in April. Before the first of May, Jim Randolph had gone to Oglethorpe. He came back to see them once or twice while he was in training. He came back once again when school took up in Autumn, a week or two before he went to France. He was a first lieutenant now. He was the finest-looking man in uniform George Webber ever saw. They took one look at him and they knew the war was won. He went overseas before Thanksgiving; before the New Year he was at the front.

Jim did just what they knew he would do. He was in the fighting around Château-Thierry. He was made a Captain after that. He was almost killed in the battle of the Argonne Wood They heard once that he was missing. They heard later that he was dead. They heard finally that he had been seriously wounded and his chances for recovery were slight, and that if he did recover he would never be the same man again. He was in a hospital at Tours for almost a year. Later on, he was in a hospital at Newport News for several months. They did not see him again, in fact, till the Spring of 1920.

He came back then, handsome as ever, magnificent in his Captain's bars and uniform, walking with a cane, but looking as he always did. Nevertheless he was a very sick man. He had been wounded near the spine. He wore a leather corset. He improved, however; was even able to play a little basketball. The name and fame of him was as great as ever.

And yet, indefinably, they knew that there was something lacking, something had gone by; they had lost something, something priceless, precious, irrecoverable. And when they looked at Jim, their look was somehow touched with sadness and regret. It would have been better for him had he died in France. He had suffered the sad fate of men who live to see themselves become a legend. And now the legend lived. The man was just a ghost to them.

Jim was probably a member of what the intellectuals since have called "the lost generation." But Jim really was not destroyed by war. He was ended by it. Jim was really not a member of the generation that was lost, but of a generation that was belated. Jim's life had begun and had been lived before the war, and it was ended with the war. At the age of twenty-six or twenty-seven, Jim was out of date. He had lived too long. He belonged to another time. They all knew it, too, although none of them could speak about it then.

The truth is that the war formed a spiritual frontier in the lives of all the students at Pine Rock in Webber's day. It cut straight across the face of time and history, a dividing line that was as clear and certain as a wall. The life they had before the war was not the life that they were going to have after the war. The way they felt and thought and be-lieved about things before the war was different from the way they felt and thought and believed after the war. The America that they knew before the war, the vision of America that they had before the war, was so different from the America and the vision of America they had after the war. It was all so strange, so sad, and so confusing.

It all began so hopefully. Monk can still remember the boys stripping for the doctors in the old gymnasium. He can remember those young winds that echoed the first coming of the blade and leaf, and all his comrades jubilantly going to war. He can remember the boys coming from the dormitories with their valises in their hands, Jim Randolph coming down the steps of South, and across the campus towards him, and his cheerful:

"So long, kid. You'll get in too. I'll be seeing you in France."

He can remember how they came back from the training camps, spotless, new-commissioned shavetails, proud and handsome with their silver bars and well-cut uniforms. He can remember all of it—the fire, the fever, the devotion and the loyalty, the joy of it, the pride of it, the jubilation and the thrill of it. The wild excitement when they knew that we were winning. The excitement—and the sorrow—when we won.

Yes, the sorrow. Does anyone really think that they were glad? Does anyone think they wanted the war to end? He is mistaken. They loved the war, they hung on to it, and they cherished it. They said the things with lips that lips were meant to say, but in their hearts they prayed:

"Dear God, please let the war continue. Don't let the war be over until we younger ones get in."

They can deny it now. Let them deny it if they like. This is the truth.

Monk can still remember how the news came that the war was over. He can remember swinging on the rope as the great bell itself began to ring. He can still feel the great pull of the rope and how it lifted him clear off the ground, and how the rope went slanting in its hole, and how the great bell swung and tolled the news there in the darkness far above him, and how all of the boys were running out of doors upon the campus, and how the tears rolled down his face.

Monk was not the only one who wept that night. Later on they may have said they wept for joy, but this is not the truth. They wept because they were so sorrowful. They wept because the war was over, and because they knew that we had won, and because every victory of this sort brings so much sorrow with it. And they wept because they knew that something in the world had ended, that something else had in the world begun. They wept because they knew that something in their lives had gone forever, that something else was coming in their lives, and that their lives would never be the same again.

CHAPTER II

The Priestly One

Gerald Alsop, at the time Monk came to college, had become a kind of Mother Machree of the campus, the brood hen of yearling innocents, the guide and mentor of a whole flock of fledgeling lives.

At first sight he looked enormous. A youth of nineteen or twenty at this time, he weighed close to three hundred pounds. But when one really observed him closely, one saw that this enormous weight was carried on a very small frame. In height he could not have been more than five feet six or seven. His feet, for a person of his bulk, were amazingly small, and his hands, had it not been for their soft padding, were almost the tiny hands of a child. His belly, of course, was enormous. His great fat throat went right back in fold after fold of double chins. When he laughed, his laugh came from him in a high, choking, explosive scream that set the throat and the enormous belly into jellied tremors.

He had a very rich, a very instant sense of humor, and this humor, with the high, choking laugh and the great, shaking belly, had given him among many students a reputation for hearty good nature. But more observant people would find out that this impression of hearty and whole-souled good nature was not wholly true. If Gerald's antagonism and prejudice were aroused, he could still scream with his great fat whah-whah of choking laughter, but this time the laugh had something else in it, for the great belly that shook with such convulsive mirth was also soured with bile. It was a strange and curiously mixed and twisted personality, a character that had much that was good, much that was high and fine, much that was warm, affectionate, and even generous in it, but also much that was vindictive and unforgiving, prejudiced and sentimental. It was, in the end, a character that had too much of the feminine in it to be wholly masculine, and this perhaps was its essential defect.

Pine Rock—the small Baptist college of red brick, in its setiting of Catawba clay and pine—had released him. In this new and somewhat freer world, he had expanded rapidly. His quick mind and his ready wit, his great scream of belly laughter, and something comfortable about him that made him very easy company, also made him a considerable favorite. He came to college in the fall of 1914. Two years later, when Monk joined him there, he was a junior, and well-founded: the ruling member, as it were, of a coterie; the director of a clique; already priestly, paternal, and all-fatherly, the father-confessor to a group of younger boys, most of them freshmen, that he herded under his protective wing, who came to him, as just recently they must have come to mother's knee, to pour out on his receiving breast the burden of their woe.

Jerry—for so he was called—loved confession. It was, and would remain, the greatest single stimulus of his life. And in a way, it was the perfect role for him: nature had framed him for the receiving part. He was always fond of saying afterward that it was not until his second year at college that he really "found" himself; strictly measured, that process of finding was almost wholly included in the process of being confessed to. He was like a kind of enormous, never sated, never saturated sponge. The more he got, the more he wanted. His whole manner, figure, personality, under the inner impulsion of this need, took on a kind of receptive urgency. By his twentieth year he was a master in the art of leading on. The broad brow, the jowled face, the fat hand holding a moist cigarette, the great head occasionally turned to take a long, luxurious drag, the eyes behind their polished frames of glass a little misty, the mouth imprinted faintly by a little smile that can only be described as tender, a little whimsical, as who should say, "Ah, life. Life. How bad and mad and sad it is, but then, ah, me, how sweet!"—it was all so irresistible that the freshmen simply ran bleating to the fold. There was nothing of which they did not unbosom themselves, and if, as often happened, they had nothing in particular to unbosom themselves of, they invented something. In this process of spiritual evacuation, it is to be feared the temptations of carnal vice came first.

It was, in fact, simply astounding how many of Jerry's freshmen had been sorely tempted by beautiful but depraved women—if the siren was mysterious and unknown, all the better. In one variant of the story, the innocent had been on his way to college, and had stopped over for the night at a hotel in a neighboring town. On his way to his room, a door along the corridor was opened: before him stood a beautiful specimen of the female sex, without a stitch of clothing on, inviting him with sweet smiles and honeyed words into her nest of silken skin. For a moment the freshman was shaken, his senses reeled, all that he had learned, all he had been taught to respect and keep holy, whirled around him in a dizzy rout: before he realized what he was doing, he found himself inside the accursed den of wickedness, half-fainting in the embraces of this modern whore of Babylon.

And then—then—he saw the image of his mother's face, or the features of the pure, sweet girl for whom he was "keeping himself." The freshmen of Pine Rock were usually in a careful state of refrigeration— nearly all of them were "keeping themselves" for a whole regiment of pure, sweet girls, to whose virginity they would someday add the accolade of their own penil sanctification. At any rate, during Jerry's regime at Pine Rock the number of lovely but depraved females who were cruising around through the hotel corridors of the state in a condition of original sin and utter nakedness was really astonishing. The census figures for this type of temptation were never before, or after, so high.

The usual end was well, however: the redemptive physiognomies of the Mother or the Chosen Girl usually intervened fortuitously at the fifty-ninth minute of the eleventh hour—and all was saved. As for Jerry, his final benediction to this triumph of virtue was simply beautiful to watch and hear:

"I knew you would! Yes, suh!" Here he would shake his head and chuckle tenderly. "You're too fine a pusson evah to be taken in by anything like that! . . . And if you had, think how you'd feel now! You wouldn't be able to hold yoah haid up and look me in the eye! You know you wouldn't! And every time you thought of your Mothah"— (it is impossible to convey within the comparatively simple vocabulary of the English language just quite what Jerry managed to put into that one word "Mothah"; however, it can be said without exaggeration that it represented the final and masterly conquest of the vocal chords, beside which such efforts, say, as those of the late Senor Caruso striking the high C seem fairly paltry by comparison)—"Every time you thought of your Mothah,— you'd have felt lowah than a snake's belly. Yes, suh! You know you would! And if you'd gone ahead and married that girl—" he pronounced it "gul," with a vocal unction only slightly inferior to this pronunciation of the sainted name of "Mothah"— "you'd have felt like a louse every time you'd look at her! Yes, suh, you'd have been livin' a lie that would have wrecked yoah whole life! . . . Besides that, boy . . . you look a-heah, you scannel! You don't know how lucky you are! You keep away hereafter from that stuff! Yes, suh! I know what I'm talkin' about!" Here he shook his big jowled head again, and laughed with a kind of foreboding ominousness. "You might have gone and got yourself all ruined for life!"

He was preparing himself eventually, he thought, although he later gave up the idea, for the practice of medicine, in which he had already done considerable isolated reading of his own; the chief effects of which, apparently, were now to warn guileless freshmen of the awful consequences of carnal indulgence. He fairly reveled in this form of grisly description. His descriptions of disease, death, and madness which resulted from stray encounters with unknown females in the

corridors of hotels were so graphic and compelling that he had the h
standing up on their young pates "like quills upon the fretful porp
tine."

In Gerald's picture of things as they were, there was no escape,
pardon for the erring. The wages of sin were not only always and i
evitably death, but the wages of seduction were inevitably fatherhoo
man's guilty doom, and the utter ruination of another "pure, swe
girl."

Thus, early, Gerald had formed a picture of the world that w;
pontifical in its absolute and unquestioning acceptance of all forms (
established and respectable authority—not only as they affected man
civic and political conduct, but as they affected his inner and person;
life as well. In this scheme of things—call it rather, this mythology—
the saintly figure of The Mother was supreme. A female, by virtue (
the fact that in the process of lawful matrimony she had created prog
eny, became, in some divinely mysterious way, not only the author o
all wisdom, but the spotless custodian of all morality as well. To hav
suggested that a woman was not necessarily an incorruptible divinit;
because she had given birth to a child was a dangerous heresy; to hav
argued this point doggedly to more far-reaching conclusions would
have branded one in Jerry's sight as a dissolute or irresponsible membe
of society. From that time on, Jerry's hand and his heart would be se
stubbornly against the infidel.

True, his enmity would be devious. Openly, for Jerry really had
a good mind, which was clear enough to see, but not brave enough
to confess the falsehood of his sentiment, he would be tolerant—hi
tolerance consisting of a form of benevolent I-see-your-point-but
then-let's-try-to-look-at-all-sides-of-the-question attitude, which wa
really more intolerant than any form of open bigotry could hav
been, because it masked the unyielding and unforgiving hostility o
his wounded sentimentality. But hiddenly and deviously, his enmit;
would be bitter and unpardoning from that time on. It would tak
the form of sly gossip, rumor, whispering, swift mockery maske

behind a play of innocence, a sudden twist upon a word, a quick, apparently guileless, misinterpretation of a meaning, the pontifical face schooled in grave and even respectful attentiveness, the whole ending suddenly with the explosion of mirth, the high, choking scream of laughter, which, as anyone who had been its victim could testify, was more devastating and unanswerable than any logic of cold argument could be.

He was a creature who, first and foremost, above all other things, hated trouble and abhorred pain—as what decent man does not?—except that here, in this great belly of a man, his hatred and abhorrence were so great that he would never face the things he hated. Thus, from an early age, he had learned to wear rose-colored blinders against life, and it was only natural that his own stubborn and unyielding hostility should be turned against anything—any person, any conflict, any situation, any evidence, or any idea—that would tend to take those blinders off.

In spite of this, in so many rich and wonderful ways Gerald Alsop was an extraordinary man. The thing that was most attractive about him was his genuine and warm humanity. In the most true sense of the word, he was a man who loved "the good things of life"—good food, good conversation, good humor, good fellowship, good books, the whole sound and happy aura of good living. His fault was, he loved them so well that he was unwilling to admit or accept the presence of any conflict that might disturb his own enjoyment of them. He was probably wise enough to see, but too sentimental to admit, that his enjoyment of them would have been enriched immeasurably by his recognition of the elements of conflict and denial, even where "the good things of life" were concerned.

Hence, there was no single virtue of his nature—and his nature was with virtue generously endowed—that was not in the end touched with this taint. He had, for example, a genuine and deep appreciation of good writing, a love of literature, an excellent and discriminating taste; but where his judgment warred with sentiment, his judgment

came off second best. The result was chaos. He not only could see no merit in the work of the great Russian writers—Tolstoy, Dostoevski, Turgenev, even Chekhov—he had never even made an effort to understand them. In some strange way, his heart was set against them; he was afraid of them. He had long ago conceived the prejudice that a Russian writer stood for unbroken gloom, grim tragedy, what gradually he began to rationalize in a phrase that he called "the morbid and distorted view of life," in contradistinction to the works of those writers of whom he approved, and who, correspondingly of course, represented "the more wholesome and well-rounded point of view."

Of this latter kind, Dickens probably stood first and highest in his affections. His knowledge of the works of Charles Dickens was almost encyclopædic. He had read them all so many times, and with such devotion, that there was scarcely an obscure character in that whole crowded and amazing gallery with which he was not instantly familiar—which he could not instantly tag with the word, quote with the exact and descriptive phrase, with which Dickens himself had tagged him.

But, here again, the nature of Alsop's fault was evident. Equipped with the intelligence, the knowledge, and the taste to form a true and accurate judgment of the work of a great writer, his sentiment had nevertheless contrived to create a completely false and spurious Dickens, a Dickens world that never was. Dickens himself, in Gerald's view, was a kind of enormous super-Mr. Pickwick; and the world he had created in his books was a Pickwickian world—a jovial world, a ruddy, humorous, jolly, inn-and-tavern sort of world, full of good food and musty ale, full of sunlight and good cheer, of fellowship and love and friendship, of wonderful humorous characters, and of pleasing, somewhat misty sentiment—a total picture that Gerald had now framed in the descriptive phrase, "the more wholesome and well-rounded view of life." It was a world very much like that depicted in those jolly Christmas cards one sees so often: shining stage coaches loaded with red-cheeked passengers, bundled in red scarves, dashing up before the

gabled entrance of a cheerful inn, mine host with pip
them, and hollied sprigs above the postern doors.

Of the other Dickens—the greater Dickens
had seen so much sin and poverty and misery and op
been moved to deep compassion for the suffering am
and who had been roused to powerful indignation
injustice in the life he knew—Gerald knew almost
did know, he had refused to see it as it was, had close
it, because it was unpleasant and distasteful to him,
not fit in with his own rosy vision of "the more wh
rounded view of things."

The result was chaos. It might be likened, rathe
truth swimming around in a sea of molasses. Alsop
in discussing and estimating the prodigious beaut
of Shelley, Shakespeare, Chaucer, and Kit Marlowe
grow lyrical and ecstatic in the same way and to t
estimating the prodigious beauties of Winnie the
quis, F.P.A., last night's moving picture show, and t
Lamb-kins of a man named Morley:

"Sure damn genius—yes, suh!—sheer, damn
genius!" Here, he would read some treasured bit, c
upward until light shimmered on the glasspoints
and, with a laugh that was half-sob, and all compact
treacle of his own self-appeasement, he would cry
God—it's sure damn elfin genius!"

Even in these early days of his apprenticeship
begun to accumulate a library. And that library was
ture of his mind and taste, a symbol of his inner ch
the soothing and combining solvent of his own syru

It contained a large number of good books—bo
others of which one had heard and would like to re
been preserved and saved with the intelligence of
discriminating taste. Alsop was a voracious reader

bookshelves even at that Baptist college showed selective power, and an eager curiosity into the best of the new work that was being produced. It was astonishing in a man so young, and in such a place.

But his library also included a world of trash: towering stacks of newspapers, containing morsels of choice taffy that had appealed to him; great piles of magazines, containing pieces of whimsey or of sentiment that were preserved in the mothering fullness of his bosom; hundreds of newspaper clippings, embalming some sentiment that was particularly dear to him; as well as many other things which were really valuable and good, and showed a welter of bewildering contradictions—a good mind and a keen and penetrating sense of judgment swimming around upon a sea of slop.

Brought down to simple fact, "the more wholesome and well-rounded view of things" resolved itself into an utter acceptance of things as they were, because things as they were, no matter how ugly, wasteful, cruel, or unjust, were "life"—hence, inevitable, once one understood them "in their full perspective" and saw "how essentially fine and sweet" (a phrase that did him valiant service) "life" was.

THUS JERRY ALSOP became the devoted champion of the conventions, the accepted and established scheme of things. If a picture could have been made of his mind during the war and post-war years, it would have revealed the following record of faith and of belief:

The President of the United States, Woodrow Wilson, was not only "the greatest man since Jesus Christ," but his career and final martyrdom—for so did Alsop speak of it—were also closely comparable to the career and martyrdom of Christ. The President had been the perfect man, pure in conduct, irreproachable in wisdom, and faultless in his management of affairs. He had been deceived, tricked, and done to death by villains—by unscrupulous and contriving politicians in his own land, jealous of his fame, and by the unprincipled charlatans of diplomacy in others.

"The second greatest man since Jesus Christ" was the president of

the college, a tall, pale man with a pure and suffering face, who got
up in Chapel and agonized over his boys, making frequent use of such
words as "service," "democracy," and "ideals of leadership"—all popular evidences of enlightened—nay, inspired!—thought, in the jargon of
the time. What it all meant, reduced to concrete terms of conduct, was
a little puzzling. "Character," "education for the good life," seemed to
boil down in practice to a non-drinking, non-smoking, non-gambling,
non-card-playing, non-fornicating state of single blessedness, leading
up eventually to "the life of service and of leadership for which Pine
Rock prepares a man"—namely, the eventual sacrament of matrimony
with a spotless female, variously referred to in the lexicon of idealism as
"a fine woman," or "a pure, sweet girl."

"An intelligent and liberal interest in the affairs of government and
politics" seemed to mean supporting the Democratic or Republican
tickets and voting for the candidates which the political machines that
dominated these two parties put up at election time.

"A serious and enlightened attitude towards religion" did not mean
hide-bound fundamentalism, for Pine Rock under its idealistic president prided itself on the liberalism of its thought. God, for example,
might be understood as "a great idea," or "an ocean of consciousness,"
instead of the usual old gentleman with the long beard—but one went
to church on Sunday just the same.

In fact, in spite of all this high-sounding talk about "service,"
"ideals of leadership," and "democracy," one could not see that it
made much actual difference in the way things were. Children still
worked fourteen hours a day in the cotton mills of the state. Tens of
thousands of men and women and children were born, suffered, lived,
and died in damnable poverty, bondage, and the exploitation of the
tenant farm. One million black inhabitants of the state, about a third
of the entire population, were still denied the rights of free suffrage—
even though "the second greatest man since Jesus Christ" frequently
declared that that right was one of the proudest triumphs of Anglo-
Saxon law, and of the nation's own great Constitution. One million

black inhabitants of the state were denied the right to the blessings of the higher education—although "the second greatest man since Jesus Christ" often declared that it was for this ideal that Pine Rock College lived and had its being, and that the right of education would be denied to no fit person at old Pine Rock, "regardless of creed, color, race, or other distinction of any kind whatsoever." In spite of the sounding phrases, the idealism, the martyred look, the inspired assurances, and all the rest of it, life went on according to the old formula, and in the old way, pretty much as it had always done. Class after class of pure young idealists marched forth from Pine Rock bearing the torch, prepared to bare their breasts and to die nobly, if necessary, at the barricades, no matter what sinister influences menaced them, or what overwhelming forces outnumbered them—in defense of monogamy, matrimony, pure sweet women, children, the Baptist Church, the Constitution, and the splendid ideals of the Democratic and Republican parties; aye, resolved furthermore, if they were challenged, so great was this, their devotion to the right, to die there at the barricades in the defense of the splendid institution of child labor, cotton mills, tenant farmers, poverty, misery, squalor, damnation, death, and all the rest of it—rather than recant for a moment, be recreant for a single second to the pure ideals that had been fostered in them, the shining star of conduct to which their youthful gaze had been directed by "the second greatest man since Jesus Christ."

And in the idolatry of this reverence, Gerald Alsop, like his distinguished predecessor, Adhem, led all the rest.

"THE THIRD GREATEST man since Jesus Christ" was a clergyman, pastor of the Pine Rock Episcopal Church, affectionately known to the boys as "Preacher" Reed. It was a name he had encouraged them to use himself. In a way, Jerry Alsop always looked upon Preacher as one of his own private discoveries. He certainly regarded him as another proof of his own liberalism, for Pine Rock was admittedly and professionally Baptist in its sympathies, but Jerry had been big enough to leap across the wall of orthodoxy and to fold the new Messiah to his breast.

Not that Preacher would not have done very nicely for himself had he been left solely to his own devices. For his own devices were unusual ones. To the boys they seemed at first amazing, then sensational, finally enchanting—until there was hardly a student in the college who had not enthusiastically succumbed to them.

At the outset, one would have said that the odds were a thousand to one against Preacher's getting anywhere. He was in Episcopalian—no one seemed to know quite what that was, but it sounded risky. He had just a little church, and almost no congregation. In addition to this, he was "a Northern man." The situation looked hopeless, and yet before six months were out Preacher had the whole campus eating from his hand, and black looks and angry mutterings from every other preacher in the town.

No one knew exactly how he did it; he went about it all so quietly that the thing was done before they knew that it was done. But probably the greatest asset that he had was that from the very beginning no one thought of him as a preacher. And the proof of this was that they called him one. They would not have dared to take such liberties with any other clergyman in town. Besides this, Preacher didn't preach to them; he didn't sermonize in hour-long harangues; he didn't pray for them in twenty-minute invocations; he did not thunder at them from the pulpit, nor did he work all the stops upon his ministerial vocal chords: he did not coo like a dove, roar like a lion, or bleat like a lamb. He had a trick worth six or eight of these.

He began to drop in to see the boys in their rooms. There was something so casual and so friendly in his visits that he put everyone at ease at once. In the most pleasant way he managed to convey to them that he was one of them. He was a well-conditioned man of fifty years, with sandy hair, and a lean face that had great dignity, but also a quality that was very friendly and attractive. In addition to this, he dressed in rather casual-looking clothes—rough, shaggy tweeds, grey flannel trousers, thick-soled shoes—all somewhat worn-looking, but

THE WEB AND THE WORLD   233

making the boys wish vaguely that they knew where he got them, and
wonder if they could get some like them. He would come by and sing
out cheerfully:

"Working? I'll not stay if you are. I was just passing by."

At this, there would be an instant scraping of chairs, the scramble
of feet, and a chorus of voices assuring him most earnestly that no one
was working, and would he please sit down.

Upon receiving these assurances, he would sit down, tossing his
hat as he did so upon the top tier of the double-decker cot, tilt back
comfortably against the wall in an old creaking chair, one foot hinged
on the bottom round, and produce his pipe—a blackened old briar
that seemed to have been seasoned in the forge of Vulcan—load it with
fragrant tobacco from an oil-skin pouch, strike a match, and begin to
puff contentedly, speaking in between the puffs:

"Now   I—I—like—a   pipe!"—puff,   puff—"You—younger—
blades"—puff,   puff—"can—have—your—cigarettes"—puff,   puff,
puff—"but as for me"—he puffed vigorously for a moment—"there's—
nothing—that—can—give—me"—puff, puff puff—"quite the comfort—of this—old—briar—pipe!"

Oh, the gusto of it! The appeasement of it! The deep, fragrant,
pungent, and soul-filling contentment of it! Could anyone think that
such a man as this would fail? Or doubt that within a week half the
boys would be smoking pipes?

So Preacher would have got along anyway without Jerry Alsop's
help, and yet Jerry surely played a part in it. It was Jerry who had
largely inaugurated the series of friendly meetings in students' rooms,
in which Preacher took the leading and most honored role. Preacher, in
fact, was one of those men who at the time were so busily engaged in the
work of "relating the Church to modern life"—in his own more pungent phrase, of "bringing God to the campus." His methods of doing
so were, as Jerry said, "perfectly delightful."

"Christ," Preacher would begin in one of those charming gather-
ings in student rooms, which found eight or ten eager youths sprawled

around the floor in various postures, a half-dozen more perched up on the rickety tiers of a double-decker cot, a few more hanging out the windows, eagerly drinking in the whole pungent brew of wit, of humor, of good-natured practicality, life, and Christianity, through shifting planes of pipe and cigarette smoke—"Christ," Preacher would continue, puffing on his pipe in that delightfully whimsical way of his, "was a fellow who never made a Six in philosophy. He was a fellow who started out on the scrub team, and wound up playing quarterback on the Varsity. But if He'd had to go on playing with the scrubs"—this was thrown out perhaps, as a kind of sop of encouragement to certain potentially permanent scrubs who might be within the range of hearing—"if Christ had had to go on playing with the scrubs, why," said Preacher Reed, "He would have made a go of it. You see"—here he puffed thoughtfully on his seasoned pipe for a moment—"the point is, fellows—that's the thing I want you to understand—Christ was a fellow who always made a go of everything. Now Paul"—for a moment more Preacher puffed meditatively on his blackened briar, and then, chuckling suddenly in his delightful way, he shook his head and cried—"now Paul! Ah-hah-hah—that's a different story! Paul was a bird of a different feather! There's a horse of quite another color! Paul was a fellow who flunked out."

By this time the eager young faces were fairly hanging on these inspired words.

"Paul was a fellow who started out on the scrub team, and should have stayed there," said Preacher Reed. "But he couldn't stand the gaff! He was eating his heart out all the time because he couldn't make the Varsity—and when there was a vacancy—when they needed a new quarterback, because, you see, fellow," said Preacher quietly, "the Old One had died"—he paused for a moment to let this subtle bit sink in—"they put Paul in his place. And he couldn't make the grade! He simply couldn't make the grade. And in the end—what did he do? Well, fellows, I'll tell you," said Preacher. "When he found he couldn't make the grade—he invented a new game. The old one was too tough.

Paul couldn't play it—it was too much for him! And so he invented a new one he could play—and that's where Paul flunked out. You see, fellows, Paul was a fellow who made a Six where Christ always made a One. That's the whole difference between them," Preacher said with the easy and informative manner of "Now it can be told," and then was silent for a moment, sucking vigorously and reflectively on his old briar pipe.

"In othah words, Preachah," Jerry, who had made a One in logic and was accounted no slouch himself in the Hegelian metaphysic, now took respectful advantage of the silence that had fallen—"in othah words, Paul was a man who was defeated by his own Moment of Negation. He failed to absawb it."

"Exactly, Jerry!" Preacher cried out instantly and heartily, with the manner of one saying, "You take the words right out of my mouth!"—"That's it exactly! Paul was a man who got licked by his own Moment of Negation. He couldn't absorb it. When he found himself among the scrubs, he didn't want to play. Instead of using his Moment of Negation—realizing that the Moment of Negation is really the greatest friend and ally that a man can have—Paul let it get him down. He flunked. Now, Christ," Preacher went on, paused a moment to suck reflectively at his pipe, and then abruptly—"You see, fellows, that's the Whole Thing about Jesus. Christ never flunked. He always made his One. It was first down with him every time whether he was playing with the scrubs or with the Varsity. He was just as happy playing with one side as with the other. It didn't matter to Him where he played . . . and if Christ had been there," Preacher Reed went on, "everything would have been all right, no matter where He played."

And again Preacher puffed vigorously on his pipe before he spoke:

"You see, Jesus would have kept Paul from making that Six. He'd have said to him, 'Now, see here, Paul, if you want to play quarterback on the Varsity, that's all right with Me. It doesn't matter to Me where I play—all I'm interested in is the Game.' " Preacher paused here just perceptibly to let this sink in. " 'I'd just as lief' "—Preacher was noted for his gift of homely phrase—" 'I'd just as lief play with the scrubs as with the Varsity. So let's change places if you want to. The only thing, Paul, *let's have a good Game.*' " Preacher puffed a moment. " 'Let's play according to the rules.' " He puffed again. " 'You may think you can change them, Paul—but, uh-uh, no you can't—ah-hah-hah—' " again Preacher shook his head with a sharp, short movement, with a sharp, short laugh—" 'you cant do it, Paul. It won't work. You can't change the rules. That's not playing the Game. If the rules are changed, Paul, that's not up to us—that's up to Some-one Else—so let's all get together now, no matter which team we're on, and play the game the way it should be played.' . . . But," his fine lean face was grave now, he paused and sucked his pipe a moment longer—then: "that didn't happen, did it? . . . Alas, alas, the real Quarterback was gone!"

And in the awed hush that followed, he knocked his pipe out smartly on his heel, then straightened briskly, and got up, saying jauntily:

"Well! So silent, gentlemen? Come, come! For lusty fellows of our kidney this is very sad!"

So signified, the whole gathering would break up in general dis-cussion, excited voices, laughter, young figures shifting through the smoke, plates of sandwiches, and lemonade. And in the center of it all stood Preacher Reed, his spare figure splendidly erect, his lean face finely and attentively aware, the clamor of the younger voices broken by his deeper resonance, his sandy and engaging warmth, the jolly brevity of his short and sudden laugh. And like moths infatu-ated by a shining light, all these moving and gesticulating groups would return inevitably to the magic ring of which he was himself the center.

Monk didn't know what it was, but they all felt happy and elated and excited and raised up and inspired, and liberal and enlightened and in touch with life and the high truth; and getting at last what they had come to college for.

As for Jerry Alsop, he was simply content to wait and watch, his fat chuckle sounding out occasionally from one corner of the room, where he, too, would be engaged in conversation with a group of freshmen, and yet betraying just perceptibly, by the shadow of a little smile, a little moisture in the eye, an occasional quiet but observant glance out towards the center of the room, that he knew his beloved master was still there and functioning, and that this was all the glory he himself could ask.

And as Alsop would himself say later, when the last reluctant footsteps died away, and there were the last "good nights" upon the campus, and he stood there in the now deserted room, polishing his misty glasses, and a little husky in the throat:

" . . . It was puffectly delightful! Puffectly God-damned delightful! Yes, suh! That's the only word for it!"

And it was.

CHAPTER 12

The Torch

Alsop had taken Monk Webber under his protective wing when the younger boy had arrived at Pine Rock in his freshman year, and for a period the association between them was pretty close. The younger one had quickly become a member of the coterie of devoted freshmen who clustered about their leader like chicks around a mother hen. For some months definitely he was sealed of the tribe of Alsop.

Evidences of what journalists call a "rift" began to appear, however, before the end of the first year—began to appear when the younger student began to look around him and ask questions of this small but new and comparatively liberal world in which, for the first time in his life, he began to feel himself untrammeled, free, the beginning of a man. The questions multiplied themselves furiously.

MONK HAD HEARD the president of the college, the late Hunter Griswold McCoy, described by Alsop not only as "the second greatest man since Jesus Christ," but as a thinker and philosopher of the first water, a speaker of the most eloquent persuasion, and the master of a literary style which, along with that of Woodrow Wilson, by which he was undoubtedly strongly influenced, as unsurpassed in the whole range of English literature. Now, having, as most boys of that age do have, a very active and questioning mind, he began to feel distinctly uncomfortable when Alsop said these things, to squirm uneasily in his chair, to keep silence, or to mumble respectful agreements, while all the time he asked himself rather desperately what was wrong with him. Because, the truth of the matter was that "the second greatest man since Jesus Christ" bored him passionately, even at the tender age of seventeen.

And as for that triumphant style which Alsop assured him was practically unsurpassed in the whole field of English letters, he had made repeated attempts to read it and digest it—it had been fittingly embalmed in a volume which bore the title of *Democracy and Leadership*—and he simply could not get through it. As for the famous Chapel talks, which were considered masterpieces of simple eloquence and gems of philosophy, he hated them. He would rather have taken a bitter laxative than sit through one of them: but sit through them he did, hundreds of times, and endured them, until he came to have a positive dislike for Hunter Griswold McCoy. His pale, pure face, somewhat gaunt and emaciated, a subtle air he conveyed always of bearing some deep, secret sorrow, and of suffering in some subtle, complicated way for humanity, began to afflict Monk with a sensation that was akin to, and in fact was scarcely distinguishable from, the less acute stages of nausea. And when Alsop assured him, and the rest of the reverent clique, that Hunter Griswold McCoy was and had always been "as pure and sweet as a fine, sweet gul—yes, suh!"—his dislike for Hunter Griswold McCoy became miserably acute. He disliked him because Hunter Griswold McCoy made him feel so unworthy, like the bird that fouls its own nest, and because he felt miserably and doggedly that there must be something monstrously wicked and base and perverse in his own life if he could not see the shining virtue of this perfect man, and because he realized that he could never be in any way like him.

In addition to this, the glittering phrases of Hunter Griswold McCoy, which, Alsop assured him, were not only pearls of eloquence and poetry, but the very sounding board of life itself—and that whoever was fortunate enough to hear one of these Chapel talks was not only being told about truth and reality, but was given a kind of magic pass key to the whole mystery of life and the complex problem of humanity which he could use forevermore—well, Monk sat miserably in his seat in Chapel day after day and week after week, and the blunt and bitter truth was, he could make nothing out of it. If the wine of life was here, he squeezed the grape desperately, and it shattered in his fingers like a rusty pod. "Democracy and leadership," "education for the good life," "service," "ideals," all the rest of it—did not mean a damn thing to him. He could not find out, although he strained desperately to hear, what "the good life" was, except when it was connected in some very intimate and personal way with Hunter Griswold McCoy, sexual chastity, matrimony, "fine women," drinking water, and Chapel talks. And yet he felt wretchedly that if he wanted any life at all it was assuredly "the good life"—except "the good life" for him, vaguely phrased and indefinitely etched, but flaming in his vision with all the ardor, passion, aspiration of his youth, had so much in it that Hunter Griswold McCoy had never spoken of, and that he dumbly, miserably felt, Hunter Griswold McCoy would not approve.

The shape, the frame, the pattern, the definition of this "good life" was still painfully obscure: but he did feel, inchoately but powerfully, that it had so much flesh and blood in it. It had in it the promise of thick sirloin steaks, and golden, mealy, fried potatoes. It had in it, alas, the flesh of lavish women, the quickening enigma of a smile, the thrilling promise of a touch, the secret confirmation of the pressure of a hand. It had in it great rooms sealed to rich quietness, and the universe of mighty books. But it had in it much tobacco smoke as well—alas, alas, such sinful dreams of fleshly comforts!—and the flavors of strong wine. It had in it the magic of the Jason quest: the thought of golden artisans; almost intolerably a vision of the proud breast, the racing slant, of the great liners as they swung out into the stream at noon on Saturday in their imperial cavalcade, to slide past the chasm slant, the splintered helms and ramparts of a swarming rock, world-appointed and delivered to the sea. It had in it, at last and always, the magic vision of the city, the painted weather of a boy's huge dreams of glory, wealth, and triumph, and a fortunate and happy life among the greatest ones on earth.

And in the words and phrases of the perfect man, there was no word of this. Therefore, dumbly, the youth was miserable. To make the matter worse, two months before the Armistice, Hunter Griswold McCoy up and died. It was the final consummation: Alsop said immediately that it was the story of the Savior and his final martyrdom upon the Cross all over again. True, no one knew exactly just how Hunter Griswold McCoy had been martyred, except by the deadly prevalence of the influenza germ, but the whole memory of his life, the sense of inner purity shining out through his pale and martyred face through all the tedium of a thousand Chapel talks, somehow lent conviction to the final impression of martyrdom. And when Alsop announced in a choking voice that "he had laid down his life for a great Cause—to make the world safe for democracy," and that no soldier who had died in France, stopped by a hail of bullets as he moved forth to the attack against the hordes of barbarism, had been more truly a sacrifice for the great Cause than had McCoy, no single word was raised in protest; there was no single voice to say him nay.

And yet, the wicked truth is that our young sinner had a secret feeling of overwhelming relief when he knew that Hunter Griswold McCoy was gone, that there would be no more Chapel talks—at least, not by McCoy. And the knowledge of this wicked consciousness filled him with such an abysmal sense of his own degradation, of his own unworthiness, that like so many other guilty souls before him, he went it the whole hog. He began to hang around with a crowd of dissolute idlers that infested the college pharmacy; he began to gamble with them for black cows. One false step led to another. Before long he was smoking cigarettes with a dissipated leer. He began to stray away from the Alsopian circle: he began to stay up late at night—but not with Alsop, and not among the devoted neophytes who feasted nightly on the master's words. On the contrary, he fell in with a crowd of lewd-tongued, lusty fellows, who stayed up to all hours and played the phonograph; and who crowned a week of shameful indolence with a week-end of disgusting debauchery in the town of Covington, a score

242 THE WEB AND THE ROOT

of miles away. The upshot of the matter was that in no time at all these reprobates had taken the innocent, got him drunk, and then delivered him into the custody of a notorious strumpet named "Depot Lil." The story not only came back to the Pine Rock campus, it roared back— it was retailed about, guffawed and bandied back and forth by these same dissolute and conniving rascals who had deliberately contrived this tragedy of ruined innocence, and who now, of such degraded texture were they, apparently thought that the story of the fall of one of Alsop's angels was a matter fit for laughter by the gods.

This was almost the end, but not quite. Alsop did not cast him out without reprieve, without "giving him another chance," for, above all things, Alsop was tolerant—like Brutus, Alsop was an honorable man. Quietly, gravely, the master instructed his disciples not to be too hard upon their fallen brother; they were even instructed not to speak about it, to treat their erring comrade as if nothing had happened, as if he were still one of them; to let him see, by little acts of kindness, that they did not think of him as a social outcast, that he was still a member of the human race. So instructed and so inspired with Christian charity, everyone began to reek with mercy.

As for our fallen angel, it must be admitted that when the full consciousness of his guilt swept down on him, and almost drowned him—he came crawling back to the fold. There was a three-hour conference with Alsop, all alone in Alsop's room, from which everyone kept religiously away. At the end of that time. Alsop opened the door, polishing his misty glasses, and everyone came trouping solemnly in: and Alsop was heard to say in a quiet but throaty voice, and with a tender little chuckle:

"Lord God! Lord God! Life is all right!"

IT WOULD BE good to report here that the pardon was final and that the reformation was complete. Alas, this did not happen. Within a month, the reprieved—perhaps paroled is the better word—man had slid back into his former ways. He had begun to hang around the pharmacy again, to waste his time in the company of other wastrels, and to gamble for black cows. And, if he did not slide the whole way back, and there was no exact repetition of the first catastrophe, his ways were certainly now suspect. He began to show a decided preference for people who thought only of having a good time; he seemed to like their indolent ways and drawling voices, he was seen around idling in the sun on the front porch of two or three of the fraternities. And since Alsop and none of his group belonged to a fraternity, this was considered as another sign of dissolution.

In addition to this, Monk began to neglect his studies and to do a great deal of desultory reading. This was another bad sign. Not that Alsop disapproved of reading—he read constantly himself; but when he questioned the disciple as to the reading he was doing, in an effort to find out if it was sound, in accordance with "the more wholesome and well-rounded view of things"—that is, if he was "getting anything out of it"—Alsop's worst fears were realized. The fellow had begun to prowl around in the college library all by himself, and had stumbled upon certain suspect volumes that had, in some strange or accidental way, insinuated themselves into those respectable shelves. Notable among them were the works of one Dostoevski, a Russian. The situation was not only bad, but, when Alsop finally rounded up his erstwhile neophyte—for curiosity, even when the fallen were concerned, was certainly one of Alsop's strongest qualities—he found him, as he pityingly described the situation to the faithful later, "gabbling like a loon."

The truth of the matter was, the adventurer had first stumbled upon one of these books in pretty much the same way that a man groping his way through a woods at night stubs his toe against an invisible rock and falls sprawling over it. Our groping adventurer not only knew nothing about the aforesaid Dostoevski: if he had even heard of him it was in the vaguest sort of way, for certainly that strange and formidable name had never rung around the classroom walls of old Pine Rock—not while he was listening anyway. The plain truth is that he had stumbled over it because he was looking for something to read and liked big books—he was always favorably impressed with the size and weight of a volume; and this one, which bore the promising name of *Crime and Punishment*, was certainly large and heavy enough to suit his taste.

Thereupon, he began a very strange and puzzling adventure with the book. He took it home and began to read it, but after fifty pages gave it up. It all seemed so strange and puzzling to him, even the characters themselves seemed to have several different names apiece, by which they addressed one another, the whole resulting in such confusion that he did not always know who was speaking. In addition, he was not at all sure what was happening. The book, instead of following the conventional line and structure of story, plot, and pattern, to which his reading had accustomed him, seemed to boil outward from some secret, unfathomable, and subterranean source—in Coleridginal phrase, "as if this earth in fast, thick pants was breathing." The result was that the story seemed to weave out upon a dark and turbulent tide of feeling. He was not only not sure of what was happening; when he tried to go back and trace the thread of narrative, he could not always be sure that he had followed it back to its true source. As for the talk, the way the people talked, it was the most bewildering and disturbing talk he had ever heard: anyone was likely to pour out at any moment, with the most amazing frankness, everything that was in his mind and heart, everything that he had ever felt, thought, dreamed, or imagined. And even this would be broken in its full flood tide by apparently meaningless and irrelevant statements. It was all too hard and confusing to follow, and after reading forty or fifty pages he threw the book aside and looked at it no more.

And yet he could not forget it. Events, characters, speeches, incidents kept coming back to him like things remembered from some haunting dream. The upshot of it was that in a week or two he went back to the book, and in two days' time finished it. He was more amazed and bewildered than ever. Within another week he had read the book a second time. Then he went on and read *The Idiot* and *The Brothers Karamazov*. It was at this stage that Alsop hunted him out and cornered him, and, as a result of their conversation, that Alsop confided to his associates that the lost one was "gabbling like a loon."

Perhaps he was. At any rate, anything the discoverer might have said at that time did not make much coherent sense. He did not even affirm any enthusiastic conviction, or confess his passionate belief that he had discovered a great book or a great writer. None of these things occurred to him at the time. The only thing he did know and was sure of was that he had stumbled on something new and strange and overwhelming, whose existence he had never dreamed about before.

He was incoherent, but he was also now passionately eager to talk to someone and tell him all about it. When Alsop came to him, therefore, he fastened on him gratefully. Alsop was older, he was wiser, he had read a great deal, he loved literature, he knew a great deal about books. Surely, if anyone at all could talk to him about this one, it was Alsop. The result of it was that Alsop suggested that he come around, remarking good-naturedly that he had been too much a stranger lately: they would have an evening of the old-time discussion, and everyone would join in. He agreed to this most eagerly, and the time was set. Alsop, meanwhile, passed the word around quietly among the other members of the group that perhaps a useful work of rehabilitation might here be done—the phrase he used was "get him back on the right track." When the appointed time arrived, everyone had been properly and virtuously informed with a sense of duty, the consciousness of lending a helping hand.

It was an unhappy occasion. It all started out casually, as Alsop himself had planned it. Alsop sat in the center of the room, one fat arm resting on the table, and with an air of confessorial benevolence on his priestly visage, a quiet little smile that said: "Tell me about it. As you know, I am prepared to see all sides." The discipleship sat in the outer

darkness, in a circle, dutifully intent. Into this arena the luckless innocent rushed headlong. He had brought the old battered copy of *Crime
and Punishment* with him.

Alsop, amid general conversation, led up to the subject skillfully,
and finally said:

"What's this—ah—new book you were telling me about the othah
day? I mean," he said smoothly, "you were telling me—about a book
you've been reading—by—some Russian writer, wasn't it?" said Alsop
blandly, hesitating—"Dusty—Dusty—Dusty—whosky?" said Alsop
with a show of innocence, and then, before there was a chance for reply,
his great belly shook, the fat scream of laughter sounded in his throat.
The disciples joined hilariously in. "Lord God!" cried Alsop, chuckling
again, "I didn't mean to do that—it just popped out, I couldn't help
it . . . . But how do you pronounce his name, anyhow?" said Alsop
gravely. His manner was now serious, but behind his winking spectacles
his eyes were narrowed into slits of mockery—"How do you spell it?"

"I—I don't know how you pronounce it—but it's spelled Dos-to-
evski."

"I guess that would be Dos—Dos—" Alsop began. . . .

"Oh hell, Jerry, why don't you just sneeze it and let it go at that?"
said one of the disciples. And again the room sounded with their
laughter, Alsop's great belly heaving and his half-phlegmy choke of
laughter rising above the rest.

"Don't mind us," he now said tolerantly, seeing the other's reddened face. "We weren't laughing at the book—we want to hear
about it—it's only that it seems funny to talk about a book when you
can't even pronounce the name of the author." Suddenly he heaved
with laughter again—"Lord God," he said, "it may be a great book—
but that's the damnedest name I ever heard of." And the laughter of
agreement filled the room. "But go on now," he said encouragingly,
with an air of serious interest, "I'd like to hear about it. What's it
about?"

"It's—it's—it's—" Monk began confusedly, suddenly realizing how difficult it would be to put into a scheme of words just what the book *was* about, particularly since he was by no means sure himself.

"I mean," said Alsop smoothly, "could you tell us something about the plot? Give us some idea about the story?"

"Well," the other began slowly, thinking hard, "the leading character is a man named Raskalnikoff—"

"Who?" said Alsop innocently. And again there was an appreciative titter around the room. "Raskal-ni-who?" The titter grew to open laughter.

"Well, that's the way it's spelled anyhow," said the other doggedly. "Ras-kal-ni-koff—I guess you call it Raskalnikoff!"

And again Alsop heaved with laughter, the phlegmy chuckle wheezed high in his throat. "Damned if you don't pick out funny names!" he said, and then encouragingly: "Well, all right, then, go on. What does Raskal What's-His-Name do?"

"Well—he—he—kills an old woman," Monk said, now conscious of the currents of derision and amusement in the ring around him. "With an axe!" he blurted out, and instantly was crimson with anger and embarrassment at the roar of laughter that greeted his description, feeling he had told the story clumsily, and had begun his explanation in the worst possible way.

"Damned if he don't live up to his name!" wheezed Alsop. "Old Dusty—old Dusty knew what he was about when he called him Raskal What's-His-Name, didn't he?"

The other was angry now: he said hotly, "It's nothing to laugh about, Jerry, It's—"

"No," said Alsop gravely. "Killing old women with axes is not a laughing matter—no matter who does it—even if you do have to sneeze it when you say it!"

At the burst of approving laughter that greeted this sally, the younger man lost his temper completely, and turned furiously upon the group:

"You fellows make me tired! Here you're shooting off your mouths and making jokes about something you know nothing about. What's funny about it, I'd like to know?"

"It suttinly doesn't strike me as funny," Alsop quietly observed. "It sounds pretty mawbid to me."

This quiet observation was greeted by a murmur of agreement.

For the first time, however, the use of the word, which was one of Alsop's favorite definitions, stung Monk into quick and hot resentment.

"What's morbid about it?" he said furiously. "Good Lord, Jerry, you're always saying that something is morbid, just because you don't like it. A writer's got a right to tell about anything he pleases. He's not *morbid* just because he doesn't write about peaches and cream all the time."

"Yes," said Alsop with his infuriating air of instructive tolerance. "But a great writer will see all sides of the situation—"

"All sides of the situation!" the younger man now cried excitedly. "Jerry, that's another thing you're always saying. You're always talking about seeing all sides of the situation. What the hell does it mean? Maybe a situation doesn't have all sides. I don't know what you're talking about when you say it!"

At last, then, here was insurrection, open, naked insurrection, for the first time now clear and unmistaken! A kind of deadly silence had fallen on the group. Alsop continued to smile his little smile, he still maintained his air of judicial tolerance, but somehow his smile was pale, the warmth had gone out of his face, behind his spectacles his eyes had narrowed to cold slits.

"I just mean—that a great writer, a really great writer—will write about all types of people. He may write about murder and crime like this Dusty What's-His-Name that you're talking about, but he'll write about othah things as well. In othah words," said Alsop pontifically, "he'll try to see the Whole Thing in its true perspective."

"In what true perspective, Jerry?" the other burst out. "That's another thing you're always saying too—talking about the true perspective. I wish you'd tell me what it means!"

Here was heresy again, and more of it. The others held their breath while Alsop, still maintaining his judicial calm, answered quietly:

"I mean, a great writer will try to see life clearly and to see it whole. He'll try to give you the whole pictuah."

"Well, Dostoevski tries to, too," said Monk doggedly.

"Yes, I know, but does he really now? I mean does he really show you the more wholesome and well-rounded view of things?"

"Ah—ah—Jerry, that's another thing you're always sayin—the more wholesome and well-rounded view of things. What does *that* mean? Who ever did give you the more wholesome and well-rounded view of things?"

"Well," said Alsop judicially, "I think Dickens gave it to you."

There was a dutiful murmur of agreement from the disciples, broken by the rebel's angry mutter:

"Ah—Dickens! I'm tired hearing about Dickens all the time!"

This was sacrilege, and for a moment there was appalled silence, as if someone had at last committed a sin against the Holy Ghost. When Alsop spoke again his face was very grave, and his eyes had narrowed to cold points:

"You mean to say that you think this Russian fellow presents as wholesome and well-rounded a pictuah of life as Dickens does?"

"I told you," the other said in a voice that trembled with excitement, "that I don't know what you're talking about when you say that. I'm only saying that there can be other great writers in the world besides Dickens."

"And you think, then," said Alsop quietly, "that this man is a greater writer than Dickens?"

"I haven't—" the other began.

"Yes, but come on now," said Alsop. "We're all fair-minded people here—you really think he's greater, don't you?"

Monk looked at him for a moment with a kind of baffled

indignation; then, spurred to a boiling point of irrational resentment by the expression of the stern faces all about him, he suddenly shouted out:

"Yes! He was! A hell of a sight greater! It's like Pascal said—that one of the grandest surprises in life is to open a book expecting to meet an author, and to find instead a man. And that's the way it is with Dostoevski. You don't meet the author. You meet the man. You may not believe everything that is said, but you believe the man who is saying it. You are convinced by his utter sincerity, by the great, burning light of him, and in the end, no matter how confused or bewildered or unsure he may himself be, time and again you know that he is right. And you see also that it doesn't matter how people say things, so long as the feeling behind the things they say is a true one. I can give you an example of that." he went on hotly. "At the end of *The Brothers Karamazov*, where Alyosha is talking to the boys in the cemetery, the danger of falseness and sentimentality in such a scene as this is overwhelming. In the first place, the scene is in a graveyard, and Alyosha and the children are there to put flowers upon the grave of another child who has died. Then again, there is the danger of Alyosha, with his convictions of brotherly love, his doctrine of redemption through sacrifice, of salvation through humility. He makes a speech to the children, a confused and rambling speech, of which sentence after sentence could have been uttered by a Y.M.C.A. secretary or a Sunday School teacher. Why is it, then, that there is nothing sickly or disgusting about it, as there would be in the harangue of such men as these? It is because we know from the beginning that the words are honest and sincere, because we believe in the sincerity and truth and honesty of the character who is speaking the words, and of the man who wrote the words and created the character. Dostoevski was not afraid to use such words," Monk went on in the full flood of his passion, "because he had no falseness and sentimentality in him. The words are the same as the Sunday School teacher might use, but the feeling behind them is different, and that makes the difference. Therefore they express what Dostoevski wanted them to. Alyosha tells the children that we must love one another, and we believe him. He tells them never to forget their comrade who has died, to try to remember all the countless good and generous acts of his life, his love for his father, his courage and devotion. Then Alyosha tells the children that the most important thing in life, the thing that will expiate our sins, pardon all our mistakes and errors, make our lives prevail, is to have a good memory of someone. And these simple words move us more than the most elaborate rhetoric could do, because suddenly we know that we have been told something true and everlasting about life, and that the man who told it to us is right."

During the last part of this long speech, Alsop had reached over quietly to his bookshelves, taken a well-worn volume from the shelf, and, even while Monk talked, begun to thumb quietly through its pages. Now he was ready for him again. He had the book open in his hand, one fat forefinger marking the spot. He was waiting for Monk to conclude, with a patient and tolerant little smile.

"Now," he said quietly, when the other finished, "that situation which you described there interests me very much, because Charles Dickens deals with the same situation at the end of *A Tale of Two Cities*, and says the same thing that Dostoevski says." Monk noticed he got the name right this time. "Now," said Alsop, looking around at his congregation with a little misty smile that prefaced all these tributes to sentiment and, in especial, to that chief object of his idolatry, Charles Dickens—and which said to them plainer than any words could do: "Now I'm going to show you what a really great man can do with sweetness and light"—he said quietly: "I think you'll all be interested to see how Dickens handles that same situation," and immediately began to read the concluding passages of the book which are devoted to Sidney Carton's celebrated utterance as he steps up to the guillotine to sacrifice his own life in order that the life of the man beloved by the woman he himself loves may be spared:

" 'I see the lives for which I lay down my life, peaceful useful, prosperous and happy, in that England which I shall see no more. I see her with a child upon her bosom, who bears my name. I see her father, aged and bent, but otherwise restored, and faithful to all men in his healing office, and at peace. I see the good old man, so long their friend, in ten years' time enriching them with all he has, and passing tranquilly to his reward.

" 'I see that I hold a sanctuary in their hearts, and in the hearts of their descendants, generations hence. I see her, an old woman, weeping for me on the anniversary of this day. I see her and her husband, their course done, lying side by side in their last earthly bed, and I know that each was not more honored and held sacred in the other's soul, than I was in the souls of both.

" 'I see that child who lay upon her bosom and who bore my name, a man, winning his way up in that path of life which once was mine. I see him winning it so well, that my name is made illustrious there by the light of his. I see the blots I threw upon it, faded away. I see him, foremost of just judges and honored men, bringing a boy of my name, with a forehead that I know and golden hair, to this place;—then fair to look upon, with not a trace of this day's disfigurement—and I hear him tell the child my story, with a tender and a faltering voice.

" 'It is a far, far better thing that I do, than I have ever done; it is a far, far better rest that I go to, than I have ever known.' "

Alsop read these famous lines in a voice husky with emotion, and, at the end, paused a moment before speaking, to blow his nose vigorously. He was genuinely and deeply affected, and there was no doubt that his emotion and the way in which he read the passage had produced a profound effect on his audience. At the conclusion, after the vigorous salute into his handkerchief, and a moment's silence, he looked around with a misty little smile and said quietly:

"Well, what do you think of that? Do you think that comes up to Mr. Dusty What's-His-Name or not?"

There was an immediate chorus of acclamation. They all agreed vociferously that that passage not only "came up" to Mr. Dusty What's-His-Name, but far surpassed anything he had ever accomplished.

In view of the fact that none of them knew anything about Mr. Dusty What's-His-Name and were yet willing to pass judgment with such enthusiastic conviction, Monk felt his anger rising hot and quick, and broke in indignantly:

"That is not the same thing at all. The situation is altogether different."

"Well, now," said Jerry persuasively, "you must admit that fundamentally the situation is essentially the same. It's the idea of love and sacrifice in both cases. Only it seems to me that Dickens' treatment of the situation is the superior of the two. He says what Dostoevski is trying to say, but it seems to me he says it much better. He presents a more rounded pictuah, and lets you know that life is going to go on and be just as fine and sweet as it ever was in spite of everything. Now," he said, quietly and persuasively again, "don't you agree, Monk, that Dickens' method is the best? You know you do, you scannel!" Here he chortled richly, shoulders and his great belly shaking with good-natured glee. "I know how you feel at the bottom of your heart. You're just arguing to hear yourself talk."

"Why not at all, Jerry," Monk came back with hot earnestness, "I mean everything I say. And I don't see any similarity at all between the two situations. What Sidney Carton says has no relation to what Alyosha is trying to say at the end of *The Brothers Karamazov*. One book is a skillful and exciting melodrama, which makes use of some of the events of the French Revolution. The other book is, in this sense, not a story at all. It is a great vision of life and of human destiny, as seen through the spirit of a great man. What Alyosha is saying is not that man dies for love, not that he sacrifices his life for romantic love, but that he lives for love, not romantic love, but love of life, love of mankind, and that through love his spirit and his memory survive, even when his physical self is dead. That's not the same thing at all as the thing that Sidney Carton says. What you have on the one hand is a profound and simple utterance of a great spiritual truth, and what you have on the other is the rhetorical and sentimental ending to a romantic melodrama."

"No suh!" Jerry Alsop now cried hotly, his face flushed with anger and excitement. "No suh!" he cried again, and shook his big head in angered denial. "If you call that sentimental, you just don't know what you're talking about! You've just gone and got yourself completely lost! You don't even know what Dickens is trying to do!"

The upshot of it was that a cat-and-dog fight broke out at this point, a dozen angry, derisive voices clashing through the air trying to drown out the rebel, who only shouted louder as the opposition grew; and it continued until the contestants were out of breath and the entire campus was howling for quiet from a hundred windows.

It wound up with Alsop standing, pale but righteous, in the center of the room, finally restoring quiet, and saying:

"We've all tried to be your friends, we've tried to help you out. If you can't take it the way it's meant, you don't need to bothah with us any more. We all saw the way that you were going—" he went on in a trembling tone; and Monk, stung by these final words into maddening and complete revolt, cried passionately:

"Going—going hell! I'm gone!" And he stormed out of the room, clutching the battered volume underneath his arm.

When he had gone the tumult broke out anew, the loyal cohorts gathering round their wounded chief. The end of it all, when the whole tumult of bitter agreement had quieted down, was summed up in the final dismissal of Alsop's words:

"He's just an ass! He's just gone and played hell, that's what he's done! I thought there was some hope for him, but he's just gone and made a complete damned ass of himself! Leave him alone! Don't fool with him any longer, he's not wuth it!"

And that was that.

"GET THE FACTS, Brother Webber! Get the Facts!"

The square Sphinx head, shaven, paunch-jowled, putty-grey; the grim, dry mouth, puckered with surly humor; the low rasp of the voice. He sat in squat immobility, staring at them ironically.

"I am a Research Man!" he announced finally. "I get the Facts."

"What do you do with them after you get them?" said Monk.

"I put salt on their tails and get some more," said Professor Randolph Ware.

His stolid, ironic face, iron lidded, enjoyed the puzzled worship of their stare.

"Have I any imagination?" he asked. He shook his head in solemn negation. "No-o," he said with a long grunt of satisfaction. "Have I any genius? No-o. Could I have written *King Lear*? No-o. Have I more brains than Shakespeare? Yes. Do I know more about English literature than the Prince of Wales? Yes. Do I know more about Spenser than Kittredge, Manley, and Saintsbury put together? Yes. Do I know more about Spenser than God and Spenser put together? Yes. Could I have written *The Faery Queen*? No-o. Could I write a doctoral thesis about *The Faery Queen*? Yes."

"Did you ever see a doctor's thesis that was worth reading?" asked Monk.

"Yes," said the implacable monotone.

"Whose was it?"

"My own."

They answered with a young yell of worship.

"Then what's the use of the Facts?" said Monk.

"They keep a man from getting soft," said Randolph Ware grimly.

"But a Fact has no importance in itself," said Monk. "It is only a manifestation of the Concept."

"Have you had your breakfast, Brother Webber?"

"No," said Monk, "I always eat after class. That's to keep my mind fresh and active for its work."

The class snickered.

"Is your breakfast a Fact or a Concept, Brother Webber?" He stared grimly at him for a moment. "Brother Webber made a One in Logic," he said, "and he has breakfast at noon. He thinks he is another convert to Divine Philosophy, but he is wrong. Brother Webber, you have heard the bells at midnight many times. I have myself seen you below the moon, with your eyes in a fine frenzy rolling. You will never make a Philosopher, Brother Webber. You will spend several years quite pleasantly in Hell, Getting the Facts. After that, you may make a poet."

Randolph Ware was a very grand person—a tremendous scholar, a believer in the discipline of formal research. He was a scientific utilitarian to the roots of his soul: he believed in Progress and the relief of man's estate, and he spoke of Francis Bacon—who was really the first American—with a restrained but passionate wisdom.

George Webber remembered this man later—grey, stolid, ironic—as one of the strangest people he had ever known. All of the facts were so strange. He was a Middle-Westerner who went to the University of Chicago and learned more about English literature than the people at Oxford knew. It seemed strange that one should study Spenser in Chicago.

He was gigantically American—he seemed almost to foreshadow the future. George met few people who were able to make such complete and successful use of things as they are. He was a magnificent teacher, capable of fruitful and astonishing innovation. Once he set the class in composition to writing a novel, and they went to work with boiling interest. George rushed into class breathlessly three times a week with a new chapter written out on the backs of paper bags, envelopes, stray bits of paper. And Randolph Ware had the power of communicating to them the buried magic of poetry: the cold sublimity of Milton began to burgeon with life and opulent color—in Moloch, Beelzebub, Satan, without vulgarity or impertinence, he made them see a hundred figures of craft and rapacity and malice among the men of their time.

Yet it always seemed to George that there was in the man a cruelly wasted power. There was in him a strong light and a hidden glory. He seemed with deliberate fatalism to have trapped himself among petty things. Despite his great powers, he wasted himself compiling antholo-gies for use in colleges.

But the students who swarmed about him sensed the tenderness and beauty below his stolid and ironic mask. And once George, going in to see him at his house, found him at the piano, his blunt, heavy body erect, his putty face dreaming like a Buddha, as his pudgy fingers drew out with passion and wisdom the great music of Beethoven. Then George remembered what Alcibiades had said to Socrates: "You are like the god Silenus—outwardly a paunched and ugly man, but concealing inwardly the figure of a young and beautiful divinity."

IN SPITE OF the twaddle that the prominent educators of the time were always talking about "democracy and leadership," "ideals of ser-vice," "the place of the college in modern life," and so on, there wasn't much reality about the direction of such "education" as George had had. And that's not to say there had been no reality in his education. There was, of course—not only because there's reality in everything, but because he had come in contact with art, with letters, and with a few fine people. Maybe that's about as much as you can expect.

It would also be unfair to say that the real value of this, the beauti-ful and enduring thing, he had had to "dig out" for himself, and this fact was "beautiful"—a lot of young fellows all together, not sure where they were going, but sure that they were going somewhere.

So he had this, and this was a lot.

CHAPTER 13

The Rock

Some fifteen or more years ago (as men measure, by those diurnal instruments which their ingenuity has created, the immeasurable universe of time), at the end of a fine, warm, hot, fair, fresh, fragrant, lazy, furnacelike day of sweltering heat across the body, bones, sinews, tissues, juices, rivers, mountains, plains, streams, lakes, coastal regions, and compacted corporosity of the American continent, a train might have been observed by one of the lone watchers of the Jersey Flats approaching that enfabled rock, that ship of life, that swarming, million-footed, tower-masted, and sky-soaring citadel that bears the magic name of the Island of Manhattan, at terrific speed.

At this moment, indeed, one of the lone crayfishers, who ply their curious trade at this season of the year throughout the melancholy length and breadth of those swamplike moors which are characteristic of this section of the Jersey coast, lifted his seamed and weather-beaten face from some nets which he had been mending in preparation for the evening's catch, and, after gazing for a moment at the projectile fury of the Limited as it thundered past, turned and, speaking to the brown-faced lad beside him, said quietly:

"It is the Limited."

And the boy, returning his father's look with eyes as sea-far and as lonely as the old man's own, and in a voice as quiet, said:

"On time, father?"

The old man did not answer for a moment. Instead, he thrust one gnarled and weather-beaten hand into the pocket of his peajacket, fumbled a moment, and then pulled forth an enormous silver watch with compass dials, an heirloom of three generations of crayfishing folk. He regarded it a moment with a steady, reflective gaze.

"Aye, lad," he said simply, "on time—or thereabouts. She will not miss it much tonight, I reckon."

But already the great train was gone in a hurricane of sound and speed. The sound receded into silence, leaving the quiet moors as they had always been, leaving them to silence, the creaking of the gulls, the low droning of the giant mosquitoes, the melancholy and funereal pyres of burning trash here and there, and to the lonely fisher of the moors and his young son. For a moment, the old man and the lad regarded the receding projectile of the train with quiet eyes. Then, silently, they resumed their work upon their nets again. Evening was coming, and with it the full tide, and, with the coming of the tide, the cray. So all was now as it had always been. The train had come and gone and vanished, and over the face of the flats brooded as it had always done the imperturbable visage of eternity.

Within the train, however, there was a different scene, a kind of wakening of hope and of anticipation. Upon the faces of the passengers there might have been observed now all the expressions and emotions which the end of a long journey usually evokes, whether of alert readiness, eager constraint, or apprehensive dread. And on the face of one, a youth in his early twenties, there might have been observed all of the hope, fear, longing, exultancy, faith, belief, expectancy, and incredible realization that every youth on earth has always felt on his approach for the first time to the enchanted city. Although the other people in the coach were already restless, stirring, busy with their preparations for the journey's end, the boy sat there by a window like one rapt in dreams, his vision tranced and glued against the glass at the rushing landscape of the lonely moors. No detail of the scene escaped the ravenous voracity of his attention.

The train rushed past a glue factory. With the expression of one drunk with wonder the young man drank the pageant in. He saw with joy the great stacks, the glazed glass windows, the mighty furnaces of the enormous works; the pungent fragrance of the molten glue came to him and he breathed it in with rapturous appeasement.

The train swept on across a sinuous stream, itself an estuary of the infinite and all-taking sea, itself as motionless as time, scummed richly with a moveless green; the sheer beauty of the thing went home into his mind and heart forever.

He raised his eyes as men against the West once raised their eyes against the shining ramparts of the mountains. And there before him, at the edges of the marsh, rose the proud heights of Jersey City—the heights of Jersey City blazing forever to the traveler the smoldering welcome of their garbage dumps—the heights of Jersey City, raised proudly against the desolation of those lonely marshes as a token of man's fortitude, a symbol of his power, a sign of his indomitable spirit that flames forever like a great torch in the wilderness, that lifts against the darkness and the desolation of blind nature the story of its progress—the heights of Jersey, lighted for an eternal feast.

The train swept on and underneath the crests of yon proud, battlemented hill. The hill closed in around the train, the train roared in beneath the hill, into the tunnel. And suddenly darkness was upon them. The train plunged in beneath the mighty bed of the unceasing river, and dumbness smote the youth's proud, listening ears.

He turned and looked upon his fellow passengers. He saw wonder on their faces and something in their hearts that none could divine; and even as he sat there, dumb with wonder, he heard two voices, two quiet voices out of life, the voices of two nameless ciphers out of life, a woman's and a man's.

"Jeez, but I'll be glad to get back home again," the man said quietly.

For a moment the woman did not answer, then, the same quiet

tone, but with a meaning, a depth of feeling, that the boy would never after that forget, she answered simply, "You said it."

Just that, and nothing more. But, simple as those words were, they sank home into his heart, in their brief eloquence of time and of the bitter briefness of man's days, the whole compacted history of his tragic destiny.

And now, even as he paused there, rapt in wonder at this nameless eloquence, he heard another voice, close to his ears, a voice soft, low, and urgent, sweet as honey dew, and suddenly, with a start of recognition and surprise, he realized the words were meant for him, for him alone.

"Is you comin', boss?" the soft voice said. "We'se gettin' in. Shall I bresh you off?"

The boy turned slowly and surveyed his dark interrogator. In a moment he inclined his head in a slight gesture of assent and quietly replied:

"I am ready. Yes, you may."

But even now the train was slowing to a halt. Grey twilight filtered through the windows once again. The train had reached the tunnel's mouth. On both sides now were ancient walls of masonry, old storied buildings, dark as time and ancient as man's memory. The boy peered through the window, up as far as eyes could reach, at all those tiers of life, those countless cells of life, the windows, rooms, and faces of the everlasting and eternal city. They leaned above him in their ancient silence. They returned his look. He looked into their faces and said nothing, no word was spoken. The people of the city leaned upon the sills of evening and they looked at him. They looked at him from their old walls of ancient, battlemented brick. They looked at him through the silent yet attentive curtains of all their ancient and historic laundries. They looked at him through pendant sheets, through hanging underwear, through fabrics of a priceless and unknown tapestry, and he knew that all was now as it had always been, as it would be tomorrow and forever.

But now the train was slowing to a halt. Long tongues of cement now appeared, and faces, swarming figures, running forms beside the train. And all these faces, forms, and figures slowed to instancy, were held there in the alertness of expectant movement. There was a grinding screech of brakes, a slight jolt, and, for a moment, utter silence.

At this moment there was a terrific explosion.

It was New York.

THERE IS NO truer legend in the world than the one about the country boy, the provincial innocent, in his first contact with the city. Hackneyed by repetition, parodied and burlesqued by the devices of cheap fiction and the slap-stick of vaudeville humor, it is nevertheless one of the most tremendous and vital experiences in the life of a man, and in the life of the nation. It has found inspired and glorious tongues in Tolstoy and in Goethe, in Balzac and in Dickens, in Fielding and Mark Twain. It has found splendid examples in every artery of life, as well in Shakespeare as in the young Napoleon. And day after day the great cities of the world are being fed, enriched, and replenished ceaselessly with the life-blood of the nation, with all the passion, aspiration, eagerness, faith, and high imagining that youth can know, or that the tenement of life can hold.

For one like George Webber, born to the obscure village and brought up within the narrow geography of provincial ways, the city experience is such as no city man himself can ever know. It is conceived in absence and in silence and in youth; it is built up to the cloud-capped pinnacles of a boy's imagining; it is written like a golden legend in the heart of youth with a plume plucked out of an angel's wing; it lives and flames there in his heart and spirit with all the timeless faery of the magic land.

When such a man, therefore, comes first to the great city—but how can we speak of such a man coming first to the great city, when really the great city is within him, encysted in his heart, built up in all the flaming images of his brain: a symbol of his hope, the image of his high desire, the final crown, the citadel of all that he has ever dreamed of or longed for or imagined that life could bring to him? For such a man as this, there really is no coming to the city. He brings the city with him everywhere he goes, and when that final moment comes when he at last breathes in the city's air, feels his foot upon the city street, looks around him at the city's pinnacles, into the dark, unceasing tide of city faces, grips his sinews, feels his flesh, pinches himself to make sure he is really there—for such a man as this, and for such a moment, it will always be a question to be considered in its bewildering ramifications by the subtle soul psychologists to know which city is the real one, which city he has found and seen, which city for this man is really there.

For the city has a million faces, and just as it is said that no two men can really know what each is thinking of, what either sees when he speaks of "red" or "blue," so can no man ever know just what another means when he tells about the city that he sees. For the city that he sees is just the city that he brings with him, that he has within his heart; and even at that immeasurable moment of first perception, when for the first time he sees the city with his naked eye, at that tremendous moment of final apprehension when the great city smites at last upon his living sense, still no man can be certain he has seen the city as it is, because in the hairbreadth of that instant recognition a whole new city is composed, made out of sense but shaped and colored and unalterable from all that he has felt and thought and dreamed about before.

And more than this! There are so many other instant, swift, and accidental things that happen in a moment, that are gone forever, and that shape the city in the heart of youth. It may be a light that comes and goes, a grey day, or a leaf upon a bough; it may be the first image of a city face, a woman's smile, an oath, a half-heard word; it may be sunset, morning, or the crowded traffics of the street, the furious pinnacle of dusty noon; or it may be April, April, and the songs they sang that year. No one can say, except it may be something chance and swift and fleeting, as are all of these, together with the accidents of pine and clay, the weather of one's youth, the place, the structure, and the life from which one came, and all conditioned so, so memoried, built up into the vision of the city that a man first brings there in his heart.

THAT YEAR THERE were five of them. There were Jim Randolph and Monty Bellamy, a South Carolina boy named Harvey Williams and a friend of his named Perce Smead, and then Monk Webber. They were all living together in an apartment they had rented up at 123rd Street. It was on the down slope of the hill that leads from Morningside towards Harlem, the place was on the very fringes of the great Black Belt, so near, in fact, that borders interwove—the pattern of the streets was white and black. It was one of the cheap apartment houses that crowd the district, a six-story structure of caked yellow, rather grimy brick. The entrance hall flourished a show of ornate gaudiness. The floors were tile, the walls were covered halfway up with sheets of streaky-looking marble. On either side, doors opened off into apartments, the doors a kind of composition of dark-painted tin, resembling wood but deceiving no one, stamped with small numerals in dry gilt. There was an elevator at the end, and, by night, a sullen, sleepy-looking negro man; by day, the "superintendent"—an Italian in shirt-sleeves, a hardworking and good-humored factotum who made repairs and tended furnaces and mended plumbing and knew where to buy gin and was argumentative, protesting, and obliging. He was a tireless disputant with whom they wrangled constantly, just for the joy his lingo gave them, because they liked him very much. His name—"Watta the hell!"—was Joe. They liked him as the South likes people, and likes language, and likes personalities, and likes jesting and protesting and good-humored bicker—as the South likes earth and its humanity, which is one of the best things in the South.

So there were the five of them—five younglings from the South, all here together for the first time in the thrilling catacomb, all eager, passionate, aspiring—they had a merry time.

The place, which opened from the right as one went in that marble hall, ran front to rear, and was of the type known as a railroad flat. There were, if counted carefully, five rooms, a living room, three bedrooms, and kitchen. The whole place was traversed from end to end by a dark and narrow hall. It was a kind of tunnel, a sort of alleyway of graduated light. The living room was at the front and had two good windows opening on the street; it was really the only room that had any decent light at all. From there on, one advanced progressively into Stygian depths. The first bedroom had a narrow window opening on a narrow passageway two feet in width that gave on the grimy brick wall of the tenement next door. This place was favored with a kind of murky gloom, reminiscent of those atmospheres one sees in motion pictures showing Tarzan in the jungle with his friends, the apes; or, better still, in those pictures showing the first stages in the ancient world of prehistoric man, at about the time he first crawled out of the primeval ooze. Just beyond this was a bathroom, whose Stygian darkness had never been broken by any ray of outer light; beyond this, another bedroom, identical with the first in all respects, even to the properties of light; beyond this, the kitchen, a little lighter, since it was larger and had two windows; and, at the end, the last and best bedroom, since it was at the corner and had a window on each wall. This room, of course, as fitted a prince of royal blood, was by common and tacit agreement allotted to Jim Randolph. Monty Bellamy and Monk had the next one, and Harvey and his friend Perce shared the other. The rent was $80 a month, which they divided equally.

In the bathroom, when the electric light was not burning, the illusion of midnight was complete. This illusion was enhanced in a rather sinister and clammy fashion by the constant dripping of the bathtub faucet and the perpetual rattling leakage of the toilet. They tried to cure these evils a dozen times; each of them made his own private experiments on the plumbing. The results, while indicative of their ingenuity, were not any particular tribute to their efficiency. It used to worry them at first when they tried to go to sleep at night. The clammy rattling of the toilet and the punctual large drip of the faucet would get on someone's nerves at last, and they would hear him curse and hit the floor, saying:

"God-damn it! How do you expect a man to get to sleep with that damn toilet going all night long!"

Then he would pad out and down the hall and flush the toilet, pull off the lid and fume and fuss with the machinery, and swear below his breath, and finally put the lid back on, leaving the empty bowl to fill again. And he would come back with a sigh of satisfaction, saying he reckoned he got the damn thing fixed that time all right. And then he would crawl into bed again, prepare himself for blissful slumber, only to have that rattling and infuriating leak begin all over again.

But this was almost the worst of their troubles, and they soon got used to it. It is true, the two bedrooms on the hall were so small and cramped they couldn't get two single cots in them, and so had to fall back on their old college dormitory expedient of racking them boat-wise, one upon the other. It is also true that these little bedrooms had so little light that at no time of the day could one read a paper without the aid of electricity. The single window of each room looked out upon a dingy airshaft, the blank brick surface of the next-door building. And since they were on the ground floor, they were at the bottom of this shaft. Of course this gave them certain advantages in rent. As one went up, one got more light and air, and as one got more light and air, one paid more rent. The mathematics of the arrangement was beauti-fully simple, but none of them, coming as they all did from a region where the atmosphere was one commodity in which all men had equal rights, had quite recovered from their original surprise at finding them-selves in a new world where even the weather was apportioned on a cash basis.

Still, they got used to it very quickly, and they didn't mind it very much. In fact, they all thought it pretty splendid. They had an *apart-ment, a real* apartment, on the fabulous Island of Manhattan. They had their own private bathroom, even if the taps did leak. They had their kitchen, too, where they cooked meals. Every one of them had his own pass key and could come and go as he pleased.

They had the most amazing assortment of furniture Monk had ever seen. God knows where Jim Randolph had picked it up. He was their boss, their landlord, and their leader. He had already had the place a year when Monk moved in, so the furniture was there when he arrived. They had two chiffonier dressers in the best Grand Rapids style, with oval mirrors, wooden knobs, and not too much of the varnish scaling off. Jim had a genuine bureau in his room, with real bottoms in two of the drawers. In the living room they had a big, over-stuffed chair with a broken spring in it, a long davenport with part of the wadding oozing out, an old leather chair, a genuine rocking chair whose wicker bottom was split wide open, a book case with a few books in it and glass doors which rattled and which sometimes stuck together when it rained, and—what was most remarkable of all—a real upright piano.

That piano had been to the wars and showed it. It looked and sounded as if it had served a long apprenticeship around the burlesque circuit. The old ivory keys were yellowed by long years of service, the mahogany case was scarred by boots and charred by the fags of countless cigarettes. Some of the keys gave forth no sound at all, and a good number of the sounds they did give forth were pretty sour. But what did it matter? Here was a piano—*their* piano—indubitably and undeniably a genuine upright and upstanding piano in the living room of their magnificent and luxurious five-room apartment in the upper portion of the fabulous Island of Manhattan. Here they could entertain their guests. Here they could invite their friends. Here they could eat and drink and sing and laugh and give parties and have girls and play their piano.

Jim Randolph, to tell the truth, was the only one who could play it. He played it very badly, and yet he played it rather wonderfully, too. He missed a lot of notes and smashed through others. But his powerful hands and fingers held in their hard stroke a sure sense of rhythm, a swinging beat. It was good to hear him play because it was so good to *see* and *feel* him play. God knows where he learned it. It was another in that amazing list of accomplishments which he had acquired at one time or another and at one place or another in his journeyings about the earth, and which included in its range accomplishments as wide and varied as the ability to run 100 yards in less than eleven seconds, to kick a football 80 yards, to shoot a rifle and to ride a horse, to speak a little Spanish, some Italian and some French, to cook a steak, to fry a chicken, or to make a pie, to navigate a ship, to use a typewriter—and to get a girl when and where he wanted her.

Jim was a good deal older than any of the others. He was by this time nearing thirty. And his legend still clung to him. Monk never saw him walk across the room without remembering instantly how he used to look as he started one of his great sweeps around right end behind his interference. In spite of his years, he was an amazingly young and boyish person, a creature given to impulse, to the sudden bursts of passion, enthusiasm, sentiment and folly and unreason of a boy. But just as the man had so much of the boy in him, so did the boy have so much of the man. He exerted over all of them a benevolent but paternal governance, and the reason that they all looked up to him as they did, the reason that all of them, without thought or question, accepted him as their leader, was not because of the few years' difference in their ages, but because he seemed in every other way a mature and grown man.

WHAT IS IT that a young man wants? Where is the central source of that wild fury that boils up in him, that goads and drives and lashes him, that explodes his energies and strews his purpose to the wind of a thousand instant and chaotic impulses? The older and assured people of the world, who have learned to work without waste and error, think they know the reason for the chaos and confusion of a young man's life. They have learned the thing at hand, and learned to follow their single way through all the million shifting hues and tones and cadences of living, to thread neatly with unperturbed heart their single thread through that huge labyrinth of shifting forms and intersecting energies that make up life—and they say, therefore, that the reason for a young man's confusion, lack of purpose, and erratic living is because he has not "found himself."

In this the older and more certain people may be right by their own standard of appraisal, but, in this judgment on the life of youth, they have really pronounced a sterner and more cruel judgment on themselves. For when they say that some young man has not yet "found himself," they are really saying that he has not lost himself as they. For men will often say that they have "found themselves" when they have really been worn down into a groove by the brutal and compulsive force of circumstance. They speak of their life's salvation when all that they have done is blindly follow through an accidental way. They have forgotten their life's purpose, and all the faith, hope, and immortal confidence of a boy. They have forgotten that below all the apparent waste, loss, chaos, and disorder of a young man's life there is really a central purpose and a single faith which they themselves have lost.

What is it that a young man does—here in America? How does he live? What is the color, texture, substance of his life? How does he look and feel and act? What is the history of his days—the secret of the fury that devours him—the core and center of his one belief—the design and rhythm of his single life?

All of us know what it is. We have lived it with every beating of our pulse, known it with every atom of our bone, blood sinew, marrow, feeling. The knowledge of it is mixed insolubly into the substance of our lives. We have seen and recognized it instantly, not only in ourselves, but in the lives of ten thousand people all around us—as familiar as the earth on which we tread, as near as our own hearts, as certain as the light of morn. And yet we never speak of it. We cannot speak of it. We have no way to speak of it.

Why? Because the young men of this land are not, as they are often called, a "lost" race—they are a race that never yet has been discovered. And the whole secret, power, and knowledge of their own discovery is locked within them—they know it, feel it, have the whole thing in them—and they cannot utter it.

George Webber was not long in finding out that perhaps it is just here, in the iron-breasted city, that one comes closest to the enigma that haunts and curses the whole land. The city is the place where men are constantly seeking to find their door and where they are doomed to wandering forever. Of no place is this more true than of New York. Hideously ugly for the most part, one yet remembers it as a place of proud and passionate beauty: the place of everlasting hunger, it is also the place where mean feel their lives will gloriously be fulfilled and their hunger fed.

In no place in the world can the life of the lonely boy, the countryman who has been drawn northwards to the flame of his lust, be more barren, more drab, more hungry and comfortless. His life is the life of subways, of rebreathed air, of the smell of burned steel, weariness and the exhausted fetidity of a cheap rented room in the apartment of "a nice couple" on 113th Street, or perhaps the triumph of an eighty-dollar apartment in Brooklyn, upper Manhattan, or the Bronx which he rents with three or four other youths. Here they "can do as they please," a romantic aspiration which leads to Saturday night parties, to cheap gin, cheap girls, to a feverish and impotent fumbling, and perhaps to an occasional distressed, drunken, and half-public fornication.

If the youth is of a serious bent, if he has thoughts of "improving" himself, there is the gigantic desolation of the Public Library, a cut-rate ticket at Gray's and a seat in the balcony of an art-theatre play that has been highly praised and that all intellectual people will be seeing, or the grey depression of a musical Sunday afternoon at Carnegie Hall, filled with arrogant-looking little musicians with silky mustaches who hiss like vipers in the dark when the works of a hated composer are played; or there is always the Metropolitan Museum.

Again, there is something spurious and unreal in almost all attempts at established life in the city. When one enters the neat little apartment of a young married couple, and sees there on neat gaily-painted shelves neat rows of books—the solid little squares of the Everyman, and the Modern Library, the D. H. Lawrence, the *Buddenbrooks*, the Cabell, the art edition of *Penguin Island*, then

THE WEB AND THE WORLD   271

a few of the paper-backed French books, the Proust and the Gide, and so on—one feels a sense of embarrassment and shame: there is something fraudulent about it. One feels this also in the homes of wealthy people, whether they live in a "charming little house" on Ninth Street which they have rented, or in the massive rooms of a Park Avenue apartment.

No matter what atmosphere of usage, servants, habitude, ease, and solid establishment there may be, one always has this same feeling that the thing is fraudulent, that the effort to achieve permanence in this impermanent and constantly changing life is no more real than the suggested permanence in a theatrical setting: one would not be surprised to return the next morning and find the scene dismantled, the stage bare, and the actors departed. Sometimes even the simplest social acts—the act of visiting one's friends, of talking to them in a room, of sitting around a hearth-fire with them—oh, above all else, of sitting around a hearth-fire in an apartment in the city!—seem naked and pitiful. There is an enormous sadness and wistfulness about these attempts to simulate an established life in a place where the one permanent thing is change itself.

In recent years many people have felt this insistent and constant movement. Some have blamed it on the war, some on the tempo of the time, some have called it "a jazz age" and suggested that men should meet the rhythm of the age and move and live by it; but although this notion has been fashionable, it can hardly recommend itself to men who have been driven by their hunger, who have known loneliness and exile, who have wandered upon the face of the earth and found no doors that they could enter, and who would to God now that they might make an end to all their wandering and loneliness, that they might find one home and heart of all their hunger where they could live abundantly forever. Such men, and they are numbered not by thousands but by millions, are hardly prepared to understand that the agony and loneliness of the human spirit may be assuaged by the jerky automata of jazz.

Perhaps this sense of restlessness, loneliness, and hunger is intensified in the city, but if anyone remembers his own childhood and youth in America he is certain to remember these desires and movements, too. Everywhere people were driven by them. Everyone had a rocking chair, and in the months of good weather everyone was out on his front porch rocking away. People were always eager to "go somewheres," and when the automobile came in, the roads, particularly on Sunday, were choked with cars going into the country, going to another town, going anywhere, no matter how ugly or barren the excursion might be, so long as this terrible restlessness might in some measure be appeased.

In the city, it is appalling to think how much pain and hunger people—and particularly young men—have suffered, because there is no goal whatever for these feverish extravasations. They return, after their day's work to a room which, despite all efforts to trick it out with a neat bed, bright colors, a few painted bookshelves, a few pictures, is obviously only a masked cell. It becomes impossible to use the room for any purpose at all save for sleeping; the act of reading a book in it, of sitting in a chair in it, of staying in it for any period of time whatever when one is in a state of wakefulness, becomes intolerable.

Yet, what are these wretched people to do? Every instant, every deep conviction a man has for a reasonable human comfort is outraged. He knows that every man on earth should have the decency of space—of space enough to extend his limbs and draw in the air without fear or labor; and he knows that his life here in this miserable closet is base, barren, mean, and naked. He knows that men should not defile themselves in this way, so he keeps out of his room as much as possible. But what can he do? Where can he go? In the terrible streets of the city there is neither pause nor repose, there are no turnings and no place where he can detach himself from the incessant tide of the crowd, and sink unto himself in tranquil meditation. He flees from one desolation to another, he escapes by buying a seat "at some show," or snatching at food in a cafeteria, he lashes about the huge streets of the night, and he returns to his cell having found no doors that he could open, no place that he could call his own.

It is therefore astonishing that nowhere in the world can a young man feel greater hope and expectancy than here. The promise of glorious fulfillment, of love, wealth, fame—or unimaginable joy—is always impending in the air. He is torn with a thousand desires and he is unable to articulate one of them, but he is sure that he will grasp joy to his heart, that he will hold love and glory in his arms, that the intangible will be touched, the inarticulate spoken, the inapprehensible apprehended: and that this may happen at any moment.

Perhaps there is some chemistry of air that causes this exuberance and joy, but it also belongs to the enigma of the whole country, which is so rich, and yet where people starve, which is so abundant, exultant, savage, full-blooded, humorous, liquid, and magnificent, and yet where so many people are poor, meager, dry, and baffled. But the richness and depth of the place is visible, it is not an illusion; there is always the feeling that the earth is full of gold, and that who will seek and strive can mine it.

In New York there are certain wonderful seasons in which this feeling grows to a lyrical intensity. One of these are those first tender days of Spring when lovely girls and women seem suddenly to burst out of the pavements like flowers: all at once the street is peopled with them, walking along with a proud, undulant rhythm of breasts and buttocks and a look of passionate tenderness on their faces. Another season is early Autumn, in October, when the city begins to take on a magnificent flash and sparkle: there are swift whippings of bright wind, a flare of bitter leaves, the smell of frost and harvest in the air: after the enervation of Summer, the place awakens to an electric vitality, the beautiful women have come back from Europe or from the summer resorts, and the air is charged with exultancy and joy.

Finally, there is a wonderful, secret thrill of some impending ecstasy on a frozen Winter's night. On one of these nights of frozen silence when the cold is so intense that it numbs one's flesh, and the sky above the city flashes with one deep jewelry of cold stars, the whole city, no matter how ugly its parts may be, becomes a proud, passionate, Northern place: everything about it seems to soar up with an aspirant, vertical, glittering magnificence to meet the stars. One hears the hoarse notes of the great ships in the river, and one remembers suddenly the princely girdle of proud, potent tides that bind the city, and suddenly New York blazes like a magnificent jewel in its fit setting of sea, and earth, and stars.

There is no place like it, no place with an atom of its glory, pride, and exultancy. It lays its hand upon a man's bowels: he grows drunk with ecstasy; he grows young and full of glory; he feels that he can never die.

CHAPTER 14

The City Patriots

Jerry Alsop had come to New York straight out of college several years before. Monk knew that he was there, and one day he ran into him. Neither seemed disposed to remember Monk's apostasy of college days: in fact, Jerry greeted his former protege like a long lost brother and invited him around to his place. Monk went, and later went again, and for a time their relationship was reestablished, on the surface at least, on something of its former footing.

Alsop lived in the same part of town, on a cross street between Broadway and the river, and not far from Columbia University. He had two basement rooms and a dilapidated kitchenette. The place was dark, and he had collected a congeries of broken-down furniture—an old green sofa, a few chairs, a couple of tables, a folding couch or daybed, covered with a dirty cloth, for visitors, another larger bed for himself and a dirty old carpet. He thought it was wonderful, and because he communicated this sense of wonder to all his friends, they thought so, too. What it really represented to him was freedom—the glorious, intoxicating freedom that the city gave to him, to everyone. So seen and so considered, his apartment was not just a couple of dirty, dark, old rooms, filled with a hodgepodge of nondescript furniture, down in the basement of a dismal house. It was a domain, an estate, a private castle, a citadel. Jerry conveyed this magic sense to everyone who came there.

When Monk first saw him there in all the strangeness of New York, the changes in Alsop's vision and belief appeared astonishing. Only, however, at first sight. The younger man's sense of shock, the result of the blinding clarity of his first impression after the years of absence, was only momentary. For Alsop had gathered around him now a new coterie, the descendants of the clique at old Pine Rock: he was their mentor and their guiding star, and his two dark basement rooms had become their club. And so Monk saw that Alsop had not really changed at all, that below all the confusion of outer change his soul was still the same.

One of the chief objects of his hatred at this time was Mr. H. L. Mencken. He had become for Alsop the Beast of the Apocalypse. Mencken's open ridicule of pedagogy, of Mother-idolatry, of the whole civilization which he called the Bible Belt and which referred to that part of life of which Alsop was himself a member, and, most of all, perhaps, the critic's open and ungodly mockery of "the greatest man since Jesus Christ," to whom he referred variously as "the late Doctor Wilson," or "the martyred Woodrow"—all of this struck with an assassin's dirk at the heart of all that was near and dear to Alsop, and, it seemed to him, at the heart of civilization itself, at religion, at morality, at "all that men hold sacred." The result was that this smashing but essentially conservative critic, Mencken, became in Alsop's eyes the figure of the Antichrist. Month after month he would read the latest blast of the Baltimore sage with the passionate devotion of pure hate. It was really alarming just to watch him as he went about his venomous perusal: his fat and usually rather pale face would become livid and convulsed as if he were in imminent peril of an apoplectic stroke, his eyes would narrow into reptilian slits, from time to time he would burst out into infuriated laughter, the whole proceeding being punctuated by such comment as:

"Well, I'll be God-damned! . . . Of all the! . . . Why, he's just a damned ass . . . yes suh! . . . That's the only name for him! . . . A plain damned ass. For God's sake now, listen to this!" Here his voice would mount to a choking scream. "Why, he hasn't got the brains of a louse!"—the whole winding up inevitably with the final recommendation for vindictive punishment: "You know what they ought to do with a man like that? They ought to take him out and——."

He mentioned this act of mutilation with a hearty relish. It seemed to be the first act of vengeance and reprisal that popped into his head whenever anyone said or wrote or did something that aroused his hatred and antagonism. And it was as if Mr. H. L. Mencken, whom Alsop had never seen, had been a personal enemy, a malignant threat in his own life, a deadly peril not only to himself but to his friends and to the world he had shaped about him.

And yet, all the time Alsop himself was changing. His adaptive powers were remarkable. Like a certain famous Bishop, "he had a large and easy swallow." And really, what mattered most to him was not the inner substance but the outer show. He would, with no difficulty whatever, have agreed that black was white, or that two and two make four and three quarters, if the prevailing order of society had swung to the belief.

It was only that, in Alsopian phrase, his "sphere had widened." He had come from the provincial community of the Baptist college to the city. And that staggering transition, so painful, so perilous, and so confusing to so many other men had been for Alsop triumphantly easy. He had taken to the city like a duck to water. And in that complete and rapturous immersion was revealed, along with all that was shapeless in his character, also all that was warm and imaginative and good.

Some come to the city, no doubt, with wire-taut nerves, with trembling apprehension, with a resolution of grim conflict desperate struggle, and the conviction they must do or die. Some, shackled by old fears, still cumbered with the harness of old prejudice, come to it doubtfully and with mistrust. And for them, the city that they find will be a painful one. And some come to it with exultancy and hope, as men rush forward to embrace a beloved mistress, whom they have never seen but of whom they have always known, and it was in this

way that Alsop—Alsop of the bulging belly and the butter-tub of fat—
it was in just this way that Alsop came.

It never occurred to him that he might fail. And indeed with faith
like his, with such devotion as he brought, the chance of failure was
impossible. Other men might rise to greater summit in the city's life.
Other men might rise to greater substance of success, of wealth, of
fame, achievement, or reputation. But no man would ever belong more
truly to the city, or the city's life to him, than Gerald Alsop.

He was made for it; it was made for him. Here was a point that he
could swim in, a pool where he could fish. Here was the food for all
his thousand appetites, the provender for his hundred mouths. Here
was living water for the quenchless sponge that was himself: the rumor
with the million tongues that could feed forever his insatiate ear, the
chronicle of eight million lives that could appease his ceaseless thirst
for human history.

Alsop was a man who had to live through others. He was an enormous Ear, Eye, Nose, Throat, and absorptive sponge of gluttonous
humanity—he was not a thrust or arm—and in such a way as this,
and so perfectly, so completely, the city was his oyster. And in his
way he was incomparable. All that was best in him was here revealed.
He communicated to everyone around him the contagion of his own
enthusiasm, the sense of magic and of rapture which the city gave to
him. With him, an excursion of any sort was a memorable event. A
trip downtown in the subway, the gaudy lights, the thronging traffics
of Times Square, the cut-rate ticket basement of Gray's Pharmacy, the
constant nocturnal magic of the theatres, the cheap restaurants, a cafeteria or a lunchroom, a chop suey place, the strange faces, signs, and
lights, the foreign vegetables, the unknown edibles of Chinatown—all
this was simply magic. He was living in an enchanted world, he carried
it with him everywhere he went.

His was the temper of the insatiable romantic. In no time at all,
instantly, immediately, he inherited the city's hunger for celebrity. If he
could not be great himself, he wanted to be near those who were. He

lapped up every scrap of gossip about celebrated people he could read or hear. The records, diaries, comments, observations of the newspaper columnists were gospel to him. The pronouncements of a certain well-known dramatic critic, Cotswold, were like holy writ: he memorized them down to the last whimsical caprice of ornate phrasing. He went religiously to see every play the critic praised. One night he saw the great man himself, a fat and puffy little butter-ball of a man, in the interim between the acts, with another celebrated critic and a famous actress. When Alsop returned home he was transported—if he had seen Shakespeare talking to Ben Jonson, his emotion could not have been so great.

He became a watcher around stage doors. It was the period of the Ziegfeld shows, the glorified chorines, the proud, lavish flesh draped in a fold of velvet. Alsop now was everywhere, he delighted in these glorified carnalities. The girls were famous, he watched till they came out, and, like some ancient lecher, he licked his chops and gloated while the Ziegfeld Beauties and their moneyed purchasers walked away. The meeting of expensive flesh with shirt front, tails, and tall silk hatdom now delighted him. Strange work for old Pine Rock?—By no means: it was enhaloed now, set like a jewel in the great Medusa of the night, privileged by power and wealth and sanctioned by publicity. The aged lecher licking his dry lips and waiting with dead eyes for his young whore of Babylon, delighted Alsop now. He told of such a one: the beauty, already famed in print, came by—the aged lecher fawned upon her—"Oh, for Christ's sake!" said the beauty wearily, passing on.

"She meant that thing," said Alsop gloatingly. "Yes, suh! She meant that thing!" His great belly heaved, his throat rattled with its scream of phlegm. "God! The most beautiful damn woman that you ever saw!" said Alsop appetizingly as he shook his great jowled head. "She sure did get him told!" The scene delighted him.

All others, too: the rumors of a thousand tongues, the fruitage of a thousand whispered gossips: who slept with so-and-so; whose wife was faithless unto Caesar; whose wit had uttered such unprinted jest; what

famous names, what authors, had behaved in such-and-such a way
at such-and-such a party, had grown drunk there, had disappeared,
had locked themselves in bedrooms with attractive women, gone into
bathrooms with them, quarreled, fought with whom: what rather aged
actress, famous for her lustihood in roles, had gone with boys of apple-
cheeked persuasion; and who the famous fairies were, and the dance
halls where they went to dance with one another, and what they said,
the mincing syllables of their fond intercourse with one another—
here belly heaved and Alsop screamed with choking laughter—such
wickedness, together with all whimsicalities, and Morley's columns
in the purest vein of elfin whimsey—"Pure genius! Pure damned
elfin genius!"—old London in the byways of New York, Dickensian
bylights of the city ways, and the thronging chaoses of Herald Square,
Park Row; the grime of unrubbed brasses, never noticed by the man-
hordes passing by, but seen now in a certain light, and properly, the
true quaintness of the world around him: the shopgirls eating sandwiches of pimento cheese among the drug store slops of luncheon hour
were really like the clients of an inn in Eastcheap ninety years ago. So,
all together—Ziegfeld, beautiful chorines, and ancient lechers in silk
hats; hot gossip of the great, the rumor of drunken riot with the famed
and few, what Miss Parker said, and so-and-so: together with the Great
of the town, the men in subways and park benches—Lamb redivivus,
alive and prowling among unrubbed brass in the quaint byways of
Manhattan—all such as this was meat, drink, breath of life to Alsop.

So the food. His taste, like Dr. Samuel Johnson's, was not fine—he
liked abundance and he liked to slop it in. He had a love for Chinatown, chop suey, and the pungent sauce: it was abundant, it was cheap.
The strange faces of the Chinks, the moisty vapors, Oriental and
somewhat depressant, all delighted him. He loved to go with several
other people—one could order several dishes and thus share. When it
was over he would call for paper bags, slop the remainders into them,
and wheeze and choke with laughter as he did so.

When all this palled, or when he felt the belly hungers for familiar food—for home to heart and stomach was still very near—he and his cronies would buy up "a mess of stuff." There were stores everwhere, around the corner in every city block were stores, and the crowded opulence of night, and lighted windows, slanting shelves of vegetables and fruit; and butcher shops, chain groceries, bakeries, every kind of vast provisioning. They would go out upon their errands, they would buy the foods of home: a package of ground hominy—otherwise known as grits; string beans, which really were the same as they had always been, except no one knew how to cook them here, a piece of fat salt port to give them seasoning; flour for gravy and for biscuit dough—for Alsop paled not at such formidable enterprise; steak, no worse if it were cheap and tough, but with the flour gravy and the condiments; bread from the bakery, butter, coffee. Then back to the basement, the two-roomed flat, a chaos of young voices, laughter, humorous, accusal—Alsop chuckling, serious and all-governing, giving directions, bustling about in slippered feet, from whose stale socks protruded the fat hinge of his dirty heels. And then the pungency of native foods again—grits, fried steak with thick brown gravy, string beans savory, deep-hued with fatback, brown-hued biscuits, smoking hot, strong coffee, melting butter. The vigorous confusion of young, drawling voices, excited, Southern, ingrown each to each, tribal and most personal—the new adventure of each daily life told eagerly and to the common mall, with laughter, agreement, strong derision. They appraised the new world where they lived with critic tongue, and often with a strong and disapproving mockery.

They had small thought of ever going home again. At least, they seldom told their love. Their love, in fact, was mainly here—for most of them, like Alsop, were immersed in glamor now, had cottoned to this brave, new world, had taken it for their own domain as only people from the South can take it—some strange and stiff-necked pride kept them from owning it. They lived in legend now: among the thrill of all this present pageantry, they loved to descant on their former glories. "The South"—for in quotation marks they saw it—was now an exiled glory, a rich way of life, of living, and of human values which "these people up here" could never know about.

Perhaps they set this glory as a kind of reassuring palliative to their shock sense, the thrilling and yet terrifying conflict of the daily struggle. It was an occasional sop to wounded pride. The customs and the mores of the new world were examined critically and came off second best. A chicanery of the Northern ways, the suspicion of the hardened eye, the itching of the grasping palm, the machinations of the crafty Jew—all were observed upon with scorn and frequent bitterness. People in "the South" were not like this. As Alsop said, one had to come "up here" in order to find out just "how fine and swept and lovable" they were.

GEORGE WEBBER HAD observed that there is no one on earth who is more patriotically devoted—verbally, at least—to the region from which he came than the American from the Southern portion of the United States. Once he leaves it to take up his living in other, less fair and fortunate, sections of the country, he is willing to fight for the honor of the Southland at the drop of a hat, to assert her supremacy over all the other habitable parts of the globe on every occasion, to speak eloquently and passionately of the charm of her setting, the superiority of her culture, the heroism of her men, and the beauty of her women, to defend her, to protect her, to bleed and die for her, if necessary—to do almost everything, in fact, for dear old Dixie except to return permanently to her to live.

A great many, It must be owned, do return, but most of those are the sorrier and more incompetent members of the tribe, the failures, the defeated ones—the writers who cannot write, the actors who cannot act, the painters who cannot paint, the men and women of all sorts, of all professions, of all endeavors from law to soda water, who, although not wholly lacking in talent, lack in it sufficient degree to meet the greater conflict of a wider life, the shock of open battle on a foreign field, the intenser effort and the superior performances of city life. These are the stragglers of the army. They hang on for a while, are buffeted, stunned, bewildered, frightened, ultimately overwhelmed by the battle roar. One by one they falter, give way, and, dispirited, bitter, and defeated, straggle back to the familiar safety and the comforting assurance of the hinterland.

Once there, a familiar process of the South begins, a pastime at which the inhabitants of that region have long been adept—the subtle, soothing sport of rationalization. The humbler members of the routed troops—the disillusioned soda-jerkers, the defeated filing clerks, department store workers, business, bank, and brokerage employees— arrive rapidly at the conclusion that the great city is "no place for a white man." The unfortunate denizens of city life "don't know what living really is." They endure their miserable existences because they "don't know any better." The city people are an ignorant and conceited lot. They have no manners, no courtesy, no consideration for the rights of others, and no humanity. Everyone in the city is "out for himself," out to do you, out to get everything he can out of you. It is a selfish, treacherous, lonely, and self-seeking life. A man has friends as long as he has money in his pocket. Friends melt away from him like smoke when money goes. Moreover, all social pride and decency, the dignity of race, the authority of class is violated and destroyed in city life—"A nigger is as good as a white man."

When George was a child, there was a story that was current over all the South. Some local hero—some village champion of the rights of white men and the maintenance of white supremacy—told the gory adventure of his one and only, his first and last, his final, all-sufficient journey into the benighted and corrupted domains of the North. Sometimes the adventure had occurred in Washington, sometimes in Philadelphia or New York, sometimes in Boston or in Baltimore, but the essential setting was always the same. The scene for this heroic drama was always laid in a restaurant of a Northern city. The plumed knight from below the Mason-Dixon line had gone in to get something to eat and had taken his seat at a table. He had progressed no further

than his soup, when, looking up, he found to his horror and indignation that a "big buck nigger" had come in and taken a seat opposite
him, and *at his own table*. Whereupon—but let the more skillful small-
town raconteurs of twenty years ago complete the tale:

"Well, ole Jim says he took one look at him and says, 'You black
son-of-a-bitch, what do you mean by sitting at my table?' Well, the
nigger begins to talk back to him, telling him he was in the North
now, where a nigger was just as good as anyone. And ole Jim says, 'You
black bastard you, you may be as good as a Yankee, but you're talking
to a white man now!'—and with that, he says, he ups with a ketchup
bottle and he just busts it wide open over that nigger's head. Jim says
he reckoned he killed him, says he didn't wait to see, he just left him
laying there and grabbed his hat and walked out. He says he caught the
first train going South and he's never been North since, and that he
don't care if he never sees the God-damn place again."

This story was usually greeted with roars of appreciative and ad-
miring laughter, the sound of thighs smitten with enthusiastic palms,
gleeful exclamations of " 'Oddam! I'd 'a' given anything to've seen it!
Whew-w! I can just see ole Jim now as he let him have it! I'll betcha
anything you like he killed that black bastard deader'n a doornail! Yes
sir! Damned if I blame him either! I'd 'a' done the same thing!"

George must have heard this gory adventure gleefully related at
least a hundred times during his childhood and the adolescent period
of his youth. The names of the characters were sometimes different—
sometimes it was "ole Jim" or "ole Bob" or "ole Dick"—but the essential circumstance was always the same; an impudent black limb of
Satan entered, took the forbidden seat, and was promptly, ruthlessly,
and gorily annihilated with a ketchup bottle. This story, in its various
forms and with many modern innovations, was still current among
returned wanderers from the Southland at the time when George first
came to the great city to live. In more modern versions the insolent
black had been annihilated on busses and in subway trains, in railway
coaches or in moving picture theatres, in crowded elevators or upon

the street—wherever, in fact, he had dared impudently to intrude too closely upon the proud and cherished dignity of a Southern white. And the existence of this ebony malefactor was, one gathered, one of the large contributing reasons for the return of the native to his own more noble heath.

Another, and probably more intelligent, portion of this defeated—and retreated—group had other explanations for their retreat, which were, however, derived from the same basic sources of rationalized self-defense. These were the members of the more intellectual groups—the writers, painters, actors—who had tried the ardors of the city's life and who had fled from it. Their arguments and reasons were subtler, more refined. The actor or the playwright asserted that he found the integrity of his art, the authentic drama of the folk, blighted and corrupted by the baleful and unnatural influence of the Broadway drama, by artificiality, trickery, and cheap sensation, by that which struck death to native roots and gave only a waxen counterfeit of the native flower. The painter or the musician found the artist and his art delivered to the mercy of fashionable cliques, constricted with the lifeless narrowness of æsthetic schools. The writer had a similar complaint. The creator's life was menaced in the city with the sterile counterfeits of art—the poisonous ethers of "the literary life," the poisonous intrigues of the literary cliques, the poisonous politics of log-rolling and back-scratching, critic-mongering and critic-pandering, the whole nasty, crawling, parasitical world of Scribbleonia.

In these unnatural and unwholesome weathers of creation, the artist—so these rebellious challengers asserted—lost his contact with reality, forgot the living inspirations of his source, had been torn away from living union with what he had begun to call his "roots." So caught and so imperiled, held high, Antæus-wise, away from contact with his native and restoring earth, gasping for breath in the dead vapors of an enclosed and tainted atmosphere, there was only one course for the artist if he would be saved. He must return, return to that place which had given him life and from which the strengths and energies of his art had been derived. But must renounce utterly and forever the sterile precincts of the clique, the salon, and the circle, the whole unnatural domain of the city's life. He must return again to the good earth, to affirmation of his origins, to contact with his "roots."

So the refined young gentlemen of the New Confederacy shook off their degrading shackles, caught the last cobwebs of illusion from their awakened vision, and retired haughtily into the South, to the academic security of a teaching appointment at one of the universities, from which they could issue in quarterly installments very small and very precious magazines which celebrated the advantages of an agrarian society. The subtler intelligences of this rebel horde were forever formulating codes and cults in their own precincts—codes and cults which affirmed the earthly virtues of both root and source in such unearthly language, by such processes of æsthetic subtlety, that even the cult adepts of the most precious city cliques were hard put to it to extract the meaning.

All this George Webber observed and found somewhat puzzling and astonishing. Young men whose habits, tastes, and modes of thought and writing seemed to him to belong a great deal more to the atmospheres of the æsthetic cliques which they renounced than to any other now began to argue the merits of a return to "an agrarian way of life" in language which was, it seemed to him, the language of a cult, and which assuredly few dwellers on the soil, either permanent or returned, could understand. Moreover, as one who was himself derived from generations of mountain farmers who had struggled year by year to make a patch of corn grow in the hill erosions of a mountain flank, and of generations of farm workers in Pennsylvania who had toiled for fifteen hours a day behind the plow to earn a wage of fifty cents, it now came as a mild surprise to be informed by the lily-handed intellectuals of a Southern university that what he needed most of all was a return to the earthly and benevolent virtues of the society which had produced him.

The summation of it all, of course, the fundamental characteristic of this whole defeated and retreated kind—whether intellectual or creative, professional or of the working group—was the familiar ratio-nalizing self-defense of Southern fear and Southern failure: its fear of conflict and of competition in the greater world; its inability to meet or to adjust itself to the conditions, strifes, and ardors of a modern life; its old, sick, Appomattoxlike retreat into the shades of folly and delusion, of prejudice and bigotry, of florid legend and defensive casuistry, of haughty and ironic detachment from a life with which it was too obvi-ously concerned, to which it wished too obviously to belong.

So much, then, for these defeated ones—these too tender and inept detachments of the rebel horde who could not meet and take the shock of battle, and who straggled back. What of the others, the better and the larger kind, the ones who stayed? Were they defeated? Were they swept under? Were they dispersed and scattered, or routed in dismay and driven back?

By no means. Their success, in fact, in city life was astonishing. There is no other section of the country whose city immigrants suc-ceed so brilliantly when they do succeed. The quality of the South-erner's success in city life is derived, to an amazing degree, from the very nature of his handicap. If he prevails, if he conquers, he is likely to do it not only in spite of his provincialism but because of it, not only in spite of his fear but by means of it, and because that terrible and lacerating consciousness of inferiority is likely to drive him on to superhuman efforts.

The Southerner is often inspired to do his best when the odds are the heaviest against him, when he knows it, when he knows further that the world knows it and is looking on. The truth of this was dem-onstrated again and again in the Civil War, when some of the South's most brilliant victories—it is possible also to say, when some of the South's most brilliant defeats—were *won* under these circumstances. The Southerner, with all that is sensitive, tender, flashing, quick, vola-tile, and over-imaginative in his nature, is likely to know fear and to know it greatly. But also, precisely on account of his sensitivity, quick-ness, imagination, he knows fear *of* fear, and this second kind of fear is often likely to be so much stronger than the first that he will do and die before he shows it. He will fight like a madman rather than like a man, and he will often attain an almost unbelievable victory against overwhelming odds, even when few people in the world believe that victory is possible.

These facts are true, and they are likewise admirable. But in their very truth there is a kind of falseness. In their very strength there is a dangerous weakness. In the very brilliance of their victory there is a lamentable defeat. It is admirable to win against terrific odds, but it is not admirable, not well for the health and endurance of the spirit, to be able to win only against terrific odds. It is thrilling to see men roused to such a pitch of desperation that they fight like madmen, but it is also thrilling to see them resolved and strong in their ability to fight like men. It is good to be so proud and sensitive that one is more afraid of showing fear than of fear itself, but these intensities of passion, pride, and desperation also take their toll. The danger is that though they may spur men to the feverish consummation of great heights, they may also drop them, exhausted and impotent, to abysmal depth, and that one attains the shining moment of a brilliant effort at the expense of the consistent and steady achievement of a solid and protracted work.

The transplanted Southerner is likely to be a very lonely animal. For that reason his first instinctive movement in the city is likely to be in the direction of his own kind. The first thing he does when he gets to the city is to look up old college chums or boys from his home town. They form a community of mutual interests and mutual self-protection; they build a kind of wall around themselves to protect them from the howling maelstrom of the city's life. They form a Community of the South which has no parallel in city life. Certainly one does not find a similar Community of the Middle West, or a Community of the Great Plains, or a Community of the Rocky Mountain States, or a Community of the Pacific Coast. There are, perhaps, the faint rudiments of a New England Community, the section which, after the South, is most definitely marked by a native identity of culture. But the New England Community, if it exists at all, exists so faintly and so sparely as to be almost negligible.

The most obvious reason for the existence of this Community of the South within the city's life is to be found in the deep-rooted and provincial insularity of Southern life. The cleavage of ideas, the division of interests, of social customs and traditional beliefs, which were developing with a tremendous gathering velocity in American life during the first half of the nineteenth century, and which were more and more separating the life of an agrarian South from the life of the industrial North, were consummated by the bloody action of the Civil War, and were confirmed and sealed by the dark and tragic act of reconstruction. After the war and after reconstruction, the South retreated in behind its shattered walls and stayed there.

There was an image in George Webber's mind that came to him in childhood and that resumed for him the whole dark picture of those decades of defeat and darkness. He saw an old house, set far back from the traveled highway, and many passed along that road, and the troops went by, the dust rose, and the war was over. And no one passed along that road again. He saw an old man go along the path, away from the road, into the house; and the path was overgrown with grass and weeds, with thorny tangle, and with underbrush until the path was lost. And no one ever used that path again. And the man who went into that house never came out of it again. And the house stayed on. It shone faintly through that tangled growth like its own ruined spectre, its door and windows black as eyeless sockets. That was the South. That was the South for thirty years or more.

That was the South, not of George Webber's life, nor of the lives of his contemporaries—that was the South they did not know but that all of them somehow remembered. It came to them from God knows where, upon the rustling of a leaf at night, in quiet voices on a Southern porch, in a screen door slam and sudden silence, a whistle wailing down the midnight valleys to the East and the enchanted cities of the North, and Aunt Maw's droning voice and the memory of unheard voices, in the memory of the dark, ruined Helen in their blood, in something stricken, lost, and far, and long ago. They did not see it, the people of George's age and time, but they remembered it.

They had come out—another image now—into a kind of sunlight of another century. They had come out upon the road again. The road was being paved. More people came now. They cut a pathway to the door again. Some of the weeds were clear. Another house was built. They heard wheels coming and the world was *in*, yet they were not yet wholly of that world.

George would later remember all the times when he had come out of the South into the North, and always the feeling was the same—an exact, pointed, physical feeling marking the frontiers of his consciousness with a geographic precision. There was a certain tightening in the throat, a kind of dry, hard beating of the pulse, as they came up in the morning towards Virginia; a kind of pressure at the lips, a hot, hard burning in the eye, a wire-taut tension of the nerves, as the brakes slammed on, the train slowed down to take the bridge, and the banks of the Potomac River first appeared. Let them laugh at it who will, let them mock it if they can. It was a feeling sharp and physical as hunger, deep and tightening as fear. It was a geographic division of the spirit that was sharply, physically exact, as if it had been cleanly severed by a sword. When the brakes slammed on and he saw the wide flood of the Potomac River, and then went out upon the bridge and heard the low-spoked rumble of the ties and saw the vast dome of the Capitol sustained there in the light of shining morning like a burnished shell, he drew in hot and hard and sharp upon his breath, there in the middle of the river. He ducked his head a little as if he was passing through a web. He knew that he was leaving South. His hands gripped hard upon the hinges of his knees, his muscles flexed, his teeth clamped tightly, and his jaws were hard. The train rolled over, he was North again.

Every young man from the South has felt this precise and formal geography of the spirit, but few city people are familiar with it. And why this tension of the nerves, why this gritting of the teeth and hardening of the jaws, this sense of desperate anticipation as they crossed the Potomac River? Did it mean that they felt they were invading a foreign country? Did it mean they were steeling themselves for conflict? Did it mean that they were looking forward with an almost desperate apprehension to their encounter with the city? Yes, it meant all of this. It meant other things as well. It meant that they were also looking forward to that encounter with exultancy and hope, with fervor, passion, and high aspiration.

George often wondered how many people in the city realize how much the life of the great city meant to him and countless others like him: how, long ago in little towns down South, there in the barren passages of night, they listened to the wheel, the whistle, and the bell; how, there in the dark South, there on the Piedmont, in the hills, there by the slow, dark rivers, there in coastal plains, something was always burning in their hearts at night—the image of the shining city and the North. How greedily they consumed each scrap of gossip adding to their city lore, how they listened to the tales of every traveler who returned, how they drank in the words of city people, how in a thousand ways, through fiction, newspapers, and the cinema, through printed page and word of mouth, they built together bit by bit a shining image of their hunger and desire—a city that had never been, that would never be, but a city better than the one that was.

And they brought that image with them to the North. They brought it to the North with all their hope, their hunger, their devotion, with all their lust for living and with all their hot desire. They brought it to the North with all their pride, their passion, and their fervor, with all the aspirations in their shining dreams, with all the energy of their secret and determined will—somehow by every sinew of their life, by every desperate ardor of their spirit, here in the shining, ceaseless, glorious, and unending city to make their lives prevail, to win for their own lives and by their talents an honored place among the highest and the noblest life that only the great city had to offer.

Call it folly, if you will. Call it blind sentiment, if you like. But also call it passion, call it devotion, call it energy, warmth, and strength, high aspiration and an honorable pride. Call it youth, and all the glory and the wealth of youth.

And admit, my city friends, your life has been the better for it. They enriched your life in ways you may not know, in ways you never pause to estimate. They brought you—the half million or more of them who came and stayed—a warmth you lacked, a passion that God knows you needed, a belief and a devotion that was wanting in your life, an integrity of purpose that was rare in your own swarming hordes. They brought to all the multiplex and feverish life of all your ancient swarming peoples some of the warmth, the depth, the richness of the secret and unfathomed South. They brought some of its depth and mystery to those sky-shining vertices of splintered light, to all those dizzy barricades of sky-aspiring brick, to those cold, salmon-colored panes, and to all the weary grey of all those stony-hearted pavements. They brought a warmth of earth, an exultant joy of youth, a burst of living laughter, a full-bodied warmth and living energy of humor, shot through with sunlight and with Africa, and a fiery strength of living faith and hope that all the acrid jests, the bitter wisdoms, the cynical appraisals, and the old, unrighteous, and scornmaking pride of all the ancient of the earth and Israel could not destroy or weaken.

Say what you will, you needed them. They enriched your life in ways you do not know. They brought to it the whole enormous treasure of their dreams and of their hopes, the aspiration of high purposes. They were transformed, perhaps, submerged or deadened, in some ways defeated later, maybe, but they were not lost. Something of all of them, of each of them, went out into your air, diffused among the myriad tangle of your billion-footed life, wore down into the granite dullness of your pavements, sank through into the very weather of your brick, the cold anatomy of your steel and stone, into the very hue and weather of your lives, my friends, in secret and unknown ways into all you said and thought and did, into all that you had shaped and wrought.

There's not a ferry slip around Manhattan that is not grained a little with their passion. There's not a salmon flank of morning at the river's edge that does not catch you at the throat and heart a little more because the fierce excitement of their youth and of their wild imagination went into it. There's not a canyon gulch blued with the slant of morning light that lacks a little of their jubilation. They're in every little tug that slides and fetters at the wharves of morning, they're there in the huge slant of evening light, in the last old tingeings of unearthly red upon the red brick of the harbor heights. They're there in winglike soar and swoop of every bridge and humming rail in every singing cable. They're there in tunnel's depths. They're there in every cobble, every brick. They're there upon the acrid and exciting tang of smoke. They're upon the very air you breathe.

Try to forget them or deny them, if you will, but they brought your harsh flanks warmth around them, brothers. They are there.

AND SO THOSE younglings from the South did not go home except for visits. Somehow they loved the poison they had drunk: the snake that stung them was now buried in their blood.

Of all of them, Alsop played the surest role: they clustered round him like chicks about a mother hen and he was most comforting. He loved the South—and yet was not so cabined and confined as they. For while the others kept inviolate the little walls of their own province, their special language, and the safe circle of their own community, venturing forth into that great and outer strangeness day by day like Elizabethan mariners on a quest for gold, or looking for the passage to Cathay—it was, in fact, still Indian country so far as some of them could see, and at night they slept within the picket circle of their wheels—Alsop cast a wider circle. He was broadening. He was talking to new people day by day—people on park benches, on bus tops, in lunchrooms, drug stores, soda fountains; people in Manhattan and the Bronx, in Brooklyn, Queens, and Staten Island.

He had been stronger than all of them in his contempt and his derision of "damned foreigners." Now he knew Romano, a young Italian, a clerk by occupation, but a painter by profession. Now he brought him home, and Romano cooked spaghetti. He met other ones as well—Mr. Chung, a Chinese merchant on Pell Street, and a scholar of the ancient poetry; a Spaniard working as a bus boy in a restaurant; a young Jew from the East Side. Alsop was strong in the profession of his nativeness, but the new and strange—the dark, the foreign, and the mixed—appealed to him.

And yet he loved the South—no doubt of that. He went back every Christmas. First he stayed two weeks, and then ten days, and then a week, and presently he was back in three days' time. But he loved the South—and he never failed to come back with a fund of bright new stories, of warmth and sentiment and homely laughter; with the latest news of Miss Willsie, of Merriman, his cousin, and of Ed Wetherby, and of his aunt. Miss Caroline; and of all the other simple, sweet, and lovable people "down there" that he had found.

And yet, in his all-mothering nature. Alsop's soul had room for many things. He chuckled and agreed with all the others, he was himself sharp-tongued and scornful of the city ways, but suddenly he would heave and wheeze with a Pickwickian toleration, he would be filled with warm admissions for this alien place. "Still, you've got to hand it to them!" he would say. "It's the damnedest place on earth . . . the most glorious, crazy, perfectly wonderful, magnificent, goddamned town that ever was!" And he would rummage around among a pile of junk, a mountain of old magazines and clippings, until he found and read to them a poem by Don Marquis.

CHAPTER 15

Götterdämmerung

It was not a bad life that they had that year. It was, in many ways, a good one. It was, at all events, a constantly exciting one. Jim Randolph was their leader, their benevolent but stern dictator.

Jim was thirty now, and he had begun to realize what had happened to him. He could not accept it. He could not face it. He was living in the past, but the past could not come back again. Monk and the others didn't think about it at that time, but later they knew why he needed them, and why all the people that he needed were so young. They represented the lost past to him. They represented his lost fame. They represented the lost glory of his almost forgotten legend. They brought it back to him with their devotion, their idolatrous worship. They restored a little of it to him. And when they began to sense what had happened, all of them were a little sad.

Jim was a newspaper man now. He had a job working for one of the great agencies of international information, the Federal Press. He liked the work, too. He had, like almost all Southerners, an instinctive and romantic flair for news, but even in his work the nature of his thought was apparent. He had, as was natural, a desire for travel, an ambition to be sent to foreign countries as correspondent. But the others never heard him say that he would like to go to Russia, where the most important political experiment of modern times was taking place, or to England, Germany, or the Scandinavian countries. He wanted to go to places which had for him associations of romance and glamorous adventure. He wanted to be sent to South America, to Spain, to Italy, to France, or to the Balkans. He always wanted to go to a place where life was soft and warm and gallant, where romance was in the air, and where, as he thought, he could have the easy love of easy women. (And there, in fact, to one of these countries, he did go finally. There he went and lived a while, and there he died.)

Jim's feeling for news, although keen and brilliantly colorful, was, like his whole vision of life, more or less determined by the philosophy of the playing field. In spite of his experience in the World War, he was still fascinated by war, which he regarded as the embodiment of personal gallantry. A war to him was a kind of gigantic sporting contest, an international football game, which gave the star performers on both sides an opportunity to break loose around the flanks on a touchdown dash. Like a Richard Harding Davis character, he not only wanted to see a war and report a war, he wanted also to play a part in war, a central and heroic part. In his highly personal and subjective view of the news, Jim saw each event as somehow shaped for the projection of his own personality.

It was the same way with athletic contests, in which his interest was naturally keen. This was strikingly and amusingly evident at the time of the fight between Dempsey and Firpo for the heavyweight championship of the world.

The fighters were in training. The air was humming with excited speculation. The champion, Dempsey, destined later, after his defeat by Tunney, to become, according to the curious psychology of the American character, immensely popular, was at this time almost bitterly hated. For one thing, he was the champion, and the job of being champion in any walk of American life is a perilous and bitter one. Again, he enjoyed the unenviable reputation of being almost invincible. This, too, aroused hatred against him. People wanted to see him beaten. Finally, he was viciously assailed upon all sides on account of his war record. He was accused of being a slacker, of having stayed at home and worked in the shipyard while his contemporaries were risking their lives on the fields of France. And of course one heard on every hand the familiar American charge that he was "yellow." This was untrue.

Firpo, on the other hand, appealed to the popular imagination, although he had little to recommend him as a fighter except enormous physical strength and a clumsy but tremendous punch. This was enough. In fact, his very deficiencies seemed to increase the excitement over the uneven match. Firpo became, in the popular mind, "The Wild Bull of the Pampas," and it was believed he would rush in, bull-like, with head lowered, and try to annihilate his opponent with a punch of his powerful right hand.

The two men were now in training for the fight, and every day it was part of Jim's job to go out to Firpo's training camp and observe his progress. The South American took a great liking to Jim, who could speak understandable Spanish, and Jim became intensely interested in the man and in his prospects for the fight. Perhaps something helpless, dumb, and inarticulate in the big, sullen brute awakened Jim's quick sympathies. Every night, now, Jim would come in, swearing and fuming about the day's happenings at the training camp.

"Oh that poah, dumb son-of-a-bitch," he would softly swear. "He don't know any more about getting into condition than the fat woman at Barnum and Bailey's Circus. And no one around him knows anything. Christ!—they've got him out there skipping the rope!" He laughed softly and swore again. "You'd thing they were training him to be Queen of the May. Why the hell should he skip the rope to get ready for Dempsey? He's not goin' to get out of Dempsey's way. Dempsey will nail him with that right before the fight has gone five seconds. This bird don't know anything about boxing. They're trying to teach him how to weave and bob when his only chance is to get in there and slug for all he's worth. . . . And condition? All I know is about conditioning a football team, but if I couldn't take him and get him in better shape in the next three weeks than he's ever been in before, you can kick me all the way from here to the Polo Grounds." Laughing softly, he shook his head. "God almighty, it's a crime to see it! Why, dammit, they let him eat anything he likes! Any football coach that saw a half-back eat like that would drop dead. I've seen him begin with soup, go right through two big porterhouse steaks, with smothered onions and French fried potatoes, and top that off with a whole apple pie, a quart of ice cream, and foah cups of coffee! After that they expect him to go out and skip rope for a few minutes to get that belly down!"

"But why doesn't he get a good trainer, Jim?" someone asked.

"Why?" said Jim. "I'll tell you why. It's because he's too damn tight, that's why. Why that cheap——!" he laughed, shaking his head again, "—he's so tight that he's got the first nickel he ever earned when he came to this country. Dempsey may knock him the whole way from here to Argentina, but he's going to take every penny he ever made when he goes."

These daily accounts were thrilling news for the others. They became passionately excited over the career and progress of the bull-like Argentinian, and as the time for the great battle drew near they all devised and entered into a fascinating speculation for their enrichment. Under Jim's leadership, they all bought tickets for the fight. It was their plan to hold these until the very eve of battle, and then to sell them to fight enthusiasts for a fabulous profit. They hoped to get as much as fifty dollars for tickets which had cost only five or ten.

This hope might have been realized if, at the last moment, they had not committed one of their characteristic follies. None of them, of course, would admit to the others that he would like to see the fight himself. Any suggestion of this was greeted by hoots of scorn. Jim, in fact, almost exploded with outraged contempt when one of them hinted that *he* might prefer to *use* his ticket instead of selling it for fifty dollars.

And yet, they held on to the tickets until it was too late—until, at any rate, they would have had to try to sell them at the Polo Grounds to possible last-minute purchasers. They might have been able to do this, but really what they had wanted all along, the secret hope that each of them had cherished in his heart and that none of them would admit, was that they could see that fight themselves. And that is what they did. And in the light of retrospect Monk was glad they did it. That night made history in their lives, in a curious, poignant, and indefinable way, as only a popular song or a prize fight can do in America, evoking a time with blazing vividness, a host of memories that otherwise would later be only obscure, blurred fragments of a half-forgotten past.

An hour before the fight was scheduled to begin, and even after the preliminary contests had begun, they were all together in the living room of their apartment, debating with one another violently. Each accused the others of having failed to go through with the plan. Each denied vehemently that he had had any intention of weakening. Above the whole excited babble, Jim's voice could be heard passionately assert-ing that he was still out to sell his ticket, that he was going to the Polo Grounds for purposes of speculation only, that the rest of them could back down if they wished but that he would sell his ticket if it was the last thing he ever did on earth.

The upshot of it was that the more he argued and asserted, the less they believed him; and the more he shouted, the less he convinced himself. They all squabbled, argued, challenged, and denied until the final moment, which they knew somehow was coming. And then it came. Jim paused suddenly in his hot debate with himself, looked at his watch, ripped out an alarmed oath, and then, looking at them, laughed his soft and husky laugh, saying:

"Come on, boys. Who's going to this fight with me?"

It was perfect. And it was the kind of folly and unreason that was characteristic of them all: the great plans and projects and the pro-testations they were forever making, and their ultimate surrender to impulse and emotion when the moment came. And it was exactly like Jim Randloph, too. It was the kind of thing he did, the kind of thing that he had always done, the irrational impulse that wrecked his best-laid plans.

Now that the time had come, now that they had all surrendered, now that all of them had openly admitted at last what they were going to do, they went jubilantly and exultantly. And they saw the fight. They did not sit together. Their tickets were in different sections of the field. Monk's was over behind third base and well back in the upper tier. That square of roped-in canvas out there in the center of the field looked very far away, and that surrounding mass of faces was enormous, overwhelming. Yet his vision of the whole scene remained ever afterwards startling immediate and vivid.

He saw the little eddies in the crowd as the fighters and their handlers came towards the ring, then heard the great roar that rose and mounted as they climbed through the ropes. There was something terrific in the sight of young Dempsey. Over all the roar and tumult of that mighty crowd Monk could feel the currents of his savagery and nervous tension. Dempsey could not sit still. He jumped up from his stool, pranced up and down, seized the ropes and stretched and squatted several times, as skittish and as nervous as a race horse.

Then the men were called into the center of the ring to receive their last instructions. Firpo came out stolidly, his robe stretched across his massive shoulders, his great coarse shock of hair shining blackly as he stood and glowered. He had been well named. He was really like a sullen human bull. Dempsey could not be still. As he got his last instructions, he fidgeted nervously and kept his head down, a little to one side, not meeting Firpo's sullen and stolid look.

They received their instructions and turned and went back to their corners. Their robes were taken off. Dempsey flexed and squatted swiftly at the ropes, the bell clanged, and the men came out.

That was no fight, no scheduled contest for a title. It was a burning point in time, a kind of concentration of our total energies, of the blind velocity of the period, cruel, ruthless, savage, swift, bewildering as America. The fight, thus seen, resumed and focalized a period in the nation's life. It lasted six minutes. It was over almost before it had begun. In fact, the spectators had no sense of its beginning. It exploded then before them.

From that instant on, the battle raged and shifted with such savage speed, with such sudden and astounding changes of fortune, that later people were left stunned and bewildered, no one knowing clearly what had happened. No two could agree. The crowd milled and mobbed, the hundred thousand voices raised in argument. No one was certain just how many knockdowns there had been, how often Firpo had been driven to the floor by the thudding power of Dempsey's fists, or how long Dempsey had been out of the ring when Firpo drove him through the ropes. Some said there had been seven knockdowns, some said nine, some said four. Some asserted bitterly that Dempsey had been knocked out of the ring for more than fifteen seconds, that the count was late in taking up, that Firpo had been robbed of a just victory. Others asserted that Dempsey had fought with a vicious disregard for the rules, that the referee had allowed him to take ruthless and illegal openings.

Certainly it was no crafty exhibition of ring skill or strategy. It was a fight between two wild animals, each bent on the annihilation of the other, by any means, by any method, in the shortest time. What finally remained most vivid, in that kaleidoscopic whirl of violent images, was the memory of Dempsey's black and bobbing head, his teeth bared in a grin of passion, the incredible speed and power of his sledge-hammer fists, and the sound of blows that moved so swiftly that the eye could not perceive them. He was like a human riveting machine. Over the terrific roar and tumult of the crowd one could hear the steady thud, thud, thud, the sickening impact of blows delivered with the velocity of a bullet. Again and again, the great brute went down before those whizzing gloves as if he had been shot. He had been shot, too. He looked and acted just like a man who has received a bullet in the brain. For a moment, for an infinitesimal fraction of a second, he would stand erect. And then he would not fall, he would just collapse, as if his massive legs had been broken. He just looked stunned, bewildered, sullenly infuriated, like a baffled bull.

But suddenly, like a baffled and infuriated bull, he charged. He caught Dempsey solidly with a terrible right-hand blow that knocked him clear across the ring, and then he charged upon him and fairly flailed him through the ropes and out of the arena. And now, while the crowd insanely roared, Firpo was like a triumphant bull that has driven his antagonist into oblivion and has the whole arena to himself. Dempsey went hurtling through the ropes like a battered doll. The newspaper men thrust up their arms to protect themselves. The fighter came crashing down into a nest of typewriters, and, at the same moment, muttered thickly, with the instinct of a fighting animal, "Get me back in there!"

They pushed him up and back, in through the ropes. He reeled in glassy-eyed, tottering like a drunken man. He fell into a clinch and hung on desperately; his brain cleared, the fight was on again—and again the riveting thud, thud, thud of those relentless hands. The bull halted, stunned, and collapsed again like broken straw.

It was all over in the first round, really, a round that lasted for three minutes, but that had attained such a focal concentration of intensity that men asserted later that it seemed to last for hours. In the second round it was ended definitely. The killer had learned caution now. He came out craftily this time, with his black jaw tucked in below his shoulder. It was all over then. The great bull had no weapons for methods such as these. He lowered his head and charged. The riveter shot him down.

That night the city was a boiling of excitement. It was like a war, like the announcement of a general mobilization order. After the fight, Jim Randolph, Monty Bellamy, Harvey Williams, Perce Smead, and Monk got together again at one of the exits to the grounds and went downtown. By the time they reached midtown New York the news was there. Broadway and the triangulated space before the Times Building was a seething horde of wildly excited, milling, fiercely argumentative

people. Monk had never seen anything like it before. It was passionately and desperately exciting, but it was also sinister.

The crowd was composed, for the most part, of men of the Broadway type and stamp, men with vulpine faces, feverish dark eyes,
features molded by cruelty and cunning, corrupted, criminal visages
of night, derived out of the special geography, the unique texture, the
feverish and unwholesome chemistries of the city's nocturnal life of
vice and crime. Their unclean passion was appalling. They snarled and
cursed and raged at one another like a pack of mongrel curs. There
were raucous and unclean voices, snarls of accusation and suspicion,
with hatred and infuriating loathing, with phrases of insane obscenity
and filth.

Monk could not understand it. He was so new to the city, and the
image of those livid faces, those convulsed and snarling mouths, those
feverish eyes shining there in the glare of night, evoked a sense of some
sinister and yet completely meaningless passion. He listened to their
words. He heard their epithets of hatred and of filth. He tried to find
the meaning of it, and there was no meaning. Some hated Firpo, some
hated Dempsey, some hated the fight and the result. Some charged that
the fight had been "fixed," others that it should never have been held.
Some asserted that Firpo had been doped, others that he had been
bribed; still others, that he was "nothing but a tramp," that Dempsey
was "a yellow bum," that a former champion could have beaten both of
them at the same time.

But what was behind their snarling hatred? Unable to explain it
any other way, Monk at last concluded that what they really hated
was not so much the fight, the fighters, and the fight's result: it was
themselves, one another, every living thing on earth. They hated for
the sake of hate. They jeered, reviled, cursed one another because of
the black poison in their souls. They could believe in nothing, and
neither could they believe in themselves for not believing. They were
a race that had been drugged by evil, a tribe that got its only nourish-
ment from envenomed fruit. It was so blind, so willful, and so evil, so

horrible and so meaningless, that suddenly it seemed to Monk that a great snake lay coiled at the very heart and center of the city's life, that a malevolent and destructive energy was terribly alive and working there, and that he and the others who had come here from the little towns and from the country places, with such high passion and with so much hope, were confronted now with something evil and unknown at the heart of life, which they had not expected, and for which all of them were unprepared.

Monk was to see it, feel it, know it later on in almost every facet of the city's life, this huge and baffling malady of man's brain, his spirit, and his energy. But now he witnessed it for the first time. He could see no reason for this idiot and blind malevolence. Yet it was there, it was everywhere, in the hateful passion of those twisted faces and the unwholesome radiance of those fevered eyes.

And now Monk heard Jim speaking. They had moved about from group to group and listened to these hate-loving men, and, now Jim Randolph began to speak, quietly, in his rather soft and husky tones, good-naturedly and yet commandingly, telling them they were mistaken, that the fighters were not drugged, that the fight had not been fixed, that the result had been inevitable and just. And then Monk heard one of those mongrel voices snarl back at him in hatred and derision, a twisted and corrupted mouth spat out at him a filthy epithet. Then, quicker than the eye could wink, the thing had happened. Jim seized the creature with one hand, draping his garments together in his powerful fingers, lifting him clear off his feet into the air, and shaking him like a rat.

"Listen, mister!" his husky voice was now charged with a murderous intensity of passion that struck silence through the whole raucous and disputing crowd and turned the creature's face a dirty grey, "No man alive is going to say that to me! Another word from you and I'll break your dirty neck!" And he shook him once again till the creature's head snapped like a broken doll's. And then Jim dropped him like a soiled rag, and, turning to his companions, said quietly: "Come on, boys. We'll get out of here." And the creatures of the night held back before him as he passed.

Poor Jim! He, too, was like a creature from another world. With all his folly and his sentiment, with all his faults and childish vanities, he was still the heroic remnant of a generation that had already gone, and that perhaps we needed. But he was lost.

GEORGE WEBBER HAD grown into a youth somewhat above the middle height, around five feet nine or ten, but he gave the impression of being shorter than that because of the way he had been shaped and molded, and the way in which he carried himself. He walked with a slight stoop, and his head, which was carried somewhat forward with a thrusting movement, was set down solidly upon a short neck, between shoulders which, in comparison with the lower part of his figure, his thighs and legs, were extremely large and heavy. He was barrel-chested, and perhaps the most extraordinary feature of his make-up—which accounted for the nickname he had had since childhood—were the arms and hands: the arms were unusually long, and the hands, as well as the feet, were very big with long, spatulate fingers which curved naturally and deeply in like paws. The effect of this inordinate length of arms and hands, which dangled almost to the knees, together with the stooped and heavy shoulders and the out-thrust head, was to give his whole figure a somewhat prowling and half-crouching posture.

His features, his face, were small, compact—somewhat pugnosed, the eyes set very deep in beneath heavy brows, the forehead rather low, the hair beginning not far above the brows. When he was listening or talking to someone, his body prowling downward, his head thrust forward and turned upward with a kind of packed attentiveness, the simian analogy was inevitable; therefore the name of "Monk" had stuck. Moreover, it had never occurred to him, apparently, to get his figure clothed in garments suited to his real proportions. He just walked into a store somewhere and picked up and wore out the first thing he could get on. Thus, in a way of which he was not wholly conscious, the element of grotesqueness in him was exaggerated.

The truth of the matter is that he was not really grotesque at all. His dimensions, while unusual and a little startling at first sight, were not abnormal. He was not in any way a freak of nature, although some people might think so. He was simply a youth with big hands and feet, extremely long arms, a trunk somewhat too large and heavy, with legs too short, and features perhaps too small and compact for the big shoulders that supported them. Since he had added to this rather awkward but not distorted figure certain unconscious tricks and mannerisms, such as his habit of carrying his head thrust forward, and of peering upward when he was listening or talking, it was not surprising if the impression he first made on people should sometimes arouse laughter and surprise. Certainly he knew this, and he sometimes furiously and bitterly resented it; but he had never inquired sufficiently or objectively enough into the reasons for it.

Although he had a very intense and apprehensive eye for the appearance of things, the eager, passionate absorption of his interest and attention was given to the world around him. To his own appearance he had never given a thought. So when, as sometimes happened, the effect he had on people was rudely and brutally forced upon his attention, it threw him into a state of furious anger. For he was young—and had not learned the wisdom and tolerant understanding of experience and maturity. He was young—still over-sensitive. He was young—not able to forget himself, to accept the jokes and badinage good-naturedly. He was young—and did not know that personal beauty is no great virtue in a man, and that this envelope of flesh and blood, in which a spirit happened to be sheathed, could be a loyal and enduring, though ugly, friend.

All this—and many more important things besides—had got him into a lot of confusion, a lot of torture, and a lot of brute unhappiness. And the same thing was happening to a million other young men at that time. Monk was a hard-pressed kid. And because he was hard pressed, he had wangled himself into a lot of nonsense. It wouldn't be true to say, for example, that he hadn't got anything out of his "education." Such as it was, he had got a great deal out of it, but, like most of the "education" of the time, it had been full of waste, foolishness, and misplaced emphasis.

The plain, blunt truth of the matter was that, essentially, although he did not know it, Monk was an explorer. And so were a million other young people at that time. Well, exploring is a thrilling thing. But, even for the physical explorers, it is a hard thing, too. Monk had the true faith, the true heroism, of an explorer. He was a lot more lonely than Columbus ever was, and for this reason he was desperately confused, groping, compromising, and unsure.

It would be nice to report that he was swift and certain as a flame, always shot true to the mark, and knew what he knew. But this wasn't true. He knew what he knew, but he admitted that he knew it only seldom. Then when he did, he asserted it; like every other kid, he "went to town." He said it, he shot it home, he made no apologies—he was passionate and fierce and proud, and true—but the next morning he would wake up feeling that he had made a fool of himself and that he had something to explain.

He "knew," for example, that freight cars were beautiful; that a spur of rusty box cars on a siding, curving off somewhere into a flat of barren pine and clay, was as beautiful as anything could be, as anything has ever been. He knew all the depths and levels of it, all the time evocations of it—but he couldn't say so. He hadn't found the language for it. He had even been told, by implication, that it wasn't so. That was where his "education" came in. It wasn't really that his teachers had told him that a freight car was not beautiful. But they had told him that Keats, Shelley, the Taj Mahal, the Acropolis, Westminister Abbey, the Louvre, the Isles of Greece, were beautiful. And they had told it to him so often and in such a way that he not only thought it true—which it is—but that these things were everything that beauty is.

When the freight car occurred to him, he had to argue to himself about it, and then argue with other people about it. Then he would become ashamed of himself and shut up. Like everyone who is a poet, and there really are a lot of poets, he was an immensely practical young man, and suddenly he would get tired of arguing, because he knew there was not anything to argue about, and then shut up. Furthermore, he had the sense that some people who *said* that a freight car was beautiful were fake æsthetes—which they were. It was a time when smart people were going around saying that ragtime or jazz music were the real American rhythms, and likening them to Beethoven and Wagner; that the comic strip was a true expression of American art; that Charlie Chaplin was really a great tragedian and ought to play Hamlet; that advertising was the only "real" American literature.

The fellow who went around saying that advertising was the only "real" American literature might be either one of two things: a successful writer or an unsuccessful one. If he was a successful one—a writer, say, of detective stories which had had an enormous vogue and had earned the man a fortune—he had argued himself into believing that he was really a great novelist. But "the times were out of joint," and the reason he did not write great novels was because it was impossible to write great novels in such times: "the genius of America was in advertising," and since there was no use doing anything else, the whole spirit of the times being against it, he had become a writer of successful detective stories.

That was one form of it. Then there was the fellow who was not quite good enough to be good at anything. He sneered at the writer of detective stories, but he also sneered at Dreiser and O'Neill and Sinclair Lewis and Edwin Arlington Robinson. He was a poet, or a novelist, or a critic, or a member of Professor George Pierce Baker's playwriting class at Harvard or at Yale, but nothing that he did came off; and the reason that it didn't was because "the times were out of joint," and "the real literature of America was in the advertising in popular magazines." So this fellow sneered at everything from a superior elevation. Dreiser, Lewis, Robinson, O'Neill, and the advertising in the *Saturday Evening Post* were all the same, really—*"Plus ça change, plus c'est la même chose."*

AT THAT TIME in George Webber's life, amidst all the nonsense, confusion, torture, and brute unhappiness that he was subject to, he was for the first time trying to articulate something immense and terrible in life which he had always known and felt, and for which he thought he must now find some speech, or drown. And yet it seemed that this thing which was so immense could have no speech, that it burst through the limits of all recorded languages, and that it could never be rounded, uttered, and contained in words. It was a feeling that every man on earth held in the little tenement of his flesh and spirit the whole ocean of human life and time, and that he must drown in this ocean unless, somehow, he "got it out of him"—unless he mapped and charted it, fenced and defined it, plumbed it to its uttermost depths, and knew it to its smallest pockets upon the remotest cores of the everlasting earth.

The greater part of his life had been lived in the confines of a little town, but he now saw plainly that he could never live long enough to tell the thousandth part of all he knew about its life and people—a knowledge that was not merely encylopædic and mountainous, but that was as congruent and single as one gigantic plant, which was alive in all its million roots and branches, and must be shown so, or not at all. It now seemed that what had been given to him was not only his father's sturdy, solid power, but that all the million fibrous arms and branches of his Joyner blood, which had sprung from the everlasting earth, growing, thrusting, pushing, spreading out its octopal feelers in unceasing weft and thread, were also rooted into the structure of his life; and that this dark inheritance of blood and passion, of fixity and unceasing variousness, of wandering forever and the earth again—this strange legacy which by its power and richness might have saved him and given him the best life anyone had ever had—had now burst from the limits of his control and was going to tear him to pieces, limb from limb, like maddened horses running wild.

His memory, which had always been encyclopædic, so that he could remember in their minutest details and from his earliest years of childhood all that people had said and done and all that had happened at any moment, had been so whetted, sharpened, and enlarged by his years away from home, so stimulated by his reading and by a terrible hunger that drove him through a thousand streets, staring with madman's eyes into a million faces, listening with madman's ears to a million words, that it had now become, instead of a mighty weapon with a blade of razored sharpness which he might use magnificently to his life's advantage, a gigantic, fibrous, million-rooted plant of time which spread and flowered like a cancerous growth. It mastered his will and fed on his entrails until he lost the power to act and lay inert in its tentacles, while all his soaring projects came to naught, and hours, days, months, and years flowed by him like a stream.

The year before he had grown sick and weary in his heart of his clumsy attempts to write. He began to see that nothing he wrote had anything to do with what he had seen and felt and known, and that he might as well try to pour the ocean in a sanitary drinking cup as try to put the full and palpable integument of human life into such efforts. So now, for the first time, he tried to set down a fractional part of his vision of the earth. For some time, a vague but powerful unrest had urged him on to the attempt, and now, without knowledge or experience, but with some uneasy premonition of the terrific labor he was attempting to accomplish, he began—deliberately choosing a subject that seemed so modest and limited in its proportions that he thought he could complete it with the greatest ease. The subject he chose for his first effort was a boy's vision of life over a ten-month period between his twelfth and thirteenth year, and the title was, "The End of the Golden Weather."

By this title he meant to describe that change in the *color* of life which every child has known—the change from the enchanted light and weather of his soul, the full golden light, the magic green and gold in which he sees the earth in childhood, and, far away, the fabulous vision of the golden city, blazing forever in his vision and at the end of all his dreams, in whose enchanted streets he thinks that he shall some day walk a conqueror, a proud and honored figure in a life more glorious, fortunate, and happy than any he has ever known. In this brief story he prepared to tell how, at this period in a child's life, this strange and magic light—this "golden weather"—begins to change, and, for the first time, some of the troubling weathers of a man's soul are revealed to him; and how, for the first time, he becomes aware of the thousand changing visages of time; and how his clear and radiant legend of the earth is, for the first time, touched with confusion and bewilderment, menaced by terrible depths and enigmas of experience he has never known before. He wanted to tell the story of this year exactly as he remembered it, and with all the things and people he had known that year.

Accordingly, he began to write about it, starting the story at three o'clock in the afternoon in the yard before his uncle's house.

JERRY ALSOP WAS changing. More than any of the others, he had plunged into the sea of life. As he said, his "sphere had widened," and now it was ready to burst through the little clinging circle he had so carefully built up around himself. His disciples hung on for a time, then, one by one, like leaves straying in a swirling flood, were swept away. And Alsop let them go. The truth was that the constant devotions of the old fellowship had begun to bore him. He was heard to mutter that he was getting "damned tired of having the place used as a clubhouse all the time."

There was a final scene with Monk. The younger man's first story had been rejected, and a word that Monk had spoken had come back to Alsop and stung him. It was some bitter, youthful word, spoken with youth's wounded vanity, about "the artist" in a "world of Philistines," and of the artist's "right." The foolish word, just salve to wounded pride, with its arrogant implication of superiority, infuriated Alsop. But, characteristically, when he saw Monk again he did not make the direct attack. Instead, he referred venomously to a book that he had been reading by one of the æsthetic critics of the period, putting into his mouth, exaggerating and destroying, the foolish words of wounded vanity and youth.

" 'I'm an artist,' " Alsop sneered. " 'I'm better than these God-damned other people. Philistines can't understand me.' "

He laughed venomously, and then, his pale eyes narrowed into slits, he said:

"Do you know what he is? He's just an ass! A man who'd talk that way is just a *complete* ass! 'An artist!' " and again he laughed sneeringly, "My God!"

His eyes were really now so full of rancor and injured self-esteem that the other knew it was the end. There was no further warmth of friendship here. He, too, felt a cold fury: envenomed words rose to his lips, he wanted to sneer, to stab, to ridicule and mock as Alsop had; a poison of cold anger sweltered in his heart, but when he got up his lips were cold and dry, he said stiffly:

"Good-bye."

And he went out from that basement room forever.

Alsop said nothing, but sat there with a pale smile on his face, a feeling of bitter triumph gnawing at his heart that was its own reprisal. As the lost disciple closed the door, he heard for the fast time the jeering words:

" 'An artist!' Jesus Christ!"—then the choking fury of his belly-laugh.

JIM RANDOLPH FELT for the four youths who lived with him a paternal affection. He governed them, he directed them, as a father might direct the destinies of his own sons. He was always the first one up in the morning. He needed very little sleep, no matter how late he had been up the night before. Four or five hours' sleep always seemed to be enough for him. He would bathe, shave, dress himself, put coffee on to boil, then he would come and wake the others up. He would stand in the doorway looking at them, smiling a little, with his powerful hands arched lightly on his hips. Then in a soft, vibrant, and strangely tender tone he would sing:

"Get up, get up, you lazy devils. Get up, get up, it's break o' day." Jim would cast his head back and laugh a little. "That's the song my father used to sing to me every morning when I was a kid way down there in Ashley County, South Carolina. . . . All right," he now said, matter-of-factly, and with a tone of quiet finality and command: "You boys get up. It's almost half-past eight. Come on, get dressed now. You've slept long enough."

They would get up then—all except Monty, who did not go to work till five o'clock in the afternoon; he was employed in a midtown hotel and didn't get home until one or two o'clock in the morning. Their governor allowed him to sleep later, and, in fact, quietly but sternly enjoined them to silence in order that Monty's rest be not disturbed.

Jim himself would be out of the place and away by eight-thirty. He was gone all day.

They ate together a great deal at the apartment. They liked the life, its community of fellowship and of comfort. It was tacitly assumed that they would gather together in the evening and formulate a program for the night. Jim, as usual, ruled the roost. They never knew what his plans were. They awaited his arrival with expectancy and sharp interest.

At six-thirty his key would rattle in the lock. He would come in, hang up his hat, and without preliminary say with authority:

"All right, boys. Dig down in your pockets, now. Everyone's chipping in with fifty cents."

"What for, for God's sake?" someone would protest.

"For the best damn steak you ever sunk yo' teeth into," Jim would say. "I saw it in the butcher shop as I came by. We're going to have a

314 THE WEB AND THE ROOT

six-pound sirloin for supper tonight or I miss my guess. . . . Perce," he said, "you go to the grocery store and buy the fixings. Get us two loaves of bread, a pound of butter, and ten cents' worth of grits. We've got potatoes. . . . Monk," he said, "you get busy and peel those potatoes, and don't cut away two-thirds of 'em like you did last time. . . . I'm going to get the steak," he said, "I'll cook the steak. That nurse of mine is coming over. She said she'll make biscuits."

And, having instantly energized the evening and dispatched them on the commission of their respective duties, he went off upon his own.

They were constantly having girls in. Each of them would bring in recruits of his own discovery, and Jim, of course, knew dozens of them. God knows where he picked them up or when he found the time and opportunity to meet them, but women swarmed around him like bees around a honeycomb. He always had a new one. He brought them in singly, doubly, by squadrons, and by scores. It was a motley crew. They ranged all the way from trained nurses, for whom he seemed to have a decided flair, to shop girls and stenographers, waitresses in Childs restaurants, Irish girls from the remotest purlieus of Brooklyn, inclined to rowdy outcries in their drink, to chorines both past and present, and the strip woman of a burlesque show.

Monk never learned where he got this last one, but she was a remarkable specimen. She was a voluptuous creature, a woman of such carnal and sensuous magnetism that she could arouse the fiercest intensity of amorous desire just by coming in a room. She was a dark, luscious kind of woman, probably of some Latin or Oriental extraction. She might have been a Jewess, or a mixture of several breeds. She pretended to be French, which was ridiculous. She spoke a kind of concocted patter of broken English, interspersed with such classic phrases as *"Oo là là," "Mais oui, monsieur," "Merci beaucoup," "pardonnez-moi,"* and *"Toute de suite."* She had learned this jargon on the burlesque stage.

Monk went with Jim to see her play one time when she was appearing at a burlesque house on 125th Street. Her stage manner, her presence, the French phrases, and the broken speech were the same upon the stage as when she visited them. Like so many people in the theatre, she acted her part continually. Nevertheless, she was the best thing in the show. She used her patter skillfully, with sensual and voluptuous weavings of her hips, and the familiar carnal roughhouse of burlesque comedy. She came out and did her strip act while the audience roared its approval, and Jim swore softly under his breath, and, as the old ballad of Chevy Chase has it, "A vow to God made he"—a vow which, by the way, was never consummated.

She was an extraordinary person, and in the end an amazingly chaste one. She liked all the boys at the apartment and enjoyed coming there. She had them in a state of frenzy. But in the end the result was the same as if they'd been members of her burlesque audience. It was the strip act, nothing more.

Jim also had a nurse who used to come to see him all the time. His struggles with this girl were epic. There was a naked bluntness of approach and purpose in his attack. She was immensely fond of him, and, up to a certain point, immensely willing, but after that he got no further. He used to rage and fume up and down the place like a maddened tiger. He used to swear his oaths and make his vows. The others would howl with laughter at his anguish, but nothing came of it.

In the end it began to be a shoddy business. All of them except Jim began to get a little tired of it, and to feel a little ashamed and soiled by his shoddy community of carnal effort.

Their life together could not go on forever. All of them were growing up, becoming deeper in experience, more confident and knowing in the great flood of the city's life. The time was fast approaching when each, in his own way, would break loose for himself, detach himself from the fold, assert the independence of his own and separate life. And when that time came, they knew that they would all be lost to Jim.

It was a fault and weakness of his nature that he could not brook equality. He was too much the king, too kingly Southern, and too

Southern for a king. It was the weakness of his strength, this taint of manhood and this faulty Southernness. He was so shaped in the heroic and romantic mold that he always had to be the leader. He needed satellites as a planet needs them. He had to be central and invincibly first in all the life of which he was a part. He had to have the praise, the worship, and the obedience of his fellows or he was lost.

And Jim was lost. The period of his fame was past. The brightness of his star had waned. He had become only a memory to those for whom he once had been the embodiment of heroic action. His contemporaries had entered life, had taken it and used it, had gone past him, had forgotten him. And Jim could not forget. He lived now in a world of bitter memory. He spoke with irony of his triumphs of the past. He spoke with resentment against those who had, he thought, deserted him. He viewed with bitter humor the exploits of the idols of the moment, the athletic heroes who were now the pampered favorites of popular applause. He waited grimly for their disillusionment, and, waiting, unable to forget the past, he hung on pitifully to the tattered remnants of his greatness, the adoration of a group of boys.

Besides themselves, he had few intimates, and certainly none with men of his own age. His fierce and wounded vanity now feared the open conflict with the world, feared association with men of his own years, with men of his own or greater capacity. He feared and hated the possibility that he might have to yield to anyone, play second fiddle, admit the superior wisdom or ability of another person. In the whole city's life he had formed only one other intimate acquaintance. This was a little man named Dexter Briggs, and Dexter, appropriately enough, was a little, amiably good-natured newspaper drunk who lacked every heroic quality of character or appearance that Jim had, and who, accordingly, adored Jim to the point of idolatry for the possession of them.

As for the four youths, the fascination of apartment life in the great city was beginning to wear off. The freedom that had seemed so thrilling and so wonderful to all of them at first now had its obvious limitations. They were not so free as they had thought. They were getting tired of a freedom which always expressed itself in the monotonous repetition of sordid entertainments, of cheap girls or easy girls, of paid women or of unpaid women, of drunk Irish girls or half-drunk Irish girls, of chorines or burlesque queens or trained nurses, of the whole smiled and shoddy business, of its degraded lack of privacy, its "parties," its Saturday-night gin-drinking and love-making, its constant efforts towards the consummation of a sterile and meaningless seduction.

The rest of them were growing tired of it. There were times when they wanted to sleep and a party would be going on. There were times when they wanted privacy and there was no privacy. There were times when they were so tired and fed up with it that they wanted to clear out. They had begun to get on one another's nerves. They had begun to wrangle, to snap back, to be irritable, to rub one another the wrong way. The end had come.

Jim felt it. And this final knowledge of defeat embittered him. He felt that all of them had turned against him, and that the last remnant of his tattered fame was gone. He turned upon them. He asserted violently and profanely that the place was his, that he was the boss, that he'd run the place as he pleased, and that anyone who didn't like it could clear out. As for his shoddy girls, he got small pleasure from them now. But he had reached the point where even such poor conquests as these gave some bolstering of confidence to his lacerated pride. So the parties continued, the rabble rout of shabby women streamed in and out. He had gone over the edge now. There was no retreat.

The end came when he announced one night that he had applied for and had received an appointment from the news agency to one of its obscure posts in South America. He was bitterly, resentfully triumphant. He was going, he said, to "get out of this damn town and tell them all to go to hell." In another month or two he'd be in South America, where a man could do as he blank, blank pleased, without being watched and hindered all the time. To hell with all of it anyway!

318 THE WEB AND THE ROOT

He'd lived long enough to find out one thing for himself—that most of the people who call themselves your friends are nothing but a bunch of crooked, double-crossing blank, blank, blanks, who stabbed you in the back the moment your back was turned. Well, to hell with 'em and the whole country! They could take it and——

Bitterly he drank, and drank again.

About ten o'clock Dexter Briggs came in, already half-drunk. They drank some more together. Jim was in an ugly mood. Furiously he asserted he was going to have some girls. He demanded that some girls be found. He dispatched the others to round up the girls. But even they, the whole shabby carnival of them, had turned on Jim at last. The nurse excused herself, pleading another engagement. The burlesque woman could not be reached. The Brooklyn girls could not be found. One by one the youths made all the calls, exhausted all the possibilities. One by one they straggled back to admit dejectedly their failure.

Jim raged up and down, while Dexter Briggs sat in a drunken haze about Jim's battered-up old typewriter, picking out upon the worn keys the following threnody:

"The boys are here without the girls—
Oh God, strike me dead!
The boys are here without the girls—
Oh God, strike me dead!
Strike, strike, strike me dead.
For the boys are here without the girls—
So, God, strike me dead!"

Having composed this masterpiece, Dexter removed it from the machine, held it up and squinted at it owlishly, and, after a preliminary belch or two, read it slowly and impressively, with deep earnestness of feeling.

Jim's answer to this effort, and to the shouts of laughter of the others, was a savage curse. He snatched the offending sheet of paper out of Dexter's hands, crumpled it up and hurled it on the floor and stamped on it, while the poet looked at him wistfully, with an expression of melancholy and slightly befuddled sorrow. Jim assailed the boys savagely. He accused them of betraying and double-crossing him. A bitter quarrel broke out all around. The room was filled with the angry clamor of their excited voices.

And while the battle raged, Dexter continued to sit there, weeping quietly. The result of this emotion was another poem, which he now began to tap out with one finger on the battered old typewriter, sobbing gently as he did so. This dirge ran reproachfully as follows:

> *"Boys, boys,*
> *Be Southern gentlemen,*
> *Do not say such things to one another,*
> *For, boys, boys,*
> *You are Southern gentlemen,*
> *Southern gentlemen, all."*

This effort, which Dexter appropriately entitled "Southern Gentlemen All," he now removed from the typewriter, and, when a lull had come in their exhausted clamor, he cleared his throat gently and read it to them with deep and melancholy feeling.

"Yes, sir," said Jim, paying no attention to Dexter. He was now standing in the middle of the floor with a gin glass in his hand, talking to himself. "Three weeks from now I'll be on my way. And I want to tell you all something—the whole damn lot of you," he went on dangerously.

"Boys, boys," said Dexter sadly, and hiccoughed.

"When I walk out that door," said Jim, "there's going to be a little sprig of mistletoe hanging on my coat-tails, and you all know what you can do about it!"

"Southern gentlemen, all," said Dexter sadly, then sorrowfully belched.

"If anyone don't like my way of doing," Jim continued, "he knows what he can do about it! He can pack up his stuff right now and cart his little tail right out of here! I'm boss here, and as long as I stay I'm going to keep on being boss! I've played football all over the South! They may not remember me now, but they knew who I was seven or eight years ago, all right!"

"Oh, for God's sake!" someone muttered. "That's all over now! We're tired hearing of it all the time! Grow up!"

Jim answered bitterly: "I've fought all over France, and I've been in every state of the Union but one, and I've had women in all of 'em, and if anyone thinks I'm going to come back here now and be dictated to by a bunch of little half-baked squirts that never got out of their own state until a year ago, I'll damn soon teach 'em they're mistaken! Yessir!" He wagged his head with drunken truculence and drank again. "I'm a better man right now—physically—" he hiccoughed slightly "—mentally——"

"Boys, boys," Dexter Briggs swam briefly out of the fog at this point and sorrowfully began, "Remember that you're Southern——"

"—and—and—morally—" cried Jim triumphantly.

"—gentlemen all," said Dexter sadly.

"—than the whole damn lot of you put together—" Jim continued fiercely.

"—so be gentlemen, boys, and remember that you're gentlemen. Always remember that—" Dexter went on morbidly.

"—so to hell with you!" cried Jim. He glared around fiercely, wildly, at them, with bloodshot eyes, his great fist knotted in his anger. "The hell with all of you!" He paused, swaying for a moment, furious, baffled, his fist knotted, not knowing what to do. "Ahhh!" he cried suddenly, high in his throat, a passionate, choking cry, "To hell with everything! To hell with all of it!" and he hurled his empty gin glass at the wall, where it shivered in a thousand fragments.

"—Southern gentlemen all," said Dexter sadly, and collapsed into his cups.

Poor Jim.

Two of them left next day. Then, singly, the others went.

So all were gone at last, one by one, each swept out into the mighty flood tide of the city's life, there to prove, to test, to find, to lose himself, as each man must—alone.

CHAPTER 16

Alone

George went to live by himself in a little room he rented in house downtown near Fourteenth Street. Here he worked feverishly, furiously, day by day, week by week, and month by month, until another year went by—and at the end of it there was nothing done, nothing really accomplished, nothing finished, in all that plan of writing which, begun so modestly the year before, had spread and flowered like a cancerous growth until now it had engulfed him. From his childhood he could remember all that people said or did, but as he tried to set it down his memory opened up enormous vistas and associations, going from depth to limitless depth, until the simplest incident conjured up a buried continent of experience, and he was overwhelmed by a project of discovery and revelation that would have broken the strength and used up the lives of a regiment of men.

The thing that drove him on was nothing new. Even in early childhood some stern compulsion, a burning thirst to know just how things were, had made him go about a duty of observing people with such fanatical devotion that they had often looked at him resentfully, wondering what was wrong with him, or them. And in his years at college, under the same relentless drive, he had grown so mad and all-observing that he had tried to read ten thousand books, and finally had begun to stare straight through language like a man who, from the very fury of his looking, gains a superhuman intensity of vision, so that he no longer sees merely the surfaces of things but seems to look straight through a wall. A furious hunger had driven him on day after day until his eye seemed to eat into the printed page like a ravenous mouth. Words—even the words of the greatest poets—lost all the magic and the mystery they had had for him, and what the poet said seemed only a shallow and meager figuration of what he might have said, had some superhuman energy and desperation of his soul, greater than any man had ever known or attempted, driven him on to empty out the content of the ocean in him.

And he had felt this even with the greatest sorcerer of words the earth has ever known. Even when he read Shakespeare, that ravenous eye of his kept eating with so desperate a hunger into the substance of his lives that they began to look grey, shabby, and almost common, as they had never done before. George had been assured that Shakespeare was a living universe, an ocean of thought whose shores touched every continent in the world, a fathomless cosmos which held in it the full and final measure of all human life. But now it did not seem to him that this was true.

Rather, as if Shakespeare himself had recognized the hopelessness of ever putting down the millionth part of what he had seen and known about this earth, or of ever giving wholly and magnificently the full content of one moment in man's life, it now seemed that his will had finally surrendered to a genius which he knew was so soaring, so far beyond the range of any other man, that it could overwhelm men with its power and magic even when its owner knew he had shirked the desperate labor of mining from his entrails the huge substance of all life he really had within him.

Thus, even in the great passage in Macbeth in which he speaks of time—

> . . . . *that but this blow*
> *Might be the be-all and the end-all here,*
> *But here, upon this bank and shoal of time,*
> *We'd jump the life to come. . . .*

—in this tremendous passage where he mounts from power to power, from one incredible magic to another, hurling in twenty lines at the astounded earth a treasure that would fill out the works and make the fame of a dozen lesser men—it seemed to George that Shakespeare had not yet said the thousandth part of all he knew about the terror, mystery, and strangeness of time, dark time, nor done more than sketch the lineaments of one of time's million faces, depending on the tremendous enchantments of his genius to cover the surrender of his will before a labor too great for human flesh to bear.

And now as time, grey time, wore slowly, softly, and intolerably about him, rubbing at the edges of his spirit like a great unfathomable cloud, he thought of all these things. And as he thought of them, grey time washed over him, and drowned him in the sea-depths of its unutterable horror, until he became nothing but a wretched and impotent cipher, a microscopic atom, a bloodless, eyeless grope-thing crawling on the sea-floors of the immense, without strength or power ever to know a hand's breadth of the domain in which he dwelt, and with no life except a life-in-death, a life of drowning horror, as he scuttled, headless, eyeless, blind and ignorant and groping, his way to the grey but merciful extinction of death. For, if the greatest poet that had ever lived had found the task too great for him, what could one do who had not a fraction of his power, and who could not conceal the task, as he had done, behind the enchantments of an overwhelming genius?

It was a desperate and lonely year he lived there by himself. He had come to the city with a shout of triumph and of victory in his blood, and the belief that he would conquer it, be taller and more mighty than its greatest towers. But now he knew a loneliness unutterable. Alone, he tried to hold all the hunger and madness of the earth within the limits of a little room, and beat his fists against the walls, only to hurl his body savagely into the streets again, those terrible streets that had neither pause nor curve, nor any door that he could enter.

In the blind lashings of his fury, he strove with all the sinews of his heart and spirit trying to master, to devour, and utterly to possess the great, the million-footed, the invincible and unceasing city. He almost went mad with loneliness among its million faces. His heart sank down in atomic desolation before the overwhelming vision of its immense, inhuman, and terrific architectures. A terrible thirst parched his burning throat and hunger ate into his flesh with a vulture's beak as, tortured by the thousand images of glory, love, and power which the city holds forever to a starving man, he thought that he would perish— only a hand's breadth off from love if he could span it, only a moment away from friendship if he knew it, only an inch, a door, a word away from all the glory of the earth, if he only knew the way.

WHY WAS HE so unhappy? The hills were beautiful as they had always been, the everlasting earth was still beneath his feet, and April would come back again. Yet he was wretched, tortured, and forlorn, filled with fury and unrest, doing the ill thing always when the good lay ready to his hand, choosing the way of misery, torment, waste, and madness, when joy, peace, certitude, and power were his, were his forever, if only he would take and use them for his own.

Why was he so unhappy? Suddenly he remembered the streets of noon some dozen years ago, and the solid, lonely, liquid leather shuffle of men's feet as they came home at noon to dinner; the welcoming shout of their children, the humid warmth and fragrance of the turnip greens, the sound of screen doors being slammed, and then the brooding hush and peace and full-fed apathy of noon again.

Where were they now? And where was all that ancient certitude and peace: the quietness of summer evenings, and people talking on their porches, the smell of the honeysuckles, roses, and the grapes that ripened in thick leaves above the porch, the dew-sweet freshness and repose of night, the sound of a street car stopping on the corner of the hill above them, and the lonely absence of departure that it left behind it when it had gone, far sounds and laughter, music, casual voices, all so near and far, so strange and so familiar, the huge million-noted ululation of the night, and Aunt Maw's voice droning in the darkness of the porch; finally the sound of voices going, people leaving, streets and houses settling into utter quietness; and sleep, then, sleep—the sweet, clean mercy and repose of healthful sleep—had these things vanished from the earth forever?

Why was he so unhappy? Where had it come from—this mad coil and fury of his life? It was, he knew, in everyone, not only in himself, but in people everywhere. He had been and known it in a thousand streets, a million faces: it had become the general weather of their lives. Where had it come from—this fury of unrest and longing, driven flight and agonized return, terrific speed and smashing movement that went nowhere?

Each day they swarmed into the brutal stupefaction of a million streets, were hurled like vermin through the foul, fetid air of roaring tunnels, and swarmed up out of the earth like rats to thrust, push, claw, sweat, curse, cringe, menace, or contrive, in a furious round of dirty, futile, little efforts that got them nowhere, brought them nothing.

At night they rushed out again with the idiot and unwearied pertinacity of a race that was damned and lost, and gutted of the vital substance of its life, to seek, with a weary, frenzied, exacerbated fury, new pleasures and sensations that, when found, filled them with weariness, boredom, and horror of the spirit, and that were viler and baser than the pleasures of a dog. Yet, with this weary hopelessness of hope, this frenzied longing of despair, they would swarm back into their obscene streets of night again.

And for what? For what? To push, thrust, throng, and jostle up and down past the thousand tawdry pomps and dreary entertainments of those streets. To throng back and forth incessantly on the grimy, grey, weary pavements, filling the air with raucous jibe and jeer, and with harsh, barren laughter, from which all the blood and life of mirth and cheer, the exultant, swelling goat-cry of their youth, or the good, full guffaw of the belly-laugh, had died!

For what? For what? To drive the huge exasperation of their weary bodies, their tortured nerves, their bewildered, overladen hearts, back to those barren, furious avenues of night again, spurred on forever by this fruitless hopelessness of hope. To embrace again the painted shell of the old delusion, hurling themselves onward towards that huge, sterile shine and glitter of the night as feverishly as if some great reward of fortune, love or living joy was waiting for them there.

And for what? For what? What was the reward of all this frenzied searching? To be shone on lividly by the lights of death, to walk with jaunty swagger and a knowing wink past all the gaudy desolations of the hot-dog, fruit-drink stands, past the blazing enticements, the trickster's finery of the eight-foot hole-in-the-wall Jew shops, and to cram their dead grey jaws in the gaudy restaurants with the lifeless husks of dead grey food. Proudly to thrust their way into the lurid maws, the dreary, impotent escapes, the feeble, half-hid nastiness of the moving picture shows, and then to thrust and swagger it upon the streets again. To know nothing, yet to look with knowing looks upon the faces of their fellow nighttime dead, to look at them with sneering lips and scornful faces, and with hard, dark, slimy eyes, and jeering tongues. Each night to see and be seen—oh, priceless triumph!—displaying the rich quality of their wit, the keen humor of their fertile minds, with such gems of repartee as:

"Jesus!"

"*Ho-ly* Chee!"

"Oh, yeah?"

"Yeah!"

"*Wich* guy?"

"*Dat* guy! Nah—not *him*! Duh *otheh* guy!"

"*Dat* guy? *Je*-sus! Is dat duh guy yuh mean?"

"Wich guy?"

"Duh guy dat said he was a friend of yours."

"A *friend* of mine! *Je*-sus! Who said he was a friend of mine?"

"He said so."

"G'*wan*! Where d'yah get dat stuff? Dat son-of-a-bitch ain't no friend of mine!"

"No?"

"No."

"Holy *Chee*!"

"*Je*-sus!"

Oh, to hurl that stony gravel of their barren tongues forever, forever, with a million million barren repetitions into the barren ears of their fellow dead men, into the livid, sterile wink of night, hating their ugly, barren lives, their guts, and the faces of their fellow dead men— hating, hating, always hating and unhappy! And then, having prowled the streets again in that ancient, fruitless, and unceasing quest, having hugged the husks of desolation to the bone, to be hurled back into their cells again, as furiously as they had come!

Oh, dear friends, is that not the abundant life of glory, power, and wild, exultant joy, the great vision of the shining and enchanted city, the fortunate and happy life, and all the heroic men and lovely women, that George Webber dreamed of finding in his youth?

Then why was he unhappy? Great God, was it beyond their power—a race that flung up ninety-story buildings in the air, and shot projectiles bearing twenty thousand men through tunnels at every moment of the day—to find a little door that he could enter? Was it beyond the power of people who had done these gigantic things to make a chair where he could sit, a table where he might be fed on food and not on lifeless husks, and a room, a room of peace, repose, and certitude, where for a little moment he could pause from all the anguish, fury, and unrest of the world around him, drawing his breath calmly for a moment without agony, weariness, and damnation of the soul!

AT OTHER TIMES his mood would change, and he would walk the swarming streets for hours at a time and find in the crowds that thronged about him nothing but delight, the promise of some glorious adventure. At such a time he would sink himself wholly and exultantly into the city's life. The great crowds stirred him with a feeling of ecstasy and anticipation. With senses unnaturally absorptive, he drank in every detail of the mighty parade, forever alert for the pretty face and seductive figure of a woman. Every woman with a well-shaped leg, or with a strong, attractive, sexual energy in her appearance, was invested at once with the glamorous robe of beauty, wisdom, and romance which he threw around her.

He had a hundred unspoken meetings and adventures in a day. Each passed and was lost in the crowd, and the brevity of that meeting and departure pierced him with an intolerable sense of pain and joy, of triumph and of loss. Into each lovely mouth he put words of tenderness and understanding. A sales girl in a department store became eloquent and seductive with poignant and beautiful speech; the vulgar, loose mouth of an Irish waitress uttered enchanted music for him when it spoke. In these adventures of his fancy, it never occurred to him that he would have any difficulty in winning the admiration of these beauties—that he was nothing but an ungainly youth, with small features, large shoulders, legs too short, a prowling, simian look about the outthrust head, and an incredible length of flailing arms. No: instead he cut a very handsome and heroic figure in these fantasies, and dreamed of an instant marriage of noble souls, of an immediate and tremendous seduction, ennobled by a beautiful and poetic intensity of feeling.

Sometimes, in these golden fantasies, it was a great lady who yielded herself to him—a lady rich, twenty-four or five years of age (for he could not stand them younger than he was), and widowed recently from an old man that she did not love but had been forced to marry by some bitter constraint and hard occasion dear. The circumstances of his meeting with her varied from repelling with a single annihilating blow of the fist the proffered violence of some Irish thug, to finding quite by accident in the gutter, already half obscured by the dead leaves of Autumn, a wallet or a mesh-bag containing not only ten or twenty thousand dollars in bank notes of huge denominations, but also a rope of pearls, some loose, uncut gems, an emerald of great size mounted on

330 THE WEB AND THE ROOT

a ring, and a number of stocks or bonds, together with letters of the most valuable and distressing privacy. This form of meeting he preferred to any other, for, although it deprived him of heroism, it enabled him to show equivalent virtues of honesty and manly dignity. Also by means of it he could pay his way.

Thus, having picked up the bag on a lonely walk in Central Park, he would see at once the value of its contents—so huge as to make even a modest reward a substantial thing—and, thrusting it quickly into his pocket, he would go at once, though by a rather circuitous route which he had all planned out, to his room, where carefully and exactly he would itemize everything upon the back of an envelope, noting that the initials upon the clasp agreed with the name upon the visiting card he should find within.

This done, he would summon a taxicab and drive at once and at great speed to the indicated address. It would be a modest house in the East Sixties, or again it would be a large, grim pile on Fifth Avenue. He preferred the modest house, high storied, but with a narrow facade, not glaringly obtrusive, but almost gloomily mellow and dark. The furnishing would be masculine, the house still bearing the mark of its dead master's character—walnut and mahogany, with heavy, worn leather cushions on the chairs. To the right of the entrance hall would be the library, a gloomy room in walnut, completely lined up to its high ceiling with ten or fifteen thousand books save for the interstices of recessed, narrow windows.

Having arrived before the house, he would dismiss the taxicab and mount the steps. The door would be opened by a maid, a well-made girl of twenty-one or two, who obviously bathed frequently, and who wore expensive black silk stockings—which her mistress gave her—on her heavy but shapely legs. Smiling, she would usher him into the library, pausing, before she went to inform her mistress, to poke up the glowing coals in a small grate, revealing as she bent before him, the heavy white flesh of her under leg, just above the knee, where her garters of ruffled green silk (probably a gift from her mistress) furrowed deeply into the smooth column of her thigh. Then she would depart, one side of her face prettily flushed by the heat, casting him a swift and provocative glance as she went, while he grew conscious of the rhythmical undulations of her heavy breasts.

Presently he would hear the maid's low voice upstairs, and the nervous, irritable voice of another woman:

"Oh, who is it? Some young man? Tell him I can't see him today! I'm much too upset by this whole affair!"

Ablaze with fierce but righteous anger at this unhandsome return for his labor and honesty, he would stride to the foot of the stairway in time to find the maid descending, and to address her in a proud, harsh voice, not loud but almost metallic—a voice of great carrying power.

"Tell your mistress that it is imperative she give me the honor of her attendance. If I am intruding here, it is certainly against my will, and at a cost of considerable anxiety, care, and labor to myself. But I have information concerning a loss she may have sustained, which I believe may be of the greatest interest to her."

He would get no further. There would be a sharp cry above, and she would come down the stairs regardless of safety, her tense face very pale, her voice almost stricken. She would seize him so fiercely with her small, strong hands that she made a white circle around his wrists, speaking in a tone that was no more than a trembling breath:

"What is it? You must tell me at once, do you hear? Have you found it?"

Gently, soothingly, but with implacable firmness, he would answer:

"I have found something which may be your property. But so serious are the possibilities of this matter, to me, that I must ask you first of all to submit yourself to a few questions that I am going to ask you."

"Anything—anything you like!"

"You have suffered a loss. Describe that loss—the time and the place."

"I lost a silver mesh-bag two days ago between 8:20 and 8:35 in the morning, while riding in Central Park, just back of the Museum. The bag had been put in the right-hand pocket of my riding jacket; it was dislodged during my ride."

"Describe as carefully and exactly as you can the contents of the bag."

"There were $16,400 in bank notes—140 hundred dollar bills, the rest in fifties and twenties. There was also a necklace with a platinum clasp, containing ninety-one pearls of graduated size, the largest about the size of a large grape; a plain gold ring set with a diamond-shaped emerald——"

"Of what size?"

"About the size of a lump of sugar. There were, in addition, eight Bethlehem Steel stock certificates, and, what I value most of all, several letters written by friends and business associates to my late husband, which contain matter of the most private sort."

Meanwhile he would be checking the list off, envelope in hand. Now he would say quietly, taking the bag from his pocket and presenting it to her:

"I think you will find your property intact."

Seizing the bag with a cry, she would sink quickly upon a leather divan, opening it with trembling fingers and hastily counting through the contents. He would watch her with nervous constraint, conscious of the personal risk he took, the unanswerable suspicion that might be attached to him if everything was not there. But everything would be!

Finally looking up, her voice filled with fatigue and unutterable relief, she would say:

"Everything is here! Everything! Oh! I feel as if I had been born again!"

Bowing coldly and ironically, he would answer:

"Then, madam, you will pardon me the more willingly if I leave you now to enjoy the first happy hours of your childhood alone."

And, taking his battered but adventurous-looking old hat from a table, he would start for the door. She would follow immediately and interrupt his passage, seizing him again by the arms in her excitement:

"No, you *shall not* go yet. You shall *not go* until you tell me what your name is. What is your name? You *must* tell me your name!"

Very coldly he would answer:

"The name would not matter to you. I am not known yet. I am only a poor writer."

She would see, of course, from his ragged clothing—the same suit he was now wearing—that he was neither a wealthy nor fashionable person, but she would also see, from the great sense of style with which his frame carried these rags, as if indifferent or unconscious of them, that there was some proud royalty of nature in him that had no need of worldly dignities. She would say:

"Then, if you are a poor writer, there is one thing I can do—one very small return I can make for your splendid honesty. You must accept the reward that I have offered."

"Reward?" He would say in an astounded tone. "Is there a *reward*?"

"Five thousand dollars. I—I—hope—if you wouldn't mind—" she would falter, frightened by the stern frown on his forehead.

"I accept, of course," he would answer, harshly and proudly. "The service I rendered was worth it. I am not ashamed to take my wage. At any rate, it is better invested with me than it would be among a group of Irish policemen. Let me congratulate you on what you have done today for the future of art."

"I am so glad—so happy—that you'll take it—that it will be of any help to you. Won't you come to dinner tonight? I want to talk to you."

He would accept.

Before he left they would have opportunity to observe each other more closely. He would see that she was rather tall for a woman—about

five feet six or seven inches, but giving the impression of being somewhat taller. She would have a heavy weight of rather blondish hair, but
perhaps with a reddish tint in it, also—perhaps it would be the color
of very pale amber. It would be piled compactly and heavily upon her
head, so as to suggest somewhat a molten or malleable weight, and it
would be innumerably various with little winking lights.

This weight would rest like a heavy coronal above a small, deli-
cately-moulded face, remarkably but not unhealthily pale, and saved
from unpleasant exoticism by the rapid and boyish daring of its movements, a smile like a flick of golden light across a small, full, incredibly
sensitive mouth—a swift, twisted smile, revealing small, milk-white,
but not too even teeth. The face would usually be cast in an intense,
slightly humorous earnestness. Her conversation would be boyishly
direct and sincere, delivered half while looking seriously at the auditor
and half with the eyes turned thoughtfully away: at the conclusion of
each remark, however, the eyes, of a luminous blue-grey depth, a catlike health and sensuousness, would steal thievishly sideways up to the
face of the listener.

She would be dressed in a close-fitting blouse of knitted green silk,
with pockets into which she occasionally thrust her small, brown, com-
petent hands (unjeweled). Her breasts would not be like the slow, rich
melons of the maid, but eager and compact—each springing forward
lithely and passionately, their crisp and tender nozzles half defined
against the silk. She would wear a short, straight skirt of blue serge;
her long, graceful legs would be covered with silk hose; her small feet
sheathed in velvet shoes clasped by old buckles.

Before he left, she would tell him that he must come as often as he
liked—daily, if possible—to use the library: it was rarely used now,
and that he might have it all to himself. He would depart, the door
being closed behind him by the voluptuous and softly smiling maid.

Then, in a fever of excitement and rapt contemplation, he would
walk, a furnace of energy, through the streets and up the broad prom-
enade in the middle of Central Park. It would be a slate-colored day in

late Autumn, dripping with small, cold rain, pungent with smoke, and as inchoate as Spring with unknown prophecy and indefinable hope. A few lone, wet, withered leaves would hang from bare boughs; occasionally he would burst into a bounding run, leaping high in the air and tearing with tooth or hand at some solitary leaf.

Finally, late in the afternoon, he would become conscious of delightful physical exhaustion, which, ministered by the golden wine of his fancy, could easily be translated into voluptuous ease, just as the flesh of certain fowl becomes more dainty when slightly old. Then turning towards Lexington Avenue, his face chill with beaded rain, he would take the subway to Fourteenth Street, go home to his room, enjoy the soaking luxury of a hot bath, shave, put on clean underwear, socks, shirt, and tie; and then wait with trembling limbs and a heart thudding with strong joy for the impending meeting.

Then, at half-past eight, he would present himself at her door again. The rain would fall coldly and remotely from bare branches, and from all the eaves. The first floor of the house would be dark, but behind drawn curtains the second floor would be warm with mellow light. Again the maid would open the door for him, leading him past the dark library, up the broad, carpeted stairs, where a single dim lamp was burning at the landing. He would follow, not too close, but a step or two behind, in order to watch the pleasant rhythm of her hips and the slipping back and forth of her rather tight skirt up her comely but somewhat heavy legs.

At the top of the stairs, waiting to greet him, the lady would he waiting. Taking him quickly by the hand with a warm, momentary pressure, and drawing him slightly towards her, she led the way into the living room, probably without saying a word, but with only the liquid stealth of the eyes. There would *be* none of that cold, remote, well-bred iciness of courtesy that chills and freezes up the warm glow of affection, such as "I'm *so* glad you could come!" or "It's *so* nice of you to come"—they would have begun almost instantly with a natural and casual intimacy, full of dignity and ease and beauty.

The boyishness of her morning garb and manner would have disappeared entirely. In unadorned but costly evening dress, of heavy, pearl-colored silk, with silver hose, and black, jeweled slippers, she would reveal an unsuspected maturity, depth of breast, and fullness of limb. Her sloping shoulders, round, firm arms, and long throat, in which a pulse would be beating slowly and warmly, in that light would be pearl-tinted, suffused, however, with a delicate bone color.

The living room would be a high, spacious room, masculine in its dimensions, but touched by her delicate taste, as the library had not been, into a room which was, although not frillishly, obviously, or offensively so, feminine.

There would be a huge divan, a chaise-longue, several large, deep chairs, luxuriously upholstered and covered with a dull, flowered pattern of old satin. A warm, bright fire of coals would be burning in a hearth of small dimensions, with a sturdy and sensible alignment of shovels, pokers, and tongs to one side, their brass very highly polished, and with no revolting antiqueyness of pseudo-Revolutionary bed warmers. The mantel would be an unadorned piece of creamy marble; above, extending the entire distance to the ceiling, there would be an eighteenth-century French mirror, with a simple gilded border, somewhat mottled with small brown patches at the lower edges. The sole object upon the mantle would be an ornate, gilded, eighteenth-century clock, very feminine and delicate. All of the furniture would have strong but delicate proportions. There would be a table behind the divan—a round leaf of polished walnut. Scattered about its surface would be several periodicals and magazines: a copy of *The Dial, Vanity Fair,* which he might pick up without comment, tossing them back carelessly with a slight ironical lifting of the eybrows, copies of *The Century, Harper's,* and *Scribner's,* but none of *The Atlantic Monthly.* There would also be copies of *Punch,* of *Sketch, The Tatler,* or sporting and dramatic magazines, filled with pictures of hunt and chase, and many small photographs showing members of the English aristocracy, gaunt, toothy men and women standing, talking, tailored into squares and checks with the toes of their large feet turned inwards, or caught walking, with their open mouths awry, and an arm or leg cutting angularly the air with such legends below as, "Captain McDingle and the Lady Jessica Houndsditch caught last week enjoying a chat at the Chipping-Sodbury Shoot."

On a small table at one end of the divan there would be materials for making various kinds of cocktails and iced drinks—a rich, squat bottle of mellow rum, a bottle of Kentucky Bourbon whiskey matured for more than twenty years in oaken casks, and pungent gin, faintly nostalgic with orange bitters. There would be as well a cocktail shaker, a small bucket of cracked ice, and dishes of olives and salted almonds.

After drinking a chill and heady liquor, infused with her own certain intoxication, he would have another, his senses roused to controlled ecstasy, his brain leaping with a fiery and golden energy. Then they would go in to dinner.

The dining room, on the same floor, would be in semi-darkness, save for the golden light that bathed a round table, covered with a snowy and capacious cover, and two small, shaded lamps upon a huge buffet, gleaming with glassware, and various bottles containing whiskey, wines, liqueurs, vermouth, and rum. They would be attended at table by the maid. There would be only one other servant, the cook, a middle-aged New Hampshire woman, who had added to her native art things she had learned when the family had spent the Summer on Cape Cod, or in Paris, where the lady would have lived for several years. In the daytime there would be a man as well, who tended the furnace and did the heavier chores.

This would be all the service. The estate would not be unhappily and laboriously wealthy, extending into several millions of dollars: there would only be seven or eight hundred thousand dollars, solidly founded in tax-free bonds, yielding an annual income of twenty or twenty-five thousand, the whole intention and purpose of the fortune being total expenditure of the income for simple luxury.

The dishes would be few in number; the food would be man's food simply and incomparably cooked. They would begin with a heavy tomato soup, the color of mahogany, or with a thick pea soup of semi-solid consistency, or with a noble dish of onion soup with a solid crust of toasted bread and cheese upon it, which she had made herself. There would be no fish, but, upon a huge silver platter, a thick sirloin or por-terhouse, slightly charred and printed with the grid at the edges and center. Small pats of butter previously mixed with chopped mint and a dash of cinnamon would be dissolving visibly upon its surface. She would carve the steak into tender three-inch strips, revealing the rich, juicy, but not pasty, red of its texture. Then she would help his plate to mealy fried potatoes and tender, young boiled onions, exfoliating their delicate and pungent skins evenly at the touch of a fork. She would cover them with a rich butter sauce, touched with paprika.

There would be as well a salad—a firm heart of lettuce, or an arti-choke, or, better still, crisp white endive. She would prepare the dress-ing in a deep mixing bowl, cutting small fragments of mint or onion into the vinegar, oil and mustard to give it pungency. Finally, there would be deep-dish apple pie, spiced with nutmeg and cinnamon and gummed with its own syrups along its crisped, wavy crust; this would be served with a thick hunk of yellow American cheese. They would have also a large cup of strong, fragrant coffee, with heavy cream. He would watch the cream coil through the black surface like thick smoke, changing finally into mellow brown. He would say little during the course of the meal. He would eat his food decently, but with en-thusiastic relish, looking up from time to time to find her eyes fastened upon him with a subtly humorous and yet tender look.

Later, in the living room, they would sit before the fire, he in a deep upholstered chair, she on the chaise-longue, where they would have small cups of black coffee, a glass of green Chartreuse, or of Grand Marnier, and cigarettes. He would smoke fragrant, toasted, loose-drawing Lucky Strikes; she would smoke Melachrinos. From time to time she would move her limbs slightly, and her silken calves, sliding gently apart or together, would cause an audible and voluptuous friction.

There would be little other sound save the enveloping and quieting drip of rain from eaves and boughs, a brief gaseous spurt from the red coals, and the minute ticking of the little clock. From time to time he would hear the maid clearing the table in the dining room. Presently she would appear, ask if anything more was wanted, say good-night, and mount the stairs to her room on the top floor. Then they would be left alone.

They would begin to talk at first, if not with constraint, at least with some difficulty. She would speak of her education—in a convent—of her life abroad, of stupid and greedy parents, now dead, of her great devotion to an aunt, a wise and kindly woman, her only friend against her family in her difficult youth, and of her marriage at twenty to a man in his late forties, good, devoted, but vacant of any interest for her. He had died the year before.

Then she would ask him about his life, his home, his childhood, his age, and his ambition. Then he would talk, at first in short spurts and rushes. At length, language bursting like a torrent at the gates of speech, he would make a passionate avowal of what he had done, believed, felt, loved, hated, and desired, of all he wanted to do and be. Then he would light another cigarette, get up restlessly before the fire, sit down again beside her on the chaise-longue, and take her hand in a natural and casual way, at which she would give a responsive squeeze to his. Then, throwing his cigarette into the grate, he would put his arms around her quite naturally and easily, and kiss her, first for about forty seconds upon the mouth, then in a circle upon the cheeks, eyes, forehead, nose, chin, and throat, about the place where the pulse was beating. After this, he would gently insinuate his hand into her breasts, beginning near the deep and fragrant channel that parted them. Meanwhile, she would ruffle his hair gently and stroke his face with her delicate fingers. Their passion would have them chained in a silent drunkenness; she would submit to every action of his embrace without thought of resistance.

Lying beside her now, wound in her long arms, he would pass his hand along her silken, swelling hips, down the silken seam of her calf, and gently up her thigh below her skirt, lingering for a moment upon the tender, heavy flesh of her under leg. Then he would loosen one breast over the neck of her gown, holding its tender weight and teat gently and lovingly in one hand. The nipples of her firm breasts would not be leathery, stained brown, and flaccid, like those of a woman who has borne children; they would end briefly in a tender pink bud, as did those of the ladies in old French paintings—those of Boucher, for example.

Then he would lift her arms, observing the delicate silken whorls and screws of blonde hair in the arm pits. He would kiss and perhaps bite her tender shoulder haunch, and smell the pungent but not un-pleasant odor, already slightly moist with passion. And this odor of an erotic female would have neither the rank stench of a coarse-bodied woman, nor some impossible and inhuman bouquet, disgusting to a healthy taste. It would be delicately vulgar: the odor of a healthy woman and a fine lady, who has not only been housed, clothed, fed, and attended with the simple best, but has been derived from ances-tral loins similarly nourished, so that now the marrow of her bones, the substance of her flesh, the quality of her blood, the perspiration of her skin, the liquor of her tongue, the moulding of her limbs—all the delicate joinings and bindings of ligament and muscle, and the cementing jellies, the whole incorporate loveliness of her body—were of rarer, subtler, and more golden stuff than would be found elsewhere the world over.

And lying thus, warmed by the silent, glowing coals, he would perform on her the glorious act of love. He would dedicate to her the full service of his love and energy, and find upon her mouth double oblivion.

Later, reviving slowly, he would lie in her embrace, his head heavily sunk upon her neck, feel the slow, unsteady respiration of her breast, and hear, his senses somewhat drugged, the faint, incessant beating of the rain.

And he would stay with her that night, and on many nights thereafter. He would come to her in the darkness, softly and quietly, although there was no need for silence, conscious that in the dark there was waiting a central energy of life and beauty; in the darkness they would listen to the million skipping feet of rain.

Shortly after this night, he would come and live with her in the house. This would be all right because he would insist on paying for his board. He would pay, against all protests, fifteen dollars a week, saying:

"This is all I can afford—this is what I would pay elsewhere. I could not eat and drink and sleep as I do here, but I could live. Therefore, take it!"

His days would be spent in the library. There he would do stupendous quantities of reading, going voraciously and completely through those things he desired most to know, but effecting combinations, mélanges, woven fabrics of many other books, keeping a piled circle about him and tearing chunks hungrily from several at random.

The library would be based solidly, first, on five or six thouand volumes, which would cover excellently but not minutely the range of English and American literature. There would be standard editions of Thackeray, the Cruikshank and Phiz Dickenses, Meredith, James, Sir Walter Scott, and so on. In addition to the well-known literature of the Elizabethans, such as Shakespeare, the handy Mermaid collection of the dramatists, and the even more condensed anthologies with Jonson's *Volpone, The Alchemist*, and *Bartholomew Fair*, Dekker's *Shoemaker's Holiday*, Chapman's *Bussy d'Ambois*, there would be several hundred of the lesser-known plays, bad, silly, and formless as they were, but filled with the bawdy, beautiful, and turbulent speech of that time.

There would be prose pamphlets, such as the romances after Bandello of Robert Greene, the dramatist, or his quarrel with Gabriel Harvey, or his confessions, Dekker's *Guls Horne-booke*, the remnant of Jonson's *Sad Shepherd*, his *Underwoods*. There would be such books as Coleridge's *Anima Poetae*, the *Biographia Literaria, The Table Talk of S. T. C.*, and the sermons of the Puritan divines, particularly of Jonathan Edwards. There would be books of voyages, Hakluyt, Purchas, Bartram's *Travels in North America*.

And there would be facsimile reproductions of all the scientific manuscripts of Leonardo da Vinci, the great *Codice Atlantico*, written backwards and reversed across the page, scribbled with hundreds of drawings, including his flying machines, canals, catapults, fire towers, spiral staircases, anatomical dissections of human bodies, diagrams of the act of copulation while standing erect, researches in the movement of waves, fossilized remains, sea shells on a mountain side, notes on the enormous antiquity of the world, the leafless and blasted age of the earth which he put in the background of his paintings—as he did in Mona Lisa. With the aid of mirrors and of Italian grammars and dictionaries, he would spell out the words and translate them, using as a guide the partial deciphering already made by a German. Then, in his spare moments between writing novels, he would show how Leonardo regarded painting only as a means of support for his investigation into all movement, all life, and was only incidentally an artist and an engineer, and how what he was really doing was tracing with a giant's brush the map of the universe, showing the possibility of Man becoming God.

There would also be books of anatomical drawings, besides those of Leonardo, of the fifteenth and sixteenth centuries, showing ladies lying on divans, gazing wistfully through their open bellies at their entrails, and maps out of the medieval geographers, compounded of scraps of fact, hypothesis, and wild imaginings, with the different quarters of the sea peopled by various monsters, some without heads, but with a single eye and with a mouth between the shoulders.

Then there would be some of those books that Coleridge "was deep in" at the time he wrote *The Ancient Mariner*, such as Iamblichus, Porphyry, Plotinus, Josephus, Jeremy Taylor, "the English Metaphysicum"—the whole school of the neoplatonists; all the works that could be collected on the histories of demons, witches, fairies, elves, gnomes, witches' sabbaths, black magic, alchemy, spirits—all the Elizabethans had to say about it, particularly Reginald Scott; and all the works of Roger Bacon: all legends and books of customs and superstition whatever, and works of quaint and learned lore, Burton's *Anatomy of Melancholy*, Frazer's *Golden Bough, The Encyclopedia Britannica*, in which, when he was tired of other reading, he could plunge luxuriously—picking out first the plums, such as Stevenson on Berenger, or Theodore Watts-Dunton on poetry, or Carlyle, if any of him was left, on various things, or Swinburne on Keats, Chapman, Congreve, Webster, Beaumont and Fletcher.

He would have the *Magnalia* of Cotton Mather, the *Voyages of Dr. Syntax*, with illustrations, Surtees' sporting novels. He would have the complete works of Fielding, Smollett, Sterne, and Richardson, and everything of Daniel Defoe's he could lay his hands on. He would have the entire corpus of Greek and Latin literature, so far as it might be obtained in Loeb's library and in the coffee-colored india paper Oxford classical texts, with footnotes and introduction all in Latin, as well as cross-references to all the manuscripts. And he would have several editions each of the Carmina of Catullus (with Lamb's translations and settings to verse); Plato, with Jowett's great rendering—in particular, of the *Apology* and the *Phaedo*; the histories of Herodotus, and in general all lying and entertaining histories and voyages whatever, as Strabo, Pausanias, Froissart, Josephus, Holinshed, Marco Polo, Swift, Homer, Dante, Xenophon in his *Anabasis*, Chaucer, Sterne, Voltaire in his voyage to England, *With Stanley in Africa*, Baron Munchausen.

There would be as well the Oxford and Cambridge University texts of the poets, with other editions when lacking for men like Donne, Crashaw, Herbert, Carew, Herrick, Prior. And in the drama there would be several hundred volumes besides the Elizabethans, including everyone from the early Greeks to the liturgical plays of the Middle Ages, to the great periods in France, Germany, Spain, Italy, Scandinavia, Russia, including all newer dramatists of the art theatre—Ibsen, Shaw, Chekhov, Benavente, Molnar, Toller, Wedekind, the Irish, Pirandello, O'Neill, Sardou, Romains, including others from the Bulgarian, Peruvian, and Lithuanian never heard of. There would also be complete bound editions of *Punch, Blackwood's, Harper's Weekly, L'Illustration, The Police Gazette, The Literary Digest,* and *Frank Leslie's Illustrated Weekly.*

Walled by these noble, life-giving books, he would work furiously throughout the day, drawing sustenance and courage, when not reading them, from their presence. Here in the midst of life, but of life flowing in regular and tranquil patterns, he could make his rapid and violent sorties into the world, retiring when exhausted by its tumult and fury to this established place.

And at night again, he would dine with rich hunger and thirst, and, through the hours of darkness, lie in the restorative arms of his beautiful mistress. And sometimes at night when the snow came muffling in its soft fall all of the noises of the earth and isolating them from all its people, they would stand in darkness, only a dying flicker of coal fire behind them, watching the transforming drift and flurry of white snow outside.

Thus, being loved and being secure, working always within a circle of comfort and belief, he would become celebrated as well. And to be loved and to be celebrated—was there more than this in life for any man?

After the success of his first book, he would travel, leaving her forever steadfast, while he drifted and wandered like a ghost around the world, coming unknown, on an unplanned journey, to some village at dusk, and finding there a peasant woman with large ox eyes. He would go everywhere, see everything, eating, drinking, and devouring his way across the earth, returning every year or so to make another book.

He would own no property save a small lodge with thirty acres of woodland, upon a lake in Maine or New Hampshire. He would not keep a motor—he would signal a taxi whenever he wanted to go any-where. His clothing, laundry, personal attentions, and, when he was alone at the lodge, his cooking, would be cared for by a negro man, thirty-five years old, black, good-humored, loyal, and clean.

When he was himself thirty or thirty-five years old, having used up and driven out all the wild frenzy and fury in him by that time, or con-trolled it somehow by flinging and batting, eating and drinking and whoring his way about the world, he would return to abide always with the faithful woman, who would now be deep-breasted and steadfast like the one who waited for Peer Gynt.

And they would descend, year by year, from depth to depth in each other's spirit; they would know each other more completely than two people ever had before, and love each other better all the time. And as they grew older, they would become even younger in spirit, triumphing above all the weariness, dullness, and emptiness of youth. When he was thirty-five he would marry her, getting on her blonde and fruitful body two or three children.

He would wear her love like a most invulnerable target over his heart. She would be the heart of his desire, the well of all his pas-sion. He would triumph over the furious welter of the days during the healing and merciful nights: he would be spent, and there would always be sanctuary for him; weary, a place of rest; sorrowful, a place of joy.

So was it with him during that year, when, for the first time and with their full strength, the elements of fury, hunger, thirst, wild hope, and savage loneliness worked like a madness in the adyts of his brain. So was it when, for the first time, he walked the furious streets of life, a manswarm atom, a nameless cipher, who in an instant could clothe his life with all the wealth and glory of the earth. So was it with him that year when he was twenty-three years old, and when he walked the pavements of the city—a beggar and a king. Has it been otherwise with any man?

WORKS BY THOMAS WOLFE

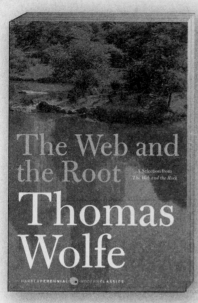

THE WEB AND THE ROOT

ISBN 978-0-06-157955-4 (paperback)

"Wolfe has written passage after passage that you want to read aloud, to memorize; no novelist since Conrad has more verbal effectiveness."
—*Saturday Review*

"Wolfe wrote as one inspired. No one of his generation had his command of language, his passion, his energy."
—*The New Yorker*

YOU CAN'T GO HOME AGAIN

ISBN 978-0-06-093005-9 (paperback)

"*You Can't Go Home Again* will stand apart from everything else that he wrote because this is the book of a man who had come to terms with himself, who has something profoundly important to say."
—*New York Times Book Review*

"If there stills lingers any doubt as to Wolfe's right to a place among the immortals of American letters, this work should dispel it."
—*Cleveland News*